RESOUNDING ACCLAIM FOR
ROBERT K. TANENBAUM AND
ACT OF REVENGE

By Robert K. Tanenbaum

ROBERT K. TANENBAUM

ACT OF REVENGE

HARPER

An Imprint of HarperCollinsPublishers

HARPER

An Imprint of HarperCollins*Publishers*
10 East 53rd Street
New York, New York 10022-5299

Copyright © 1999 by Robert K. Tanenbaum
ISBN 978-0-06-206839-2

First Harper premium printing: June 2011
First HarperTorch mass market printing: June 2000
First Harper hardcover printing: June 1999

HarperCollins ® and Harper ® are registered trademarks of Harper-Collins Publishers.

Printed in the United States of America

Visit Harper paperbacks on the World Wide Web at
www.harpercollins.com

10 9 8 7 6 5 4 3 2 1

To those most special,
Rachael, Roger, Billy, and Patti
and in memory of our friend,
Homicide Detective Don Baeszler

ACKNOWLEDGMENTS

Again, and yet again, all praise belongs
to Michael Gruber whose genuis and
scholarship flows throughout and who is
primarily and solely responsible for the
excellence of this manuscript and whose
contribution cannot be overstated.

Special thanks to Paul McCarthy who,
like Henry Robbins before him, shares
the same vision and offers the same caring
literary guidance and encouragement.

And special recognition belongs to
Georgia di Donato, my confidential
assistant without whose patience,
friendship and able assistance
none of this would be possible.

1

IN AND OUT, WAS HIS THOUGHT AS HE stood in the dusty storeroom of the Asia Mall. The targets would be *there*, and I'll be *here*, and the Vietnamese guy would come in through the rear entrance, off of Howard Street, down that little hallway, and do it. Then the Vietnamese guy would leave the way he came in, and I'll walk out through the store. The man strolled back and forth, pacing off the distances, humming softly. He was a slight Chinese man in a cheap blue suit and a white nylon short-sleeved shirt buttoned to the top. On his feet he wore twelve-dollar Kinney loafers over white cotton socks. Nobody would have looked twice at him on any street in Chinatown, which was one of the things he now counted on. Walking out through the mall, through the throngs of Asian people buying cheap clothes, household items, and fabrics, and out into Canal Street. No one would ever have seen him with the men from Hong Kong.

A rattle announced a stock clerk coming in from the store with a hand truck. The man in the blue suit stayed where he was, and the stock clerk looked right through him, hoisted a carton of woks onto his truck, and departed. The stock clerk had seen the man any number of times, on the street or in the mall talking to the boss, and he had also never seen him before in his life, depending on who was asking.

After the stock clerk left, the man clapped his hands hard, three times, as they do before a shrine to frighten the demons who tend to lurk by shrines, and listened carefully after each clap. This section of the stockroom was composed largely of ceiling-high shelves made of steel pipes, rough planks, and chicken wire, stuffed plump with pillows and bean-bag chairs, making effective baffles for loud, sharp sounds. It was likely that no one in the mall would hear anything out of the ordinary. Smiling a vague and modest smile, the man in the blue suit came out of the storeroom. He asked the girl at the front counter for a pack of Salems, and she gave it to him. She did not ask him for any money, nor did he offer any. She was another of the very many people who did not recall ever seeing this man while doing him various favors. He walked out onto Canal Street, crowded with shoppers on this sunny Friday in early June, crowded by American standards, near empty by the standards the man had grown up with in China. This afternoon, in the back room of the Asia Mall, he would complete a plan five years in the making, a tower of mahjong tiles that required the delicate placing of a last exquisitely balanced piece to hold it together. With that last ivory click, his life would change.

The man walked down Canal toward Lafayette, smoking, his mind calm. He knew he was good at this, that his plan was sound and would bring forth the results he desired. Of course, the men from Hong Kong might not come at all, but that could not be helped. Everything else had been considered and accounted for, and it all would have worked exactly as planned, except for the little girl. And who could have imagined such a girl?

The girl, at about that moment, was up at Columbia University's College of Physicians and Surgeons getting her head examined. Dr. Morris Shadkin, a small, youngish, plump man with a friendly pop-eyed look and unfashionable black sideburns, was doing the examining. The girl said, in an exaggerated nervous voice, "Okay, doc, don't beat around the bush. Am I . . . am I . . . going to make it?"

Shadkin looked up from the sonogram strips he was studying and adopted a grave mien. "I'm afraid not, Lucy," he intoned in a good replication of the voice used by the elderly scientists in fifties monster movies. "I'm afraid your brain will have to be removed for further study. I'm sorry."

"Oh, no problem, doc," said the girl. "Could I say good-bye to my dollies first?"

He laughed. "Yes, but be quick about it! This is big science. What do you think of this?" He handed her a couple of sonogram strips stapled together. "Check out 102 and 102b."

The girl looked at the patterns. "They look the same," she said.

"Yeah. Those are phoneme prints corrected for pitch and timbre. One of them is a native Cantonese speaker, and the other is you."

"So I speak perfect Cantonese. We knew that already."

"Hey, who's the doctor here? Now look at these, wise guy."

"What's this, the Russian?"

"Yeah, which you don't speak at all. Look at the sequence down the page." He pointed with a pencil. "This is the tape, this is you. See: rough at first, but you got a learning curve like a rocket, kid. Down there on the bottom it's nearly a perfect match."

"Oh, yes, I'm this big prodigy," said Lucy in affected boredom, "but will it bring me true happiness?"

Shadkin twiddled an imaginary cigar and bounced his eyebrows Groucho-like.

"Stick with me, kid, you'll be wearing diamonds. Want to see the EEG results?"

"From the thing with the green shower cap and the wires?"

"Yo, that." He tapped with the pencil at various places on a life-size plaster model of a human brain. "You seem to have an unusually active Wernicke's area. That's the chunk of brain we think is responsible for comprehension of language. Same with Heschl's gyri, which is right here. Now, we're no longer strict localizers, that is, we no longer think that there's a little smidgen of brain meat with 'car' on it and another with 'sassafras,' but it's pretty clear there are, even at this gross level, some differences between your EEG output and those of ordinary mortals. It's hard to explain right now. It's not a simple bilingualism. But as I understand it, you've always been bilingual in Cantonese."

"As far back as I can remember."

"This was a child-care worker—the one who taught you?"

"Sort of. It's a little more complicated. My mother dumped me on the Chen family starting at about six weeks. She's very career-oriented, my mother."

"And why did the Chen family take you in? I bet that's an interesting story."

She shrugged. "One of my mother's heroic deeds. She was running the rape and sex crimes unit at the D.A. Mrs. Chen's younger sister came over from China, and she was in the country about ten days when some guys snatched her off the street and gang-raped her. The next day she jumped in front of a train."

"Jesus!"

"Yeah. Chinese people don't like to mess with the cops, and the Chens didn't tell anybody about the rape, or even report it. But my mother figured it for a rape and found the guys and put them away. It was a big case."

"How did she . . . ?"

"The vic had bite marks on her," said Lucy shortly. She changed the subject. "So my brain is different, huh?"

Shadkin took the hint and picked up a sheaf of EEG printouts, and began to point out what the various peaks and flats meant about the busy neurons beneath the electrodes. After a bit, the girl found out more than she wanted to know. It was good that Shadkin treated her like an adult, but there were limits to her interest in neurophysiology, even that of her own brain. Her attention wandered as he went on

summarizing what was known about the neural sub-
strate of language formation (not a hell of a lot, apparently) and the importance of studying someone
who had preserved so late in life something close to
the language-absorptive capacities of very young
children.

Her gaze drifted around the small office, a typical academic's rat hole—papers and journals piled
on every available surface, strips of EEG and sonogram paper hanging from the ceiling, odd bits of
handmade machinery, posters from drug compa-
nies on the walls, along with diplomas and framed
awards.

"Are you married or anything?" she asked abruptly,
catching him in the middle of a trip down the Fis-
sure of Rolando.

He said, "No, I'm not. Why do you ask?"

"Just nosy. How come? Are you, like, gay?"

"Nope. I guess I was just waiting for someone
like you to come along."

She rolled her eyes and blushed charmingly. "You
know, you could get arrested for stuff like that," she
said primly.

"Hey, I can wait. Listen, it'll be great. After I describe your brain and make you famous and win the
Nobel prize, you can push me around in a wheelchair for twenty years. Trust me, you'll love it."

At that point the phone rang. Shadkin picked it up
and said, "Hello. Yeah, it went great. Yeah, we're just
about finished for today. Uh-huh. Yeah, here she is."

He handed the receiver across the desk. "Your
mom."

While Lucy spoke on the phone, Shadkin took

the opportunity to study his electroencephalo-
grams, but his eyes kept sliding over to study the
girl. This was their first session, and already he was
making plans to write up a major grant, with her as
its chief object of study. Ronnie Chau, his post-doc,
had found her; apparently she was quite a figure in
Chinatown, where a lot of Chau's relatives still
lived. Even from the scant data he had already, he
could see that she was a true linguistic prodigy,
possibly the rarest quirk of which the human brain
was capable, far rarer than math whizzes or plain
vanilla geniuses. It really seemed as though in Lucy
Karp's head the hard-wired apparatus that enables
babies to learn their native tongues, and which
switches off in most people at about age five, had
stayed on. She claimed that she had learned French
in a couple of weeks and, from what Shadkin had
already heard, she was perfectly fluent.

The talent seemed to have affected the rest of her
personality, too. Shadkin liked children and, as a
student of the development of language, he naturally
had much to do with them. He could tell that there
was something odd about Lucy Karp, fascinating-
odd, not annoying-odd. The body language: straight
in the chair, hands folded and still on her lap, none
of the extravagant slumps, tics, and gestures normally associated with American kids. Her look was
direct, remarkably so, as if she had contrived to let a
thirty-year-old woman peer out from her twelve-
year-old eyes. Funny eyes, too, the color of cigarette
tobacco and set slightly aslant in the face, richly
lashed above prominent cheekbones. But aside from
those eyes and the good cheekbones, an unlovely

child, unnaturally thin and dull of complexion, with a nose and mouth too large for the pointed little face. Not what he would have called a cute girl in his own dimly recalled adolescence, no, nothing cute about Lucy Karp. There was also a certain air of neglect about her. She wore baggy black cotton trousers, cheap black high-top Asian sneakers, a red T-shirt with Chinese characters in white on the front, and a worn black velvet vest over it, covered on the front with ragged embroidery. Her hair, which was dark, neck-length, thick and curly, and not terribly clean, was parted severely in the middle and drawn back over her broad forehead by two barrettes, green plastic alligators, a little remnant of childhood there, Shadkin thought, and thought further, this kid has something negative going with the mom. Lucy was answering whatever her mother had to say in tense monosyllables, and a sharp, deep line had appeared between her brows. Another short volley of uh-huhs and yes, moms, and she hung up the phone, looking pinched around the nostrils.

"A problem?" Shadkin asked.

Her expression resumed its neutrality. "Oh, not really. She's involved in a case and can't come to pick me up. She wants me to take a cab home."

"Do you have cab fare? I'd be glad to—"

"No, thank you, I have enough," she replied quickly. "So, what now? Do you want to examine me some more?"

"Oh, yeah. In fact, I was just thinking about writing a grant, just for you. How would that be? A couple, three times a week? I mean, you'd have to check with your parents . . ."

"They won't mind. Is there folding money involved?"

Shadkin let out a startled laugh. "For you? Yeah, I guess. What did you have in mind?"

"How about twenty-five an hour? Plus expenses."

He whistled. "That's pretty steep for a kid."

"A unique kid. You said it." She looked at him coolly.

I wonder where she learned that look, he thought, and then he agreed, and they shook hands. Her grip was firm and strangely hot. A metabolism like a vole, he thought. No wonder she can't put on any weight.

She said good-bye and left. Shadkin let out a long breath, laughed, and sang "Sank heav-ahn for leetle gurrls . . ." and the rest of the verse in the same stupid accent. Then he rummaged out a lined pad and a pen from the clutter and began the process of asking the Defense Advanced Research Projects Agency for an enormous shitload of cash.

Lucy Karp had no intention of taking a cab, although a slow cab caught in midtown traffic was going to be part of the cover story. Instead she slipped into the subway at 168th Street and took the A train downtown. She would pocket the cab fare, of course. Money had lately become more significant. She was assembling a trove, for what purpose she could not quite articulate, but it had something to do with her mother, with breaking away. At some level, of course, she understood that she was twelve, that she was not, in fact, going to light out for the territory anytime soon, even that her lot was not in the least comparable to that of kids with serious problems, but still there was that itch to have a little secret pile. Shadkin's money, which would remain a private matter to the extent possible, would make a nice addition.

When the train came roaring in, she boarded the first car and settled herself in the corner seat across from the motorman's booth. She amused herself by memorizing the appearances of the other people in the car, closing her eyes and describing them to herself, then checking to see if she'd got it right. She was pretty good at it by now. She had learned it a year or so ago from a middle-aged Vietnamese gentleman with an interesting past, an employee of her mother's. It was an art useful if one is liable to be followed by people of evil intent. Lucy had not to her knowledge ever been so followed, but given her mother's activities, it was not excessively paranoid to think that she might one day be on some psychopath's list.

At 125th Street the first wave of rush hour boarded the car, ending her game, and she took a worn yellow-covered paperback book from her backpack. One of her great disappointments had been the discovery that facility in learning to speak foreign languages did not mean that she could automatically read them as easily. She had to learn to read French and Chinese and Arabic with sweat, just as little French and Chinese and Arab children did. Most pedagogues would not have started a young girl off with *Claudine à l'école*, Colette's racy account of sexual silliness at a girls' school circa 1890, but Lucy had rifled it from her mother's bookshelf, attracted by the title, and had thereafter fallen under its spell. The book had immediately become her favorite, alongside *Kim*, for it supplied the girl-specific material in which the Kipling novel was lamentably void. Lucy had consigned *Catcher in the Rye*, her favorite of the previous year, to the closet bottom; compared to Claudine and Kim, Holden was a gormless dickhead. The problem was how to combine the two into a model for life. It was rather easier to imagine a turbaned, filthy Claudine slipping through the alleys of Lahore, speaking all the languages of the bazaar, the Little Friend of All the World, than it was to imagine Kim having thrills in the washroom in the Montigny school, but the problem remained. That her own mother had confronted the same quandary at about the same age and had solved it, after a fashion, was an idea that did not occur to Lucy, for her relations with that woman had degenerated into a series of border skirmishes, with the prospect of a major battle to come.

Lost in the story and struggling with the antiquated provincial slang of the French, she almost missed her stop, and had to shove her narrow body through a dense mass of strap hangers to the almost closing doors. Lucy did not mind the subway in the least, and rode it at most hours, especially enjoying those rides when, as now, her mother thought she was safe in a stuffy cab. None of the things that were supposed to happen to lone young girls on subways had yet happened to her. No one had even pinched her, but then, she admitted to herself, she had little enough yet that was pinchable. She caught a glimpse of herself in the glass of a wall ad and grimaced. This was something the lovely Claudine had no reason to worry about, and Lucy was of two minds about it. Boys ignored her, which was good, because she *certainly* didn't want them nosing after her as they were starting to do to her friend, Janice Chen. On the other hand . . . on the other hand, what? She couldn't fully articulate it, not yet, but the thing was there, beneath her conscious mind, fueled by the menace of hormones coiled in ambush: sexual rivalry, the ever ignored issue in the lives of mothers and daughters. It did not help that she looked like a geeky boy, and her mother looked like a baroque saint as imagined by Bernini.

Lucy stepped out of the subway station, blinked in the bright June sunlight, took a left, and walked into Asia. The outposts of Chinatown had taken over much of Canal Street in her own lifetime, pushing up from the south via Mott and Mulberry streets and spreading east and west on the broad thoroughfare. Lucy knew Chinatown. She was practically a native, having been born a few streets north on Crosby Street, where Little Italy meets Soho, and had from an early age been a presence on its streets, gadding about with the four Chen children and their parents, cousins, in-laws, and associates. And Chinatown knew Lucy. Hardly a merchant on its streets had not done a double-take when the *gwailo* infant had addressed him or her in the clanging accents of Guangdong. For when Lucy's mother had unexpectedly rescued the Chen family's honor, she had created an enormous burden of *bao*, a debt of reciprocity owed to her not only by the Chen family proper, but by the Chen name association, its allied name associations, the tong to which the family belonged, and, to a lesser extent, the county and village associations of the fifty-millionfold Chens. That Lucy's mother had only been doing her job was a laughable concept to the old-country Chinese, to whom life was largely a meshwork of unspoken obligations. Thus it happened that Lucy Karp, being first her mother's daughter, and second, the foster daughter of the Chen clan, and thirdly a miraculous and rather spooky speaker of perfect Cantonese (and arguably not less than a reincarnation of Chen Renmi, the dead sister), had achieved a status that few Caucasians are ever granted in that community: she had become a real person, someone with *mihnhai*, with face, and no longer merely a white ghost.

She had emerged into a fine New York summer evening, Canal Street packed with trucks and cars going to the tunnel or the bridges, sending up a fine stink of fumes to the sky, which was just going slatey blue, the stink mixing with the higher notes of fried fat, starch, spice, and decay to make the true Chinatown perfume. The wide sidewalks teemed with shoppers just out of work, enough of them Asians of various tribes to make the *gwailo* among them stand out. Lucy threaded through the crowd and into the Asia Mall, a wide double storefront on the north side of Canal, and a typical enterprise of the district. Its show-windows were nearly covered with hand-lettered ads on white butcher paper, Chinese characters in red paint touting shoes, clothing, fabric, drugstore items, and food specialties of the Orient. It was a great success and the result of over twenty years of backbreaking labor by the Chen family.

As she passed through the Asia Mall, she greeted the checkout ladies in Cantonese, assured them she had eaten, inquired after their families, and they about hers (their hands never stopping to punch in and stuff bags, never pausing in the accumulation of wealth), and she moved on to the back of the store, and through the swinging door to the storeroom. She made her way down the aisles of the cavernous space, treading familiar pathways until she came to the pillow section. She scampered up the pipe scaffolding like a young monkey, crawled through a space in the chicken wire, and wriggled through fake-fur passages until she came to a void, a cave about ten feet on a side, entirely surrounded by fluffy beanbags dyed colors so garish that they were hardly salable, even to Filipinos. A space had been left above, like a hairy skylight, through which a sickly fluorescent glow penetrated, enough to read by. It was a perfect hideout, if you ignored the stink of cheap plastic, and here she found, as she had expected, Janice Chen and Mary Ma.

They say that two boys is half a boy and three boys is no boy at all; it is as true of girls. Janice Chen was supposed to be "helping" in the stockroom and had asked Mary Ma to share the burden and goof off. The two—Lucy's closest friends, Janice as good as a sister—might have stood in a pattern book for the two most familiar types of Chinese girls. Mary had the flat moon face, rosebud mouth, cheeks like peaches, and the bowl cut with bangs, while Janice was slender and golden as a flute, with high cheek-bones, a sharp small nose, and forty inches of black hair running down her back in a braid like a python.

"Lucy!" the other girls both cried, but not too loudly. "We thought you were getting your brains scrambled at Columbia," Janice added.

"I was, but I got out early and took the train."

"What did he make you do?"

"Strip naked and walk around on my hands. He's really a little bit of a sex maniac."

"No, really!" Mary insisted.

"Oh, just science stuff. I had to wear this like old-fashioned bathing cap with wires coming out of it and translate from *Guóndùngwá* and *guoyu* and French and Vietnamese, back and forth. Totally boring. But he's going to pay me. A lot."

"Really?" asked Janice. "Are you going to keep it?" In her world earnings were the property of the family.

"Of course," said Lucy, "and don't tell anyone, okay? What're you guys doing?"

"We're supposed to be breaking boxes," answered Janice. "My brother's being a total dork about it. He loves to give orders—big deal, he's in *charge* of us. So we're hiding."

Mary added responsibly, "We should go back. He'll tell your dad."

"Oh, let him wait," said Lucy. "Later we'll all do it together and get it finished. You want me to read you more Claudine?"

Glittering eyes and giggles. Lucy got out her book and translated the part where the schoolgirls have a fight in a hotel room with their chemises rucking naughtily up around their various interesting parts. The rural dialect in which much of it was written gave her some trouble, but she bulled through, in the process adding some lubricious details omitted by Colette. Like the girls in the novel, the three of them were, in fact, as pure as boiled eggs, but, in the manner of many such children, they very much wished to think of themselves as sexy devils. Of course, they had swiped copies of *Playgirl*, and they had weathered copies of *Zap Comix*—they were 1980s rather than 1880s girls, after all—but still the lush and sensuous language of a ninety-year-old French novel provided them with the required combination of secrecy and salaciousness. The three of them lay stretched out, belly down on the fur, with Lucy in the center, their bodies touching, and Lucy toyed with Janice's long rope of hair as she read. Each would remember this span of time—it could not have been more than forty minutes—with regret and a certain longing, as the pinnacle of something sweet and absolutely lost. So intent were they on what they were doing, so deliciously close and intimate was the atmosphere of the furry cave they had made, that it took some little time for it to register that strange voices were rising through the beanbags from directly below them. Lucy stopped reading, and they all listened.

"*Sssh!* Listen!" Janet interrupted in a hoarse whisper.

"Your brother?" asked Mary.

"No, dummy! It's two people, right below us." They all listened.

"That's not your dad, is it?" Lucy asked Janice in a low voice.

"No, it's strangers," whispered Janice.

Lucy said, "Let's go and see who they are." With that, she stashed her book and wriggled away through the bags, but not the way she had come in. Instead, she pushed her way to the face of the bin that over-looked the main aisle of the stockroom. Shortly, Janice followed, and then Mary, their three faces pressing against the wire mesh through a narrow slit between a pair of beanbags.

Looking down, they saw three men, two youthful and one elderly, all Chinese. One of the young men and the older man were standing together, and were dressed in cream silk suits. The other young man, clad in a blue suit, was addressing them in Canton-ese, in the accents of rural Guangzhou. He was using extremely courteous language, flattering words, something about staying, about others who would arrive soon. The older man replied in the same tongue, but with a Hong Kong accent, a heated reply to the effect that he had come a long way, and did not appreciate the waste of time. His younger compan-ion concurred, but more vigorously. The blue-suited man resumed his appeals. From their high angle, the girls could not see the faces of the men below, but it was clear from the body language of the two Hong Kong men that they were not mollified.

What happened next happened so fast that for a stunned instant the girls could not believe what they had witnessed. A slightly built man, wearing a dark sweatshirt with the hood pulled up and tied in place, walked around the corner from an adjoining aisle and, holding a pistol stiffly at arm's length, shot the two Hong Kong men in the back, and when they fell down he shot them both in the head. *Pop-pop. Pop-pop.* Then he was gone.

Lucy heard Mary Ma take a sharp breath, and knew that in another half second a scream would burst out and so she twisted like a fish and clapped a hand over the other girl's mouth. This quick motion made the beanbags shift, and the man in the blue suit lifted his head up and looked right at them. Hours seemed to pass. Lucy could feel Mary's rapid, boiling-hot breath swish past her hand. Her palm was soaked with drool, and Mary's breathing was starting to make a nasty bubbling sound against it, which Lucy was sure could be heard across Canal Street.

"Be quiet!" she hissed into Mary's ear. The other girl took one long, shuddering breath and was still. The man stared for a little longer, then turned on his heel and walked away. The two Hong Kong men stayed where they had fallen, the runnels of blood from their heads joining into one round, ghastly pool, black as tar under the harsh fluorescent lights.

Janice Chen was the first to move, sliding backward through the sticky, clinging vinyl and the whispering fake fur. Back in the hideout, Mary Ma burst into blubbering tears, and the two other girls threw themselves on her to get her to stop, Lucy going so far as to grab a handful of Day-Glo pink fur and hold it over her mouth. In a minute or so, Mary had regained control and they got off her.

"Oh, God, what are we going to do?" she whimpered.

"I know that guy," said Janice, ignoring this. The other two stared at her.

"What guy?" Lucy asked.

"The guy in the blue suit, the guy who walked away. I don't know his name, but he's always hanging around with my father."

"A tong guy?"

Janice nodded, eyes dropping. Lucy understood Chinatown well enough to understand this. No important Chinatown businessman, especially not a first-generation Chinese immigrant like Louie Chen, was unconnected to the tongs. The Chens' tong was the Hap Tai Association, but Lucy had never heard a breath that they might be involved in murder, at least not recently. The tongs worked their wills far more subtly nowadays. On the other hand, there were certainly gangs in Chinatown, and gangs killed people, and nearly every gang had some affiliation with a tong.

"What are we going to *do*, Lòuhsì?"

Lucy became aware that both of her friends were watching her expectantly. She expected this. The word for "teacher" in Cantonese is *lòuhsì*, and Lucy had been called that, as a joke, by the Chens and by every other Cantonese speaker she had met from an early age. At first it had been amusing to give a little mite (and a female at that) such a name. Later, as Lucy's personality developed, it seemed more appropriate, sometimes disturbingly so. Lucy was, in fact, the leader of the little band, both of the inner circle here assembled and of a satellite clique of a half dozen girls at school. There was nothing racial in this; Lucy would have been a leader anywhere, and added to that there was the thing with the languages, and also (although no one mentioned this to her) she was the daughter of the legendary Shenpei Meilin, the one-eyed, who shot people, and crushed evildoers without mercy, like a warrior woman from the old tales. So they looked at her to see what she would do.

"Well, so first of all, we're not going to tell anyone about this," Lucy said firmly, and she detected tiny sighs of relief from her companions. No explanation of this was necessary, but she gave one anyway, to make sure the reasons were fixed in both their minds. "Mr. Chen didn't know what was going down here" (this to save Janice's face), "but if the cops know about Janice seeing this guy with him, he's going to be in big trouble. *Big* trouble." She meant with the tong, not the police. There was no question in any of their minds about this.

"And, of course, *Mary* can't say anything either," said Lucy, and they all knew what *that* meant, too, because they knew that Mary and her family were *ren she*, smuggled illegals, with phony papers that would not survive any official inspection.

There was a long pause after this, a silence broken only by Mary's snuffling. Lucy felt the eyes. "Oh, right!" she said indignantly to the silence. "*I'm* really going to rat you out. *Cào dàn! Fàng gou pì!* . . ." and more of the same, for although in English Lucy was as clean-mouthed as could be wished, in either Cantonese or Mandarin she could strip the chrome off a trailer hitch. "If you think that," she continued,

switching from Mandarin to Cantonese and moder-
ating her tone, "the pair of you are dumb as wooden
chickens. Do you think I would get my foster father
in trouble? Or get Mary's family kicked out?"

Shamefaced, the other girls agreed that this was
not to be thought of.

"Okay, then, we have to swear never to tell *anyone* about this. Not your family or anyone. And
believe me, they're going to come after you."

"What! How!"

"Silly turtles! When they find the bodies, they'll
want to talk to everyone who was back here, and
Janice's parents know you both were back here. Nobody knows I'm here, and I want you to keep it that
way. Now, swear it! Give me your hands!"

The three clasped their hands in a knot. Lucy felt
imbued with a rich excitement, as the situation combined the best aspects of Claudine and Kim, girlish
intimacy and deadly danger. She thought briefly of
pulling her little pocket knife and extracting a blood
oath, but her natural practicality and her apprehension that, confronted with additional gore, Mary Ma
would lose it again, decided her in favor of a purely
verbal ritual. In Chinese, of course.

"Mary, you go first!" she ordered.

Mary, quavering, said, "I swear."

Janice said, "I swear to the sky."

Lucy said, "I swear, and if I go back on my word,
let me be executed by heaven and destroyed by
earth!"

Under this profound doom, Lucy led the way out
of the secret nest and out the rear door onto Crosby
Street.

"Go around to the front entrance and get lost in the store. Find something to do—like, grab some cartons and move them around until somebody notices you. Then you say, if they ask you, you were in the front the whole time. You didn't see anything. They might not believe you, but if you stick to the story, they can't do anything. And look, they'll get each of you alone and they'll say, like, 'Janice, Mary told us the whole story, why don't you tell us what went down.' They always do that trick. Just keep saying you didn't see anything. And cry a lot, and have to go pee every ten minutes."

With this good advice, they dashed off. Lucy walked the two short blocks to her home. The Karp family lived in a fifth-floor floor-through loft on Crosby at Grand, which Lucy's mother had occupied since the late sixties, when Soho was barely a gleam in some speculator's eye and regular people (not to mention rich ones) did not dwell in disused factory space. It had been beautifully modified some years back as a result of a parental windfall: Swedish finish on the floor, track lighting on the ceiling, a kitchen out of a magazine spread, climate control, and a hot tub. The building had gone condo and put in an elevator entered from the street with a special key. Lucy wore hers around her neck. She twisted this, waited, ascended, and emerged. There she was greeted by, in order, her twin four-year-old brothers, Giancarlo and Isaac (called, in a deplorable excess of cute, Zik and Zak), their so-called nanny, a retired street person in her early twenties (Posie), and her father, Roger Karp (called Butch), the chief assistant district attorney for the County of New York.

All these save the last she disposed of with dispatch: a sloppy kiss and a couple of tickle rhymes for the boys, a how-was-your-day and a critical note on the Violent Femmes with Posie. Then she sidled up to her dad and clutched him about the waist, rather harder than was her habit. He looked down at her.

"Something wrong?"

"No, not really. Just need a hug."

This was supplied, with enthusiasm. He asked, "How did the brain thing go?"

"All right, I guess. He seemed pretty excited about me. Apparently, I'm a total freak show."

"How would you like a hit in the head?"

"Well, I *am*."

Karp aimed a mock back-hander at his daughter's head, which she ducked, and then they sparred around a little, a familiar game and one that Karp knew did not have long to run. He was glad to get in as many bouts of affectionate roughhousing as time and biology would allow.

When he, after many shifting moves, had her in a clinch and had tormented her in the usual way by rubbing his five o'clock shadow across her tender cheek, to the usual howls, he said, "You want to know a secret? Everybody thinks they're a freak. Everybody thinks people are staring at them. Everybody thinks everybody else is better off or happier, especially kids. You want me to give you a pep talk? You want me to make a list of all your good points?"

"Not really," she said, her gaze sliding away from his.

"Anything go wrong today, Luce?" asked Karp, his fatherly antennae vibrating.

"No, just the usual," Lucy lied, and then changed the subject to "Are you going to cook those?"

She pointed at the counter in the gleaming kitchen where sat a pair of icy brownish Tupperware oblongs.

"Yeah, we have a choice of lamb stew or lasagna."

"*Com'é ripugnanti,*" said Lucy, wrinkling her nose. "Where's Mom?"

"She said she was tied up. Didn't she call you? She said she was going to tell you to take a cab home."

"Yeah, she did."

"You got a cab all right?"

Lucy felt her face flush. Another lie in the offing, and Lucy tried as hard as ever she could not to lie to her father. The scrupulous honesty of this man was one of the foundation stones of her moral universe. In contrast, her mother had a more fluid relationship with veracity. As Lucy herself did, she had to admit. "I never lie, never, but the truth is not for everyone," was one of her mother's sayings, delivered always in Italian.

So she uttered a vague mumble that she hoped would suffice to pass the question, which it did, and then she asked, "Can we order out? Please? I'll call Pho Bác. I'm dying for *chà giò.* Spring rolls? And noodles and lemon chicken?" She looked disdainfully at the hearty meals her mother had prepared in her weekly marathon cooking sessions. "I don't see why she bothers. Posie cooks for the boys, and we live in the take-out capital of the galaxy. Please?"

Karp laughed and said, "Hell, yeah! Let's live a little," because by and large he agreed with his daughter about take-out, and the absurdity of a woman who worked as hard as his wife did worrying about home cooking. Besides that, he was feeling bushed and was not looking forward to eating a microwaved meal liable to be chilly in the center and dry on the edges and have to clean up after.

Lucy ran to the phone and put in the order, in Vietnamese.

Karp watched his remarkable daughter do this with his usual mix of love and concern, a little heavier on the concern this evening because he had spent fifteen years with the D.A. and knew from a few thousand confrontations what someone who had something to hide looked like. Lucy had something to hide.

2

IT WAS KARP'S HABIT WHEN THE weather was fine to pick up the *News* and skim through it as he strode along the eight-block distance between the loft and the New York County courthouse at 100 Centre Street. He relied on his size and the determination of his walk to clear the way of all smaller mobile objects and his remarkable peripheral vision to steer clear of the larger ones, like trucks. Karp walked with the loping, graceful stride of the American athlete, which also served to sweep people from his way. Karp had, in fact, been an athlete, a very good one in his youth, a high school All-American in basketball and a Pac 10 star at Berkeley. A horrific injury to his knee had cut that career short, eliminating the jock arrogance from his personality and the knee itself from his body. Having had the orthopedic replacement, he was after nearly twenty years quite pain-free, except, on occasions, around the heart. Suffering does not always ennoble, but in Karp's case it actually had, although it would never have occurred to him (as it would have and did to his wife) to think of it that way. What he felt was a rediscovered plea-

sure in his body, evinced now, as it was every work-
day morning, in the recovery of his swift, charging,
aggressive New York pace. He could usually get
through his usual reading—sports and crime—by
the time he reached the trash can at Foley Square,
where the courthouse stood.

The weather was indeed fine, and he flew more
or less blind down Centre Street from Grand,
clutching the tattered red cardboard folder he used
for a briefcase under his arm like a running back's
football, and snapping through the pages of the
tabloid. Karp had a real briefcase, a lush cordovan
Mark Cross, given to him by his father for his law
school graduation gift, but he never used it. This
had to do with Karp's extraordinary (and in that
era of luxuriant self-promotion, near-pathological)
conservatism with regard to personal show, which
had prevented him from appearing with a shiny
new briefcase on his first day at the D.A.'s years
ago, and continued to generate excuses for not now
showing up with it. Lugging the tacky cardboard
gave him a vague satisfaction, and also served to
distinguish him in his own mind from those members of his profession not famously devoted to justice, who had been richly rewarded by society for
their scumbaggery, and who typically hauled their
vile shenanigans about in the finest morocco.

As for the rest of his equipage, Karp was dressed
at that moment in a natural shoulder, three-button,
navy tropical wool suit with the faintest of pinstripes,
one virtually identical to the other nine suits he
owned (half winter- and half summer-weight). With
this he wore a plain-collar white silk shirt and a tie

that Richard Nixon might have rejected as being a shade too understated, and a pair of black cap-toe wing tips. Except for the tie, everything visible he had on was custom-made and of the highest possible quality, which bought at retail would have set him back well over five grand. He had spent nothing like that, however, since the clothing and shoes came from Chen connections in Hong Kong and Taipei, who had supplied it at cost or less. Thus did Karp reap the benefits of being, through marriage, an honorary Chen, and therefore he read with more than usual concentration the story of the murders in the Asia Mall, and not without a sharp pang of fear, since he knew that the murder scene was one of the usual hangouts of his little girl. He parked the tabloid in his usual waste can and walked into Foley Square.

Two centuries ago, Foley Square had been Collect Pond, a body of water that early New Yorkers had soon converted into an open sewer. Hardly had the colonial filth jelled when they built the city jail on it, which sank into the mire, and then they built another one on top of it, the infamous Tombs. The four towers that Karp saw as he walked through the tiny park with its incomprehensible orange steel sculpture was the third grim structure on the site, and no longer the main New York jail, although one tower was still used as a holding facility for prisoners undergoing justice and was still called the Tombs. It was a gray and hulking fascist ziggurat, and Karp, who had slight interest in architecture, rather liked it. He thought that, considering what transpired within, a pretty building would have been an obscenity.

There was an entrance on the south side of the Criminal Courts building reserved for its staff, but Karp ordinarily preferred to come in through the main door facing Foley Square. Here he was exposed to the sentiments carved in marble on the sides of the entranceway, and, as a ritual, he read one or two of them, like a tourist. This morning it was *Why should there not be a patient confidence in the ultimate justice of the people*, which always gave Karp a chuckle, since what was just on the other side of the swinging glass doors was a pretty good argument why not. The lobby here had been known since the late sixties as the Streets of Calcutta. When someone in the D.A. said, "Hey, I saw Bernie Popkin in Calcutta yesterday," they referred not to the Asian metropolis but to this melancholy hallway, murmurous with sighs, cries of outrage, confidential whispers, and other noises associated with a criminal-justice apparatus rusted and crumbling like the West Side Highway, and suffused, not unlike the actual Calcutta, with a peculiar and diagnostic odor, constructed of old paint, musty papers, disinfectant, the snack bar's grease-and-burnt-coffee, the expensive cologne of rich lawyers, the cheap scent of whores, and the immemorial effluvium of the unwashed poor.

This was, of course, Karp's native air, and a tonic; breathing it in and rubbing against Calcutta was the reason he took this route. In his present job he spent a lot of time handling clean paper and harrying the neatly dressed. He felt his edge slowly dulling and wanted grit, and this walk was, most days, all he would get of it. He passed the several thick lines of people waiting to traverse the guard station and its metal detectors and went toward the left side of the entryway, where there was a special gate for the anointed. People were lined up there, too, showing their passes. Karp did not show his pass, because the guard and all the other court officers knew him by sight. This was not hard to do, because Karp was six-five, with big hands and long arms on a solidly built lean frame, a tall dark slab like the one that amazed the ape men in *2001*. On top of this was an equally memorable face, a bony, sallow one with a broad, heavy brow under crisp brown hair unfashionably cut by an ancient Italian person on Mulberry Street, and high cheekbones, not the good type sported by the people who drank crystalline martinis in Connecticut, but the less prestigious kind seen on those who drank fermented mare's milk east of Odessa. A determined chin under a surprisingly sensual mouth, a nose too large and too often broken—now resembling a sock toe full of pebbles—and, his most striking feature, odd, long, slightly slanted eyes, colored gray with yellow flecks. Karp flashed this face at the guard, greeted her by name, and was waved on through. The usual murmur of resentment issued from some of the other people waiting before the gate, this being democratic New York, and *standing on line*, as they say there, being one of the last remaining flecks of cultural glue, but no actual challenges. Karp was not above taking this privilege of rank.

Another one of these was the office. It was located on the eighth floor in the suite occupied by the district attorney, and it contained rugs and paneling and wooden furniture and a big leather chair and two large windows looking out on Foley Square. Karp greeted Mary O'Malley, the D.A.'s formidable secretary, went by the supply room for a cup of her excellent coffee, and went back to his office. Karp had recently been made, somewhat to his own surprise, *chief* assistant district attorney. Before that he had held a meaningless staff post into which he had been stuffed to rescue him from a political firestorm arising out of a racially charged murder case. Since then there had been an election, which the D.A., Jack Keegan, had won by a 71 percent plurality and could thereafter do as he damn pleased, and what he pleased to do was to appoint Karp as what was essentially the chief operating officer of the entire prosecutorial organization. Karp did not particularly enjoy the bureaucratic aspects of the job, but he was vitally interested in maintaining the integrity of the D.A.'s office against all assaults, of which in the present corrupt age there were many. What Karp really liked doing, what he did better than practically anyone in the city, was trying homicide cases, and in the negotiations that had led to his present position he had arranged with Keegan, in a manner rather like some medieval symbol of a feudal obligation (the gill of pepper or the five silver fox pelts) that he would get his pick of one case per annum, to prepare and to bring before a jury. Meanwhile, he was a team player, and he discovered, also to his surprise, that he was reasonably competent at a variety of unpleasant bureaucratic tasks. He hired, he fired. He caused the drafting and distribution and approval of policy documents. He spread terror among the incompetent and lazy. He kibitzed on important trials. He distributed largesse—office furniture, remodeling, space, and staff—where he thought it would do the most good, he spied discreetly, and he passed on to his boss what he considered it proper for the big guy to know. And occasionally he had dumped in his lap an affair so tormented, so covered with poisonous spines and excrement, that only someone with insane bravery and no detectable ambition for higher office would touch it with a barge pole.

Then O'Malley came in abruptly, her wrist with its watch held up in front of her face. Karp stared at her. She tapped the watch dial with a blunt fingernail.

"The Hilton? It's nine-fifty."

"Oh, *shit*!" cried Karp, leaping up. He ran for the door, grabbing his jacket on the way. The secretary slapped an envelope into his hand, like the baton of a relay racer, as he flew by.

"Ed's waiting out on Leonard Street," shouted O'Malley, and received a shouted thanks.

Of all of Karp's duties, the most irritating (which is why he often had to be reminded of it, as now) was representing the district attorney at public events that the district attorney did not think quite important enough to require the exhibition of his actual body, but not negligible either, so that someone from the office had to go eat the chicken and peas. Karp was almost always this eater.

At least he got to go to these in a cop car. Ed Morris, his driver, goosed lights and siren to clear a

path uptown. Karp dabbed his brow with his handkerchief, used the rearview to fix his tie, and pulled
out the contents of the envelope. Oh, yeah, *this*, he
recalled: the Metropolitan Council's annual awards
luncheon. This was an assembly of the great and the
good dedicated to civic improvements of all types,
one of the older and less interesting of the innumerable groups doing the same in New York. It was
dominated by slightly right-of-center academics,
didn't give political contributions, and was not likely
to soon give an award to Jack Keegan, which was
why he wasn't going and Karp was. The person who
was getting this year's award was Thomas Colombo,
the U.S. attorney for the Southern District of New
York, a registered Republican. Karp ran his eyes
down the list of speakers and discovered "John J.
Keegan (invited)," who was to discourse on "The
New York D.A. and Organized Crime" for fifteen
minutes as a warm-up to the actual award and the
main address by its distinguished recipient, whose
subject was listed as "Using the Racketeer Influenced and Corrupt Organizations Act Against
Criminal Infiltrators."

Karp cursed briefly, pulled out a pen, and started
to make notes on the back of the flyer. Public speaking held no fears for him, and he was an extempore
speaker of real talent. By the time he had arrived at
the Hilton at 53rd and Sixth, he had a beginning,
middle, and closing indicated by telegraphic sentences, and single-word indications referring to
appropriate jokes—frog, farmer, clam—all guaranteed not to offend any conceivable ethnic, religious,
disadvantaged, or sexual group.

He was late to the dais table—the fruit cup had already been proffered—but he shook hands with the owlish professor who ran the outfit, made a gracious apology for his boss's unavailability and his own lateness, and told the man who he was. He sat down between a Methodist bishop and an attractive woman whose name card said she was the president of one of the city university's colleges. The college president immediately engaged him in a conversation about Marlene Ciampi, his wife, about whom she had an unbounded curiosity, this soon shared by the bishop, and Karp found himself reluctantly recounting the inside skinny on some of her cases, and after that began to grow tedious ("But how do you stand it, the violence? And what about the children?") he skillfully turned the subject to college presidenting and bishopry. One good thing about the people you met at these operations, he reflected, it was never hard to get them to start talking about themselves.

The owlish professor tapped a glass as Latinos carted away the remains of the meal and introduced Karp and his subject. There was no sigh of disappointment in the crowd. Karp was very nearly as well-known among the city's crime buffs as the D.A. himself, and had perhaps the more colorful background.

He rose to the podium, told the frog joke, got a mild laugh, presented the take of the man Karp considered the finest of the city's D.A.s, the late, great Francis P. Garrahy, on the Mob (They want to kill each other? I'll hire Yankee Stadium for them, and I'll pay for the bullets), and then delivered a precise and lucid talk about the origins of organized crime in New York and why it was inevitable given the predilection of Americans to legislate sin into the criminal code, and why the alternative to organized crime was not necessarily law and order, but was more often an increase in disorganized crime, verging on anarchy and the conversion of streets into war zones. He reminded his audience that when Murder Incorporated did its work back in the thirties and forties, it killed discreetly and accurately, and did not spray the streets with gunfire, wiping out kids and old ladies. Reverse course now, tell the farmer joke, remarks not meant as an endorsement of the Mob, *The Godfather* only a movie, the real guys nasty, unattractive, fortunately mostly dumb as a load of bricks, then a brief summary of the D.A.'s approach to organized crime, which was not that different from its approach to regular crime—if someone did a crime, they got prosecuted, whether their name was Gambino, Colombo, or Ishkabibble. Tell some goombah stories, the big New York cases, Tom Dewey, Garrahy, more modestly, Karp himself (moral: we don't necessarily need the feds to help us deal with these fellas), tell the clam joke, big laugh, but not from Tommy Colombo, who never liked to hear the name of that particular crime family uttered in a public place, and Karp had indeed used it as a mildly nasty zinger, see if the guy was awake there, and move to close. Burst of applause, actual, not polite hand slapping.

Then the professor introduced Colombo, introduced the award, told everyone why Tommy C. was getting it, and handed it over (a crystal plaque with a bronze shield embedded within). Colombo moved to the podium. He was a stocky man of thirty-eight with thinning brown hair, a bony, big-nosed hatchet face, and a wide, lipless mouth. Under heavy eyebrows his eyes were large, heavy-lidded, and protuberant. He had a strong tenor voice and a New York accent. Karp had meanly left the microphone up so that Colombo had to bring it down seven inches, thus illustrating the difference between Karp's height and his own.

Colombo spoke RICO for twenty-five minutes, reading from a sheaf of papers, squeezing in as many invidious comparisons as possible between the old, ineffective, case-by-case way of dealing with the Mob (broadly implied: just what the New York D.A. still did, the *patzers*) and the RICO way: gigantic, thermonuclear-strength prosecutions with multiple indictments that could wipe out whole crime families at a blow. His applause was noticeably less intense than that which had followed Karp's effort.

Afterward, politeness required Karp to mingle and shake, people coming up and exclaiming how much they liked his talk and would he consent to speak at their school, church, club, retreat, picnic, commencement? He collected business cards and distributed noncommittal answers. He got vamped in a civilized way by the college president (which had the virtue of keeping others away), and after that he made his escape.

As he wrongly imagined. There was a blond, burly crew cut standing by the elevator. Karp observed that he had a little radio device in his ear. When Karp approached, the crew cut mashed the elevator button, the door slid open, Karp entered, but the crew cut didn't. Tommy Colombo was in the car.

"Nice speech, Butch," he said, mirthlessly smiling. They shook.

"Thanks. I'm going down," said Karp.

Colombo pushed **L**. "I always thought Jack was lucky to have you," said Colombo. "Of course, it's a hell of a waste, you running errands like this. It's like using Reggie Jackson as a bat boy."

"How about those Yankees?" said Karp tonelessly.

"Seriously, I never figured it out, how come you don't move somewhere where you could try cases?"

"Seriously? I tried private for a while. I didn't much like it."

"I don't mean private," said Colombo. "I don't mean Brooklyn or Nassau either."

The elevator stopped. Colombo put his finger on the door-close button. "You taking up career counseling, Tom?" Karp asked.

"Like the Marines, I'm always looking for a few good men. My trial division chief is about to transfer out. You should come by, we'll talk. About trial work, major cases."

Karp nodded and said, as to a child, "Tom, let me explain a few things. First of all, I'm controlling a case load approximately a hundred times the size of yours. I could run your whole trial division in my lunch hour. Second, I can try any case I like, and when I do I get to try it my way, without having to think about what it means to anybody's political ambitions down in D.C., or even right here in the city. Third, I work for a guy I respect." Here he looked down at Colombo and stared expressionlessly as he would have at a felon who had just told a whopper, waiting for the skel to lose the attitude. Colombo stared back at him, a look of disbelief on his face. He was not often spoken to in this manner. Karp said, "Tom, take your finger off the button. And the next time you want to talk to me, use the phone and make an appointment. The elevator and the FBI guy business is for the movies."

After a few seconds' hiatus to demonstrate who was in control, or something like that, Colombo released the button and Karp walked out.

On the ride downtown, he mused about the impossibility of his ever working for somebody like Tommy Colombo. Keegan was very nearly as ambitious as the other man, but Karp thought he could usually shame Jack Keegan into behaving by playing the Francis P. Garrahy card. Keegan needed at some level to feel himself right with Garrahy, his mentor, the greatest D.A. in New York's history. Over Colombo Karp would have no such control. He dismissed the man from his mind and pulled out his calendar. A meeting about handicapped accessibility around the courthouse. Wonderful!

At his office, there were two people in wheelchairs and a guy with black glasses and a white stick waiting for him. He smiled, sighed, and waved them in.

• • •

Back at the Crosby Street loft, Mrs. Karp, née and still to all the world Marlene Ciampi, sat at her kitchen table and gazed mindlessly at the smoky surface of a cup of Medaglia D'Oro coffee the color and consistency of tire paint, waiting for her personality to reassemble itself from the chaos of sleep. Flanking her were Zak and Giancarlo, four and identical, sloppily munching a brand of cartoon cereal sugary enough to cause hypoglycemia in the average adult and with little nutritional value. An enormous black Neapolitan mastiff circulated under the table, grunting and licking up spills. Mrs. Karp disapproved, mildly, but she was not in charge of breakfast.

The person who was, Posie the Hippie Slut Nanny, sat opposite, crunching the same garbage, and regally handling the remote for the small Sony depending from a corner of the ceiling. She switched channels rapidly, in a manner designed to mollify the twins, who, though alike as two eggs to the eye, had radically different tastes in morning TV, Zak preferring trashy cartoon violence, Giancarlo doting on *Sesame Street* and, strangely, game shows. Mrs. Karp ordinarily found such channel surfing unbearable, but said nothing. Officially, she was not really there, and she was bottomlessly grateful to Posie for handling the boys' mornings. The girl could have fed them human flesh and run little Satanic rituals without Marlene making much of a fuss. Morning was not her best time.

She was snapped into real consciousness because Posie's thumb happened to falter on the switch and the set rested for a moment on a morning news program. Marlene heard, ". . . further developments in last night's double murder in the stockroom of a Chinatown shopping center. The police are questioning Mr. Louie Chen, owner of the Asia Mall, where the bodies of two men reported. . . . *zzsk* . . . He-Man, we've got to get to the castle before Skeletor uses his death ray—"

"Wait! Posie, go back!" cried Marlene.

"What, the news?"

"Yeah, do it!"

But when the morning show came back, the screen showed only the front of the Asia Mall with an attractive young Chinese-American newscaster named Gloria Eng standing in front of it, saying, ". . . the possibility of a gang war in Chinatown. Back to you, Ron."

Posie grinned broadly and pointed. "Hey, that's the Chens' place on the TV. Wow! I was just there the other day."

Giancarlo said, "I was there, too."

"That's where we get lichee nuts," Zak added. "Posie, could we go there today?"

"Today is probably not a great idea, kids," said Marlene, rising. She slurped some more coffee and took the cup down the length of the loft to her home office, where she put in a call to the Chen residence. As she had feared, she got nothing but a busy signal. After the fifth call she gave up and dialed another number which, since it was a police station, was answered. Marlene asked to speak to Detective James Raney, waited, was told he was out, and left a message. After that she trotted through the shower and dressed in her informal work outfit: black cotton slacks, black Converse footwear, and one of her large collection of Hawaiian shirts, the discreet pistol-covering kind, this with mauve orchids, clouds, and moons against bright yellow.

She was checking out this outfit in her mirror when the phone rang and it was Raney returning her call.

"You've decided to leave him and marry me," said Raney. "I knew today was going to be my lucky day."

"Yeah, well, we're almost there, Raney; as soon as the pope comes around on divorce, I'm yours. Meanwhile, what have you got on the thing yesterday at the Asia Mall on Canal?"

"Oh, no small talk? No how's it going, Jim, how's your life been, no tell me the secrets of your inner heart, Jim, we been pals for I forget how many years?"

"I'm sorry, Jim," said Marlene, adopting a concerned therapist's tone, "please, tell me the secrets of your inner heart. Did you ever get help for that sexual thing? The dribble?"

Raney cracked up at this, and they chatted amiably for a few minutes. Raney was Marlene's best friend on the cops and, of course, her primary source of cop information. She quizzed him again on the Chinatown killings, and he made some information-free noises.

"Are you going to make me describe my underwear again, Raney?"

"Um, always a thrill, but I don't think I know enough for a fair trade. A mystery, is what I hear. Two guys, Hong Kong passports, shot twice each, head and back, in the stockroom of the Asia Mall. Nobody saw nothing, as usual."

"The news said something about a gangland slaying."

"The news would. But it's possible. Like the man said, it's Chinatown. What's your interest? Oh, wait, it's *your* Chens, right?"

"Right. My Chens. Is there any idea that they're involved?"

"This I don't know. I could find out who caught the case and what they know, if you want."

"Oh, that'd be great, Jim! I'll owe you one."

"And I'll collect, too," he said, laughed a nasty laugh, and hung up.

Marlene got her gun from the gun safe, clipped it on, logged thirty seconds of quality time with her boys, whistled up the dog, and punched for the elevator. Marlene was in the security business, although the Chens were not clients.

They lived in Confucius Plaza, a seven-year-old structure that had been fully rented before the first spadeful of earth turned over. That the Chens had a nice apartment was an indication that the family was somebody in Chinatown. There were a couple of news vans parked on the street outside, and a small crowd of photo and video journalists lying in wait. Clearly, the cops had suggested, or maybe it was just a media rumor, that the Chens were connected to the "gangland slaying." Hype about a new tong war was in the air, and the press was drooling. As was Sweety, of course. Marlene hooked him to his leash and walked toward the building entrance.

"Sweety, *si brutto!*" she ordered, and the dog

went into his rabies impersonation, heaving at the leash, snarling and flinging long, disgusting ropes of sticky saliva. The media backed away in panic, tripping over cables and dropping mike poles.

"Oh, sorry, oh, gosh, excuse me," Marlene chirped. "Oh, dear! Monster, behave yourself! . . ." until she was at the glass doors. The security guy, who knew Marlene well, was having a hard time keeping his face straight as he opened it for her.

"Way to go, Meilin," he said. "I'll call up for you."

Marlene had known the Chens for nearly fifteen years and had been to their home—originally an apartment on Mott and now this one—innumerable times, to deliver and pick up her daughter. On every occasion she had been offered tea and cigarettes and engaged in a short conversation, almost always about children and the unbearable difficulties brought on by their slovenliness and ingratitude. She had thought that she had, through her daughter at least, a good relationship with the Chen family, not intimate, but sufficient to make this visit perfectly natural and, with the offer of help she had in mind, even welcome. She was soon disabused of this idea. At her ring, Walter, the Chens' eldest son, came to the door and stood there, looking at her as at a stranger. Walter was a senior at Columbia, and Marlene knew him as a bright, often amusing, regular (by which she meant Americanized, predictable) kid.

"Hi, Walter," she said, expecting him to move away from the door and usher her in. He didn't move. His eyes were very black, and flat and (she actually thought the word) inscrutable. "Walter," she said, urging a smile to her lips, "aren't you going to let me in?"

He did not return the smile, but said, as to a stranger, "Marlene, that's not a good idea right now. My parents are extremely upset . . ."

"I bet they are. That's why I came over, to see if I—"

". . . and they can't see anyone today," he concluded, and closed the door firmly in her face.

Karp's intercom buzzed. The handicapped were gone and he was dealing with the aftermath, drafting a memo. He threw down his pencil, pushed the button. O'Malley said, "They're ready for you."

"This is the Catalano meeting?" asked Karp, well knowing it was.

"At long last, and may God have mercy on your soul," said O'Malley fervently.

As a symbol of his authority, Karp got to use the D.A.'s conference room, a stately, paneled office with a long, mellow oaken table and high, stately green leather chairs. The D.A., on attaining the office, had attempted to reproduce, in detail, in the whole executive suite, the decor favored by his predecessor-but-one, Francis P. Garrahy, of sacred memory. Keegan had run the Homicide Bureau under Garrahy, and Karp had been trained in it, and both men were subject to nostalgia for those departed times, when crime seemed slightly less overwhelming. Both men entertained the suspicion, unvoiced to be sure, that even Phil Garrahy might have trimmed a little more than he did, might have had trouble keeping his integrity untarnished under such a collapse of civil order. To his credit, Keegan tried to keep up the standards, and if his own integrity had a grungy spot or two, the symbols were at least kept brightly polished and dusted. For the conference room Keegan had even located in some forgotten Centre Street attic the framed oil portraits of Franklin Roosevelt and Fiorello LaGuardia that Garrahy had hung on his walls and had added one of Garrahy himself, done from a photograph.

It was not a good portrait. In it the old man looked stiff and surprised, neither of which was a characteristic of himself, but it was what they had. This painting looked down upon where Keegan himself now sat at the head of the long table, in his shirtsleeves, toying with a large claro cigar that he never smoked. He was a big, florid Irishman, heavy-shouldered, carrying an elegant head: the requisite pol's mane of white hair, blue, deep-set eyes, an aristocratic beak, no lips to speak of, and a chin like an anvil. He'd played offensive end for Fordham, and retained the grace and the twisty moves. He looked up and popped the cigar into his mouth when Karp walked in, smiling cordially around it. (He never got the end damp, and so no one knew whether he didn't smoke the same one every day or retired the thing at intervals.) Karp nodded to Keegan and to the other three men, and took a seat at the end of the table, where he always sat.

Karp took the notes at these meetings, a somewhat unusual role for someone with his rank, this necessary task being regarded by the average legal bureaucrat as suitable only for peasants, or women. Karp had assumed it for two reasons. First, it made him appear to pompous idiots less important than he was, which made them tend to ignore him, which made it easier for him to sneak up behind them if need be and yank their pants down. Besides that, he understood that who takes the notes at executive meetings controls the memory of an organization, and since Karp had never cultivated a political base, any control he could develop was welcome. While he respected Jack Keegan's skill and competence, and actually liked him well enough as a man, Karp was under no illusions about the district attorney's ambitions. He understood perfectly (for Keegan, to his credit, had made it no secret) that if a sacrifice had to be made to that altar and if Karp was at hand and unprotected, the D.A. would not hesitate for a New York minute before yanking his plug.

Karp took meeting notes in thick accountant's ledgers bound in pale green cloth, items not much in demand at the supply room since computers had come in. He had rows of them in his office in a locked steel cabinet whose sole key was ever in his custody, and he never showed the notes therein to anyone. Thus no one knew what Karp had written down, which tended to make Keegan's more haughty satraps less willing to get into arguments about who had promised what to whom. The note business was an absurdly simple ploy, but it worked to the D.A.'s advantage and polished the luster of Karp. Swiftly, using his idiosyncratic quasi-shorthand, Karp wrote down the purpose of the meeting—"strategy for

Catalano murder"—and the date and the names of the three participants besides himself and the D.A.

The first of these, sitting to Keegan's right was Roland Hrcany, the chief of the Homicide Bureau. Hrcany had the look and build of a professional wrestler, and, like many of them, he wore his straight blond hair combed back from a cave-man brow ridge and long enough to reach past his collar in back. Despite this brutish appearance (or perhaps because of it) he was the best homicide prosecutor in the office, next to Karp, a fact that rankled him, as did Karp's former incumbency as homicide chief. Some months ago he had been shot by a Mexican felon trying to introduce south-of-the-border criminal justice practices to the New York area, and he was still not back on duty full-time. The event, and its wasting effects on his massive body, of which he was inordinately proud, had oddly enough improved his disposition, which had been churlish and of an aggressiveness outstanding even in the testosterone-rich precincts of the D.A.'s office.

Opposite Roland sat Frank Anselmo, the chief of the Rackets Bureau. He was a dapper, dark man with a full head of thick black hair, well cut, and small, active, manicured hands. Anselmo, the son of a police inspector, and thus a man with important cop credibility, had pitched for Fordham during the same years that Keegan had played football. The two men were cronies from way back, and Keegan had brought him in as Rackets chief from the Queens D.A. shortly after taking over the New York office. This made sense, since the D.A. had to trust more than anyone else in his office the person responsible for, among other things, investigating public officials. Karp did not know him well. Rackets was a small bureau, its work was perforce somewhat secret, and it brought few cases to trial. The book on Anselmo around the office was that he was smart, ambitious, and, it seemed, temporarily content to play in the shade cast by Jack Keegan's lofty oak. The relationship with the boss was, of course, well-known, and hardly anyone gave him any trouble. He was smiling and joshing with Keegan about a sports bet. He smiled a lot. In general, Karp was suspicious of people in the criminal justice business who smiled a lot, as he himself did not see much to be happy about there, but Anselmo always seemed to put Keegan in a better mood, which was never to be sneezed at.

The last man at the meeting was clearly not in a good mood and not amused by Anselmo's patter. Raymond Guma, slumped like a bag of dirty laundry in the chair just to Karp's left, was one of the few ADAs who did not at all mind giving Anselmo trouble. Guma had on occasion been mistaken for the former Yankee catcher Yogi Berra, although he was less pretty than Berra, and unlike Berra he had shown (during a tryout for the Yanks, for he had been quite the star at St. John's) that he could not reliably hit a major league breaking ball. He was nearly the same age as Keegan and Anselmo—late fifties—but carried his years more heavily, for unlike the other men there he had never been promoted to any position of authority, and never would be. He had been a homicide prosecutor for over twenty-five years, and he knew more about the New York Mafia than anyone in the building, which was why he was at the meeting. Some said he knew rather too much about the New York Mafia, which was one of the many reasons he had never been promoted. He was a sloppy, ill-disciplined man, a sexist in the current parlance, sour and cynical, but—and this is why Karp loved him—with boundless heart and a sense of humor made of Kevlar.

In the normal course of things, Guma should have been in Rackets under Anselmo, but between the two men lay a morass of near visceral antipathy. This, even more than the hazards of the case on the agenda, accounted for the tension in the room. Keegan let the sports talk peter away. "Guys, you all know how important this one is. We're going to come under a lot of pressure, and I want some early resolution. Butch has my full authority on this one." He looked up as O'Malley came in looking concerned and tapped her wristwatch. "The goddamn lieutenant governor," growled Keegan. He stood, said, "I'll be back," and left. All faces rotated to the other end of the table. Karp nodded to Anselmo.

"Frank, your meeting."

Anselmo's smile broadened by an inch, showing even, small white teeth, and he ducked his head in a fetching gesture of humility. He shuffled some papers on his lap and passed out a set of neatly bound blue manila folders stamped CONFIDENTIAL in big red letters. Guma turned his face toward Karp, out of Anselmo's view, and flashed his gargoyle imitation—a convincing one, given his physiognomy.

"All right: Catalano," said Anselmo. "To review the bare facts: on the night of June ninth, a body later identified as that of Edward Catalano was found in a car parked under the West Side Highway at Vestry Street. He'd been shot from behind at close range with a small-caliber weapon. Five shots to the head, a typical gangland murder."

Here what might have been construed by an unsympathetic listener as a snort of derision issued from Guma's direction. It was a low sort of snort, however, and if Anselmo heard it, he paid no attention.

"That method," he resumed, "and the fact that Catalano is known to be a *capo regime* of the Bollano family suggested that this was a professional hit having to do with the politics of the New York Mob. So—as you probably know, when they start hitting *capos*, it means that the power balances are shifting. There's disorder in the ranks, shifting loyalties, the wise guys are all looking for where they're going to end up after the dust settles, and so this is a prime time for us to do ourselves some good. Now, the first question we have to ask when something like this goes down is, naturally, *cui bono*. We look inside the family first, table one in your handout."

Shuffling of papers. Karp cast an eye on Guma, who had leaned back in his chair, the unopened file on his lap, and seemed to be getting set for a snooze. It was not unknown for Guma to drop off in meetings, and Karp hoped that he would not break out in snores. That too was not unknown.

"At the top, of course, we have the don, Salvatore Bollano, known as Big Sally. He's seventy something and not in good shape. Last of the breed, by the way, actually born in Sicily. There's some question as to whether he's still in control. Next in line is Salvatore Bollano, Jr., Little Sally, but not to his face, ha-ha, aka, Sally Jump, age forty-three. You have his arrest record there. Assault, rape, jury tampering, bribery, dozens of collars, never convicted. Violent, short-tempered, little son of a bitch; he may be mentally unstable, in fact."

Here came a snort from Guma. This time Anselmo paused and directed his attention to Guma's chair. "Um, Ray? Did you have a point to make?"

"Uh-uh, Frank," said Guma. "You're doing fine."

"Thank you. Next came Carlo Tonnati, street name Charlie Tuna, currently serving a life stretch in Attica for ordering the murder of Vinnie Ferro a dozen or so years ago."

Karp knew this, as he had personally put Charlie Tuna away, and everyone else did, too. Anselmo was often excessively thorough. He listened with half an ear and took precise notes on autopilot as the man ran through the order of battle of the Bollano crime family and presented his Machiavellian analysis of their various rivalries. The Bollanos were the smallest of New York's Mafia families, not looking to expand at all, but what they held, they held very hard. Their base was the Lower East Side, and Anselmo had charts and tables showing their various estimated sources of income, so much from drugs, so much from prostitution, so much from shakedowns and loan sharking. This was boring. Who cared about the enterprises or politics of thugs, except someone planning to write one of those inside-the-Mob books? Karp's instinct was for the concrete, for the facts, for the evidence. They had a crime; was there a case? Anselmo came to the end of his aria. In the silence that followed, Karp asked, "So you like Joe Pigetti for it?"

"Yeah, I do. It's the only scenario that makes sense. Pigetti and Catalano were the two most powerful *capos*. Catalano was tight with Little Sally, Pigetti was on the outs with both of them, but he was Charlie Tuna's protégé and he had more or less replaced Tonnati with Big Sally. If the old don were to kick off, though, he'd be up shit's creek. Or maybe he heard that the two of them were going to do him. So he goes to the don and lays something bad on Catalano. Some betrayal, he's skimming—whatever. The old guy's not so sharp, so he gives the okay. For Pigetti it was a good career move."

Karp seemed to give this serious attention. "Roland?"

"Well, Pigetti's out as the actual trigger," said Roland. "He's alibied to the neck. Apparently there was a big party the night of. One of the don's nephews was getting married, and the goombahs threw him a party at the Casa D'Oro on Elizabeth. Pigetti was there until two or so, and then he and a bunch of them went out clubbing until four-thirty. Catalano was at the party and he left around one-thirty, or it could've been an hour earlier or later, because all the boys were feeling pretty good by then and vague about the time. In any case, it happens that we know the exact time of death because one of the bullets fired into the back of Catalano's

skull came out through his eye and broke the dash-
board clock at three-fourteen A.M." He paused to see
what effect this detail had on the assembled group.

"That's a fancy touch," said Karp carefully.

"It *is* a fancy touch," Roland agreed. "A little fan-
cier than we're used to from the wise guys. Call me
cynical, but you might suspect that it was done on
purpose that way to give Joe an alibi. It turns out
that a little before three, Joe was checking into the
valet parking at a club at 57th off Eighth. So clearly
the cops are looking for an associate of Joe's who
doesn't have an alibi for the time of, and they come
up with Marco Moletti. Moletti was also seen leaving the Casa D'Oro with Catalano and a couple of
other guys. Catalano was going to drop by his girlfriend's house, and he took this bunch along for the
ride, maybe call up some ladies and continue the
party. But Mutt and Jeff got talking to some girls at
a light and they bailed. According to Mutt and Jeff,
Marco was the last guy in the car. According to
Marco, Marco wasn't feeling so hot, having overin-
dulged at the fiesta, so after dropping Catalano at
the girl's place at Park and 36th, he handed over the
keys, walked to his place, Lex and 49th, and crashed.
He says."

"That's a long walk, you're not feeling so good,"
said Karp.

"The cops thought so, too," said Roland. "Besides that, Catalano never made it to the girlfriend
that night. The cops think Marco stuck a gun in
Catalano's back, made him drive to under the highway, and popped him there. Then either someone

picked him up or he walked away and took a cab or the subway home. In any case, Marco was the last person to see Catalano alive."

"The second to last if he wasn't the shooter," said Karp. "Are you charging him?"

Roland waggled a hand and twisted his face into a doubtful expression. "It's thin. He was in the car, but they all admit that. The search found a box of .22 longs in his place, but no gun. The vic was killed with .22 longs. There was also a bag with a little short of fifty K in it. Payoff money? Ordinarily, I'd give it a pass, but . . ." Here he looked over at Anselmo, who put in, "Right, but this is not an ordinary case. I'm pushing Roland to charge him and then squeeze him to give us Pigetti. This could be the thing that cracks the whole Bollano family."

Karp looked at the faces: Anselmo avid, smiling like a kid at the circus; Hrcany pretending forbearance, willing to go along as long as no one made him responsible for a weak case, and perfectly willing to see Anselmo carry this freight; and Guma? Was the jerk actually asleep or just pretending the most elaborate boredom? Under the shelter of the conference table Karp's cap toe reached out and gave Guma one in the ankle. The monkey eyes opened, the floppy mouth yawned, showing more bridgework than anyone wanted to see.

Hrcany said, "Now that you mention it, Frank, Guma has some thoughts on that. Ray?"

"Yeah, Frank," said Guma pleasantly, "my thoughts are that you try to squeeze Moletti, you might get some of that scungilli he scarfed down at the party there, but nothing else."

"Why?" snapped Anselmo. "Because of the sacred code of *omerta*? They don't do that shit anymore, Guma. They sing just like anyone else when you push them."

Guma looked up at the ceiling as if he thought the answer to this question might be inscribed there, and when he responded it was in the sort of voice a kindergarten teacher might use to explain that D came after C. "Actually, Frank, I wasn't thinking of any high-tone Mafia stuff like that. I was thinking about Marco. You know what they call Marco Moletti on the street? No, don't look in the file, Frank, I'll tell you. If they sort of like him, they call him Slo Mo. If they're annoyed at him, like if the pizza they sent him out for is cold, they call him Marky Moron. He's a gofer, Frank. He's also real honest, because he's too dumb to steal and he knows it, which is why the guys sometimes leave stuff with him, cash, like your bag of money, or hot property. He's got his niche, you could say, and he's happy in it. But to put it mildly, Frank, he ain't a player. So anyone who thinks that Marky knows fuck-all about what goes on in the Bollanos is stupid. You want to squeeze something, squeeze the hubcap on Eddie Catalano's Lincoln, you'll get more out of it. And anybody who thinks that Marky Moron would get tagged to whack a *capo regime* is . . . words fail me. *Felony* stupid? Besides all that, in my opinion, you're doing great."

Anselmo shot to his feet and flung his papers to the floor. "Ah, come on, Butch, what the *hell*!"

"Sit down, Frank," said Karp. "Guma?"

"I apologize, Frank," said Guma instantly, in monotone.

"All right, now that we've all had our fun," said Karp, "let me remind you why we're here. Eddie Catalano was killed the day before he was scheduled to appear pursuant to a subpoena before a federal grand jury investigating Mob involvement in local businesses. This has greatly vexed our colleague on the other side of the square. The U.S. attorney believes that Mr. Catalano was slain to prevent his testimony—"

"Horseshit," said Guma.

"We're aware of your opinion on that subject, Guma," Karp snapped, "but would you put a goddamn cork in it just for now? Thank you. And since the U.S. attorney has been kept from his goal of, as he so elegantly puts it, 'breaking the Mob in New York,' he has devoted his time and talent to breaking our boss's balls instead. Why is Jack Keegan not pursuing this obvious gangland slaying with more alacrity and success? Why have we not seen the Mafia scumbags dragged into court? How come his crusade is stopped in its tracks? Is it that maybe Jack Keegan's not up to the job? And so forth, as you know. Now, in order to get Tommy Colombo off our ass, we need to show movement on this goddamn murder. Either we have to have a plausible defendant behind bars, or, failing that, we have to find out why the scumbag got killed. Roland, what are the cops doing besides sniffing around this Moletti character?"

Hrcany rolled his massive shoulders in a shrug. Not as massive as they used to be, Karp observed, but still meaty. The eighteen-inch collar of his shirt was loose on his neck.

"Well, Butch," he said, "you know how it is— they fall in love with a perp, it's forever, unless they dig up something new. I got enough for an arrest warrant and an indictment. When he's in the can, who knows? A pal of his could drop a dime—Marky didn't do it, I heard it was X. Or he could talk in jail. Maybe he knows from nothing, like Guma said, but still, he's around those guys. Even waiters pick up stuff. And then one of the regular jailhouse snitches could grab it. I don't know—"

"Roland, cut the horseshit," said Karp. "Don't give me warrants and indictments. We wanted to, you know damn well we could arrest and indict the cardinal archbishop for this one. What I'm interested in is, do you believe that this putz is a legitimate suspect? Did he fucking *do the crime*?"

Hrcany looked down for a moment as if gathering himself and then met Karp's gaze. "Since you ask, I don't and he didn't. Guma's right. He's a retard."

"Then forget him!" Karp ordered, and then, to nearly everyone's surprise, he turned to Guma. "Ray, what really happened?" he asked, almost casually. Frank Anselmo's smile became noticeably more false.

"Oh, they brought in somebody," Guma answered confidently, as if giving the correct time. "Probably a pair of guys. They picked him up in the girlfriend's lobby, hustled him out to his car, tossed him in the trunk, and drove to the scene of in two cars. Then they stuck him in the driver's seat and did him so it would look like he got popped by a buddy in the backseat. All these guys watched *The Godfather* fifty times, so they know how it's supposed to go down. The clock's a nice touch, and it ties it to somebody who might need an alibi."

"Like Pigetti?" asked Karp.

"Oh, either Joey was involved, or somebody wanted to make it look like Joey was involved. If he did do it, though, the important thing is, did he clear it through the don? My guess is no, he didn't. It's hard to think why Big Sally would want to take out Eddie Cat." He looked at Anselmo. "See, Little Sal doesn't *have* any friends to speak of. Eddie was Little Sal's baby-sitter. This is well-known. Used to be Charlie Tuna, then Eddie got the job when Charlie went upstate. Little Sal needs a lot of watching. He gets testy when he doesn't get his way, and it interferes with business. So this is perfect for the don. He got one of his *capos* tight with his kid, the heir, keeping him in line, but also the kid is watching Eddie, of course. Neither of them can make a move against him without the other knowing. And he's got his other *capo* right there in his pocket, Pigetti. Anyway, whoever did it, Pigetti, Little Sal, the don, or some combination thereof, it's a sure bet it's a family thing, got nothing to do with the federal grand jury. Eddie Cat would go to jail if he had to, but not into a witness program, which anyone who knew the guy would tell you in a second."

"So who did the deed, Guma? You probably already have a name for us." Anselmo spoke sarcastically, but Guma took the question on, knitting his brows as if trying to think of an actual name.

"Not a Sicilian, Frank. No Sicilian would hit a made guy and a *capo* in his own family without an order from his don, and if he was from another family, not unless he wanted to start a major war, which we got no evidence at all is what's involved here. So who? Well, if Murder Incorporated was still in business, this is the kind of stuff they used to contract out to the Jewish fellas, but I don't think Jews are into whacking anymore."

"Only whacking off," said Karp. "You're suggesting that Pigetti would reach out to one of our fine non-Sicilian ethnic groups?"

"I am," said Guma. "As far as which one . . ." He shrugged. "It's a whachamacallit . . . an embarrassment of riches out there."

The meeting broke up soon afterward. Guma and Hrcany vanished into the hallway, and Anselmo walked through the door that led to the D.A.'s office. Karp finished cleaning up his notes. When he went a few minutes later into Keegan's office, he observed Anselmo talking vigorously at the D.A., in undertones, and the D.A. not liking what he was hearing, shaking his noble head. When Anselmo ran down and left, Keegan hooked a finger, and Karp followed him to the other end of the office, where Keegan sat down in his chair with a snarling kind of sigh.

"What did Frank want?"

"Oh, he was pissed off about Ray, needless to relate. Christ, the pair of them are like a couple of brats. No, Frank, you can't be in charge of Guma, for the ninetieth time. And of course Roland set the whole thing up, just to show Frank who's got the biggest dick. Jesus!"

"You could put Guma in charge of Frank," Karp suggested.

Keegan goggled at him until he saw Karp was joking, and then he barked out a laugh and grinned. "Oh, yeah! That'd be rare, our own junior Mafioso in charge of Rackets. Tell me, did Guma really once stash a material witness with an out-of-town wise guy?"

"I've heard that story, too," said Karp in a non-committal tone. "You got a minute for this?"

Keegan had, and Karp epitomized what had just happened in a little under two.

"So you're telling me we got bullshit."

"What can I say? Police baffled, as the headlines used to say."

"Well, that can't be," said Keegan, putting away all smiles. "No chance that this Marky guy was involved?" He sounded wistful.

Karp said, "It doesn't even pass the laugh test."

For an instant Karp was afraid that Keegan was going to reverse him on arresting the fool, but the man's better angels chimed in and he merely cursed under his breath and said, "This isn't your everyday public service Mob hit. Tommy is running for whatever the fuck he's running for on fighting the big bad Mob, showing that although he's an Italian-American gentleman he's not *that* kind of Italian-American gentleman, and if he's got to run all over me to do it, that's fine with him. This is not one we can afford to lose." A steely glare, before which Karp did not in the least flinch, and then he added, the grin returning, "Say, 'Yes, boss,' so I know you understand you have complete charge of this shit pile."

"Yes, boss," said the good soldier.

3

MARLENE CIAMPI WAS WEARING A RED
T-shirt with white Chinese calligraphy on it, similar to the one her daughter owned. Unlike her
daughter (as far as she knew) she was also wearing a
pistol, a slim Italian 9mm semi-auto, in a nylon belt
holster, and a blue cotton blazer to conceal it. This
T-shirt had been a gift from Lucy on Marlene's last
birthday, back when she and her daughter were still
friends. The child had ordered the shirt from a copy
shop on Lafayette Street, where they would turn any
design you wanted into a shirt, and the calligraphy
was in Lucy's own hand. It supposedly read, "What
is the most important duty? The duty to one's parents. What is the most important thing to guard?
One's own character." Below this was the colophon
(Meng Ke) of the author, Mencius, and that of the
calligrapher (Kap Lòuhsì), the kid herself.

Marlene stared at the pay phone in whose demi-
booth she stood and let the events of the previous
two days rankle in her mind. The Lucy business.
The Chen business, now tangled together. She
thought of calling home and talking directly to
Lucy. She had two potential conversations in mind:

one a cold interrogation, using all her considerable investigatory skills to determine what her daughter was doing between 3:45 P.M., when she had spoken with her at Columbia-Presby, and 6:10 P.M. when, according to her husband's report, the little wretch had sashayed into the loft, or, alternatively, one that included some magical combination of frankness, wisdom, and empathy that would turn Lucy into the agreeable little girl she once was, and give to that vexed segment of Marlene's motherhood a fresh start.

She sighed, after a few dithering moments, then cursed, and turned her attention to the corner of 23rd Street and Tenth Avenue. The fire engines had left, and the crime scene unit cops were loading equipment into their van. The yellow tape that surrounded the brick storefront was by now bedraggled, drooping to the ground in places, and a couple of detectives were standing amid broken glass and blackened trash, talking to a uniformed patrolman. Above the entrance a charred sign— Chelsea Women's Clinic—was still legible. Abortions were among the services provided there, and someone objecting to the practice had, a few hours before, blasted out the storefront window with a shotgun and tossed in a gasoline bomb. The staff had been able to smother the flames with extinguishers, however, and no one, oddly enough, had been badly injured. The director of the clinic had thereafter been informed by the police that, despite the attack, the NYPD could not post a permanent guard at the site henceforward until forever. So she had called Marlene.

She crossed the street and walked up to the group of cops. She knew one of the detectives from the time she had spent some years ago as head of the Rape Bureau at the New York D.A.

"How's it going, Shanahan?"

"Marlene Ciampi! See, guys, I knew this was gonna get more interesting. I hope you're not here for an abortion, Marlene, 'cause I think they're closed for the day. However, if you're interested in a simple gynecological examination, I think Patrolman Vargas and I can accommodate you."

The uniformed kid snorted in surprise and looked nervously away. The other detective chuckled and said, "Vargas, watch this—now she's gonna sue us for sexual harassment. This is good training, Vargas. Get your notebook out."

"Also, Patrolman Vargas," Marlene said, "you'll want to note that aging detectives whose sexual function has been all but destroyed by excess consumption of alcohol often try to compensate by making vulgar remarks to women, including, as in the present case, decent Catholic mothers. It's something you'll want to avoid as you rise through the ranks. What happened here, Shanahan?"

The two detectives were grinning broadly. They didn't get to do this much anymore. "You wouldn't think it to look at her, Vargas, but this woman has the dirtiest mouth in the five boroughs, not excluding Margo the Transvestite down by Manhattan Bridge. What's your interest?"

"I'm not sure I have any, Shanahan. The people here called me, asked me to come by. Anything cooking yet on the perp?"

"You see how these cheap P.I.s operate, Vargas? Trying to get confidential information off the Job? They use bribes, threats, even fading sexual allure, like now . . . what's that on your shirt, Marlene, stick out your chest a little. Oh, yeah, Confucius say, man with erection who enter airplane door sideways going to Bangkok."

"That and, 'Kiss my ass, I'm Irish,' but, really . . . ?"

"Really? Well, it's a highly skilled master criminal terrorist we got here, if you want my opinion. They didn't want to use their own vehicle for the job, oh, no, so they rented a van from Penske over in Jersey somewhere. That's 'cause Penske don't ask for any personal information or anything, you just give them your watch or your dog and drive away."

"A grounder."

"Uh-huh. They're probably closing in on the desperadoes as we speak. Too bad you won't get to use your sleuthing powers in this one, Marlene. Officer Vargas, when Marlene uses her sleuthing powers, it usually ends up with hair on the walls. You want to keep your hand on your weapon around Marlene here. So to speak."

Marlene grinned, waved, and stepped over the crime tape.

Shanahan called after her, "And may I say, Marlene, that your ass is holding up pretty good, considering your age."

She wiggled that unit parodically in the interest of good police relations and entered the building.

The pattern of shot had come in high, judging

from the pits marking the wall above the receptionist's desk. Either the guy had rushed his shot or he intended to miss; in any case the woman sitting behind the desk had retained her brains in her skull. She was still at her post, carefully sorting through charred files. A couple of other women and a man in rough work clothes were sweeping burnt trash into a barrel. Marlene asked the receptionist where the director's office was; a weary motion pointed her down the hall, toward where a television crew—camera, sound, and glistening reporter—was recording an interview with Alice Reiss-Kessler, the director herself. The reporter, the same Gloria Eng who had reported on the Asia Mall killings, was wearing a peach-colored suit miraculously free of the fine soot that covered every other surface in the place, and at the moment she was asking the inane and inevitable "How do you feel" question. Ms. Reiss-Kessler, a good-sized brunette with a strong, plain face that tended to go jowly under ten-thousand-candlepower light, was not looking her best, but she was gamely doing her duty as a patriotic American by allowing television to share her pain. Marlene wished fervently for her to say something like, "I feel really great, Gloria. We've wanted to redecorate this crummy barn for ages, and since we're insured up to the nipples, we'll be able to do it right and also pay for about six hundred late-term abortions." Instead, she did the usual victim moan, and Marlene could see Eng calculating behind her faux-sympathetic matte face how to get an eight-second sound bite out of this farrago. Marlene backed away, intending to lurk in a corner until the newsies left, but her heel came down on a pile of trash and she stumbled noisily.

At the sound Eng looked up and, without missing a beat, broke in with, "Is it true that you've retained a private investigator in this matter?"

Reiss-Kessler hesitated. "Ah, well, we're looking into increased security, but—"

"Does that mean you approve of counter-violence against the kind of people who might want to bomb abortion clinics?"

"No, I believe that the police should do their job and protect the legally recognized right to choose."

"Then why have you hired Marlene Ciampi? Isn't Ms. Ciampi associated with the kind of 'security' not very distinguishable from vigilantism?"

"We haven't hired anyone," said Reiss-Kessler. "We're talking to consultants."

Nice block, girl, thought Marlene, but a moment later she was bathed in the unforgiving light herself, as the reporter directed camera and microphones toward an even more interesting subject.

"One of those consultants is apparently Marlene Ciampi, who has just entered this ruined clinic," Eng said. "Ms. Ciampi has been involved in several fatal shootings in the last few years, and in other acts of violence against people she claimed were harassing her clients. Marlene! Could you tell us what your response will be to whoever perpetrated this attack?"

"No comment," said Marlene, and moved to pass the reporter, who counter-moved to remain in her path.

"Give me something, Marlene," said the reporter.

"Have you spoken with the police? How do they feel about your involvement?"

Marlene kept her smile, checked, faked, got by, and in a moment had clutched Ms. Reiss-Kessler by the elbow and steered her into her own office, kicking the door shut in the camera's face.

"Well," said the director, "you certainly know how to make an entrance. I'd offer you coffee, but the coffee room was a casualty. Have a seat."

Marlene brushed plaster dust off a side chair and sat down. Reiss-Kessler settled on the edge of her desk. "You don't care for the media, I take it."

"They do their job, I do mine," Marlene said. "In fact, I had no comment."

"I'd think that getting your face on television would be good for business."

"I have enough business, Ms. Reiss-Kessler—"

"Please, Alice."

". . . Alice, and I don't particularly want to encourage the kind of business Gloria is interested in promoting for me. I'm here representing the Osborne Group. Security? I assume that's what you're interested in." She indicated the wreckage with a wave.

The woman let out a bitter chuckle. "Yes, locking the barn door. Security, but mainly I want the people who did this caught and punished."

"Uh-huh. I bet. Fortunately, you don't need me for that. The cops have a good lead on the perps here, and they should make an arrest fairly soon."

Reiss-Kessler's eyes widened. "Really? They didn't say anything about that to *me*."

"I try to cultivate good relations with the police."

An expression of astonishment tending toward sneer appeared on the woman's face. "You *like* those chauvinist bastards?"

Marlene stiffened and smiled falsely to cover. "Not like. They're hard to like. A great many of them are boorish, violent, corrupt, and stupid. But I do love them. In a manner of speaking. My heart goes out to them. They see stuff and do stuff every day that if you did it, it would make you cry for a week, and they've got no real training to deal with it and they get no support for it, except that silly macho cynical business they're all into, which makes it all worse, and includes the idea that only the penis-equipped can do the job. So they make comments to me, technically sexual harassment, technically clear violations of the Patrol Guide, and what I do is, I mean within limits, I don't give them the 'that's not funny' line and utter threats, I grin like a bimbo and give them a shot back or two. And when I need some help from them, which I do a lot in my business, I usually get it."

"It's nice that you're one of the boys," said Reiss-Kessler.

Marlene ignored the icy tone, kept her smile, and replied, "Yes, it *is* nice. Let's turn to business, Alice, if you don't mind. We both have a lot to do."

Alice gave a stiff nod, and Marlene went into her spiel, laying out what the Osborne Group could and could not do in the way of protection and site hardening. This included building surveys, installation of equipment and architectural mods, security seminars for clinic staff, and the provision of bonded square-badge guards. The woman listened, took some notes, asked the usual questions. Marlene could see she was disappointed, had expected something else, something more ardently feminist, a source of emotional support rather than a security firm functionary, which is why she had called Osborne and asked for Marlene by name. Marlene couldn't help that (it happened a lot), nor could she help what she felt about the clinic. This emerged, too, in the conversation.

At the end, the director made some noncommittal remarks that they'd be in touch. Marlene doubted this; she was being given the boot. She was not exactly famous, but she'd been in the news enough over the past decade so that there were people who would call for an appointment just to take a look, and others who wanted the cachet of having her guard their bodies, and others who thought she was in the business of shooting unwanted males on order. Marlene figured that Alice Reiss-Kessler's initial thought in the immediate aftermath of the attack had been punishment and revenge, and since she came from a class and subculture that did not trust the police to have the right attitude toward feminist issues, she had sought a private enforcer.

Which Marlene was not, and had made that clear, and now, leaving the sooty storefront, wondered why it was easier for her to be nice to horrible male-chauvinist cops than to a perfectly decent woman with the right liberal opinions on every subject. To be fair, she was just as impatient with the right-wing verities of most cops. And of her mother.

She walked now, head down and grumpy, to her

car, an old Volvo 240 ___ faded orange, parked illeg___ sonal assistant was sitting in ___ grunted a greeting as she ente___

"I don't know, Sweets," she sai___ moving in the south-bound flow. "___ ___t up for no reason. I had to give that dumb ___ch about the cops, and what she wanted was the us girls against the men business, oh, bite my tongue, not *girls*, of course, and I had to sound off about abortion, but when she said that about those abortion-is-murder nuts, and said well, it is and they're not all nuts, and she gave me that you can't be serious look, and I said well, yeah, legal, safe, and available, sure, I'm for that, but you're also killing babies, you should stand up for that, and be sad, I'd like to see more tears, more anguish, I mean it's not a haircut and a rinse, is it? And she got chillier and chillier, and then I cracked wise about me participating in a number of post-natal abortions and I didn't care for those either, and then we went back to talking about doors and bomb barriers. And of course, she's big in New York feminist circles, and she's going to spread the word about what a traitor I am to the cause, which will not help with the celebrity jobs either, and Osborne is going to start having second thoughts about bringing me in. I mean, really, Sweets, what is going on here? How can you be more of a feminist than me? Huh?"

Sweety offered a shrug and a sympathetic look.

"Do I put my fucking *body* on the line? Do I actually protect *women* from *men*? I do. And what do I get for it, huh? I'll tell you what I don't get. I don't

. My husband hates what I do. My
just hates me *whatever* I do, *poor Marlene*,
after today I doubt I'll be invited to sit on the
dais at the NOW meeting, and I bought the most
darling little black dress. . . . Sweety! Talk to me! I
need advice."

In response to this, Sweety dropped his massive
head on her lap and dispensed a half cup of saliva
directly onto her crotch. Marlene hooted maniacal
laughter and made a dramatic turn across two lanes
to catch her left onto 14th.

Marlene was about to meet (speaking of her peculiar problems with feminism) a woman who made
Ms. Reiss-Kessler look like Nancy Reagan. This
person lived and worked in a five-story tenement-
plus-storefront on Avenue B in the neighborhood
called the East Village, if you were placing real estate ads, and Alphabet City if you were a resident, or
a cop. Unlike other poor and crime-plagued sec-
tions of New York, most of which had declined
from better days, this one had been designed as a
slum in the previous century and was a slum still.
Marlene parked her car behind a burned sofa across
the street, and walked blithely away with the window open and the doors unlocked. A 200-pound
dull black, red-eyed, attack-trained Neapolitan mastiff in the front seat is the sort of car alarm that still
works in Alphabet City.

The building had a small sign over the door that
said EAST VILLAGE WOMEN'S SHELTER, and the door
itself was a steel industrial model in a steel frame.
In the center of this door was a bell button and a
small notice:

RING. WE ARE ALWAYS OPEN.

IF YOU'RE LOOKING FOR SHELTER,
   YOU ARE WELCOME,

AND IF YOU'RE LOOKING FOR TROUBLE
   WE HAVE THAT, TOO.

The former shop windows had been replaced by bolted-on galvanized sheets backed by thick plywood. Marlene rang the bell. A whirring noise from above. She looked up and waved to the camera. *Buzz. Ke-chunk.* The outer door opened, and Marlene walked through and down a short blank entry corridor faced by a windowed door, behind which was a steel desk, behind which was a fullback-sized brown woman with beaded hair. This person ascertained that Marlene was really Marlene and not the spearhead of an invasion, and clicked her through the glass. The EVWC was hard to get into. Its clientele consisted exclusively of women and children under credible threat of death from that small class of men who will not be deterred from expressing their devotion to their loved ones in this unusual way even by the full pressure of the law. Almost all women's shelters are at secret locations, to prevent the loved ones from coming by and trying to get in. This one was blatantly public, because its proprietor rather hoped the loved ones would try something, and especially that they would engage in the sort of behavior that entitles the invaded party to use lethal force.

"What's up, Vonda?"

"Besides the murder rate? Not that much. We got a rare one last night. Buck-ass naked and beat."

"Really? Anyone I know?"

The woman shrugged and shifted the Remington 870 on her lap. "She'll tell you about it. I just got on."

Marlene went through another door into the shelter proper and was hit first by the smell—cooking and disinfectant and too many people—and second by a four-year-old on a Big Wheels. A thin woman chasing the child apologized in heavily accented English and dragged the child away to the play area that took up much of the first floor of the building. The children who lived here did not get out much.

The owner was in the kitchen, dressed in her usual black jumpsuit, supervising the preparation of the evening meal, which, like most meals at the EVWS, was highly spiced, hearty, and well balanced, if plain. Marlene often reflected on the medieval aspects of this establishment: noise, squabbling, gouts of steam, the sound of a slap and a wail, hectic activity under the command of a benevolent tyrant. It must have been so in the castle when the knights were away at war. Mattie Duran was a strong, stocky Mexican woman with a fierce *indio* ax face set off by two thick black braids tied with red wool. She looked up, saw Marlene, nodded, settled the business she had begun, and walked out of the kitchen, Marlene following.

Duran had a tiny office off the dining room fitted with a steel desk, industrial shelving holding what passed for her record system, a swivel chair for her, and a ratty armchair for guests. She drew a couple of cups of black coffee from an urn, sat behind the desk with a grateful sigh, and gave her guest the once-over, focusing on Marlene's soaked crotch.

"What happened, you piss yourself or are you just glad to see me?"

"The dog."

Mattie raised an eyebrow. Then they both guffawed. Mattie had a deep, wet laugh, like an old man. Marlene had worked with the EVWS for a couple of years. Their clientele overlapped to some extent, and they more or less agreed on the principle that guys who persisted in trying to kill women should get their lumps. They were both unindicted felons, but Marlene was guilty about it and Mattie was not. Marlene related her recent experiences at the Chelsea clinic. Mattie was not sympathetic.

"That's what they get for having glass windows. Uptown assholes!"

"I think they were trying to make the place more inviting. Not everybody likes to work in a fort."

"Let 'em open a goddamn yarn shop, then. Speaking of uptown assholes, your pal Brenda Nero is back with us."

"How nice for you."

"You got to help me out, Marlene. The bitch is driving me crazy."

"Uh-huh. The solution is simple. Walk up to her and say, 'Sugar, get your young white ass out of my shelter.'"

Mattie frowned, taking on even more of the aspect of a Toltec idol than she normally carried. "Marlene, hell, you know I can't do that."

Marlene did know. "What's she done now?"

"Oh, you know. Nothing you can put your finger on, but I got three women threatening to leave if I don't get rid of her. That's a laugh, huh?" She laughed dully to illustrate. "They're threatened with death and dismemberment, and they'd rather skip than hang with Brenda."

"That's Brenda," said Marlene, and looked long at her pal, and observed that she was genuinely suffering under the hard-girl mask. Blaming the victim was one of the three remaining cardinal sins among the liberati of New York, along with littering and smoking in restaurants, and Marlene struggled daily to resist it. That it was always the Man was not, however, an article of faith for her, as it was for Mattie. In many cases it turned out to be an unconscious conspiracy between a man and a woman to continue mutual torture until they were both dead. Thus she could see Brenda as a mere problem and not as a holy cause.

"You've talked with her, naturally."

"I've talked with her, I yelled at her, I made her cry. I came *this* close"—Mattie held thumb and index finger a pea-diameter apart—"to punching her face out." She snorted. "That'd be rich, huh? Shelter operator pounds victim."

"Why's she here?" asked Marlene with a surreptitious glance at her watch.

"Oh, the usual. Chester's acting up again."

"She says."

"She's got a big bruise on her jaw, goddammit!"

Marlene adopted the calming tone she used with dangerous fanatics, of which there were some few in her life. "Okay. Well, why don't I go and have a little talk with Chester this afternoon? Maybe we can work things out."

"Break his legs."

"It's an option. Was that why you wanted to see me today?"

"No, it's this new one. Won't talk, won't say who she is. Looks like she's been pimp-beat, but don't look like a hooker."

"What, with a wire hanger?"

"Some kind of thin whip anyway. Looks like it's been going on for a while, the scars. She says he put his cigar out on her ass."

"And she won't say who she is?"

"No, but—"

"But me no buts, girl. You got rules, I got rules. You know I don't touch a client unless she goes for the whole legal business . . ."

"Marlene, just see her . . ."

". . . naming the abuser, prosecuting for assault . . ."

"Marlene, five minutes. She asked if she could see you."

". . . and so on. What is this now, the cute puppy school of bodyguarding? If I like her looks, I'll waive the rules?"

Mattie turned up her glower a notch and thrust forward her heavy jaw. "Don't be a bitch, Marlene."

"Oh, that's delightful, coming from you." She rose and gathered up her bag. "I have to go. I will drive out and see Chester, and then I will go home. I have children. And a husband."

Mattie's face darkened to mahogany, and her heavy brows almost met in the middle. An interesting moment passed, during which both of them realized that, manlike as were some of their doings, they were not in fact men and didn't have to carry on so. The big woman sucked in breath and said, "Marlene, please. For me. Just see her and maybe she'll talk to you. If she don't, no harm. You can just forget her, okay?"

A request in these terms from Mattie Duran was so unusual as to stun Marlene's normal prudence, and, of course, she was intrigued.

"Okay, I'll see her."

Mattie smiled, brightening the room with a show of gold and bright enamel against her dark skin. "Great! You're a pal, *chica*. She's in 37."

She would be. Room 37 was the only single room for clients in the EVWS, tiny, in the center of the building, windowless, its doors and walls heavily reinforced. It was the most secure place in the shelter, and was reserved for people that Mattie had determined were under threat from people who knew what they were doing when it came to dispensing lethal violence. Some time back, the shelter had been attacked by a group of actual international terrorists, who had made off with a young girl, and Mattie wanted to make sure it would not happen again.

Marlene climbed the stairs against the flow of women and children descending for the evening meal. She greeted those she knew, a substantial proportion. Marlene's role at the EVWS was to represent clients in court, to move them to (they hoped) safe apartments, to train them in self-defense, and to provide her brand of counseling to the significant others. Given Marlene's rep around town, this often sufficed. Marlene had not lost a client in some years, and her clientele was selected from among the most endangered women in the city, or rather those of the most endangered who had the sense and the nerve to get out.

The woman who opened the door of 37 to Marlene's knock was still lovely in the frozen way that some wealthy women adopt, a look that peaked in the Kennedy years. Not a mark was visible on the face, which didn't mean much. A lot of guys were careful about the face, wanting to preserve the trophy value of the arm piece. Her eyes, a nice china blue, and big ones, showed more mileage around the edges than one might gather from a first look at the face and body. A well-preserved forty, was Marlene's thought, three days a week at the gym, a few surgical tucks maybe, strict diet, winters in the Islands. She was dressed in a ratty purple sweatshirt and jeans several sizes too large for her, and a pair of cheap tennis shoes, all clearly out of the shelter slop box.

"You wanted to see me," said Marlene, and introduced herself, extending a hand. The woman's grip was soft and hesitant, and her eyes, which Marlene now observed were fuzzy and unfocused, slid away from contact. Oh, pharmaceuticals! thought Marlene. She loved these types.

The woman did not give her own name, but turned away and sat on the narrow bed. Marlene shut the door and sat beside her, there being nowhere else to sit. The room was tiny, a cell eight feet on a side, holding only a steel cot, a varnished deal bureau, a rag rug, and a rickety night table.

"So, what do I call you?"

The woman paused, as if trying to remember. "Vivian," she said.

"Last name?"

The woman shook her head and looked down at the rag rug.

"Look, I can't begin to help you unless you talk to me." Nothing. "I have to have your name at least." Marlene waited. She observed that the woman had fragments of nail polish still clinging to her nails, which bore the signs of having had the frequent attention of a manicurist. Her hair, too, though lank from a recent washing, showed the mass and shaping of a first-class cut. Marlene felt a pulse of irritation, which she knew she would not have felt had the woman been poor. She stood up and announced, "Okay, sorry, but I'm leaving."

"Fein," said the woman.

"Fine? You don't want help? You want me to leave?"

"No, Fein is the name. My name is Vivian Fein." The crying started.

Marlene always said that she was one of the few women in New York for whom both Kleenex and bullets were a deductible business expense. She gave over a wad of the former to stem the drench and waited, making soothing sounds.

"I'm sorry," said Vivian Fein, after some minutes. "It's hard to explain. I was thinking about my father." She paused, glanced at Marlene in a way that seemed to demand some recognition, as if this father were so well-known as to require no further explanation, and then she blushed and said, "Ah, shit, you must think I'm crazy"—here she uttered a shrill laughlike sound. "Oh, yeah, why would you think that, just because I ran out of my house dressed in a blanket and a pair of panties? Of course, I assume you know all about my father, just because that's what's rattling around in my head all the time. Isn't there a disease where people think they're transparent? That everyone can see their thoughts?" A spate of silent shaking laughter, dissolving into liquid weeping.

Marlene adopted a neutral expression and waited. The father thing was interesting. Maybe it wasn't the S.O. this time, for a change. Or maybe Dad was both—not at all unknown in the business. The Fein woman stopped being semi-hysterical and drew away, and leaned against the wall. She wiped her eyes and blew her nose on Marlene's wad of tissues. To her surprise, Marlene now found herself subject to an appraising look, with a hint of hardness. A quick recovery. Or the waterworks was an act. Or the woman was deep in tranquilizer psychosis.

"You don't look like what I thought you would," she said.

"I never do," said Marlene coolly. "Let's cut the horseshit, Ms. Fein. I presume you wanted to see me about whoever beat you up. I'll need his name and details of the incident, plus any information about past abuses, with documentation."

"Documentation?" The woman was staring at her as if she were speaking in a foreign tongue.

"Yes. Visits to the emergency room or private doctors. Calls to the police. Any witnesses to the violence . . . I'm sorry, you find this *amusing*?"

The woman brought her giggling under control. Definitely pills, thought Marlene. "No, I'm sorry, really. I realize I must seem crazy to you. But . . . no, there's no witnesses. No documentation. And that's not why . . . whew!" Fein took several deep breaths. "We got off on the wrong foot, Ms. Ciampi. I don't want you to pursue my husband in any way. I want to hire you for something else altogether."

Marlene cocked her head, the attitude of disbelief, and also, in her particular case, the way in which she focused attention with her one good eye. "Excuse me. It's a reasonable assumption. This is a battered women's shelter you're in."

"Yes, and I do need protection, and I'm incredibly grateful for it, but this is something I have to do, and I can't do it from home. My husband would not approve, and he's an extremely watchful and suspicious man."

"Uh-huh. And what is it you want to hire me to do?"

"I want you to investigate the death of my father, Gerald Fein. He was a lawyer. He supposedly committed suicide in 1960."

"And you think there's something suspicious about his death, that it wasn't a suicide? How did he die?"

A bleak smile. "I see you're not a New Yorker."

"But I *am*, born and raised. You mean you think I should recall a suicide twenty-odd years ago, of a—" Marlene clapped her hand to her mouth. "Oh, shit! You don't mean Jumping Jerry was . . . Oh, Christ, I'm sorry, that was crude of me."

"Oh, please, we're used to it. Well, I don't think you ever *get* used to it, but you learn to live with it. You must have jumped rope to the, whatever, the rhyme, if you were a city kid."

"I was a little old. My younger sister did, though. It must have been unbelievably bad for you."

"Yes. We loved him very much. And we thought he loved us."

Marlene did not know what to say to this, and she did not particularly want to learn. The story now percolated back up from deep storage from where it had lain alongside Brooklyn Dodgers team rosters and the Ozone Park rules for ring-a-levio. And jump-rope rhymes, of course. Gerald Fein had gone to his office building one day and instead of getting off at the 57th floor, where his firm had its suite, he had traveled up to the observation deck, where he had somehow gotten past the barrier and, achieving the actual parapet, had walked into space, thus becoming the last man to jump successfully from the Empire State Building. After some moments of uncomfortable silence Marlene said, "Ah, Ms. Fein, regarding this investigation—I don't, that is, in my connection with the shelter, I don't do investigations, except for things like locating a spouse for child-support payment. But my firm, the Osborne Group, has an investigations division. I could put you in touch with them."

The woman was shaking her head. "No, I want you to do it."

"I'm sorry, Ms. Fein, but I don't have the time or the resources to handle a serious investigation into something that happened twenty-three years ago. Osborne does, and I ought to tell you now that if they take the case it's going to cost you. And, not to be harsh, but you don't look like you have a whole lot of bucks at your disposal."

"I can pay!" the woman cried. Moving like a frightened bird, she darted her hand under the pillow of the narrow bed and snatched out a crumpled paper bag, which rattled as she brought it to her lap, and reached in. Light flashed in her hand.

"That's real, I presume," said Marlene, who could not help a thick swallow at what she saw.

"Oh, yeah, it's real. One thing about Sa—my husband, he only buys the best stones. This is a six-and-a-half carat D color VVS2 quality stone in platinum. It's worth at least a hundred forty grand."

There was something about the way this statement popped out of Vivian Fein's lush little mouth that raised for Marlene the notion that perhaps the deserted hubby was not one of society's ornaments, though filthy rich, that perhaps Ms. Fein (and what *was* her married name, after all?) had spent some time around the hard boys. Come to that, Marlene thought further, wasn't old Jumping Jerry mobbed up in some way? Another reason to avoid additional involvement. She stood up again and pulled her eye away from the fabulous glitter of the ring.

"You want to put that in a safe, Ms. Fein. Some of the ladies here are fairly hard types. I'll have someone from our investigations division give you a ring. A call, I mean."

"Take it!" said the woman. "You *have* to, you *have* to . . ." She leaped up and grabbed Marlene's sleeve, and tried to press the diamond into the pockets of Marlene's shirt. They shuffled around the floor for a while like a pair of folk dancers from a particularly ungraceful folk, and Marlene thought, absurdly, of her tiny grandmother trying to press packets of leftovers on recalcitrant relatives, both of them doing the same sort of dance. Vivian was again weeping, Marlene saying, "Please . . . excuse me . . . please," and wondering whether she would have to get rough to make her escape, when a long, full-throated scream sounded in the hallway outside.

Vivian froze. All the pink drained from her face, and her eyes showed white all around their blue centers. From outside another yell and the sound of cursing and shrill cries. Vivian jumped back from Marlene and, with crazed stupidity, looked around for somewhere to hide in the tiny cell. In a hoarse, high-pitched whisper she said, "Oh, shit, oh God, oh shit . . . it's him, oh, shit, oh, God . . ."

"Stay here," Marlene commanded inanely, pulled her pistol from its holster, and stepped out of the room. At the end of the narrow hallway a small crowd of women and kids had formed a yelling circle around what was obviously a fight. Marlene crouched down and looked between the legs of the spectators. As she had expected, one of the combatants, the one on the bottom, getting creamed by a hefty brown woman, was Brenda Nero. Marlene replaced her pistol. Heavy treads on the stairway and here came Mattie Duran at the trot, darkness on her brow. The spectators scattered before her as she pierced the circle and grabbed a handful of each combatant, heaving them to their feet and holding them apart like a pair of squabbling puppies.

"What the hell is going on here?" she yelled.

Marlene heard a familiar voice wail, "I didn't do *anything*!" Brenda's old refrain. Brenda never did anything, yet where she dwelt chaos reigned. On her last unlamented visit to the shelter she had, among other stunts, spilled a bottle of nail polish (borrowed without asking, of course) and wiped it up with "an old rag" that proved to be her roommate's baby's baptismal dress, the last pathetic remnant of the poor woman's lost respectability. Marlene imagined it was something like that this time, too, or a remark at just the wrong moment, or a secret casually revealed. What her life with Chester Durrell was like, Marlene could barely imagine, yet she was prepared to talk to Chester about keeping his temper and not going with the fists. In fact, she had to admit, she would rather deal with Chester than with Brenda. Let Mattie deal with Brenda.

As for Vivian Fein, Marlene suspected that her case made Brenda and Chester look like Ozzie and Harriet. Not interested, was Marlene's thought, not even in why Vivian Fein So-and-So had decided to split from an abusive man at just that time and look into her father's long-ago death, and she took the opportunity to slip-slide away, down the stairs and out of the shelter, into a nice, warm, smelly New York purple evening. But of course, now she couldn't get the damn skipping rhyme out of her head.

Jumping Jerry jump so high
Really thought that he could fly
Jumping Jerry couldn't wait
He jumped off the Empire State
Down and down and down he flew
Landed on Fifth Avenue
Hundred-ninety-eighty-seventy-sixty-
   fifty-forty-thirty-twenty
SPLAT!

Or alternatively, you could end with the most disgusting possible raspberry noise. She entered her car. The dog made a companionable whine and panted.

"Don't ask, Sweets. Just don't ask," she said as she cranked up the car and pulled away from the curb. In fact, as she now recalled, she *had* skipped to it, when alone with her sister Pat and her younger cousins, and not standing on the dignity of twelve years. She had been a damn good double-dutch skipper, too. All the Ciampis had skipped, including the boys. Her dad had been a welter-weight club fighter in the forties for a couple of years, and skipping was macho training rather than a girl thing at *casa* Ciampi, where everyone also learned to box. Marlene had kept up training, too. She had a speed bag and a heavy bag set up at home, and she worked out a couple, three times a week—not a Jazzercise girl, Marlene—still including skipping. And, naturally, Marlene had taught her daughter. Lucy still skipped, and was brilliant at it, but she did it in private, not with Mom anymore. It's just a phase, Marlene thought, trying to generate a little self-comfort.

But really, who knew? Who knew, for example, what Jumping Jerry Fein's spectacular suicide had done to his daughter? Clearly, she was in a marriage made elsewhere than in heaven, but did that follow necessarily from the big jump? Flash forward twenty years—Lucy sitting all beat up in room 37: "Yeah, well, my mom was this hard-rock feminazi with a gun, so I guess I just became a doormat to get back at her."

"Is that why I don't want to do this silly woman's investigation, Sweety?" she asked. "Because I don't want to get *into* it? Some other miserable family. I am a simple person, basically. No, really, don't laugh! I love my husband, I love my children, even that rotten brat, I don't try to change the world, I'm not an ideologue, I don't tear cigarettes out of people's mouths in restaurants, I don't throw paint on furs. All I do is I try to keep a tiny fraction of the violent shitheads of the world from hurting their loved ones. This is simple, no? Yell, scream, be depressed, but no hitting, no stabbing, don't shoot them with guns. It's kindergarten."

Marlene waited for the light at Houston and Lafayette and turned to face the mastiff, who turned his contemplative, sag-faced, red-eyed gaze on her, the better to concentrate his canine wisdom on her kvetching.

"But I always seem to get involved. I'm down *in* it all the time, slopping around with the toxic worms, who did what to who, back when, why—Brenda fucking Nero, this new one . . . I don't know, Sweets, this is not what I bargained for. If I wanted to do social work, I would have a little office with light oak and nubbly tweed furniture, and my MSW diploma and some soothing abstracts on the walls, and a black plastic thingie on my desk with my name engraved, or maybe a wooden one, with the swoopy carved letters. Do you see me doing that? Of course you don't. It's not me. I don't have good listening skills. I have good *shooting* skills, although God knows I never asked for that either. So? Any sage advice?" She waited. "What's that? Eat decayed corn dogs and sniff anuses? Okay, it sounds extreme, but if it works for you, I'll try it. I tried everything else."

4

ONE OF THE HABITS THAT KARP HAD retained from his days as a worker bee was culinary, or rather anti-culinary. In the lunch hour, in fine weather when he had no unavoidable business luncheon, he repaired to one of the shiny cancer wagons lined up along the edges of Foley Square, and there consumed remarkable quantities of what his mother always called *chazerei*, or pig swill. Today he was eating macerated beef lips and pork by-products forced into a condom and served in a piquant mustard sauce on lozenges of absorbent cotton, with kraut, washing this (the second of a matched pair) down with fizzy orange sugar water. Next to him, on the bench, there rested a yellowish square in waxed paper, the shape and very nearly the taste of paving material, which had been purveyed as a knish.

As he ate, he read through a stack of files, moving them, after reading, from one side of his seated position to the other, using the knish as a convenient paperweight. Although Karp could not possibly keep abreast of the thousands of live felony cases handled by the D.A.'s office, he made an effort to examine enough of a sample to give him a feeling for the tone of the office as a whole. From time to time he found some funny business and he pounced. As now. This, from Felony Bureau, was a major prosecution against a car-theft ring, an interstate operation involving numerous chop shops, crooked parts dealers, and gangs of thieves who functioned as suppliers. It was an elaborate case that had required many months to develop and involved cooperation with the FBI.

Karp muttered and made notes on a legal pad, ripped off the pages, stuck them in the folder, and was about to move on to the next one when he looked up and was startled to see an elderly woman sitting on a bench across the path from him who was also muttering and making notes on a legal pad. Her pad was tattered and faded, and she was using a stumpy pencil instead of an office ballpoint, and she was wearing more than one dress and had next to her a shopping cart stacked with boxes and black plastic bags. Like most New Yorkers, Karp was careful to give the homeless their privacy and did not ordinarily stare, but this woman's face was interesting, plain, large-nosed, but with deep-set, large dark eyes, rimmed with brownish skin, like rust stains. Her drawn cheeks were decorated with spots of cherry rouge, and there were flakes of bright lipstick clinging to her lips and the skin surrounding them. Her hair was frizzy and dirty gray, and upon it she wore a black velvet hat with a tiny veil, such as his mother had worn back in the fifties. The woman stopped and looked up just then, and met his gaze, hers turning wary. He smiled and indicated his pad and hers.

"Nice day to work outside," he said.

"Are you a counselor, sir?" she asked after rather a long pause. Her voice was cracked from disuse, but she spoke with the exaggerated clarity of the New York native who has been at pains to disguise the accent.

"I'm with the D.A.," said Karp.

"Oh. I have such an interesting case here," she said, waving a thick and filthy manila folder. "Maybe you would be so kind as to give me your legal opinion. I believe a great injustice has been done, a very great, a very great, great injustice, and they're getting away with it." She lowered her voice and glanced theatrically over both shoulders. "With murder."

"Would you care for a knish?" Karp asked, hoping by this gesture to forestall what he knew could be an unpleasant encounter. The courthouse area was, naturally enough, well supplied with those of the mad whose nuttiness came out in legal colors, and this person was clearly one of them.

"Oh, no, I couldn't take your lunch," she fluttered.

"Please." He stood and extended the brick to her in its square of waxed paper, meanwhile slapping his (actually quite flat) stomach with his other hand. "I don't need it," he said heartily. "It'd only go to waste."

"Oh, well, in that case, thank you very much," she said, and accepted it and took a first small bite, closing her eyes as if she were tasting a spoonful of *molossal* at Le Pavillon.

Karp took this opportunity to make his escape,

feeling somewhat ratty about it, but not too ratty, and not really regretting his lost knish.

Back in the office, he called the ADA in charge of the car-theft-ring prosecution, a luminary of the Felony Bureau named Weingarten, and asked him to stop by if he had no other commitments. Officially, Karp should have called Weingarten's bureau chief, Tim Sullivan, and taken it through channels, or, failing that, he should have had O'Malley call the Felony office secretary to set up an appointment, but he chose not to. Sullivan would bitch to Keegan, of course, and Keegan would answer that the chief assistant could call anyone in the office he damn pleased, and then yell at Karp to for chrissake go through the chain of command, and Karp would forget to do so the next time, and thus each of the hundreds of attorneys in the office would learn that they could at any moment expect such a call and have to answer instantly for any of the cases under their control, which, of course, was the point of Karp doing it in so outrageously unbureaucratic a fashion.

Weingarten said the only thing he could say, which was that he had no other commitments and would be right up, and then he spent a frantic five minutes juggling his many commitments, and arrived at Karp's door breathless, a long-faced young man with pale eyes and thinning blondish hair. Karp pointed him to a seat and held up the case file.

"*People* v. *Ragosi*, nice job," Karp said.

A smile pulled tentatively at Weingarten's mouth and the ginger mustache that sat upon it. "Uh, thanks."

"Yeah, how long did it take you to build the case, a year?"

"Fourteen months, including the grand jury."

"Yeah, this Ragosi seems to be the kingpin, all right. And you got him the usual way, by turning each layer of his organization. The cops went undercover, posed as car thieves, got the evidence on the chop shops, the chop shops gave you the parts brokers, and one particular parts broker, what was his name? I got it right here . . ." He thumbed through the thick file.

"Ortiz, Luis Ortiz," said Weingarten.

"Yeah, here it is. I see Luis was a very bad boy. You started him out on fifty-seven separate B-felony counts, criminal possession of stolen property, first-degree—wow, this was a multimillion-dollar operation—plus forgery of a VIN, forty counts, plus odds and ends: falsifying business records, illegal possession of a VIN, and then you let him plead down to, let's see here, three counts of CPSP four, an E felony, plus some misdemeanor trash, and the payoff was he gave you Mr. Ragosi, who is the mastermind behind the ring. Is that right?"

Weingarten said, "Yeah, we thought that was a good deal for us. The cops and the feds have been after Ragosi for years, but he was always too sharp."

"Yeah, I see where Ortiz testifies to the grand jury the guy always used cutouts for cash transfers, would never meet face to face with his suppliers. And I don't see any evidence from the phone taps and mail covers, so I presume you got zip. A careful guy, Ragosi. So it was real fortunate that Mr. Ragosi decides one fine day to personally hand a manila envelope with forty grand in it to your pal Ortiz, and even more fortunate that Ortiz decides to keep that envelope, and sure enough, it's got Mr. Ragosi's prints on it. And on that evidence the cops get a warrant and raid Mr. Ragosi's place of business, and what do they find? All sorts of incriminating paperwork from our boy Ortiz. None from all the other limbs of his vast criminal enterprise, only from Ortiz. What do you make of that, Weingarten?"

"What can I say? The guy got sloppy for once, and we got lucky. It happens."

"Yeah, it does. It also happens that defendants under the hammer of a big jolt perjure themselves, and it also happens that cops anxious to close out a big one encourage that perjury and plant evidence. Ragosi may be a criminal mastermind, like you say, but I would be willing to bet my next paycheck that in this case he was framed."

Weingarten felt sweat bead up on his hairline and resisted the urge to wipe at it. "Wait a minute, you don't seriously think I—"

"Suborned perjury? No, I don't. I think the cops arranged it, and you bought it. Be more careful next time. Do you realize that you have no real independent corroboration of Ragosi's personal involvement in a criminal enterprise?"

"But we have half a dozen of his employees—"

"The same as Ortiz. They're ratting the boss out to save their asses. No, as far as I can see from this, you have a legitimate case against Ragosi for a number of counts of falsifying business records, period."

The young prosecutor gaped. "But that's . . . *nothing*!"

"It's not much," agreed Karp, "but it's all I'm going to let you go ahead with on Ragosi. The shame of it is that this is a really good operation. Ortiz and the other chop kings are bad guys and you got them. You broke up a major car-theft ring. If the big guy beat you, hey, you might get him the next time. There's no shame in getting whipped. The shame would be in this office bringing a case that stinks of perjury and manufactured evidence. If you're still set on Ragosi, my advice to you is go back to his operation and look harder."

"But we *did*!" cried Weingarten in a strangled tone. "We looked everywhere, his wife, his banks, his daughter, his fucking cousins, we bugged his house, his office . . . Jesus Christ, every skank, drugged-out car thief on the East Coast knows Ragosi is the man, and we didn't find a fucking mark on him, and if it wasn't for Ortiz . . ." He stopped, flushed, and hissed, "Ah, shit!"

"I rest my case," said Karp.

When Weingarten had slunk off, Karp made a note to talk to Keegan and Sullivan about canning the Ragosi trial, and also to let the police chain of command know in the nicest possible way that he wasn't having any of that particular brand of horseshit this month. Then he picked up the phone and called his wife.

"Where are you?" Karp asked when she answered. Marlene's car phone was still enough of a novelty that Karp always asked, even though he had been talking to cops in their cars for years without querying their 10–20 unless necessary. It was different when it was your wife.

"I'm on Woodhaven in Queens," said Marlene.

"Oh, yeah? Seeing the folks?"

"No, an old boyfriend. Rocco Lopata."

"Uh-huh. Is this like something I should be worrying about?"

"Nah, it's just that every so often I have to get it on in a grease pit with a short, hairy, overweight body-shop manager. I'll be in and out of there in twenty minutes."

"Hey, no problem, I'm an eighties guy. You'll wash up after?"

"Of course. Oh, also, I had a charming conversation with your daughter on the subject of how the Chens are taking this shooting thing. I happened to mention I had been by there, and she went ballistic on me. Apparently, I totally destroyed her life, and none of her friends will ever talk to her again."

"What? By offering to help?"

"Yes, and don't ask me to explain it because half of it was in Chinese. What I sort of gathered was that by appearing there I implied that I wished them to incur even more obligation to me than they already owed, which is sort of an insult, if you can figure that out. Also, she'd already heard through some grapevine that I was wearing a yellow shirt, which made it worse, yellow being an inauspicious color in time of trouble. Anyway, I was elaborately cursed out and had the phone slammed in my ear. I called back right away, and Posie said she'd stormed out."

"Wait a second—Lucy? She used *language* to you?"

"Oh, not in English, she's not *that* crazy, but I got the tone through whatever she was speaking—Cantonese or Tibetan, for all I know. Butch, we've got to do something about that kid."

"I'll talk to her," Karp said grumpily, thinking, as he did often these days, why can't she for God's sakes get along with the kid—Lucy's perfectly okay with *me*. The family drama was something of a closed book to Karp, who still thought that mere kindness and honesty would suffice to untangle that tale.

Marlene worked to keep the snap from her voice. "Yeah, well, I was thinking more along the lines of a Catholic military school in Alabama, but give it a try."

"I guess that wasn't the moment to bring up Sacred Heart again," Karp said.

Marlene laughed bitterly. "Oh, right. The last time I did she bit my head off. I explain the advantages, I tell her she's not going to be happy in public school ninth grade, and I get, I'm not going to leave my *friends* and that's final, *Mother*."

"It's her life," said Karp.

"It's *not* her life," cried Marlene, and then sighed and in a tone of false brightness she asked, "And how was *your* day, darling?"

"Great. I just shit-canned a case out of Felony that took a year and a half to construct, and probably drove some kid ADA to drink or worse."

"Was it fun?"

"Made my week. I'm going to have to ream Jimmy

Sullivan's ass again. The thing never should've gotten this far in the first place. But look, why I called, whatever the Chens say, I'm going to find the ADA on this Chinatown thing and get the full story. I assume you're looking into it, too."

"I have Jim on it—he hasn't got back to me yet," said Marlene, after which static intervened and she clicked the thing off.

Atlantic Avenue Paint & Body was located on that thoroughfare just after it crosses Woodlawn Avenue, in the Ozone Park neighborhood in the borough of Queens, and consisted of the usual one-story concrete-block loft, with an asphalt apron in front packed with vehicles. It was painted bright blue, with the name of the firm picked out in fancy shadowed white lettering. Marlene had grown up six blocks away and would never have considered taking her trade anywhere but Lopata's, as the place was called locally. Although at this point both her paint and her body were fine.

Marlene sat in her car for a while, feeling the sun through the windshield, warm but not unpleasantly so, listening to the rumble of the dog's breathing from the back and the sounds of metal bashing from inside Lopata's, and letting the old neighborhood soak in. Contra the famous saying, Marlene, unlike New Yorkers from Iowa, say, *could* go home again and did so fairly often. Her family and their neighbors thought she was crazy but not a danger to anyone but herself, and the mild celebrity she enjoyed did not hurt. Lately, her mother had started asking why Marlene did not appear on the talk shows, since she "knew more than all of those idiots they got on there put together." Also, although she would have denied it, the stability of this neighborhood was a comfort. Ozone Park had been inhabited by Italians and other Catholics of the old immigration when Marlene was born, and it was inhabited by them and their children still. Ordinarily, Marlene rather enjoyed dwelling in one of the districts of the city most boiling with ethnic weirdness, but sometimes not, as now; in the wake of the Chen unpleasantness she had *paisan* hunger, and had semiconsciously contrived a business excuse for a journey here to assuage it.

Through the dusty window of the garage she could see a burly man in a filthy pinstriped mechanic's coverall speaking on the phone. His gestures as he spoke were eloquently violent, and she could imagine the tenor of his language. Remembered, more than imagined, and that went for the gestures, too. Rocky Lopata as a high school junior had been a lean, cocky, mildly criminal kid with a duck-tail haircut and a black motorcycle jacket, the heartthrob of the whole girls' eighth grade at St. Joseph's parochial school. He hung with the kind of bad girls who wore their collars up in back and hung Chesterfields from their scarlet mouths, and it was a known thing that Terry Riccio had gone all the way with him. It was therefore a wonder to the school when little Marlene, of the straight A's and perfect behavior record, laid a heavy flirt on him at the Holy Martyrs basketball game (to which he, of course, responded, she being at the time as beautiful as the dawn) and even more of a wonder when Terry came after her with claws out after the game and Marlene knocked her sprawling with three punches. This, naturally, won the heart of Rocky, and there followed three months of educational evenings in the back of Rocky's chopped Plymouth out by the airport, the planes roaring overhead, while Marlene learned what she wanted to know about the physical aspects of love. Rocky never got her to go all the way, but he wasn't complaining, considering what he *was* getting, and thinking himself in love until the day when she skillfully dumped him. It was his first heartbreak, and Marlene's first as a breaker, though far, far from her last.

Rocky finished his call, slammed down the phone, felt eyes on him, cocked his hand to shade a peering look through the window, and then walked out to her car. He grinned as he came closer.

"I thought to myself, that can't be Marlene Ciampi in a orange *Volvo*," he said, "but I was wrong. All right, she had the VW, she's a old hippie, I can live with that, but a *Volvo*?"

Marlene grinned back and got out of the car. "They're very reliable," she said primly.

"Oh, yeah, and *safe*. Hey, I got a cherry '78 Trans I could put you in. Silver flake lacquer?"

"Rocky, give me a break. I'm an old lady with a big dog."

"So get a poodle. You belong in serious wheels, Marlene." He looked her boldly up and down. "Meanwhile, you're still the hottest thing in the borough."

"Thank you. You probably clean up pretty good yourself. How's Terry?"

After that they spent a pleasant fifteen minutes

catching up on the old gang, many of whom had stayed close to home.

"So, what're you, visiting the folks?" Rocky asked when that had run its course.

"Yeah, I'll fall by after, but really, I needed to talk with Chester."

Rocky's face took on a pained expression. "Ah, shit, Marlene . . ."

"No trouble this time, honest to God, Rocky, I just want to talk to him."

"He quit on me, Marlene. I ain't seen him in a week."

"Horseshit, Rocky." She gave him that look, the one they had both learned from the nuns. He sagged, sighed, said, "Not with the dog, Marlene."

"No dog, and there wouldn't have been one last time, if he hadn't tried to bash my head in with a body hammer."

Rocky was still frowning and shaking his head when Marlene leaned into him, grabbed the collar of his coverall at an unsoiled spot, and said, "And I also came by to see a real good old friend," with which she planted a semi-sisterly kiss full on his mouth.

He gasped. He rolled his eyes to heaven and flapped his hand, as if it were on fire. "Oh, *marone*!" he said, and then, "Marlene, you're gonna burn in Hell, you know that."

"Yeah, but they'll have to catch me first. Where is he?"

Rocky punched a thumb over his shoulder. "Back in bay three. Be nice, now."

Marlene stood in the doorway of the cinder-block room and watched Chester Durrell fill a dent. He was a small, narrow, dark man of mixed Latin and Irish ancestry, with long black hair tucked under a reversed ball cap. His sleeves were rolled back, showing muscular forearms, the dun skin elaborately illustrated with blue, red, and green tattooing. His long fingers worked a pad of wet sandpaper back and forth on a gray patch of Bondo on the neatly masked rear fender of a new black Lincoln. Marlene knew that Chester had a city-wide rep as a body guy, and that in a couple of hours you would need an electron microscope to know that the bright black surface had ever been marred.

Marlene loved to watch a competent craftsman mold the physical world. As a girl she had begged her father to be allowed along on weekend plumbing jobs, where if the old man was feeling good, she would get a shot at turning a pipe cutter. Chester rubbed his patch to perfection, tossed his sandpaper into the water bowl, stretched, scratched, and reached behind him for a spray can of primer, at which point he saw Marlene.

He's looking for the dog, thought Marlene as she observed the tension in Chester's body and the jerking of his head. His pleasantly goofy face showed a near ludicrous apprehension, like the kind you see the doomed bit-part actors wearing just before the jaws snap shut in the early scenes of a monster movie.

"He's in the car, Chester," Marlene called out. "I just want to talk. Why don't you put your first coat down and we'll chat while it dries?"

After an uncertain pause he did that, in a dozen smooth strokes, the solvent smell filling the room despite the roaring fans.

He put the can down and leaned against the draped fender of the big car. "She sent you, right?"

"No, actually, I came on my own. You probably figured out Brenda's at the shelter again. Chester, I thought we talked about your hand problem. I thought that was all over."

"Hey, it wasn't like that, I swear to Christ, Marlene. You want to hear how it went down? Okay. We get invited to this party, right? Up in Inwood, man, my cousin Clarisse's. I say, Brenda, let's go, we'll have some laughs, but she says, no, she don't like Clarisse. Okay, so I say, I'll drop by myself, fuck it, she invited me and all, and she says, okay, go. Fine. So I go. A couple hours, I'm there, feeling good, I had a couple, few drinks, what happens? Bam! In walks Brenda, dressed up and all, so I go over to talk with her and so forth, why she changed her mind, and I see she's coked to the ears. So, fine, right away I knew there's gonna be trouble, and sure enough, pretty soon she's mixing it up with Clarisse, Brenda made some remark. You know like she does?"

"Yeah, I do."

"So Clarisse and her start scuffling, and we all break it up, and I pull Brenda into the bedroom, and I try to talk to her, you know, but now she's like yelling shit, all kinds of personal stuff. I mean really yelling so's everybody could hear it. So I like lost it and I popped her a couple, not hard, and she runs out, crying. So I had a few more and I take the subway home."

"That's it?"

"No, later back at our place, she comes in, maybe three in the morning, stoned. She takes her fuckin' *panties*, which I actually *bought* her, out of her bag in front of me and tosses them on the floor. In *front* of me, you understand? And . . . fuck, man, I don't want to get into what she was saying, but it was real bad, mean stuff, and like I must've blacked out because the next thing I knew, there's blood all over the bed, and I'm standing there in my shorts and she's gone."

"You busted her face up pretty good, Chester."

He hung his head and then lifted it abruptly and stared at her. The beginning of panic showed in his eyes. "Are you gonna get me arrested again?"

"No. Look, let me explain something. You know what I do, right?"

"Yeah. You beat up on guys who pound their old ladies."

"Not exactly. Chester, there's bad guys out there. Sick guys. Guys who get their rocks giving women grief, guys who don't feel like men unless they got a woman who's a slave. There's guys who just pick a woman off the street, or in a store or a bank, they see her and they stalk her, and they make her life hell. I can stop that kind of guy sometimes."

"With one through the skull is what I hear."

"If necessary," Marlene said coldly, "but my point is, you're *not* a bad guy. You're a *good* guy. You're just in a bad relationship. I'm telling you now that if you stay with Brenda Nero, one day you're going to wake up next to her corpse. No, wait, I know what you're going to say. She's great a lot of the time and you love her, and you're right, she *is* great. She's sexy, pretty, she's classy, she's smart—but she's also crazy, Chester. Disaster happens around her. You got to break it up. I mean now. You understand what I'm saying?"

She wanted to shake him as he stood there by his fender, rolling his eyes and shaking his head, like an unusually stupid horse shying from a proffered halter. I'm no good at this, she thought. He's right, one through the head is where my true talent lies. But eventually she got him to promise more or less that he'd ditch the woman, and she left him, thinking that she would have to do the same thing with Brenda, too, with even less chance of success. Marlene had met more than one woman whose life was a disorganized sprint toward an early grave, and most often they got some poor schmuck to help them into it. Tragedy, whereas Marlene did best at melodrama, with a clear villain in the black suit and the tender maiden in white pining for rescue. Depressing, and she had wanted to be cheery for Mom, or so she thought, and naturally, there was no question of coming to the old neighborhood and neglecting a family visit. The NSA would be happy if it could track Chinese missile tests as accurately as Marlene's family recorded the trajectories of their absent children.

The elder Ciampis dwelt in a pre-war two-story bungalow, built of dark brick, the sort of sturdy, simple house that working-stiff vets could buy in the late 1940s when the nation was still poor enough to afford it. In the front, two small patches of immaculate clipped lawn greenly gleamed behind low privet growing through a chain-link fence. To the left the lawn patch was decorated with the usual Virgin w/blue mirror ball and birdbath, and on the right there was the fig tree, stunted and twisted but still alive, still throwing out green shoots. These items demonstrated, as they did in all the old boroughs of the city, that second-generation Italian-Americans lived here.

Marlene hitched herself around in the car seat, removed her pistol and its holster, and locked them in the glove compartment. Marlene had a new gun. The old gun had killed two men and it had started giving her the sick shivers when she touched it, so she had sold it and bought this thing, a SITES AW9 "Resolver," one of the lightest 9mm semiautomatic pistols available, made in Turin, sleekly Italian in design. She prayed daily and sincerely that it would never have to resolve anything, would forever remain a shooting-range virgin. It was a little less than twice as long as a king-sized cigarette and about twice as thick and weighed about the same as an office stapler. This made it much too heavy to carry into her mother's house.

The front door was, as always, unlocked. Marlene went in and passed directly into the kitchen.

"Hi, Mom."

"Good, you can help me hang," said her mother, indicating the wicker basket of wet wash on the kitchen table, as if this visit had been arranged, or as if Marlene had never left home. Mrs. Ciampi, despite the book on Italians, had never been a physically demonstrative parent.

Marlene heaved the basket up on her hip and

followed her mother out through the screen door
to the tiny backyard. She and Mrs. Ciampi began
to hang clothes on plastic lines strung between two
T-shaped poles.

"Didn't we get you a dryer, Ma?"

"I like it better when they hang. They don't smell
right from the dryer."

Marlene was out of practice, being totally dryer
dependent herself, and her mother placed four
clothespins to every one of hers. Marlene cast
glances at her mother through the flapping linen.
Aside from the hair, which had gone pepper and
salt, and a thickening middle, she looked more or
less as she had looked during Marlene's youth, or
perhaps it was merely imagination. She had the
kind of face that holds age well, Marlene thought,
handsome rather than beautiful, too bony for that,
the features too prominent. The main difference
seemed to be the track suit she was wearing instead
of the flowered housedresses she had worn every
day back then. Mrs. Ciampi had discovered track
suits late in life and had adopted them for every occasion that did not involve the Roman Catholic
Church. She had a dozen, this one being aqua with
a beige stripe. Combined with her mother's ener-
getic movements, the outfits suggested that she
was about to strip and run the five-hundred-meter
hurdles.

While they worked, Mrs. Ciampi wormed into,
with a skill that the KGB would not have disdained,
every cranny of her daughter's life, having already
detected on her secret mother radar the unidenti-
fied bogey menacing Marlene's heart. The twins

first, their little doings elaborated, discussed, the peculiar difference between them made light of, on the basis of other family twins, not to worry; Marlene's own work, deplored sadly, the infant Marlene, her brilliance and hoped-for future recalled, with the familiar anecdotes, the necessary dollop of guilt offered and accepted; the brothers and sisters analyzed, their recent triumphs and travails recounted, nor could one neglect highlights from the lives of Marlene's twenty-three first cousins, none of whom, it seemed, was required to shoot people in their chosen fields of endeavor.

The wash hung, the two women entered the house. Mrs. Ciampi offered coffee, which Marlene accepted with an internal shudder. It would be instant, with water barely boiled. Marlene's mother, unlike Marlene, had no interest in cuisine beyond assuring quantity, and had raised six children on canned and frozen, on Kraft dinners and Velveeta and Pepsi, unlike her own mother, who was a *maestra assoluta* of south Italian cuisine. Marlene thought about generations, about inheritance, about what she was doing here, really, as she sipped the weak and bitter cup.

"And how's my doll?" asked Mrs. Ciampi, feigning innocence, comprehending perfectly, of course, that the one person they hadn't discussed was the one most on Marlene's mind. "What's with Lucy?"

So it all came out, the rudeness, the disobedience, the sullen contempt. Mrs. Ciampi listened, gently encouraging, withholding comment. Marlene felt some of the misery lift and wondered how women her age who were estranged from their own mothers managed to raise children—who could they talk to? Books? Therapists? Not that Marlene considered Teresa Ciampi any great expert on child rearing: look how Marlene had turned out, after all, but she had the history, she'd been there, when the seeds were planted that—so Marlene believed in her deepest heart—were bearing in Lucy such unlikely fruit.

"Tell me," Mrs. Ciampi said after her daughter had run down, "does she still go to church?"

"Oh, does she ever! I can't get her out of there. She makes the Little Flower look like Lenny Bruce."

Her mother shot her a look dense with meaning. Decoded: you and your wise mouth, I told you a million times, you mock the church, you're going to get trouble and here it is.

Aloud, she said, "And you? Or you just drop her off?"

"I go, Ma. You know me. I punch the clock even if I don't work the shift. What, you think it's a punishment from *God* Lucy's giving me grief?"

"No, she's just taking after her mother."

"Get out of here! I was a little angel compared to Lucy. I never opened my mouth."

"Oh, I beg your pardon. I must have been in amnesia eighteen years, I wasn't really here."

"When? Give me one time!"

"One time? Oh, let's see . . . you were fourteen, because it was the summer your great-aunt Angela passed away, God rest her soul. I came home from shopping and you were in the kitchen leaned over the ironing board, ironing your hair like you used to do, the hair God gave you wasn't good enough. You remember that?"

"I remember ironing my hair."

Mrs. Ciampi raised her eyes. "Oh, thank you, Madonna, I'm not losing my mind. So I come in, I put my bags down, and I say, because it was a weekday, and you were working at Uncle Manny's, why're you doing that on a Tuesday, or whatever it was, you got work tomorrow, you're not going out, and you don't say anything, like a mule. So I ask you, where're you going you're ironing your hair. Still no answer. So I think, this is my house, my kitchen, and this little *strega*'s pretending I'm not there? So I yank the cord from the iron out of the wall."

She paused for effect, nodding, took a sip of coffee, assured herself that she had Marlene's full and fascinated attention, and resumed.

"You let out a yell like I never heard, and you called me a bad word, I won't even say what it was, and then you threw the iron at me. At my head."

"No!"

"Yes. You think I'm making this up? Look over there on the door post, on the left. See that mark? It's painted two times since then, but you could still see it. That's the mark. Then you ran out, we didn't see you until God knows when at night. That was when you were climbing in and out up the drainpipe."

"Oh, Jesus, you *knew* about the drainpipe?"

"Don't swear. Yeah, I know you think my head's full of lasagna, but I got eyes."

"And you never said anything. Did you tell Pop about the drainpipe?"

Mrs. Ciampi sniffed disdainfully. "Are you joking? You'd be six feet underground I ever told him the things you pulled. I didn't tell him about the iron either. He came home and saw the mark, I said I was changing the kitchen bulb and the ladder fell."

"I can't believe this," said Marlene. She felt an odd constriction in her chest, and the room seemed to be growing warmer. "I don't remember *any* of that. And you didn't do *anything* about it?"

"I prayed, Marlene. I sent up so many novenas . . . Father Martini, if you remember him, let him rest in peace, Father Martini said, 'Teresa, you wore out the roof on the church. That's why we need a new roof, Teresa Ciampi.' What else could I do? Whip you like a dog? Lock you up?" She sighed, sipped the cooling coffee. "Anyway, it turned out better than I expected, tell you the honest truth. You stopped with those bums with the motorcycles, you won the scholarship to Sacred Heart . . . I'm not saying you're not still *pazza*, but it's your life, darling. But what I'm saying, about Lucy, the apple doesn't fall far from the tree. Have patience and bring her by more, I'll talk to her."

Marlene nodded, hardly hearing. "I'm stunned, Ma. Now you're going to tell me *you* were out of your skull when you were Lucy's age, too." Silence at this. "Well, *were* you?"

"That's none of your business," said Mrs. Ciampi, and looked away.

• • • •

The object of this discussion, having calmed her fury just enough so that she was no longer shaking, dressed in her usual jeans, sneakers, and embroidered vest over a T-shirt, this one imprinted with a color rendition of a can of Chung-King Chicken Chow Mein, and fled the loft. On an ordinary summer vacation day she would have headed, of course, for the Asia Mall to hang out and help out, but this was, naturally, impossible, her mother having ruined her life forever. She had her musette bag stocked with her favorite books, her journal, pens, a compact dictionary or two, and something less than $200 in crumpled bills, her stash.

She walked in a northerly direction, up Crosby, over to Broadway on Spring, up Broadway, through the heart of cast-iron Soho. She almost headed for Old St. Patrick's, where she might dump some part of her burden of pain, but decided against doing so until the wrath had left her heart. Father Dugan was a smart fellow, and he would snatch the secret from her in no time, as one could not lie to a priest, and she did not want to give it up just yet. She began playing with the idea of going to Washington Square Park and making a start as a junkie prostitute street person. Pro: it would focus the entire energy and attention of the family on Lucy, where it truly belonged, and would make her mother utterly miserable, which she deserved. Con: hideous pain and early death. Still, she had to do *something*. . . .

At Prince Street she became aware that someone was following her. In an instant the stupid adolescent maundering left her mind by the nearest exit. Her true self popped up out of the mire, looked around, and took charge.

Lucy paused, as she had learned to do, at a corner window and checked the reflection, and then turned east on Prince. Halfway down the block, she suddenly dashed across the street, as if attracted by the display in a gallery window opposite. She saw an oriental man in dark clothes and a cheap straw hat walk past on the north side of Prince and stop to examine some rugs on display in a window. He could see her reflection as she could see his. When Lucy moved west again, he followed, keeping to the opposite side of the street. Then, between one of her sideways glances and another, he vanished.

Lucy was impressed. She had been taught that (non-crazy) people follow other people for one of two reasons: either they wish to know where the target is going and what she's doing there, or they wish to find her in a vulnerable position, alone, for example, in the classic dark alley, and there do her mischief. In both cases, of course, the follower must be careful not to let the target know she is being followed, while the target should perform various maneuvers when she suspects she is, so as to break the follower from cover. This Lucy had just done, and the follower, spotted, had broken off his follow.

Or maybe not. Back on Broadway by this time, she waited until the light had just turned red against her and flew across the honking street and down into the Prince Street subway station. There she did the standard drill, waiting for a downtown train, boarding it, jumping off an instant before the doors closed. The platform was empty. She crossed to the other platform, waited for an uptown local, and took it to Eighth Street. From there she walked over to Washington Square and found a bench by the chess tables.

This park was, like many another in the city, a drug market and urban squalor demo. Around the noble arch, dingy and scrawled upon, a fake cake in the window of an unprosperous baker, bored Guatemalan nannies of bond trader/ad executives' babies alternated with crack dealers, with their zoned-out clients, with bemused Asian architecture students, with kids from the Tisch School making videos about the collapse of civilization, the soundtrack provided by folk singers encouraging people to join the coal miners' union, their warbles competing with a half dozen boom boxes blasting salsa, ska, punk, R&B, and heavy metal into the innocent green canopy, echoing back, mixing strangely, assaulting the ears of those who were not yet used to the love songs of the city, hardly disturbing the slumber of the bond trader/ad executives' babies, as the Guatemalan nannies gently rocked them to whatever transient beat penetrated, their flat brown faces closed tight against America.

For Lucy, child of the city, all this was as a wheat field to a Kansas kid, an unremarkable background, against which only a few objects had any chance of standing out. A disheveled person holding an automatic weapon might engage her interest, for example, or the guy who had been following her. Meanwhile, she sat and read *Claudine en Menage*. It would be hard for anyone who has never been captivated by a fictional character to comprehend the depths of Lucy's disappointment in Claudine, or to credit that the end of the second book in the series—in which Claudine agrees to marry a man old enough to be her father—had contributed considerably to the recent explosion with her mother. In one corner of her mind she had imagined (while understanding at some level the absurdity of the notion) that Claudine would marry Kim, and somehow combine a life of intimate sensuality with exotic adventures involving a large number of foreign languages.

Her devotion to the series was such, however, that she read grimly on, and after a while found some satisfaction in Claudine's discovery that marriage to the old fart was not what she had expected, and increasing fascination in the prospect of her lesbian affair with the delicious Rézi. Naturally these juicy parts made her think of spinning it all out to her friends in the fur room, and the recollection that all that was lost forever, and probably her friends with it, pierced her heart anew, and the pages blurred.

She dabbed her eyes and then gasped, for standing right in front of her was the oriental man in the straw hat.

"You know," he said in French, "it does little good to make your escape so brilliantly and then to come sit here all oblivious like an eggplant on a windowsill. Would you care for a peanut?"

She took one from the proffered bag, and he sat down next to her.

"How did you do that?" she asked grumpily. "I thought I got away clean on the subway."

"So you did, but, as you are aware, my study of the secrets of the Orient has given me certain mystic powers far beyond your puny Western abilities." With this he slitted his eyes mysteriously and waggled his thick eyebrows. This person, who called himself Tran Vinh Din, was a medium-sized Vietnamese of unprepossessing appearance, somewhat more than fifty years old, wiry of build, calm of demeanor. Except for the shallow dent in the side of his head and the scars on his hands and the oddly twisted fingernails, he looked like someone to whom nothing interesting had happened, a schoolteacher, say, or a cook in a noodle joint. In fact, he had been a schoolteacher and a cook in a noodle joint, but between those two occupations, in the years between 1954 and 1975, he had been a member, and eventually quite a senior member, of the Vietnamese National Liberation Front, known inaccurately as the Viet Cong. After that he had been a political prisoner of the People's Republic of Vietnam and after that a boat person and after that a fraudulent immigrant under his false name (a common enough story at the time in New York, save the Viet Cong part), and now was a sometime employee of Marlene Ciampi, as well as her daughter's best friend over the age of thirteen.

"*Merde*," responded Lucy with assurance and took a handful of nuts.

"So you respond with the word of Cambronne, and properly in this case. In fact, I meet you here entirely by accident, although you still should not have let me approach. I could have been two rough fellows with a big sack."

"In full day in the middle of a crowded park?"

"Oh, yes, these chess players would have leaped to your defense, I have no doubt. Many unpleasant things may happen in the full light of day."

She sighed, for this was familiar, and asked, "So, what *are* you doing here, Uncle Tran?"

He gestured with the bag. "I come for the peanuts. The man there on the corner sells freshly roasted ones, which I enjoy. So, truthfully, it was entirely happenstance that I found you here. What is that book in which you were so abandoned as to forget your caution? Hm! A fine writer, but with no political ideas, mere decadent sensuality; also, that is not her best work. Yet, in any case, it is better than condescending oriental fantasies by Kipling."

"I like oriental fantasies, and I don't care about condescending. Everyone condescends to someone. What I would really like is an oriental fantasy with decadent sensuality."

"I'm sure, but then you would have something like Ouida, unreadable even by your deplorable standards. What is going on between you and your mother?"

An old interrogator's trick, slipping the zinger in among trivialities, but it struck. Lucy flushed and said, "Nothing."

"Not nothing," said Tran, "a great deal, I think. Will you tell me about it? No? Then I will have to use my mystical oriental arts. First, you have been angry and sullen with your mother for some time. Americans tolerate this in their children, as I have observed on the television, and it is of no consequence—fireworks on Tet, as we say: boom, boom, and it passes, leaving everything as before. But today it is much worse. Your mother visited the Chens yesterday and was turned away, quite properly, but on hearing of it, you attack her with your tongue. Also, I find you alone and aimlessly wandering instead of plotting outrages with your two friends. The two events are connected, isn't it so?"

"She ruined my life," Lucy mumbled, staring down at a smear of old gum on the pavement between her sneakers. "I'll never be able to go to the Chens anymore—"

"What, because you think your mother has lost face and you have to because she is your mother? This is absurd. You have done nothing improper, and in this case your duty is to go to them like a good foster child and offer support. As for what your mother did, it never happened. No one pays any attention to your mother, except as they do to a thunderstorm or an earthquake."

"Really? So you think I would be welcomed at Janice's."

"I believe so," said Tran. "Of course, as they are Cantonese, they may cut you up in small pieces and fry you with green onions and garlic."

This brought a smile to her face, and seeing it, Tran felt a warm current in the place his heart used to be. His own daughter had never reached thirteen, having been incinerated by a B–52 along with his wife in 1968. He had no photographs of them anymore, and to his dismay their faces were fading from his mind. When he dreamed of his daughter now, she had Lucy's face. Pathetic and sentimental, he thought, but there it was.

"Perhaps I'll call her and go over now."

"A fine idea, after you have apologized to your mother. In a harmonious world, parents should teach children, and it is an unfortunate thing when the child knows more than the parent about certain things. I have observed that this is more common in America than elsewhere, especially among those from foreign lands. Nevertheless, you must apologize. Agreed?"

"Agreed," said Lucy. It had not occurred to her that her mother was in any way imperfect, and the knowledge both intrigued and appalled her.

"Now," said Tran, "of what are you so afraid?"

Lucy's heart performed an unpleasant leap. "What makes you say that?"

"In the instant you spotted me awhile ago, before you understood that it was me playing a game, you had a look of terror on your face and in the stance of your body. Is it possible that someone is after you in earnest, my child?"

Lucy waited some long seconds before answering. "You won't tell my mother?"

Tran looked down at his devastated hands. "I believe I can keep a secret."

"I can't tell you the whole thing because I swore not to, but . . . it might be a good thing if you watched my back for a while." She placed her hand in his.

Tran nodded and rose, and they walked out of the park hand in hand.

"Who is Cambronne?" Lucy asked abruptly.

"Ah, Cambronne. Marshal Cambronne was the commander of the Old Guard at Waterloo. At school all of us little *mites* were taught that when the British called upon him to surrender, he said, 'The Guard dies, it does not surrender.'"

"What is *mites*?"

"Oh, that is just a word the French used. From Annamites. That is to say, we Vietnamese. You would say 'gooks.' But, naturally, we also knew this expression, 'the word of Cambronne.'"

"You mean, he really didn't say that heroic thing, he just said, *'merde'*?"

"So it seems. Another thing among many that confirmed for us the absolute hypocrisy of the French. You Americans are insane, but far less developed in your hypocrisy. This is refreshing. I am proud to be an illegal immigrant in your country."

5

THE CHEN FAMILY EMERGED FROM SE-
clusion early in the afternoon of the next day and
reopened their emporium, the police having finished with it. They did a remarkably good business
for a weekday, as people in the community flocked
in to demonstrate ethnic solidarity and assuage
morbid curiosity. Lucy Karp walked in somewhat
later, and after a brief conversation with one of the
checkout bag girls, put on an apron, replaced her,
and started stuffing. As she had promised, she had
called her mother on the car phone and offered a
formal apology, and said dutifully that she was
about to visit the Chens. Her mother was still suf-
ficiently stunned by her conversation with her own
mother to accept this without asking any questions.
Lucy's tone had been cool and polite, which was in
itself something these days.

In a break between customers, Lucy waved to
Mrs. Chen, standing watchfully in her elevated
glass booth, and Mrs. Chen smiled and waved back.
Tran had been right, Lucy saw with vast relief. For
her part, Mrs. Chen understood what Lucy was doing and understood its benefits to her daughter. As

she had often before this, Lucy would take half a shift for free, so that the bag girl would work a half shift for Janice, thus giving Janice four hours of free time. Mrs. Chen had never had any free time when she was Janice's age, and if Mr. Chen had his way, neither would Janice. Mrs. Chen had heard, however, that most American children did not work twelve hours a day, every day, during school vacations, and so she was prepared to be indulgent, as long as nothing interfered with the intake of cash. Not that the Chens were greedy, not compared to those operating a quarter mile to the south of the Asia Mall in Wall Street, but they had obligations. In China a vast Chen cousinage awaited opportunity, sponsorship, transportation to Gold Mountain, so that they in their turn could prosper and achieve glory and honor and add luster to the name of Chen. A few hours of leisure for her daughter, Mrs. Chen thought, would take little enough from this enterprise.

The two girls walked in companionable silence along Canal Street, both of them inexpressibly glad that normal relationships had been reestablished after the disaster.

"You want to go listen to music at Sounds Like?" Janice asked.

"Yeah, later," said Lucy, "but first I have to do something. Let's cross here."

She dashed south across Canal, dodging slow-moving cars and trucks, Janice in her wake, and continued south on Mott.

"Where're we going?" Janice asked.

"You'll see."

"I hate it when you get mysterious, Lucy."

"That's too bad, girl, because I'm mysterious a lot."

Janice stopped in her tracks. "Tell me this isn't about . . . you know, because no way am I . . ."

"No, this is personal. I have to open a bank account."

They kept walking south into the heart of old Chinatown, herb shop and gambling cellar country, and other stuff, too, that the girls were not supposed to know about but did.

"Are we going to the Republic bank on the Bowery?" Janice asked.

"No, there's one in there," said Lucy, pointing down the narrow opening of Doyers Street. Originally an eighteenth-century cart track and not much improved since, narrow and twisted as a lane in Guangdong, Doyers is the shortest street in Chinatown. The sharp bend in its middle was known around the turn of the century as the Bloody Angle, because it was there that the hatchet men of warring tongs would wait to ambush one another, and for a while more people were killed here than on any other street in the nation. The tongs were respectable business associations now, of course, and didn't employ hatchet men anymore. If you asked.

At Number 10 on this street, just across from where the original Chinese opera house used to be, stood a grimy building barely ten feet wide, fronted by a dusty glass window showing off three desiccated snake plants and bearing the legend in red characters "Kuen and Sons, Importing and Exporting." No English translation was provided.

"This is a bank?" asked Janice.

"Kind of," said Lucy. "Tran told me about it. The Kuens are pretty famous."

"I never heard of them," said Janice.

"Famous among mysterious people," Lucy amended. She opened the door and they went in. A bell tinkled. They were in a small room lit by the streaked window and an overhead fluorescent fixture with two tubes dark and the remaining pair buzzing and flickering. A settee and two chairs in brown-painted rattan and a low lacquered table on which sat an old copy of *China Today* made up the room's furniture. A calendar from a Chinese food company and the sort of cheap framed chinoiserie prints available in any shop in the district made up the wall decor. A ceiling fan hung motionless above them.

They heard soft footsteps. An elderly Chinese man stuck his head out of a door. Reading glasses were pushed up on his freckled, nearly bald pate, and he held a Chinese newspaper. He frowned when he saw Lucy and said to Janice in Cantonese, "What do you want? I am busy."

In the same language Lucy said, "Venerable Kuen, forgive me for interrupting you, but I wish to deposit some money with your house."

The man's eyes opened wide at this, then narrowed. He calculated swiftly, a well-honed skill of his. Clearly this was the famous spirit-possessed daughter of the she-demon Shan-pei, and the other one must therefore be the eldest daughter of Chen. An interesting opportunity—it would not hurt to put the Shan-pei in his debt, and the Chens were also numerous, prosperous, and attentive of their obligations. He stepped back from the door and motioned them forward.

This room held a scratched table, three oak desks, with accompanying swivel chairs, one desk with a manual Underwood on it, the two others supplied with abacuses, two steel tube chairs with green oil-cloth seats, several oak filing cabinets, a Barca-lounger in green leatherette, a television on a metal stand, a typewriter table with a large many-keyed machine that Lucy recognized as a Chinese type-writer, and a tangerine tree in a big round blue ceramic pot. The walls were stained dark yellow-brown with decades of cigarette smoke. It smelled of boiled rice and old paper and tobacco and ink.

Mr. Kuen sat in one of the swivel chairs and favored the girls with a smile, about which the only genuine thing was the gold in three of the front teeth.

"An account, you said?" he inquired.

"Yes, Venerable Kuen. I have one hundred and ninety-two dollars."

Mr. Kuen nodded and held out his hand. It was not a contemptible sum. Some of Mr. Kuen's clients made that every week, others every two minutes. Mr. Kuen paid no interest on deposits, nor did he pay attention to the Internal Revenue Service or to the currency regulations of the United States of America. The house of Kuen had therefore many customers. He counted the bills and placed them in a desk drawer. Then he got out a cheap pad and a ballpoint pen. Passing them across the desk to Lucy, he said in Cantonese, "Write your name."

Lucy wrote the character equivalent to the sound *káp* in Cantonese, which means grade or rank, and then the characters for old and poetry, or teacher, *lòuhsì*. Mr. Kuen took a ledger from the desk drawer, made a notation in a three-hundred-year-old code, wrote some characters on the pad, tore the slip off, and handed it over. Lucy tucked it away without impolitely studying it. She knew very well that it would be honored for $192 or its equivalent in goods in every Chinese community from Penang to Panama. After some ritual words expressing the honor that the house of Kuen realized from her patronage and Lucy's declining of that honor, instead expressing the deep obligation she felt toward the house of Kuen (which was more nearly true), the girls left.

"Would you mind telling me what that was about?" Janice demanded.

"That guy at the med school is going to pay me big bucks, and I need a place to run my checks through without going through a regular bank."

"Why don't you just give them to your mom to cash?"

"Because I don't want my mom to know."

"What! Why not?" Janice was astounded. She could imagine having secrets from her mother, but not about money.

Lucy shrugged. "I don't know," she said. Which was true; that was the problem.

Janice dropped the subject, and they walked out of Doyers and back the way they had come. They were just past Pell on Mott, weaving through the increasingly crowded streets, when Lucy picked up the tail.

"I want something to drink," said Lucy suddenly, and grabbed Janice's arm.

"A soda? We can get one—"

"No, I want tea, and food, I want to sit down." So saying, she hustled her friend down the short flight of stairs to one of the street's many tea and bun shops. The place was sparsely occupied, a couple of old people at the counter and a few at tables. It was not a tourist place. Lucy pushed Janice into a chair facing the mirrored wall at the rearmost table, and Lucy used the pay phone briefly. Then she sat down with her back to the wall, watching. A sullen waiter came over; without being asked, he placed a steel quart pot of fresh boiling tea in front of them and departed.

"Lucy, what's going on? Why are we in this joint?"

"We're being followed by a couple of *ma jai*. Here they come. For God's sake, don't look around. Speak in Cantonese and play along with whatever I say."

The two *ma jai*, little horses, gang members, swaggered in and sat at the next table. They called out loudly for tea and steamed pastry. Both of them wore sunglasses and black shirts worn outside dark trousers and opened to the chest, showing bridal white T-shirts. One had a broad, pockmarked face, a beefy guy in his early twenties. His companion looked younger, a teenager, thin-faced and jumpy. Lucy could feel their eyes on her through their dark glasses. She poured tea, took a scalding sip, and said, in a noticeable voice, ". . . anyway, I'll never do that again." She gave Janice eye signals.

"Um, no, me neither," said Janice haltingly.

"Damn it, I was wasted! How much did you drink?"

"Oh, a lot. Four cans."

"Four! I had six, and Mary Ma had the same. We must have finished half a case. I completely lost track of time."

From an early age Lucy Karp had been able to make up stories, precociously sophisticated ones about little girls who slipped between the cracks in reality, and expansions of traditional fairy tales, in which Cinderella, Tarzan, and the Wolfman would visit Mars to rescue Barbie. So she had no difficulty making up a yarn in which the three of them, Mary Ma, Janice Chen, and herself, had slipped away to the West Street docks, where the bad boys and the hustlers hung out (although not in the early afternoon, as a rule) and gotten drunk on beer, and become sick, and staggered back to the Asia Mall to find there (Surprise! Horror!) the uproar of the shootings. Once Janice saw where the theme was headed, she had no difficulty embellishing the plot with many an amusing detail. The gangsters were glowering and mumbling to each other, an ideal audience for this lie. Janice was growing more nervous by the second, however, and Lucy was not confident that her friend would keep up the fiction without letting out something harmful. Janice was not a liar in Lucy's league. What was needed now was a graceful, or at least a plausible, exit.

Lucy found it after five tense minutes of stiff, false chatter. She pointed past the steamy window to the street. "Look," she cried, "there's Warren

Wang. Oh, God, how do I look? Pay the bill! No, give me a mirror."

"Warren *Wang*?" said Janice in an astonished voice, and received a sharp kick under the table.

"My boyfriend, you idiot," said Lucy in English under her breath, and then louder in Cantonese, "Come on, Jen-dai, let's catch up with him." Lucy stood and, using the mirror Janice handed her (for she did not carry one herself) pretended to primp, after which she attempted to mime the appearance of young love, in the style of *Gidget* reruns. The disgusting little squeals that issued from her throat rang absurdly false to her own ears, but she hoped they would convince a pair of Chinese nogoodniks just off the boat.

Warren Wang, an eighth grader with plump cheeks, thick spectacles and a bad haircut, a Spider-man devotee and the vice president of the math club, was a well-known dweeb, and to be considered a dweeb in a Chinese-American environment is to have achieved dweebness in its most refined form. That Janice Chen, the most beautiful girl in eighth grade, and Lucy Karp, the weirdest, might suddenly accost him on Mott Street in the light of day, gripping his arms and cooing, was not something he had ever expected outside the world of teenage boy dreams. He knew Mary Ma, another math club stalwart, and he knew that these two hung around with her, but heretofore he had only gazed at her two friends from a distance. Yet here was Lucy's bony little hip pressing in on one side and Janice's softer one on the other, their arms linked in his, the both of them chattering gaily, how you doing, Warren, want to go somewhere, Warren, listen to records, a movie? Warren had heard about dog dates, of course, and was well informed about the boundless and inventive cruelty of incrowd girls. He stiffened, like a hen in the jaws of a fox, waiting for the punch line.

Lucy was in contrast feeling loose and on top of things. It was a Kim moment, combining as it did the yanking of wool over the eyes of vaguely defined malign forces and impressing her peers with her brilliance and mystery. And she was enjoying talking to this boy, something she hardly ever did, would never be caught dead doing as the grotesque beanpole Lucy Karp, but now, in the urgency of the situation, she was mobilizing Claudine as well as Kim, so the charm just gushed out, delightful dirty nonsense: "Warren, I know you're interested in sexual perversions. Have you been to the new place on Broome that caters to Asian sadomasochists?"

Blushing giggles. "You're the only perverted one here, Lucy," said Janice.

"More than you know, my dear," said Lucy, "although Warren could probably both teach us something, eh, Warren? Anyway there is one."

"There is not. Don't listen to her, Warren."

"Yes, it's called Thais That Bind," said Lucy casually, at which Warren, who took an inordinate delight in puns (in English—any fool could pun in Chinese), cracked up and fell in love, in that order. Warren's laughter infected the two girls, and soon they were all three staggering against walls, clinging to each other, convulsed by the hysteria—so irritating to the adult world—that is peculiar to the adolescent psyche.

Lucy was not entirely lost in herself, however, and had been keeping an eye on the two *ma jai.* They were standing a half block away, conversing and glaring at the three kids through their dark glasses. They did not like that there was laughter going on, since there was at least a possibility that some of it was directed against them. As Lucy watched, they seemed to make a decision and started to move rapidly toward the group, pushing through the Mott Street crowds, who were quick to yield the way.

Lucy sobered instantly, grabbed the two other kids by their arms, and tugged them north on Mott Street. The two gangsters now pulled close enough to nearly tread on their heels and started to talk nasty.

"Look at the three girls," said the thin one. "Which one do you want?"

Pockface said, "Only one girl has an ass worth fucking. One is too big and the other has none at all."

And much worse as they moved up Mott and across Canal. Warren kept mumbling out of the side of his mouth, asking for an explanation: Why are these guys following you? Why don't you call a cop? What's going on? Where are we going? To all of which Lucy replied with soothing words and urged them all along west on the north side of Canal Street, nearly running, Warren pale and tripping over his feet, the thugs dancing around them, poking them, calling out the colorful obscenities with which Chinese is so plentifully supplied. They collected disapproving glances from the shoppers and merchants along the way, but no one interfered.

Lucy judged her distances and nudged Warren in the ribs.

"Warren, the Pearl River Market is coming up. When we get there, cut and run in. They won't follow you."

"No, I'll stay with you," said Warren, surprising both of them as the words came out. His glasses were misted with strenuous perspiration. Lucy frowned. She had never been gazed at with devotion before, and it made her cross.

"Warren, just go! It's a plan. We'll be all right. Now . . . run!" She shoved him away, and he vanished into the large Chinese food store. In the same motion she spun and shouted at the gangsters, *"Gou pi! Cao ni ma bi!"*

It took a second for the gangsters to understand that a skinny white girl had yelled at them, in public, "Dog fart! Fuck your mother's pussy!" In that instant Lucy (and a split second later, Janice) were off like deer, the gangsters pursuing. So intent were they on the chase that they failed to notice when they crossed Baxter Street, which marks the border, in gangland, between China and Vietnam.

Halfway to the next street, Lucy slowed; Janice looked in panic over her shoulder to see what was wrong and discovered that the two *ma jai* had disappeared.

Gasping for breath, hands on her knees, Janice demanded, "What happened? Where are they?"

"Someplace they'd probably rather not be," Lucy replied, gasping. "It's okay, we're cool now."

At this Janice Chen, who had been holding herself in with great effort since Doyers Street, exploded.

"Cool? What the hell do you mean, *cool*? What are you *doing* to me? What's *happening*? Who were those guys and what did they want? Where did they go? I swear, Lucy, I'll *strangle* you if you ever pull anything like this again." And more in the same vein, with the waterworks thrown in. Janice finally collapsed into a heap on the pavement, leaning against a wall. Lucy squatted next to her.

"They were trying to send you a message, Janice."

"What? Who? What message?"

"Whoever shot those guys. They want your family to know they can pick you up whenever they want."

"Why me? Why not you?"

"Because it's your store, Janice. They might have figured that if somebody saw something, it was a family member. Remember how that guy looked up when Mary panicked? And nobody knows I was there. Which is good, because they won't be keeping an eye on me and maybe I can find out what's going—"

"*Stop it!*" Janice shrieked. "I can't stand this mystery stuff like it was some *game* you're amusing yourself with. It's not TV, Lucy. It's not one of your books."

She stood up abruptly and brushed herself off. "I don't *want* this to be happening. I just want to be a regular person and let other people worry about murders and shit."

She looked so miserable standing there, weeping, that Lucy reached out to put an arm around her shoulder, but the other girl shrugged it away.

"No! Just leave us alone, huh? Just leave us alone!"

She ran off in the direction of the Asia Mall. Thus did Lucy learn what her mother well knew about the heroine business: that, unlike in books and movies, the people one saved were not always grateful. Rather the opposite, in fact.

It was part of Karp's management style to appear unannounced at various bureau offices at the end of the day, to pick up the kind of gossip that would not ordinarily reach the ears of the D.A. and to generally spread the sort of terror without which prosecutorial organizations tend to get lazy and sloppy, as he had recently demonstrated in the case of *People* v. *Ragosi.* He stopped by the Felony Bureau, to find the Felony chief, Sullivan, gone for the day, amused himself by poking a few sticks into various anthills, and then went down the hall to Homicide.

Ray Guma was sprawled out on the green couch in the bureau chief's office when Karp walked in, not dissuaded by Roland's growled "Go away!" Guma was drinking from a giant container of coffee, and Karp could smell the bourbon in it from the doorway. It was known that Guma often softened the day with a snort after the Supreme Court judges had gone home, which they all liked to do around four, and the place reverted to its natural proprietors. No one begrudged Guma this frailty.

He had not been known to appear drunk and incapable in court (drunk, yes; incapable, never) and besides, he was from another age, which the younger men, reared on the movies of that epoch, suspected was tougher, cleaner, and supported a nobler masculinity than their own deplorable era.

"What can I do for you, Butch?" asked Roland, smiling like a haberdashery salesman.

Karp smiled back and took one of Roland's side chairs. "Nothing, Roland, I just wanted to tell you guys again how much I enjoyed the performance up in Jack's conference room the other day. Did you rehearse that, or was it improvised?"

"He asked for it," said Roland dismissively. "Guy's full of shit anyway. When was the last time Rackets won a case? I don't mean bookies and that crap. He's just trying to horn in on my murder, like I'm going to deal him in."

"Meanwhile, you got shit on the case. Guma? What's the good word among the wise guys this week?"

Guma said, "The prairie dog sends signals to the hawk."

The other two men stared at him. "Goom, put away that coffee, for now," said Roland.

"The prairie dog sends *signals* to the hawk," Guma repeated with emphasis. "The hawk's trying to eat him, and he's sending up signals, help the hawk out a little. It's amazing."

"That's it," said Roland, "I'm calling 911. It's time for the rubber room."

"What're you talking about, Guma?" Karp asked.

"Prairie dogs. They live in these burrows, and they come out to feed on the ground. And the hawk flies over them, he's figuring one of the prairie dogs might not spot him up there in the sky, he dives and bang! Lunch. If he figures right, if the little guys don't really see him, he'll nail the dog before it gets into the hole. If not, no payoff. The bird has to fly up there again and start over. The only thing is, the hawk can't make too many mistakes, he'll knock himself out, maybe he'll starve, or his chicks'll starve. So—and here's the funny thing—the prairie dog *knows* this; so if it spots a hawk up there, it'll like make a little nod of its head. The hawk sees this, it doesn't dive on that prairie dog, doesn't waste the effort."

The two other men exchanged looks. Roland said, "Guma, what the *fuck* are you talking about?"

Guma ignored this and continued, his voice low and gravelly; Karp listened, fascinated. This was a different Guma. "So you have to ask, what's in it for the prairie dog? What the fuck does he care about some hawk, the hawk spends the day whacking his pals? Hey, but it's dog eat dog out there. So to speak. The prairie dogs are competing for turf, I mean real turf, 'cause they eat grass, bushes, whatever. So the dog figures, the hawk's gotta eat somebody, let him eat the guy who's a little slower than me, doesn't look around enough, too busy stuffing his face to check out the sky. I'll help him out, no skin off my ass, and plus, there'll be more leaves and shit for *me*."

He took a long swig from his cup and was silent. Roland said, "That was good, Guma. It's always nice to learn something about the world we live in. Now, would you please get the fuck out of here and sleep it off!"

Karp said, "No, Roland, Guma had a point, didn't you, Goom?"

"The point is," said Guma slowly, "the point is, things are not always like they seem. You gotta have all the connections or it don't make sense, like the prairie dog tipping off the hawk. And we don't."

"You're talking about Catalano, right?" asked Karp.

Guma gave him a long, bloodshot stare. "Of course, what the fuck else're we talking about? Like I said before, this is a family thing, it's got fuck all to do with the grand jury."

"So what's going on in the family?" Karp asked.

"Wait a minute," said Roland. "I want to know where you got all that shit about the prairie dogs. I thought you were a sports and pussy man."

"I am, Roland," said Guma with grave dignity. "But man does not live by sports and pussy alone. For your information, I got it off a PBS program."

"I don't believe this," said Roland, batting the side of his head with the heel of his hand. "Guma watches PBS? What're you, joining the ACLU, too?"

"I watch nature programs, Roland. I watch every fucking thing they got, David Attenborough, *Nature*, *National Geographic*, *Wild Kingdom*, I watch fucking *Nova*, they got an animal program on. What, you're surprised?" He finished the cup and put it down. "It's no big thing. Assuming I don't score with any beautiful young women, and you know they're all out there just looking for fat, ugly fifty-eight-year-old lawyers with no money, I go back to my miserable, shitty apartment and I watch. It's relaxing. There's a whole world out there with no fucking money involved. Eat and be eaten, just like the goddamn city, except they don't take a percentage. And the lion, or the fucking *hyena*, wants to get laid, he doesn't have to make any conversation, he doesn't have to develop his communication skills, he doesn't have to respect her in the fucking A.M., he just does it, and the bitch gets the dinner, too. What can I say, it relaxes me."

"I knew it," said Roland, "he gets off on the animal fuck scenes."

"Get back to the family, Guma," said Karp. "What kind of family thing?"

"Oh, yeah. The Bollanos." He paused, as if in thought, or maybe, Karp imagined, the old cells weren't firing quite as fast as they used to.

"You know," he began musingly, not yet ready to focus, "Phil Garrahy didn't waste five minutes worrying about the Mob. He thought it was grandstanding, like Tom Dewey did. Fucking Dewey got Luciano deported for what? A nickel pimp charge, and that was the only racket Lucky wasn't even in. Had a big impact on prostitution in New York, no more whores in town after that, which is not surprising because practically the only thing Luciano *wasn't* involved in was pimping. Phil had a clear sense of what was important, and the wise guys understood that. They did their thing and Phil did his, because he knew that, whatever the fucking *New York Times* says, it's better for the city to have vice organized, private, out of sight. Which is why in the old days, you didn't have what you got today, with the drugs and the whores in your face all the time, and the punks blasting away out on the street. And this bum, Colombo, he's got a hair up his ass, he wants to make sure nobody confuses him with the Mob family. I ask you one question: Did he play any ball, Colombo? No, he was on the fucking debating club. He was the kind of kid got his face pushed in the mud in the schoolyard, probably ran to the nuns with it. Never trust a D.A. didn't play ball, they're looking to prove something, they got a dick on them—"

"The family, Goom," said Karp patiently. Ordinarily he could listen to Guma talk about the Mob and the old days for hours, but he had things he had to do. Guma switched neatly into the new track without a bump.

"Yeah, Eddie Cat. What I said up there in Jack's, I was pissed, you know? Fucking Anselmo. What I'm thinking now is, is it reasonable to assume the don was in the dark here, and the more I think about it, the more I'm thinking he *did* know, not that he told Pigetti, whack this guy, but he let it out to Joe that maybe it would be a good idea. I can't see Pigetti just whacking Eddie Cat without any cover at all, is why. If he wanted to move in on the Bollanos, he would've taken out the old man and the kid *and* Eddie. So the don's not clean, is my thinking. You know Little Sally's a nutcase, everybody knows that. But let me tell you something else: he's following in the footsteps there."

"The don, you mean?" asked Karp. "I thought he was this icy calculator."

"Oh, I'll give you icy calculator; shit, yes. But also the word is maybe the good ten and the three of hearts slipped under the couch while he's playing, he didn't notice it. Besides that, he's—Big Sally, I mean—he's not a nice guy."

Roland burst out laughing. "Oh, wait, stop the presses! He's not a nice guy? Christ, Guma, he's a fucking *Mafia don*! He's supposed to be a choir boy?"

Guma ignored this and continued talking to Karp. "These guys, they're, when you get right down to it, real conservative. The family's over in the corner there; they might whack each other, they might whack a girl gets in the way, but they leave *la famiglia* alone. You understand this, Butch, Sicilians and the family. They sell whores, they use whores, they sell dope, whatever, but they don't *think* of themselves as bad guys. Okay, so there's rumors about Big Sal, always was, that he's like *bent*, from way back. Not short eyes, not a faggot, nothing like that, but there's a twist there. Big Sally would go to some lengths to see it didn't get out. With the big guys, there can't be what they call an *infamia*, they won't do business with a guy like that, and no business means . . ." He made a thumbs-down gesture, suggesting early retirement under a layer of paving material.

"So, you're thinking what?" Karp asked. "That Eddie was going to spill this whatever? That's why he was killed?"

"No, I'm not saying that, necessarily, but it was

something *like* that," said Guma reflectively. "You hear stories, too. They don't have much domestic felicity at the Bollanos, which is not that common either, the *cugines* like peace and quiet they come home from a hard day at the rackets, and the girls ain't into calling the cops they get rapped in the chops a couple times. So, that could hook up, too, someone's fucking someone, I mean for real, in a bed. But we don't know. It's like I was saying about the prairie dogs and the hawks. There's a message there for somebody, but we can't read it yet. We don't even know who's eating who. But that kind of stuff, that's where we should be looking."

Marlene, driving back to Manhattan on autopilot, thinking about selective amnesia, thinking Jesus fucking Christ I tried to kill my mother, and about her daughter, the ticking bomb. Of course, Marlene hadn't actually connected with that hot iron, but on the other hand, the kid had access to more sophisticated weaponry. The pistol in the glove compartment was sending out malign rays. Wondering why your kids hate you is a winless game, but one with the addictive qualities of a slot machine. She turned on the stereo, cranked the volume up, punched buttons, rejected rock 'n' roll, immature mooning after love, music of youthful rebellion, yes, she really needed *more* of that just now, settled on WQXR, Haydn sweetly blaring, a symphony. She blanked her mind, a necessary technique in many professions, including hers, and let the harmonies massage her. By the time she reached the

Queens Midtown Tunnel, the yammering in her head had been reduced to the usual low buzz of demonic voices conveying the usual neurotic messages, familiar as road signs: you're wasting your life, you're making your family miserable, you're going to end up dead in an alley or in prison; your kids will get shot by a maniac, *bad* mother *baaaad* mother, worthless, worthless, worthless . . .

The traffic gelled at the entrance to the tunnel, and Marlene called the dog into the front seat. "Sweety, come talk to me. I need the wisdom of the deep animal spirits." He came up from the rear deck of the station wagon and, with a damp sigh, draped himself across the front seat, his hindquarters down on the floor and his immense, hideous head resting on Marlene's thigh, or rather upon the old towel that she had placed across her legs. She stroked him behind his velvety ears.

"Oh, tell me about memory, Sweety. How can we live with each other if we can't agree about what happened? Now that I know I'm suppressing stuff, I wonder what I suppressed with Butch, or Lucy. I realize sometimes the family walks on eggs around me, and of course Butch is the world champion of papering over, pretty rich for a professional confronter of crime, but not in the sacred hearth, oh, no, the poor bastard, and Lucy, who knows what's cooking in there? I could've done something horrible and never remembered it. It would have to be pretty bad compared to what I *can* remember. And they talk about what trauma does to kids, and I think Lucy, a year old, some maniac grabs her out of her stroller and Jim Raney blows the guy's brains all over her, four years old, her dear Mom has a little nervous breakdown over practically getting raped by her boss, drags her out of town barely functional, at seven she procures a murder weapon for a kid who kills a cop, Mom covers that up, of course, and never mention, at ten she watches Mom blow away a guy who's after one of her clients, right there on the street, and a little later a friend of hers gets murdered and stuffed in a trunk by a bent cop, and the next year she watches Tran shoot a guy dead and even helps a little, and now what? I'm upset she's a little *tense*, a little *withdrawn*? Doesn't want to make *fudge* with Mommy anymore? I should be thankful she's still in the church, but God forgive me, that irks me, *too*, like she is just doing it to piss me off, the famous religious failure, I can do it, Mom, and you can't, nonny nonny nonny, oh, Jesus, is that an unworthy thought, or what, Sweety? Christ in heaven, how does this crap get into my brain? No, she's sincere, otherwise she'd probably be a serial killer already. And why can't I, Sweety? Why doesn't the grace come to me anymore? It used to. Come on, Sweets, you must have some religious ideas. Is there a secret Church of Dog? Does Dog exist, as the dyslexic agnostics ask? No, you don't need it, because you don't know you're going to die. Or maybe you do. How the hell would we know? We can't even talk to each other and we can *talk*."

The car entered the filthy, gleaming tube, and the radio was cut off, leaving Marlene with static, with the swish of traffic outside and the stentorian breathing of the dog inside.

"Meanwhile, Sweets, let's use this moment. In a

couple minutes, unless there's a tanker explosion that fries us all to a crisp or a crack in the tube, which is also something to worry about—of course, in that case you would heroically save me by dragging me out in your mighty jaws—but absent that, we will emerge into bright sunlight on Third and go uptown to talk to Harry Bello and get a lecture full of good sense, and it really is an absolutely gorgeous day, gorgeous, far too good for New York, if you ask me, and we will feel good again, through the dark tunnel into God's light, like Dante. Here we go."

And it was so, the sunlight flooded the broad canyons, Haydn came back with the final chords, and the fruity QXR voice informed us all that it had been the Ninety-fourth Symphony, called *The Surprise*, which made Marlene chuckle and bounce the dog's head on her knee, thinking, yeah, it always *is* a surprise, the good stuff amid the shit, and how pathetically grateful I am for it. The dog shuddered in delight and slobbered into God's lap.

6

THE OFFICES OF OSBORNE GROUP, INC., were housed in a twenty-four-story building on Third in the Sixties. The building was an undistinguished crate in the usual degraded International Style (glass over steel, and on the columns and in the lobby marble facings colored like pale toast and as thick), the den of small firms in fields representative of the city's business, including especially the innumerable parasites that cling like lice to the creative spirit—agents, producers, publishers, packagers, ad agencies, tax lawyers—plus a scatter of legal and medical professionals, and on the ground floor behind glass windows a discount brokerage and a health club. It was a respectable if not prestigious building and right for a security agency that liked to think of itself as having some class.

Marlene had her own marked parking space in the underground garage, which was a nice perk, and meant, among other things, that she could shop at Bloomies and get home without schlepping packages on the bus or trying to hail a cab or taking out a second mortgage to pay for parking. Many women in New York would work for Satan to get a deal like that, and Marlene knew it and was grateful that she only had to work for Lou Osborne, who was a pretty decent guy. In fact, she only had to report to her pal and former partner, Harry Bello.

Who was in, and looking good, as he usually did these days. During his last years on the cops Harry had run into some bad luck and got into the sauce and done some dreadful things, things he couldn't live with, and been in the process of committing slow suicide. They'd called him Dead Harry then. Marlene wasn't sure whether she or God's infinite mercy had saved Harry, but saved he was, now a prosperous security executive, and good at it, and while remaining a reliable pal, not in the least willing to cut Marlene any slack. She found his paternal concern alternately chafing (she already *had*, for Christ's sake, one semi-oppressive Italian father) and comforting (he was also the smartest detective she had ever met, fearless, and loyal). The arrangement was that Marlene ran her own business how she liked and worked for Osborne under Harry's nominal supervision, straight security for organizations and the well-to-do, celebrities even, as Marlene had a rep of the kind that the golden people delighted in, a sort of violence-chic. Which she herself despised, but it paid the bills.

He was wearing an expensive-looking gray suit and a blue striped tie, and he'd gained some weight in the last year or so, which he had needed to do. Not much hair left on Harry, and he still had those dark, sunken cop eyes, but his face was now healthy, rather than damp-clay swarthy, and he no longer looked like a fresh corpse.

Marlene greeted him with a kiss, went to the little refrigerator, opened a Coke, and flopped in one of Harry's leather sling chairs.

He said, "You know, you're supposed to call in, we send you on an appointment. How did it go?"

He meant the abortion clinic. "I was my usual charming self and a credit to the firm," said Marlene. "I don't think I made a sale. In fact, I think Ms. Hyphen-Name expected something very different. More of a sister, which I was not."

"Well, you must've done something right, because she called this morning and signed up. Site hardening, security service, the works. They caught two of the guys there, did you hear?"

"Wait a minute, she *hired* us? I thought she was going to throw me out of there."

Harry indicated amusement by crinkling his eyes and twitching the left side of his mouth up a quarter of an inch.

"What's so funny?" Marlene was a skilled reader of Harry's minimalist emotional field.

"You never can tell the effect you're having on people. Back on the Job, I used to bang away at some witness, trying to get cooperation, and it was no, no, I didn't see nothing, I wasn't there, and a couple days later you get a call, they want to sing. Meanwhile, who's Vivian?"

Marlene had to laugh. "That was cute. Where did you find out about old Vivian?"

"Woman's been calling here every couple hours," said Harry. "Won't give her full name, asks for you, no, nobody else can help her. The girl up front figured it might be something we should know about, so she told me. So?"

"She's from the shelter. No, don't roll your eyes at me, Harry! Showed up in a blanket and a pair of panties, been abused. Vivian Fein, she calls herself, maiden name, and she didn't strike me as someone who normally goes by the maiden name. She tried to hire me to investigate the suicide of her father. Gerald Fein." Marlene waited for Harry to make the connection.

"Not *Jumping* Jerry? You got Jumping Jerry's daughter in that shelter?"

"Yep. She was serious about it, too. Had a diamond the size of a golf ball she was going to give me as a retainer."

Harry didn't appear to hear this. "Jesus, that takes me back. Jumping Jerry. It was what? Nineteen sixty, right? Right, yeah, because it was my last year in the city before I transferred out to Brooklyn."

"You were in on the investigation?"

"Nah, I was in Auto at the time. But there *was* an investigation. Fein was mobbed up—you knew that?"

"I recall something of that nature."

"Yeah, what they call a Mafia lawyer. So the thought was that he might've had some help going off. But nothing turned up, and we had to let it go down as a legit suicide. Arnie Mulhausen had the investigation."

"You remember this? I'm impressed, Harry."

Bello smiled deprecatingly. "It's a habit. But I tell

you, it's not that impressive because stuff is starting to slip. I'm trying to think of Mulhausen's partner and I can't. Stocky guy, Irish, thin red hair. Donovan? Donohue? Something like that, and he had a nickname, B something . . . Billy-club? No. Anyway, Mulhausen passed while I was still working out of Bed-Stuy, so what's-his-name would be the guy to see. Dolan? I'll think of it."

"Guy to see? What, you *want* me to do this?"

"Why not?" replied Bello easily. "She's got means. We're running a business here, Marlene. It's got to be a long project, lots of billable hours at the top rate, and we got participation on a sliding scale based on our billables. She wants you, we know that, so go for it."

Marlene hugged herself, wriggled in her chair, and in a breathy voice cooed, "Oooh, Harry, when you talk that business talk, it just makes me feel shivery all over."

"Don't get wise, Marlene, like you couldn't use the money," Harry grumbled. "Besides, her money, it's a public service. Donnelley? I should sing that damn song with all the Irish names in it."

"What?" said Marlene. Harry occasionally reverted to a gnomic form of communication that assumed that the person he was talking to was making the same mental leaps he was. Marlene could often follow him, but not now. "What's this about her money?"

"Just that prick of a husband. It'd be nice to put it to him. On the other hand, he's not going to be happy she split on him. I hope your pal's ready for action there, got her six-gun oiled."

"Harry, what the hell are you talking about? You know who Vivian Fein's husband is?"

Harry snapped his fingers. "Doherty! John Doherty. They called him Black Jack. I knew there was a B in there somewhere."

"That's Vivian's *husband*?"

Harry looked at her as if she were speaking Welsh and replied in an elaborately patient tone. "No, Marlene, that's the guy on the investigation, with Mulhausen. Who you should see. The husband is Bollano. Jerry's daughter married Little Sal Bollano about two years after Fein hit the sidewalk. It was the wedding of the year for the wise guys."

Marlene could hear it through the elevator as it approached the fifth floor, the incredible volume produced by a pair of four-year-olds in full wail, and her heart shriveled inside her. As she had so many times before, she resisted the desire to head directly for the bedroom and bury herself beneath the covers, and went like a good momma bear toward the source of the noise. In the playroom she found Posie mopping vomit and her husband, still in his suit, a red-faced twin on each knee, his lapel decorated with little yellow flecks.

"I think it's coming out both ends," said Karp, which Marlene could smell for herself. The screams increased in volume when the boys spotted their mother, source of all comfort, and they reached for her like infant cuckoos.

"What did you give them?" Marlene snapped at

Posie. Toddler dietetics had never been one of the girl's strong points.

"Nothing, Marlene, honest! They just had their regular lunch and they started acting cranky around four and then Zak had the shits and I cleaned him up and then they *both* started puking just before Butch got home."

"Pick one," said Karp.

They had done this before. Marlene grabbed Zik and snapped out orders to Posie.

"There's a container of chicken barley soup in the freezer. Zap it for ten minutes!"

"I threw up, Mommy," Giancarlo wailed.

"I threw up, *too*, Mommy," said his brother. "We're sick as *dogs*."

As if cued, in pranced the mastiff, who began licking up delicious bits of yellow matter off the floor. Screams, shouted orders, startled giggles from the twins; the dog slunk off, but the cycle of hysteria was broken, which, thought Marlene, was just one more reason to have a shambling monster in the household.

The couple repaired to the bathroom, where the twin boys got stripped and cleaned and Karp held each one in turn screaming while their mother poured Kaopectate down their throats.

"What do you think?" asked Karp as he shoved Zak's arms into pajamas. "Not too hot, are they?"

She felt both their foreheads: warm, but not blazing. Diagnosis, stomach virus. After which, Mommy and Daddy pumping chirpy cheerfulness out like water from a spigot, which improved the boys' moods a good deal, then a bowl of healthful broth, a powerful dose of baby aspirin ground into apple-sauce for both of them, and a long lounge for Daddy and the twins in Zak's bed, reading one of Richard Scarry's compendiums, and, three times, the preschooler's answer to Phenobarbital, *Good-night Moon*. After the delicate little snores sounded, Daddy carried Giancarlo over to his own bed, tucked him in, and staggered down to the kitchen, where he found Mommy with a tumbler half full of red wine attempting to resume the character of Marlene.

"They are down," he said.

"Well, aren't you a light unto the Gentiles," she said, grabbing him and planting a kiss on the side of his head as he walked by to the refrigerator. She joined him and cut herself a chunk of Asiago cheese and a quarter loaf of yesterday's Italian bread, oiled and garlicked it, and ate the rest of the soup out of the Tupperware 6.

She watched Karp manufacture a roast beef on rye with his own hands, even, Marlene was amazed to see, slicing a tomato to go into it without damage to any vital organ.

"Sorry about your suit, by the way."

"Oh, no problem. It's designed to shed vomit. I'm a lawyer, you know."

"And besides that, how was your day?"

He told her then about the Catalano case, and its political ramifications, and Ray Guma's theory that it was something to do with the family, and Marlene listened, and did not tell him she suspected that at least part of the crime family's problem was sitting in room 37 at the East Village Women's Shelter. Indeed, it was common for Marlene to conceal things from her husband, although Karp was perfectly open with her about everything the law allowed. This imbalance was all right with Karp; he had no interest in learning all that his wife was up to.

"By the way," Karp continued, "I had a talk with Mimi Vasquez, the ADA who's handling the Asia Mall shootings. They've come up with some interesting stuff. The vics flew in that morning from L.A. on the red-eye. They got in the night before from Hong Kong. No known contacts in the city, so they're figuring someone followed them here to whack them. They're checking airport arrivals now, but it looks like—"

Marlene dropped her soup spoon and interrupted, "Wait a second—where's Lucy?"

"She's in her room, isn't she?" said Karp. The twins crisis had prevented either of them from thinking about the family's usual problem child.

"Is she?" Marlene got up and went down to Lucy's room, whose door was, as usual, locked. She knocked. "Lucy? Are you okay?" A grumble assured her that the girl was inside. "Come out and have something to eat."

"I'm not hungry."

"Are you sick?" No response. "Open the door, please, Lucy." More muttering, not all of it in a Christian tongue, stomping feet, the click of the lock. Marlene entered to see her daughter, dressed only in the Chung-King T-shirt and underpants, heading back toward her bed, where she jumped under the Italian flag duvet and turned to the wall.

Marlene sat on the bed and pressed the back of her hand against Lucy's cheek.

"You're not hot," said Marlene, her heart twisting as her daughter seemed to cringe away from her touch.

"Have you eaten anything?"

"I *said*, I'm not hungry."

"If you have anorexia, I'm going to kill you," said Marlene, trying to lighten it up.

"I *don't* have anorexia, Mother," said Lucy to the wall, mumble, mumble.

"What was that?" asked Marlene, comprehending very well what it was.

"Nothing, Mother. I just want to sleep, okay?"

"At eight o'clock? Lucy, did something happen today? Are you upset about something? Lucy . . . ?"

Lucy burrowed deeper under the covers and pulled a pillow up over her head. Marlene started to feel like a weasel digging a baby bunny out of a hole. She patted the mute lump and left.

At least she wasn't rude in English, thought Marlene. At least no heavy, sharp objects were flung. She was walking back down the hall to her husband when the street-level buzzer sounded. She went to the kitchen wall and asked who it was.

The tinny voice spoke in French. "Marie-Hélène, it is Tran. We should meet and talk."

"Come on up. I'll make some coffee."

A pause. "Perhaps that is not a good idea."

"Ah, *that* sort of talk. I'll come down."

Karp was used to his wife dashing off at odd hours. "Will you be late?" he asked mildly.

"No, be right back. I just have to have a word with someone."

Karp listened to the elevator descend. He got up, checked the twins, and then knocked gently on the door of Lucy's room. No answer. He entered and saw that it was dark, but heard not the calm and steady respiration of childhood sleep, but a caught breath.

"You okay, Luce?" He moved carefully toward her and sat on the bedside. He felt her forehead. Clammy. "Can't sleep?"

"I'm okay," she whispered.

"I don't think so. Why don't you tell me what's wrong?" Silence. "Is it what happened with the Chens?"

"I don't want to talk about it."

"Lucy, listen to me. There's no problem that we can't fix together. But you got to come clean. I'm worried. Your mother's worried . . ."

"Hah!"

"What, you don't think she cares about you? Are you nuts? Whatever this is between the two of you is making her miserable."

"The only way she would really care about me is if somebody was trying to kill me," said Lucy with finality, and then pulled her quilt over her head in an unambiguous signal that she wished to converse no more.

Down on the street, Tran shook hands with her formally as he always did. They walked up Crosby through the warm blue evening. They inquired after each other's health, remarked on the pleasant and seasonable weather. Marlene spoke her correct schoolgirl French, Tran his soft and nasal Vietnamese variety.

"So? What did you want to talk about?" Marlene urged when Tran seemed reluctant to begin.

"A delicate matter, I think. This afternoon Lucy called me and told me that she and the Chen girl were being followed by some Chinese boys she thought were gang members. Let me explain also that Lucy had earlier expressed to me fears that she might have been followed by someone of uncertain motives."

"And you didn't tell me?" Icily.

"I did not. The relations between you and your daughter at the present time are such that if she thought I was carrying tales to you, she would not share confidences with me; hence she would have no adult guidance at all in a certain restricted sphere. I trust that what I tell you now will not be flung in her face."

Marlene fumed briefly, but she took the point and grumblingly agreed. The score she gave herself in the motherhood category dropped yet again. "Who was following them?"

"A pair of boys associated with the White Dragons. They were hired by a man who called himself Leung Wenri. Their target was Janice Chen rather than Lucy. They were supposed to follow, and show that they were following, and put a fright into the girl. Which they did."

"This has something to do with the shootings in the Asia Mall, doesn't it?"

"That is a reasonable assumption," said Tran after a moment. "It is possible that the elder Chens are somehow involved. Perhaps they agreed to have their shop used for these assassinations. Perhaps they were not told it would be an assassination. Now they are frightened. The assassins wish to impress upon them how vulnerable they are."

They reached the end of the street, and Tran turned and started back the way they had come, Marlene at his side, as if they were some Edwardian couple taking a turn around the gardens.

"Do you think the girls are in any real danger?"

"Not from those two, at least."

These words sank in. She stopped short and blurted in English, "Oh, Christ, Tran! Don't tell me you whacked them!"

He gave her a pained look. "I assure you, Marie-Hélène, they are entirely intact, aside from a little fear. One of them soiled his underclothes, but that is, I believe, the only damage. I thought it would be useful if they went back to Mr. Leung, so that whoever hired him would understand that the girls are not entirely bereft of friends useful in such matters."

"This Leung is not the principal in the shootings, you surmise?"

"I would be startled to learn it. From what I can gather, he is a petty gangster. It is unlikely that he would dream of assassinating men such as the Sings."

"These are the victims?"

"Yes. Sing Peichi and his son, Sing Zongxian. From Hong Kong."

She stopped again and examined her friend's face. He seemed hesitant, as if unwilling to discuss the subject. This was a sure way to attract Marlene's avid attention.

"And why, pray, would one consider the Sings, father and son, as being outside the reach of the petty gangsters of the world?"

Tran saw she would not let it drop, sighed, and resumed strolling. "I suppose you know what a triad is?"

"Of course. The Chinese version of the Mafia."

"Which is what most Westerners think, but, like most aspects of China, the truth is somewhat more complex. How to explain this? A Mafia is a feudal organization: that is to say, it is a strict hierarchy, ordered and controlled from the top, bound together by loyalty and the conferring of valuable gifts, with violent sanctions for those who break its rules. In comparison, a triad is more like a trade association or a chamber of commerce, except the trade is largely criminal and the commerce illegal. And being Chinese in origin, they are naturally festooned with all manner of ritual and superstition. Shall I explain how they operate?"

"Yes, but first tell me how you came to learn all this."

Tran gave her a sidelong look and pursed his lips in a manner that reminded Marlene of Sister Marie-Michel, the elderly nun who had introduced her to the French language.

He said, "You know, Americans are the only people in the world who believe it is their natural right to know the entire history of a person with whom they converse; worse, they feel obliged to deliver their own complete annals, whether desired or not."

"Allow me to tender my apologies on behalf of Americans everywhere. You were saying . . ."

"I was not saying. But, suppose you imagine me in 1975, on a beach in the Philippines, after eighty-six days at sea, in rags, penniless, my only possessions a pistol and three books. Four years later I possess enough money to travel to New York and open a restaurant. Now, I have but two real skills: one is the teaching of literature, somewhat rusty, and the other the efficient generation of death and terror, sharp and well honed. Which do you suppose afforded me the most profit in those years?"

"You were actually *in* a triad?"

"Tchah! Don't be foolish, Marie-Hélène! I cannot be *in* a triad. I am Viet, not Han. Triads are not—you have this marvelous phrase—*equal opportunity employers*. But since the war and our diaspora, we Vietnamese have acquired a reputation throughout the Pacific and elsewhere as men of desperation, with little respect for life or property. In my case, sadly, it was even true. If something particularly nasty is to be done, the Chinese especially look for a *Viet-Kieu*. In Europe it is Albanians; in the Pacific, Vietnamese. Thus I prospered. I worked for a gang associated with the Ssu Shih K Hau triad, which was a branch of the 14K triad group of Hong Kong. Are you satisfied that I know whereof I speak? Thank you, very good. To resume: triads act like clearinghouses and substitute families for the Chinese criminal classes. They are networks and are further organized into associations of networks, triad groups—the 14K and the Wo in Hong Kong, the Hung Pang in Thailand, the Hung Men in Malaysia, and so forth. Now, imagine I am a criminal who wants someone killed, or I wish to open a house of prostitution . . ."

"That requires very little imagination, Monsieur."

"How very droll, Madame. Suppose, as I say, I am such a one. I go to my triad and they put me in touch with someone I can trust to perform the extermination, to supply the young girls. I do business with this person or gang, and the triad vouches for both parties. In return, the triad receives a grateful gift. Now, suppose I betray one of my partners, to the police, or an enemy. In that case, the triad has lost face, and it must make the betrayed party whole again, either by payment or by exacting revenge upon the traitor. Naturally, triads may take a direct hand in criminal activity, but what I have described is the more usual case. Is this clear?"

"Perfectly. And with respect to the present shootings?"

"The Sings are adherents of the Wo Hop To triad, originally from Hong Kong but now well established in other nations, although not, as far as I know, in New York. The elder Sing held the rank of White Paper Fan, which is a kind of very senior adviser. It is quite unusual for such a person to leave Hong Kong. There are a number of business connections . . . do you know what is meant by *guanxi*, or *guanhaih*, as the Cantonese say?"

"Yes, Lucy has explained it to me in painful detail."

"Of course. Well, there is considerable *guanxi* between the Wo Hop To and the Háp Tài tong here in New York. The Chens are members of the Háp Tài. Thus, it becomes somewhat more clear, doesn't it? The triad people wish to have a meeting of some importance in New York. They wish it to be entirely cryptic and anonymous, hence the selection of a storeroom as a venue. As I have pointed out, the Chens oblige their tong with the offer of the Asia Mall's back room. Then, for whatever reason, disaster; also, clearly, some betrayal by the other party to the meeting."

Marlene thought for a moment before voicing the significant word. "Betrayal. You said . . . do you think the triad will take revenge on the Chens?"

Tran shrugged. "It is possible, if they think the Chens colluded in the trap. The most immediate danger to the Chens, however, would seem to come from whoever planned the assassination, to prevent them from saying what they know, if anything. Here the only thread we possess is this Leung person."

"We should interview him at the first opportunity, don't you think?"

"We? Perhaps I have not made myself entirely clear, Marie-Hélène. With the exception of those who are insane, or are fatigued with life, no one strikes at a senior triad official unless with the support of another triad. *We*, unless I am mistaken, are not a triad, but a one-eyed woman, an old tired man, and a dog. In the normal course of events, the two contending triads will ask a third triad, from another triad group, to mediate. Harmony is an important Chinese value, as you know, and conflict is bad for business. Until then, whoever inserts himself into this affair will be like a beetle playing between two millstones. I believe the Chens have demonstrated that they do not want your help."

Marlene stopped walking and rounded on him. "So, Monsieur, you recommend that we stand by with our hands in our pockets while thugs terrorize my daughter and her best friend?"

"You have grasped my point exactly, Madame," Tran replied stiffly, "although allow me to point out that, whereas Janice may have been terrorized, Lucy considered the affair, what is your expression? *A day at the beach*." They stared at one another for some time, like duelists. Marlene controlled her temper first, and asked in a softer tone, "Truly, can nothing useful be done here?"

He dropped his eyes, nodded, and took her arm; the pair continued walking. They were almost back at the loft.

"Well, in point of fact," he said, "I have already done something, this afternoon, with those two bad boys. I have attracted the interest of M. Leung, at any rate. The next move is his, and we will respond within the scope of our resources. Speaking of these, I must report an unauthorized expenditure from the cash drawer: six hundred and twenty-six dollars, seventy-two cents. I also made long-distance calls totaling thirty-seven dollars, eighty cents."

"Not an inconsiderable sum. What, pray, did we buy with it?"

"The services of three young people of my acquaintance, countrymen of mine, with their van, and the purchase of two canvas mailbags, used, suitable for confining unwilling guests, and one U.S. Army field telephone, TA 312/PT, also used. I have the receipts."

"Thank you, but one doubts that a street abduction is a tax-deductible business expense. To whom were you sending telephone messages?"

Tran smiled. "No one at all. The useful part of the apparatus is the crank generator, which is quite powerful. I would have sent a message of a different sort to certain sensitive regions, but it was not necessary. As with the great Galileo, a mere exhibition of the instruments was sufficient. Do you wish to know the details of how this machinery is used?"

"No, not in the least," said Marlene quickly, trying to keep the distaste from her voice. "I assume the calls were to your contacts in the triads? To find out about the Sings."

"That is correct. Two calls to Hong Kong, one to Manila, one to Texas—an old comrade."

"And these three young people, how ever were you able to arrange it so quickly? Not an hour could have passed between the time Lucy called you and the kidnap."

"Oh, you know, one has contacts, here and there. These boys are from the *Hoi-Do* gang, as they call themselves. *Viet-Kieu* like myself. Their usual business is home invasions and armed robbery, but they are also willing to take on such engagements, especially against the Chinese. They were quite put out that I did not have to use wet techniques."

"How sad for them," said Marlene. They were at her doorstep. She leaned over and kissed him on the cheek; they were almost the same height.

"Thank you for this, my friend. You know, as the world judges men, you are very nearly the worst man I know, yet there is hardly a person of my acquaintance whom I like better. Why do you suppose that is?"

"It is because you are perverse, Marie-Hélène," Tran responded immediately. "You are the most perverse woman I have ever known. Whatever one expects of you, as soon as you are aware of it, you do the opposite. You act the thug among lawyers, among thugs, the lawyer. Among the liberal intelligentsia you are a Catholic mother, conservative as the pope. Should you ever be called to meet the pope, however, you would appear nude and twirling a gun. It is a peculiar way of life, and disconcerting to all around you. I wonder that you remain married or have any friends at all."

"What a condemnation! Have I no good points?"

"Several. Shall I enumerate them?"

"Do. 'To refuse to accept praise is to want to be praised twice over.'"

Tran chuckled, a rare noise. "La Rochefoucauld, maxim number 149. Very good. One of the little annoyances of fighting a war for the peasants and workers is that one must associate with so many illiterate people. Dying with you will at least be amusing. So that is the first point. One can converse with you without boredom, in French. This alone would make me your slave. Second, the esthetic appeal. A beauty, but maimed, scarred, like something out of Baudelaire. Irresistible. Were I twenty years younger and still an actual human being, I could not answer for your virtue. Third, your courage. Although unlike most heroes you have a full appreciation of the reality of death, still you behave as if you feel no fear. This is the most admirable form of courage. Finally, despite what you do, you have not amputated your moral sensibility. Therefore you suffer agonies in your deepest soul, which is above all what makes you admirable, at least to me. We Vietnamese are connoisseurs of suffering, you understand. It is our national sport and the basis of our most refined culture."

Marlene placed her hand over her heart and fluttered her eyelids dramatically. She said, "Monsieur, you have quite overwhelmed me. I must return at once to my husband, lest I be tempted to commit an indiscretion." Tran made a graceful stage bow, and they both laughed. In a more sober tone she asked, "Tran, will it really be so terrible?"

"Who can say? Maxim 310 bears on this. I wish you a good night, Marie-Hélène." He walked off without another word. Marlene took the elevator up to the loft, locked up, and went into the bedroom, a small room with large windows overlooking the back of the building, a lower structure, and a parking lot. Much of the room's floor space was occupied by an enormous brass bed that would not have disgraced a New Orleans brothel, the rest of the furnishing being the white painted "Provincial" furniture Marlene had used as a child, including a little vanity table with a pink tulle skirt. Karp thought this was weird, but one of the less objectionable parts of the Marlene package. Neither of the pair was into trendy furnishing, however, and so their loft (worth over three-quarters of a million dollars and the envy of any number of trust-fund artists and Wall Street types) was full of bits of odd junk Marlene had dragged home or inherited from Queens and, as a result, was as comfortable and as childproof as an old flannel shirt.

She found her husband stretched out on the bed, which he had converted into a desk, with folders, documents, and neat piles of paper arranged in rows and columns about his long frame.

He looked up when she entered and asked, brightly, "Was that Rocco wanting another taste?"

She ignored this and said, "I knew you were married to your job, but I didn't think that meant you actually had to take it to bed. What *is* all that?"

"Oh, it's a small part of the administration of justice, my dear. Requisitions, petitions, permissions, submissions, admonitions . . . I actually blew my day with some criminal justice work, so all this has to be looked at in my, *ha!*, spare time."

"Should I sleep in the guest room?"

"Just a second, let me think . . . is this stuff more interesting than Marlene in bed . . . well, that depends . . ."

"Very funny. I'm going in there to pee, wash, and change, and when I come out I don't want to see anything in that bed but husband."

"Yes, dear," said Karp. "No, dear, I don't know, dear." She laughed and went into the bathroom.

When she came out, smelling of Jean Naté and dressed in a worn St. John's T-shirt that descended fetchingly to just past her groin, Karp had cleared the marital deck and was making notes on a legal pad. She got into bed, snatched the pad and pencil out of his hands, and tossed them across the room, snuggling up at the same time.

"Listen, that was Tran just now," she said. "I'm a little worried."

"About . . . ?"

"Janice Chen. Tran said the girls were followed by a couple of thugs today."

"Thugs? They weren't hurt, were they?"

"No. Lucy used her head and called Tran and he took care of it, but . . ."

"He took . . . excuse me, but don't we have all those guys in blue suits who're supposed to—"

"Oh, for God's sake, Butch, it's Chinatown! I told you, Tran took care of it."

"Committing how many Class A felonies in the process?"

"Several, if you must know, but none that are likely to come within the cognizance of the law. Do you want to talk about this or not?"

"What're we talking about?"

"Lucy. I don't know if you've noticed, but she's extremely unhappy and she's taking this business with the Chens very hard. I think they've closed ranks in this crisis—family only—and she's feeling left out. She won't talk to me about it. Maybe you can get through to her. Also . . . Tran told me a lot of stuff he picked up. The details don't matter, but the Chens could be in a bind. It's tong stuff, like that. Jesus! Yet another reason for her to go to Sacred Heart, the damned obstinate puppy!"

"*Tong* stuff? You mean for *real*?" Karp was incredulous.

"So it appears. I thought maybe we could slip the word to Mimi Vasquez and the cops, to the effect that there's no point in hassling the Chens. They don't really know anything, and the guy who did it is probably sipping a sloe gin fizz in Kowloon as we speak."

"Go easy because they're our friends."

Marlene missed his tone. "Yeah. Come on, Butch, they really *don't* know anything."

"This is what they teach in Yale? You're pals with the D.A., so you get a free one? That's exactly the reason they *can't* get special treatment, Marlene. What're you thinking of?"

One thing that Karp could not bear was tension in the bedroom, and there was plenty at that moment, so he curled an arm around his wife and said, "Look, Lucy just needs some attention. We're both somewhat workaholic—"

"I'm not workaholic . . ."

"No, you're worse, you're a fanatic. We're supposed to be having a family here. Maybe you should cut down on the Wonder Woman routine and spend some more time with her."

"What about you? When was the last time you spent any time with her?"

"Okay, let's not get into it right now. Let's both spend time with her—we'll plan something for the weekend, all of us, the boys, too. And this thing with the Chens can't be that bad. If Lucy knew anything really bad was going on, she'd tell us."

Marlene thought that was about as likely as Santo

Trafficante confessing to the murder of Jimmy Hoffa out of remorse, but held her mouth, which in any case was being nibbled by that of her husband. Marlene thereafter gratefully abandoned her miasmic thoughts to the brief oblivion of sex, not all that brief in this particular case, because Karp, though no Lothario (and thank God that was something she did *not* have to worry about, him sniffing up other women's skirts), knew all her fleshly buttons and how to push them, and Marlene, for her part, had found that, contrary to every marriage manual she had read, screwing was better when she had something sneaky going on.

Afterward, they fell into the usual divine swoon, but at 3:10 Marlene popped awake from an unpleasant, unremembered dream, sweating, her heart thumping. She put on her T-shirt and went out of the room, stumbling as she always did on such sleepless excursions over the great dog who was sleeping across his mistress's doorway, as mastiffs have done for three thousand years. She stifled a curse, patted the dog, went into the dark kitchen, where she filled Zak's *Star Wars* tumbler half full of red wine.

She drank and tried to arrange her racing thoughts. Triads. The Mafia. The dead men from Hong Kong and the Chens. Jumping Jerry couldn't wait. The woman in room 37. The abortion clinic. Her mother and the flying missile. Lucy. What had she mumbled? *You have to be cute to be anorexic.* Oh, Jesus! Oh, Mary, full of grace. *Mama mia!* Motherhood, an impossibility in the present age. What a tangled web we weave. She entertained vague escape thoughts (an assumed name, a trailer west of

Tonapah, a job with the school board, blast away beer cans on the desert at night, fuck brainless cowboys, shoot crank, and drive her car into an abutment at ninety) and wondered how long she could sustain her current life. Perversity, its origins? Tran had got that right, the bastard. Thinking of that conversation, she chugged down the rest of the wine, gagged slightly, went through the long central hall of the loft to her little office. She looked out the window, pressing her moist forehead against the cool glass. Crosby Street was empty, lit by the nasty orange light from the street lamps. Free of danger, for now.

From her bookcase she took her copy of La Rochefoucauld's *Maximes*, the purple-bound Hachette edition, and thumbed through to number 310. She translated: *Sometimes in life situations develop that only the half crazy can get out of.* She laughed, her laughter sounding maniacal enough in her ears, until the dog came trotting in to see what was the matter.

7

THE CHINESE MAN IN THE BLUE SUIT believed ardently in the principle that contemplative thought should precede action, especially violent action, and so for several days after the incident with the Chen girl and the two White Dragon boys he sat and thought and did nothing. In his youth he had, in contrast, been a passionate advocate of violent action with no thought at all, thought itself having been rendered nugatory by the intellectual achievements of the Great Helmsman. Later, bobbing in the vast sludge of broken humanity left by the Cultural Revolution, he had discovered individualism, and for a while he imagined that the discovery was original. Later still, he met others, former Red Guards like him, without education, family, culture, or hope, who had also become individualists, and together they rediscovered feudalism, a system in which a few strong individualists become rich through the imposition of pain and terror upon the weak. This suited him very well, and it suited the leaders of his country, who had found, contra Marx, that feudalism was necessary for the operation of a communist state since, unlike communism, it worked.

He stared into the steam rising from his teacup and through the amber liquid to the leaves on the bottom, and tried to fit them into the shape of a character, although he knew he did not have the skill, if skill it was. He should have an oracle cast, he thought, although he had never found them useful in the past. Regrettably, their usefulness seemed to depend on the cultivation of self-knowledge, something he was disinclined to do, as he suspected, rightly, that it would interfere with his goal of accreting to himself as much raw power as he could. Still, he knew others believed, and that was what was important. After the brief bubble of chaos brought on by the Cultural Revolution, the dense substance of Chinese life had flowed back into its original immemorial spaces. It no longer paid to advertise disbelief. People might think you were unlucky, which was a disaster for any cooperative enterprise among the Chinese, at home or abroad.

He drank, slurping. The man in the blue suit spent a good deal of his time here, sitting on the lumpy bench of the rearmost of the four booths, facing the streaked window and the street. There were no other customers in the restaurant at this hour, understandable at ten in the morning, but there were few at any hour. Nevertheless, the tea room, a twelve-by-twenty-foot box on Bayard Street, was on paper enormously profitable. It was called *Li Gwún*, or Lee's Place, that is, the Chinese equivalent of "Joe's," and its primary purpose, like that of a great many similar holes in Chinatown, was not the dispensing of the world's most sophisticated cuisine but the metamorphosis of illegal cash into spendable income. It was, in fact, a Chinese laundry, and a wholly owned subsidiary of the man's organization.

He was calling himself Leung nowadays, which did not mean much, as underworld Chinese change names nearly as often as they buy shoes. What was important was what he represented, that and the plan. When Leung thought about the plan, the two words that came into his mind were *yù* and *bàng*. The first means a kind of wading bird, a snipe. The other means a clam. They are the first two words of a Chinese idiom, based on an ancient fable. The clam lies open on the shore, and the snipe grabs it. The clam closes its shell on the snipe's bill. Neither will let the other go. The snipe holds on because of greed, the clam because it fears being eaten. A fisherman comes by and catches them both. The success of the plan depended on keeping the contending parties focused on one another and not on the fisherman creeping closer.

Thus the attack on the White Dragons was disturbing. He was supposed to be invisible in his character as a no-name Chinatown gangster, a loyal vassal of the Háp Tài tong, a nobody, the creeping fisherman. Who had ordered the interference? The men who took the *ma jai* off the street so smoothly and professionally were unlikely to be local talent. Most of the people Chinatown called gangsters were petty extortionists, clowns who thought that a big score was a bunch of them ordering a meal in a restaurant and not paying. The *ma jai* had not seen the faces of their captors, which had been concealed behind ski masks, but they claimed that the leader had spoken to them in what sounded like Viet–accented Cantonese. That made more sense. One would use a Vietnamese or a Fujianese for that sort of thing. He himself had used a Vietnamese for the business in the Asia Mall. Thinking about that, he considered the possibility that Chen had hired protection for his daughter, and then dismissed it. Chen would not dare, although he did have the temerity to complain about the killings taking place on his property, which was why the demonstration against his daughter had been necessary.

If the Chens were of no consequence, who had intervened? Leung could not imagine that the thing had any other purpose than to send him a message. As he read it, it was this: we know who you are; we are watching; we can get to your people; and we can get to you. That was the message he himself would have sent with the action on Canal Street—a daylight abduction, which meant an additional footnote: we're tough and competent. The message could not be from the Wo Hop To triad. If they thought he had betrayed the Sings, he would already be dead in some particularly unpleasant way. His comrades in the Da Qan Zi triad might have sold him out. That was always a possibility, and he certainly had rivals enough. But he had carefully balanced the rivalries heretofore, and the promise to his triad leadership of what he intended to bring to them was more than sufficient to stifle with avarice any move against him, at least until the fisherman had the snipe and the clam firmly in hand. That left the Italians. The more he thought about

it, the more he felt that this was the correct solution. He had expected something like this, but not
in so subtle a fashion. That was the Vietnamese
influence. The Italian had given the contract to a
Viet gang, both to insulate himself from suspicion
and because he wanted to see what Leung would
do under pressure. He had, of course, no idea that
Leung was all by himself in New York, that he
was operating with only the barest toleration of
his triad, on speculation, that the *yù bàng* plan was
his alone. If they penetrated this veil, he was finished.

He thought briefly about the little American in
Macao, and what he had learned from him about
the absurd machinations of American law. The
man could talk for hours about it, introducing
strange concepts that had no Chinese equivalent.
*Due process. Conflict of interest. Plea bargaining. Im-
munity.* He was a drunk and an opium addict, but
he had long periods of lucidity, and Leung had listened with close attention. The man was dead now,
but what he had taught Leung had fermented like a
tub of soy beans in the young gangster's head and
become, after the passage of years, a part of the
plan.

Leung slurped the last of his tea and rose to
leave. They wanted to see what he would do under
moderate pressure, perhaps expecting a tentative
push in return. Instead he would advance his plan
and respond with a devastating counter blow, one
that would remove the Italian entirely from the
board.

• • •

Mary Ma washed dishes in the kitchen of the Golden Pheasant, a big, brightly lit, old-fashioned tourist restaurant on the second floor of a building on Mott, a few doors up from Pell. The appreciation of Chinese cuisine had recently come a long way in the city, and there were now large numbers of *gwailo* New Yorkers who could distinguish between the various regional cuisines and be boring about how to eat Peking duck. The old Golden Pheasant, however, catered to the tour-bus trade, terrified gaggles of ladies from Indiana shrieking with nervous laughter over chopsticks, soy sauce, and lobster Cantonese with flied lice. The Ma family was three years in the country, six years out of the PRC, beginning to make it in America in the good old way, working two jobs apiece, living like dogs in two tenement rooms, keeping their one kid in school, saving every penny. (Mrs. Ma was shocked to her soul when, a few days after her arrival in town, she observed a group of children tossing pennies against a wall. Playing! With real coins! What if they *lost* one?)

Aside from violating the child labor and minimum wage laws of the state of New York for eight hours a day, Mary Ma was more or less on her own. From the age of ten she had worn the latchkey necklace, that badge of striving families, and saw her parents mainly at work, where Mrs. Ma was a prep cook and Mr. Ma a waiter. Mary Ma had started school in Guangdong in the PRC, continued in Hong Kong, and had been registered in public school on the second day after the family's arrival in New York, speaking little English, and that with a faint British accent. She was lonely, as all such children are and more than most, since she was a member of the Chinese generation that has no siblings by order of the leaders of the PRC. In the fourth grade, however, she had with uncharacteristic boldness advised the *gwailo* girl at the next desk, who was having incomprehensible difficulty with a math problem that Mary Ma had solved in eight seconds, and to her immense surprise the girl had thanked her profusely in Cantonese.

Thus was born her friendship with Lucy Karp, and thus was she brought into the charmed circle of the Chens and the Karps, and supplied with the role models every immigrant child needs to become American. From Janice she learned how to be Chinese and cool, she learned that thick leather boy's oxfords are never appropriate no matter how well they wear, that iridescent blue-framed harlequin-shaped eyeglasses are a bargain for a good reason and that small wire-framed ones are better and nearly as cheap, she learned that makeup is not the unmistakable sign of prostitution, that the cheap brands of blusher are about as good as the costly ones, that it is not a sin against the ancestors to have some spending money of one's own, that parents deserve respect and obedience but do not necessarily represent the source of all earthly wisdom.

From Lucy there came lessons more thrilling, even terrifying: about films and music—who is hip, who not; that girls are the equal of boys, and often smarter, that making a boy look a fool is not a sin but amusing; that the correct response to insult is not shame but counter-insult and aggression; that the street has its own rules, some of them not thought of by Confucius; and (this, of course, indirectly, but the most important of all) that a big part of growing up in America is the invention of the self, and there are no real constraints on this choice—not class, not race, not even sex.

And Lucy introduced the immigrant child to the bosom of the American family. (With what difficulty did Mary Ma explain to her parents what a sleepover was, and its purpose, and assure them that they would not have to reciprocate, and that there was no loss of face in this!) Used to analyzing the deeper meaning of every act for political consequences, the Ma parents were flabbergasted that their offspring was being entertained in the home of a public prosecutor (the honor!), something that could never have happened in the Red mandarin society of the PRC, but naturally they were terrified that she would let something slip about the provenance of their green cards. Mary would never have revealed to her parents that Lucy Karp knew all there was to know about this aspect of the Mas' American journey, and that secret was one of the things that tied her most closely to Lucy and Janice. A certain amount of foolish secrecy is involved in most friendships among girls of that age, but in this case the secrets were not foolish at all, were real and dire. It made the friendship closer, more intimate, and as water to the thirst of Mary Ma, who had almost no one else to love. That was another lesson: there was American stuff that your folks could never, ever understand, even if, as in Lucy's case, they were Americans born.

The disaster at the Asia Mall had thus affected Mary Ma's life even more than it had that of her friends. Suddenly Janice was distant and vaguely "busy," Lucy was practically incommunicado, and the phone conversations Mary had with both of them were brief and unsatisfying. Unlike her friends, however, Mary could not afford to sulk, her social resources being much thinner. Besides this, she was compelled by a sense of shame about the way she had lost it and blubbered in the aftermath of the killings.

On a Monday morning, then, ten days after the events in the storeroom, she left her family's tenement apartment on Eldridge Street and strode down Canal, her round face as grim as a round face ever gets, her fists clenched, looking much like one of the girls marching boldly out of the picture plane on one of those flower-colored Maoist posters touting the Great Leap Forward. She was headed for Lucy's home, with what in mind she hardly knew, but resolved to fight for friendship in whatever way might present itself.

She walked by the Asia Mall, looking sideways to see if she could catch a glimpse of Janice through the windows. She thought of just bursting in and demanding to know what was up, but quailed at the thought of going into that place just yet. She was cursing herself for a spineless wretch when she spotted a familiar face emerging from the glass doors.

"Hey, Wang!" she called out, just as if she were a boy, which was permitted in America.

Warren Wang looked up, saw who it was, and waved.

She continued west on Canal, and he fell in with her. He was carrying two large plastic Asia Mall shopping bags.

"Where're you going?" he asked.

"Wherever I feel like," said Mary Ma, and added, "The highway is my home."

"No, really."

They stopped to let traffic pass on the corner of Broadway. She pointed at a phone number on the side of a passing truck. "I'll tell you if you tell me what's interesting about that number."

"What, 4937775?" His eyes unfocused briefly. "Um, it's a Smith number. The sum of the digits equals the sum of the digits of its prime factorization minus one. Forty-two. So, tell me, where?"

"I'm going to Lucy Karp's."

"Forget it. She locked herself in a closet and swallowed the key. I've been trying to talk to her for a week."

"You have? I didn't know you were a friend of hers."

He laughed ruefully. "Neither did I." Upon which he related the strange incident involving Janice and the two *ma jai*. "I called her up as soon as I got home," he continued, "but it was like nothing ever happened. 'Forget it, Warren.' Okay, I'll forget it, and then I ask her if she wants to go hang out or something, hit the arcade or the movies, but nothing." He sighed. "I guess it was like a scam, them being, you know, nice and all."

Mary was silent for so long that the boy stopped and looked into her face.

"What's wrong?" No answer. "Earth to Mary . . ."

Mary's face had gone the color of old parchment. She forgot to breathe for a long time, and when she did it came in a strangled whoop. When her mind unfroze, she found that she was running up Broadway. At Grand she looked around wildly, but all she saw was the normal street traffic and poor Warren Wang standing there, his shopping bags drooping from his hands, his mouth open in surprise. The terror she had felt in the storeroom was back again, redoubled. There was only one reason for Janice and Lucy to be followed, which was that somebody knew they all had seen the murders. This thought, once comprehended, blasted through Mary Ma's considerable intellect like a gas explosion, leaving behind it a single bare instinct, similar to the one that drives the whooping crane two thousand miles to a tiny patch of Texas. In five minutes she was at Crosby off Grand, her finger jammed into the button for Lucy Karp's loft, imploring Guan Yin, goddess of compassion, that Lucy might answer. Which she did, but coolly.

"Um, Mary, I'm kind of involved—"

"*Wah! Lòuhsì!*" Mary sobbed, and then started babbling in Cantonese, at which point Lucy, without another word, pressed the button that would send the elevator down to the street.

What Lucy had been involved in was prayer, actually on her hard little knees in her bedroom, clicking through her rosary, concentrating, hoping for an end to the fog of pain and confusion she had endured these past days, the isolation from her friends, the gnawing sense that she was letting her family down, and, barely acknowledged, the roiling pit where her feelings about her mother lurked, generating fumes of acid. Lucy prayed often. The preacher's kid as rakehell is folkloric, but that train runs in the other direction, too. Being the child of an agnostic Jew and a heterodox semi-lapsed Catholic, raised in a society growing more secular every year, it was perhaps natural that she should couch her juvenile rebellion in such terms. She was the most religious person she knew not in holy orders, and this gave her no little pride, which rather defeated the devotion, although she was only on the outer edges of understanding that.

When Mary rang, Lucy found herself annoyed at the interruption, and then, as she waited foot-tappingly for the elevator to rise, it struck her, in a wonderful wave of understanding. She had been praying, as everyone should, not for a solution to her problems, but for moral strength and the clear light, expecting something mental, some heavenly voice perhaps, such as was vouchsafed by St. Teresa, but no, here it was in the person of poor Mary Ma, the opportunity to extend loving kindness to an unhappy friend, which she immediately saw as the perfect answer to her present spiritual need, better than any amount of angelic advice, and presenting as well the opportunity to ask forgiveness for being such a complete jerk.

Mary Ma was not used to being a sign from God, and was unprepared for the enthusiasm with which she was greeted, the kisses, the embraces, the rushing, heartfelt apologies. The two repaired to Lucy's bedroom, locked the door, and exchanged tearful vows that they would not let anything tear them apart again. Besides being quite sincere, the whole business was very Colette, which gave Lucy considerable satisfaction. She was at the age when behaving spontaneously like someone in a book is particularly fine.

"So . . . what about Jan?" said Mary Ma after all this had been going on for a good while. She was quite over her fear, which had, after all, been ninety percent loneliness.

"Did you talk to her? I mean after."

"Yeah, but she was still freaked. I couldn't get ten words in a row out of her."

"Uh-huh. She's freaked out about her family. Janice wants everything to be a certain way, and if it doesn't go that way she thinks if she doesn't think about it, it'll sort of disappear."

"What should we do?" asked Mary.

"We should find the killer ourselves and bring him in!" said Lucy in a dramatic voice.

Mary Ma gave her a look. "That's ridiculous. We're a couple of kids. No, the first thing is to get Janice back together with us and find out what's going on with her family and this thing, is she getting threatened or anything. The next thing is to make sure that none of us are on the street alone in case they try anything again. We should really hang out together like we used to. Also . . ." She paused and looked closely at Lucy, her eyes glinting behind her spectacles. "How did you get rid of those gangsters?"

"A friend of mine helped us. Why?"

"Just thinking. Have you got any money?"

"What? Why?"

"We could hire our own gangsters," said Mary Ma.

"*Mary!*" cried Lucy, looking at the other girl rather as Dr. Frankenstein had at his monster when the thing first stirred.

"It's the logical thing. But first we have to grab Janice and get her back to the real world."

Lucy sprang from the bed. "Let's go now!"

Mary's face fell. "Now?" she said hesitantly, which gave Lucy some satisfaction, as signaling the retention of her leadership in action, and this was augmented when they arrived at the Asia Mall and Mary got the willies at the entrance to the storeroom.

Lucy grabbed an arm and yanked, and would not let go, presenting Mary with the choice between entering what Lucy persisted in calling the Cavern of Death and causing a face-destroying scene. Lucy kept a protective-coercive arm around the other girl as they went down the narrow aisles between the bins.

They found Janice alone in the little stock office, where she had been put to filing invoices. She yelped and tried to flee, and Lucy had to get physical with her, which was not that unusual in their long relationship. Lucy told her (into her ear, lying atop her, Mary Ma assisting with the legs) in their usual mixture of English and Cantonese that she loved her, that she was her sister forever, that her heart was breaking, and that if Janice didn't relent, she would kill herself. Thereupon she leaped up, plucked a stapler from the desk, held it to her temple, and grimaced, her eyes shut. At which point

Janice, whose own life had been as much a misery since she had walked away on Canal Street, laughed (and had missed that, too—who else made her giggle like Lucy Karp? No one), and then they were all laughing and crying, and tickling one another, until Mrs. Chen came back and threatened to beat them all with a broom, and (secretly transported with relief) gave them all something useful to do.

Marlene got the call from Raney in her car as she was traveling back to her office from the East Village Women's Shelter.

"It's about time," she said testily. She had not had a good morning.

"Do you want to hear this, or do you want to nag? You know, we're not married yet, so I don't have to take shit from you when I'm doing you a favor."

She covered the mouthpiece, let out a maniacal shriek, so that pedestrians looked over at her in alarm, and then spoke softly into it. "I'm sorry, Jim, my Irish dreamboat, but I had a hell of a morning."

"On the rag again, huh?"

"I might as well be. Men suck, Jim, you know that? You know something else? So do women. Meanwhile, what've you got?"

"Not a whole hell of a lot. Phil Wu caught it out of the Five. What he figures is a Hong Kong job. Gang wars type thing. He says he called the Hong Kong cops, and that's their take on it, too. Some gang over there, they couldn't get to these two on their own turf, they figure they wouldn't be that well guarded in New York, so they set up the hit for here. Wu figures the shooter was on the first plane back home a couple, three hours after he did it."

"So this is on the back burner?"

"Yeah, more like it fell off the back of the stove, it's down there with the roach traps and the crumbs. Plus, there is absolutely no heat on this."

"You mean from the community?"

"Right. Not like it was a couple of Germans got whacked in the Macy's stockroom. Or some tourist got hit on Mott Street. I believe this case will be transferred from Detective Wu to Detective Can, forthwith and henceforward. Like the man said—"

"Yeah, I know, *it's Chinatown*, and I'm getting so fucking tired of hearing that. Tell me something: Does anyone have any hint that there's some *local* connection here? With the community, with gang activity in the city?"

"Not that I heard, Marlene." A significant pause. She could almost hear her pal switching into detection mode. "Why do you ask? Did you hear something?"

Marlene tapped at random a couple of buttons on the handset. "Gosh, Raney, we're breaking up. Thanks—I'll get back to you later."

Stopped at a light at Houston and Lafayette, she addressed her companion. "Something doesn't jibe here, Sweets. If it was an in-and-out with some torpedo from Asia, what are they doing following Janice Chen? Why the hell is this Leung interested in her? Maybe I should go talk with Detective Can. Meanwhile, I thought my performance this morning was flawless. Flawless, but futile. So often this is the story of my life, don't you find? I lay the facts before the wretched woman. Brenda, darling, I say, it's your life, but based on my very considerable experience with relationships fucked up beyond all hope of repair, it is my strong advice to you that you kiss off Chester D. And get some help for yourself while you're at it. No licensed MSW could have put it better, don't you agree?"

The dog, catching the tone, made a sound between a growl and a whine.

"Of course you do. You are an intelligent creature. But not Brenda Nero. Not at all, especially when I told her that I had given the very same advice to her darling. What language! Well, really, I wash my hands of her. I intend to testify at Chester's trial, and I will advise him to plead justifiable homicide. Which reminds me, I have to shop around for a psychiatrist for my daughter, and while I'm at it one for the delightful gun moll Ms. Vivian Fein Bollano, my client. Can you do some research, Sweets? Hop on down to the various papers and pull clippings about Jumping Jerry? No, I better do it myself. In fact, I could get up to the *News* right now . . . oh, shit, that better not be Raney, trying his sly tricks on . . ." She picked up the buzzing phone. "Hello, Marlene Ciampi."

The voice on the phone was, however, not Raney's but that of an official-sounding woman.

"Hello, excuse me, but I'm trying to reach a Mr. Roger Karp. The answering machine gave me—"

"Right, this is his wife. Can I help you?"

"Yes, maybe. Do you know a Sophie Leontoff?

This is Beth Israel Hospital calling. Mr. Karp's number was listed as next of—"

"Oh, God! What happened to her? I mean, yes, she's our great-aunt."

"Oh, good. Sophie took a fall this morning, and I'm afraid she fractured her hip. She's in surgery now."

Marlene got the rest of the information, hung a right on Broadway, and sped uptown to the hospital, at First and 16th. She called Karp; he was out—of course, the hospital would have called him first. Sophie was Karp's maternal grandmother's younger sister and in Marlene's opinion the only one of her husband's relatives worth knowing, an assessment with which her mate concurred. A real character, Sophie—as a young woman she had been a major player in *schmatehs*, traveling to Paris to steal fashions from the couturiers, and then setting up as a dressmaker there. Caught by the war, she had spent some time in a concentration camp, which had not noticeably depressed her spirits, and had returned to America to become the driving force behind her late husband's Seventh Avenue empire. She smoked Gitanes, drank cognac, played gin with a group of louche West Side crocks, made an annual trip to Monte Carlo, and would have sewn all Marlene's and Lucy's clothes had she been allowed. It was hard to think of her as being sick, but, of course, she *was* closing in on eighty.

Reporting at the ward desk, Marlene was directed to a waiting room. There were two people there, an elderly couple. The woman was tiny, carefully made up, with huge, bright eyes, fine, sharp features like a mynah bird's and a thin cap of auburn-dyed hair that fell as a fringe across her forehead. She was dressed in a black silk T, a fawn skirt with stockings, and beautiful tan pumps. She also wore a string of pearls, a Cartier watch, a diamond tennis bracelet, and a good-sized diamond ring. Her husband—and it *had* to be her husband—was bald on top with a fringe of pepper and salt hair that descended somewhat below the collar of his knit navy sport shirt. He wore a well-cut linen jacket, also in navy, tan whipcord trousers, and alligator loafers with gold fittings. When Marlene entered, the woman was reading a paperback, which she had set into a needlepoint cover, matching her large needlepoint canvas bag, while the man was reading one of the tattered waiting room magazines—a *New York*.

They both looked up. The woman smiled. "Oh! You're . . . Oh, God, I'm so embarrassed, don't tell me . . . for Sophie Leontoff, am I right?"

"Right," said Marlene. "I think we met at her seventy-fifth birthday party." She held out her hand. "I'm Marlene Ciampi." The woman's hand in hers felt like good-quality kid leather, cool and buttery.

"Oooh! You're the . . ." The woman's hands made circular motions about their wrists (meaning? The Shiksa? The Infamous Slayer of Men, Film at Eleven? The Nephew's Wife?), and then she laughed and said, "Selma Lapidus. This is Abe, my husband. We're in 5-B."

The man rose and shook hands, mumbling the conventional. He had the sad eyes of the retired.

"Now I remember," chirped Selma. "What's wrong with me! Roger, the nephew, no, the grand-nephew." She pulled Marlene down next to her on the pink vinyl sofa. "It's so nice of you to come, and you're not even related. I tell you, these days . . . when Abe had his surgery two years ago, I had to practically commit suicide on the phone so my daughter would *bestir* herself to fly in from L.A. She's in the industry."

"Um, Mrs. Lapidus . . ."

"Don't be ridiculous—*Selma*."

"Selma. Did they say how it's going, I mean with the—"

"She's in very good hands, the best! Dr. Baumholtz is a genius. He did Abe's hip. Tell her, Abe—you were walking the next day. The next day! And so sweet, a doll! The best orthopedic man in the city, you'll meet him, you'll see. I personally am not worried in the least."

"Of course not, you're not on the table," said Abe into his magazine.

Selma rolled her eyes but did not respond to this. "We were the ones who found her. We have a card club in our building, there's a room downstairs. We play gin, canasta . . . So this morning, I ring, there's no Sophie. So I get the key—we exchange keys, I mean, you never know, God forbid, we're not so young, something could happen, and I go in, and I'm telling you, my heart almost stopped, there's Sophie, on the bathroom floor, she says, "Selma, I can't move, I knew I should've bought that thing. You know, that signal machine. Anyway, she says, thank God it was a Thursday—the cards, she meant—because a Friday, she could've been there all weekend, we could've been at the beach, we have a place in Southampton. . . ." She stopped talking and looked up. They all looked up, because someone had come into the room.

"Oh, Jake, you're here," said Selma. "Good."

"How is she?" Jake asked, and Marlene looked at him with interest. A big old guy, maybe seventy-five, massive rather than tall, chest like an oil drum, with a lumpy, large-featured face, and crinkled, close-cut white hair. He wore a double-breasted gray summer suit, old but well cut, a white shirt and bow tie, and brown-and-white shoes with decorative little holes in the toe part, highly polished. He held a straw hat in his hand.

A cop, was Marlene's first thought, and then she changed her mind. A hard guy, in any case, not a regular citizen. His eyes flicked over Marlene as they were introduced, wary but amused. Jacob Gurvitz. He didn't offer to shake. Selma Lapidus filled him in on Sophie, and he seemed concerned, perhaps more concerned than a neighbor would be. (He was in 12-D, lived there three years, not rent-controlled, a card player, single, just back from Miami; in Selma Lapidus's zone of operations, personal information leaped into view unbidden, as on a computer screen.) Marlene wondered, a love interest? Sophie would have a guy like this. Maybe a fellow camp survivor. Yes, that could be it, the look. This guy had seen things other than legal briefs and *schmatehs*.

They sat. Selma talked, a not unpleasant sound, like the whirring of a refrigerator in an empty apart-

ment. After ten minutes or so, she left for the ladies'.
The two men looked at each other and grinned, and
then Marlene grinned with them. The look said,
Selma! Gotta love her, but . . .

"You're an attorney, too, I understand, Marlene?" said Abe.

"Yes, but I don't get much practice anymore."

"Neither do I." He smiled. "You would think the
law was all in the head, but litigation is a physical
thing. A big case, when a man's liberty or even a
life, in those days, was at stake, you work your *tou-
chis* off, believe you me. So, when the body starts to
go . . ." He waved a hand, as if in farewell. "One of
our partners had a heart attack, died right there in
the office. Another dear friend, also an attorney,
had a cerebral on his way to work. Selma said, Abe,
that's it! I'm not planning on being a rich widow
my whole life. Out! So . . . my dear wife, once she
makes her mind up . . ."

"I can imagine," said Marlene, and they had another smile all around. "You were in criminal law?"

"Mainly, although in my day there wasn't so
much of this specialization." After that, the usual
exchange of stories, the big cases, how the practice
of law had changed in Abe's forty years at the bar,
Marlene's experiences at the D.A. The possibility
of mutual acquaintances was explored, and there
were, in fact, a number of these, judges, a lawyer
or two. Marlene was aware of Jake Gurvitz as an
interested presence, but he made no contribution
to the conversation.

Curious, Marlene asked, "You're not a lawyer,
too, are you, Mr. Gurvitz?"

"Nah, I always tried to stay away from lawyers. I was with the bakers' union. Retired."

Marlene tried to imagine Jake in floury whites popping a tray of danish into an oven, and came up blank. As the daughter of a union plumber, Marlene knew something about the New York unions in the relevant period, and what sort of folks staffed their upper reaches. So, a "union" guy with expensive clothes, living in an uncontrolled apartment off Central Park West. And a lawyer practicing criminal in the same interesting period. It was worth a shot.

She turned back to Lapidus and asked, "I was wondering, speaking of courthouse people, did you ever run into Jerry Fein back then?"

A pause. She could hear the sounds of the hospital clearly, the distant televisions, the clinking of bottles, the muffled noise of rubber heels and rubber-tired carts. Abe's smile faded and was replaced by a made-up one, and Jake's face went into neutral. Did they exchange a look? Maybe not.

Abe sighed. "Jerry Fein. That takes you back. Oh, sure, I knew him, to say hi to, yeah, around the courthouse, you know. A real tragedy. Why do you ask?"

"Oh, his name came up in a case I'm working on, and I remembered the, you know, the, um, tragedy. So talking about the old courthouse . . ."

"Uh-huh. Well, Jerry was a character, all right. Wore a pearl homburg in the winter, and on Memorial Day he switched to a straw boater. You could set your calendar by him. That was what they said. And then Labor Day, he'd show up with the hom-

burg on again and fly the boater out his office window. Huh! There's irony for you. The window . . .
Always beautifully dressed, the rest of it, he had a
special way of folding his breast pocket handkerchief, four little points, perfect —"

"Any truth to the rumor he was mobbed up?"
Marlene cut in.

Lapidus frowned, and his voice became more ani-
mated. "What're you talking, 'mobbed up'? What
does that mean? Look, the thirties, the forties, in
the city, into the fifties, nearly any legal work you
did you had some contact with, let's say, elements.
You work for garment people, furriers, trucking,
unions, *unions*! My God, tell her, Jake! It was pervasive. *Pervasive*. So, what—we should close down the
criminal bar? And the cops, in those days, it was
hard to tell them from the crooks, this was before
Miranda was even born, forget Escobedo! Rubber
hoses and worse. Frame-ups? They didn't like you—
pouf! You're in Sing-Sing. So it was rougher. And we
all, I mean the criminal bar at that time, the coun-
selors, we all did things, let's say, on the edge. But
there were lines. Suborning witnesses, jury tampering, concealing evidence in major felonies: some
crossed, some didn't."

"Was Fein a line crosser, do you think?"

He shrugged, and then straightened his shoulders
and fixed her with an eye, and Marlene understood
that he would have been a formidable courtroom
presence.

"Marlene, the man is dead twenty-three years,
what does it matter what he did and what he didn't?"

"It could matter to his family, if it had to do with

why he killed himself. He was disbarred, wasn't he, just before? What was that about?"

He waved a hand—New York's own getoutta-heah gesture. "Oh, don't get me started on that. It's a long, long story; I'll give you the short version. Jerry got a royal screwing. His partner set him up, that *momser*. You know what a *momser* is?"

"I believe it's a person whose ethical development leaves something to be desired."

Lapidus let out a laugh. "Ha! You I like! I'm trying to think of the case it was, that jury. Johnny Gravellotti, yeah, a big hoodlum, they hung him from a meat hook in the old Washington Market. Johnny Shoes they called him, also a sharp dresser . . ."

"Johnny Shine," said Jake Gurvitz.

Lapidus snapped his fingers. "Johnny *Shine*, right! Don't listen to a word I say, honey, I'm losing my marbles. Johnny Shine, and they had Big Sally Bollano for it—there's another sweetheart for you—and it was a tight one: good physical evidence, ballistics, a bloody *shoe* print, if you can believe it. The D.A., Garrahy at that time, was slavering. And the jury walks him on it. So, of course they figure tampering, intimidation. And Jerry was the lawyer . . ."

"Wait a second, Fein was Sally Bollano's lawyer?"

"Oh, yeah, for years. Him and Heshy Panofsky, the *momser*, that was his partner. Jerry did the courtroom work, Heshy handled the inside, the deals. They had another partner, Bernie Kusher, also a crook, but that's another story entirely. So the D.A. investigates, and they find somebody got to a couple of the jurors, money changed hands. Something about an envelope with Jerry's prints on it, with the money. I can't recall. In any case they charged him with it, and what happens? Jerry pleads guilty, cops to it for a suspended sentence. Nobody could believe it. I mean, let me tell you, Gerald Fein was a fighter, a tiger in the courtroom, and he rolls over like a poodle. Of course, they disbarred him after that. Oh, it was a complete pile of crap, excuse my French."

"Why? Because Fein wasn't the kind to tamper?"

"No, because *Heshy* was in charge of tampering at that particular firm, and everybody knew it. You want to know the kicker in this? Heshy Panofsky is now the Honorable Herschel B. Paine of the Supreme Court of the State of New York."

"*That's* Judge Paine?"

"You know the man, I see."

"Of course. They're touting him for the next opening on the Appellate Division."

"I don't doubt it. After Jerry left, Heshy changed his spots, he fixed his name, he went with a white-shoe firm downtown, lots of political connections . . . believe me, honey, some things you don't change so easy. He's still a *momser.*"

"So, wait—why do you think he set up Fein to take the fall?"

Lapidus started to answer, but at that moment, in walked Selma Lapidus, beaming, towing a forty-ish man wearing the hospital greens and the confident jock-like air of a surgeon.

"A complete success," announced Selma, as if she had handled the knife. "And everyone, *this* is Dr. Baumholtz."

Selma *kvelled*, Baumholtz pronounced upon the hip replacement and departed, the visitors all marched off to Sophie's room. They were shocked at the way she looked, tried not to show it, failed, covered this with jokes, and then Marlene's beeper sounded and she went off to call in. It was from Osborne, a complicated matter involving security at the Chelsea clinic, and when she returned to Sophie's room, the old lady was sleeping and the visitors had all gone home.

Leaving, Marlene considered the Abe and Jake show she had just enjoyed. Some information, delivered in a tone meant for casual shopping of secondhand gossip, and there was that maybe look between the two men, and Jake's silence. Silence while the lawyer talked—it felt to her like something he was used to, professionally. Yeah, she would talk to Abe Lapidus again, for sure, but only after she had accumulated more information on the big questions: Why had Gerald Fein rolled over for a trumped-up charge? Why had Vivian Fein waited over twenty years to try to clear her father's name? There was no point in talking to someone like Abe unless she knew enough to know if he was lying to her or not.

8

RETURNING HOME FROM HER HOSPI-
tal visit, Marlene felt emotionally bedraggled and
not at all looking forward to family life, especially
not to another tense evening with Lucy. But when
she arrived at the loft, she found not Sylvia Plath Jr.
but Little Mary Sunshine, happily giggling with her
brothers in her room, in *her* room, a treat almost
beyond comprehension, Lucy's room being, for the
twins at least, the domestic equivalent of the For-
bidden City. Besides that, the loft was tidied and
swept, and the table laid for dinner, also Lucy's
work, since the concept of "tidy" had never imposed
itself on Posie's custardlike mind.

"Hi, Mom!" they all chorused when Marlene
stuck her head in to view this marvel. Marlene had
often noticed the peculiar complementarity of her
moods with those of her daughter, as if they were
at either end of the same seesaw. Lucy had clearly
emerged from her recent private hell; Marlene felt
herself descending into her own. She tried to be
glad about her daughter's return to the broad, sun-
lit uplands, but as the evening passed, she could not
help feeling that Lucy's mood had an aggressive

edge to it, as if to say, "You've tried to make me miserable, wretched Mom, but I have transcended your wicked designs." Karp was charmed out of his socks, which didn't help much either. Marlene retired early with a headache and a pint of plain red wine.

Lucy retired early as well, not to sleep but to finish the last of the Claudine books, *Claudine s'en va*, which was about (and here she moved the story around in her head, describing it to herself as she would describe it to her pals) this woman Annie, and how she was married to this dork, a real conceited guy, and then she met Claudine, and Claudine had turned into this terrifically cool and sexy woman, yeah, she was still married to that guy, but it was all different somehow, she wasn't squashed by it anymore, and anyway she shows Annie that Annie doesn't really love her husband, and he doesn't love her and they should break up, which was a big deal in those days, but she does anyway, and Claudine thinks about seducing her but doesn't because she promised her own husband that she wouldn't do stuff like that (Lucy, the dirty little thing, made a mental note to maybe modify that in the retelling) and Annie does set out for the future and life goes on. She mused for a while, imagining herself installed Claudine-like in some apartment with her father, a man engaged in his work but always ready to devote his entire attention to his little girl. Claudine had not been supplied with a mom, which was one of the chief sources of the delight Lucy took in the novels.

She closed the book and placed it neatly in its proper place on her bedside shelf. A satisfactory ending, the kind she liked, and she was glad that Claudine had moved on from merely arranging her own life to arranging those of her friends. This was also Lucy's ambition, especially when her friends were in some trouble and the arranging might offer some Kim-style skulking and even a measure of violent adventure.

Mary had, of course, been sensible in her Mary way: children did not catch killers, especially not oriental professional killers, but now that she had her friends again, Lucy was not slow to imagine plots by which some satisfactory conclusion to the Asia Mall murder case could be brought about. Lucy's interest in this was not principled but personal: those murdering bastards had nearly messed up her life and should pay for it with their heart's blood. With these and similar thoughts, of a violence rather more common among young girls than their parents suspect, she drifted off to sleep.

And awoke full of energy, more than she had felt in weeks. She fed, toileted, and dressed in mere minutes, and was out of the house at just past seven and on her way to her mother's office while her brothers were still having their wake-up whine. The fine weather continued, but now she noticed it as for the first time, balmy springtime in the city, and was buoyed up by it, and it lent bounce to her step as she trotted down Broadway to Walker.

Bello & Ciampi had a suite on the second floor of an undistinguished loft building otherwise devoted to galleries and the sale of oriental rugs. The firm name was painted in gold on the large semilunar window around the portrayal of a staring eye, with INVESTIGATIONS-SECURITY below, which Lucy thought unbelievably tacky. Her mother had surrendered part of the space when the firm had contracted with Osborne and Harry Bello had moved uptown. She had an anteroom for her secretary-receptionist, one large room behind the big window with the sign on it, a toilet with shower, and a couple of windowless cubbyholes in back. One was fitted out as a kitchen, and Tran lived in the other.

Crying out a greeting in Arabic to Mr. Habibi, who ran the rug emporium on the ground floor, she ran up the steps and pounded on the door. She knelt and shouted through the brass mail slot and peeked through it, and shortly she saw a pair of feet in rubber zoris approach.

Tran greeted her and walked back through the office to his room, which contained a neatly made-up iron cot, a particle-board wardrobe, a pine table, a wooden swivel chair, and a small block-and-board bookcase, its lower shelves full of books, mainly paperbacks, in French, English, and Vietnamese. On its top shelf sat a twelve-inch black-and-white TV, with a coat hanger antenna, and a cheap clock-radio cassette player. The walls were bare and white. Tran sat in the chair, and Lucy perched herself on the edge of the bed. The office, and Tran's quarters within it, were among Lucy's favorite places. She had been coming here since early childhood, and it was here that she had developed her taste for snooping. She still came to snoop into Tran's doings, and to spy on her mother, that sink of iniquity, and it did not occur to her that her presence here also allowed her mother to keep tabs on her, both directly and through Tran. Lucy was a capable conspirator, an extraordinary one for her age, but she was not quite ready for the major leagues, where both Mom and the Vietnamese had long been players.

"What are you doing?" she asked after the usual long silence.

"I am playing pyramid, as you see. Is there something wrong with your vision?"

"I meant, what are you doing *today*?" Silence, the flap of cards. Peevishly she said, "You always play that stupid game. You never win."

"So you imagine. I like this game because it is almost impossible to cheat at it, and almost no hands play out. It is thus a good model of real life in both respects."

"One can cheat in real life," said Lucy. Tran raised his head from the cards and gave her one of his famous looks. Lucy had trained herself to meet her mother's gaze, which was powerful enough, but Tran's eyes were in a class of their own, with a range that ran from Santa-like merriment to the matte black merciless gaze of a large shark. For an instant it was like staring at hot anthracite; then it softened and he said, "Only about trivial things, money or romance. I was speaking of the essentials, that is, life itself. In any case, today I must see the boyfriend of one of our clients, who has persisted in unpleasant behavior."

"Will you pound his lights out?"

"Certainly not," replied Tran prissily. "I am a

feeble and elderly oriental person and do not, as you say, *pound out the lights* of people. No, I will simply indicate to him in a variety of ways that he is being followed, and that neither his home, nor his place of work, nor his auto, is secure, should anyone wish to do him an injury, and I will further indicate that such intrusions will cease when he ceases his unwanted attentions toward his former mistress."

"What if he doesn't?"

"In that case, we will threaten him with a visit from you. He will crumple like a dry leaf. Please be careful with that book."

Lucy had been examining the objects set on the shelf affixed to the wall behind the head of the cot, in perfect disregard of her host's privacy. She palmed a couple of Camels from a pack there, flipped through a little notebook, and opened the book in question, an octavo volume printed on vellum paper like a good Bible, bound in soft blue leather, much battered and stained. She had seen it innumerable times but had never focused upon it until now. It was, she saw, in the Vietnamese language. She read the title aloud, "*Truyen Kieu.*" Someone had written something on the flyleaf in ink, but it had run and faded and she could not make out its meaning.

" 'The Tale of Kieu,' " she translated. "What's it about, refugees?"

"In a way. Vietnamese who have fled Vietnam are called *Viet-Kieu* because *kieu* means migrant, but the association is there, because Kieu had to flee her home also. She is our patron saint, you might say. A girl who suffered much."

"It's about a girl?"

"So the title suggests. It is the Vietnamese national epic."

"Yeah? Can I borrow it?"

Tran pinched his nostrils and looked uncomfortable. "Hmm. I don't know. Except in prison, it has not been out of my possession for many years. It was a gift."

"Who from?"

"From Linh. My wife."

"Oh. Did she write in the front? What does it say?"

He spoke in Vietnamese. "It says, 'Naturally, when two kindred spirits meet, one tie/Soon binds them in a knot nothing can tear loose. From your kindred spirit, Linh. Tet, 1956.' The lines are from the poem itself."

Lucy put the book carefully back on the shelf. "I'm sorry," she said, "I thought it was just a book. I don't really read Vietnamese very well either." She was acutely uncomfortable now. Some vast and heavy and awful thing seemed to lurk at the corners of her consciousness, like a formless bogey out of a dream. It was once again the faint apprehension of the suffering of Asia, something she touched a dozen times a day, and drew away from, and ignored like other Americans. She wished very much to pull away from it again, to resume the persona of a cheeky little girl poking about the room of a crotchety old uncle, but a feeling came over her then, a feeling like watching the odometer of a car turn over to produce a clean line of white zeros, and she understood that this was no longer possible for her.

"You must have been really sad when . . ." she began, and then stopped, appalled. She didn't know how to talk about stuff like this, as she had just at the moment realized. The times when she had chattered on, casually asking him about his life, now recollected, filled her with hot shame.

He sensed this and was kind. "I was sad, of course, but I did not find out about it until some time later. I was buried alive for four days, in a tunnel. When I came out, I was not the person I was before. Perhaps I could not have gone back to being a husband and a father in the same way, or at least that is what I told myself. And they were simply gone; it was not as if I had to bury them. They were in the canteen at Bac Mai Hospital, and it received a direct hit from a thousand-pound bomb. From a B–52, you understand. They fly so high that there is no warning. Alive and unafraid at one instant, dead the next. There are many worse deaths."

"Then why did you come here?" Lucy demanded angrily, tears starting. "Why don't you hate us?"

Tran's eyes were mild and somewhat surprised, and he answered, "As to why I came here, this is the land of opportunity, and I badly needed opportunity. My life in my country was over in a way that I hope you will never be able to comprehend. Also, when my family was killed, my country was at war, the whole country, not a small band of confused young men as with America. My wife and daughter were part of the war. The Americans bombed a hospital. Why should they not? I assure you that had I access to a B–52, I would have bombed every hospital from here to California."

She started to object, but Tran turned on her a riveting stare. He said, "Listen to me, because this is important. Peace is best. You should make every sacrifice to secure peace. When you absolutely must go to war, however, you must try to kill all the enemy you can as quickly as you can, holding nothing back, until they have surrendered or you have been defeated utterly. It is a great fraud to think otherwise, as the Americans did, and it prolongs the agony. It would be better if people said, if we fight, we are going to boil babies in their own fat and blast the skin off nice old ladies, so that they die slowly in great pain, and we are *happy* to do this, because what we fight for is *so* important. And if they conclude that it is *not* as important as *that*, then they should fight no more. Your mother understands this, which is why I am able to work for her. With these men, you know, she asks, she pleads, she begs them, she warns them so that they can have no doubts, she offers help. Then, if this is to no avail, suddenly, overwhelming, merciless violence."

At the mention of her mother and how terrifically great she was, *again*, Lucy felt herself withdrawing attention. Tran sensed this as well, and resumed snapping his cards.

"I have to go to Chinese school," said Lucy, getting up.

"If you like, I will go with you. I have business in that area."

They walked in companionable silence to Mott Street and the Chinese Consolidated Benevolent Association Building, where they had the Chinese

School. Tran said, in English, "Watch yourself, beautiful. Don't take any wooden nickels," and was rewarded by the astounded look on her face as she passed in through the door. He watched a great deal of TV late at night, for he had slept badly for a very long time, and when his eyes were too tired for reading he switched on the set. He preferred the films of twenty-five years ago and earlier, because the actors spoke more slowly and the plots were simpler and the violence was not so lovingly portrayed, and sometimes a phrase would stick in his mind and he would repeat it to hear how it sounded in his mouth. He was slowly learning American, of an antiquated type that, as it happened, was well suited to his personality.

Tran went over to an address on Bayard Street, where he squatted against a wall near a grocery store and waited. It had not been particularly difficult to find Leung; gangsters have office hours like other professionals. It was necessary only to know where to inquire, and Tran knew.

The grocery opened for business: the proprietor and his sons set out bins and stocked them with fresh vegetables, and hosed down the shining produce and the sidewalk in front of the store. The man noticed Tran but ignored him, only taking care not to get him wet. All along the street, shopkeepers were doing similar things, moving window grates back, setting racks of clothes or boxes of cheap items out on the street, adjusting awnings, accepting deliveries from the usual worn, stinking trucks painted with big characters.

At just past eight, a short, stocky man wearing

white cook's pants and a dark zipper jacket came to the door of Li's, opened it, and began moving in the crates that had been delivered earlier in the morning. Tran crossed the street and spoke to the man in Cantonese. The grocery store owner, coiling his hose, watched the interaction with mild interest. The short man appeared to object. Tran leaned closer, took something from his trouser pocket, and slid it into the pocket of the man's jacket. He gripped the man's shoulder in either reassurance or menace; it was hard to tell from across the street. After a few moments, however, the short man nodded and smiled, and then both men worked together to take the cartons into the restaurant. The grocer knew what had happened. The older guy had asked for a job, and the restaurant guy had turned him down, because he didn't need a guy, because, as everyone on the street knew, Li's was a tong place and not a serious restaurant at all, but the old guy had slipped him some cash so that the restaurant manager would carry him on the books, so that the old guy could claim employment, so he could bring relatives over, or people he said were relatives. It was *wan shai kaai*, making a living, the usual mild chicanery of Chinatown. The grocer himself had done any number of similar things. He forgot the incident, and began pricing his vegetables with little paper signs.

In the kitchen of Li's, Tran put on an apron and began to set up for the day. He filled the tea urn and loaded the rice cooker. Mr. Li was surprised to see that the fellow seemed to know his way around a kitchen. Mr. Li decided to tell his employers, if they should ask, that the man was his wife's cousin, a Viet-Ching from Saigon, which would explain his accent and features. He thought the man was in actuality a Vietnamese illegal on the run, and he thought he could milk additional funds out of him without anyone being the wiser.

Tran made a pot of *juk*, or congee, the rice gruel that is the corn flakes of China, and served out two bowls of it accompanied by pickled vegetables, pickled ginger, sliced salt eggs, and white bean cheese. Mr. Li was further astounded, because it was very good *juk*, creamy and smooth, and he rather liked being served breakfast in his own restaurant. It was almost like owning a real restaurant. He left Tran to chop and clean, while he sat at the little table at the front of the place and added columns of figures.

Leung came in at his usual time and sat in his usual place. Mr. Li went to the kitchen and poured an urn of tea and laid some steamed buns on a plate and set it before Leung. He thought for a moment of offering Leung some congee but decided against it. He was not interested in interrupting any detail of the man's routine.

A half hour later another man came in, this one a smooth-looking elderly fellow in a gray sharkskin suit and a patterned tie. Mr. Leung got up from his seat and greeted this man deferentially, because of both his age and his position in the community. He addressed him as Venerable Yee. Mr. Yee was a wealthy clothing importer and the president of the Háp Tài Business Association. Háp Tài means "benevolent ladder" in Cantonese, which more or less summed up the purpose of the organization, which was, in fact, a tong, although no longer involved in criminal activities, except when necessary for benevolence or for climbing the ladder of success, as now. The Chen family was also a member of this association, which was why Mr. Yee was here this morning.

Mr. Li ushered the tong leader to Leung's table and hurried off to fetch a fresh pot and more delicacies. He returned and went back to his stool. Leung and Mr. Yee saw a thin man in an apron come out of the kitchen with a mop and bucket and start to wash the floor, but they saw him not. Leung poured tea. They began to converse, beginning with the usual compliments. Both men understood *jo yan*, a term that means "behave like a human" and which stood for the norms of behavior expected of a Chinese, even if that Chinese is a very bad human. When Leung had been a Red Guard, he had done his best to destroy the idea of *jo yan*, but had failed, and so here they were, Leung being deferential to this old jerk, Mr. Yee, confident in his ability to condescend to a man nominally more powerful.

Mr. Yee had the privilege of raising the point of their meeting, which he did after all ceremony had been satisfied.

"An unfortunate event occurred in the Asia Mall, one that brought shame upon my associates."

"The shame is mine," said Leung, "for arranging the meeting. Nevertheless, spilt water cannot be recovered. The question is what to do now. I would welcome your suggestions."

"You clearly know more than I do about such

things, but would it be possible to assure the associates and family of the lamented Sings that the Háp Tài were not involved in this affair? As you know, we were simply asked to provide a private place and we did so, without in the least expecting such a disturbing event."

"I understand," said Leung, "but rest assured, the Woh Hàp Toùh have no doubts about your honesty. It is perfectly clear that this was not done by you, or even by a Chinese. It is obviously the work of the Italians. Indeed, this is why they desired the meeting with the Sings."

Mr. Yee allowed himself to appear startled, so startled was he. "The *Italians*? But we have never ever had any trouble with them; they have their things, we have ours. Are you certain you are not losing an ax and suspecting a neighbor?"

"My information is correct and comes from a source that cannot be impeached," said Leung.

The older man busied himself with pot and teacup to gain time to arrange his thoughts. "If that is truly the case, then we must bend the chimney and shift the firewood, and without delay. I am grateful for this information."

"I am happy to provide this small crumb if you think it is of value. Let me say this, however: as usual, these killings have attracted the attention of the police. This presents a separate danger. The Woh people will deal with the Italians in their own way and in their own time, but if it is thought that the Háp Tài were party to an official investigation, one that might reveal almost anything, then their rage would be considerable and then it *would* be directed at you, both here and in China."

Leung let that sink in, and then added, almost offhandedly, "I suppose the Chens can be relied upon?"

Mr. Yee was quick to answer, "Without a doubt they will say nothing."

"I wonder. The elder daughter seems to spend all her time with a *gwailo* girl. No doubt her head is being filled with pernicious notions. It may make her unreliable." Leung had made discreet inquiries about all the Chens and was trying to confirm this odd information.

"Oh, no, that is just Lòuhsì," Mr. Yee exclaimed; then, under Leung's questioning, he explained Lucy's provenance, and finished by saying, "So, you see, she is not a real *gwailo*, she's practically Chinese herself. There is no need to worry about her."

"If you say so, and take the responsibility. But suppose I was describing her to someone, say someone in Hong Kong. I would say, perhaps, yes, yes, everything is fine here. For example, the Chens—above reproach! The Chen daughter is always in the company of an *American* girl who is the daughter of a public prosecutor, and the daughter of a woman, an *Italian* woman, an *armed* Italian woman who interferes with the proper disciplining of wives. Wah! This person might say, but surely this is yet prudent, for being a *gwaileui*, she could never learn anything of moment from the Chen. Now I must inform this person that this girl speaks Cantonese and Mandarin perfectly, and who knows what she has heard and passed on to her so-interesting parents? What do you suppose this person would say then?"

Mr. Yee was growing pale around the nostrils. His voice dropped half an octave. "Perhaps he would say that you were mistaking the shadow of a bow in the cup for a snake." He looked at his watch, a calculated rudeness, and moved his teacup aside with a sharp gesture. "I have business elsewhere, so let me say this: if you should have the honor of conversing with your elders in Hong Kong or China, please inform them that the correct behavior of the Chens and their friends is guaranteed by the Háp Tài. Also, please convey to your superiors the honor our little organization experiences in being associated with your glorious and powerful brotherhood, and assure them that our behavior will be as exemplary as our inferior abilities permit."

After Mr. Yee had gone, Leung made some notes on a paper napkin, using the triad code, and then made two telephone calls. When he came back, he had to squeeze by the man with the bucket, who was now wiping down the counter. Leung waited outside the restaurant for five minutes, leaning against the wall and picking his teeth. A dark brown sedan pulled up to the curb, and a thirtyish oriental man in a blue blazer and gray slacks got out. Leung went over to the man, and they spoke briefly.

Inside Li's, Tran looked up from his polishing and observed. He could not hear what was being said, but he had heard enough while he plied his mop. He did, however, catch the smooth, quick movement of a fat envelope from Leung's inner jacket pocket to the breast pocket of the blue blazer. The man re-entered his brown car and drove off. Leung looked down the street in both directions and then walked slowly west toward Mott Street.

Tran picked up his pail and rags and returned to the kitchen, where he doffed his apron and started out of the restaurant. Mr. Li looked up from his figures. "Where are you going?"

"I have to go to my other job," said Tran.

"What? You have another job?"

"Yes, one must struggle to survive in the Beautiful Country."

He headed quickly toward Mott Street and the Chinese School, hoping he was not too late.

Karp had first heard the name William Fogel while working downtown as a tort lawyer. The man was a prominent member of the New York bar, who had recently negotiated, against a local hospital, a malpractice settlement large enough to appear in the business section of the *New York Times*. Karp studied the name on the yellow message slip and tried to think of why Fogel would be calling him. Probably something about one of his old tort cases, was his thought as he dialed the number. The secretary put him right through. Fogel had a genial voice, like an old-fashioned radio announcer's, and had worked hard to cover a Bronx accent. He made polite inquiries after Karp's well-being, recalled the few mutual acquaintances they'd had in the tort universe, dealt with their well-being, and then, Karp having exhibited his lack of enthusiasm for this palaver, Fogel came to the point.

"I've got an odd one here, Butch, a client, a new client, in fact, says he wants to see you, says he's got some information about the shooting of Edward Catalano."

"That is odd. A little far afield from your usual run of clientele, huh? The hit on Catalano probably didn't have much to do with malpractice."

Booming laugh, within which Karp detected a core of nervousness. "No, I guess not," said Fogel. "In any case, I agreed to represent him in this matter. I imagine it's fairly routine."

"Maybe," said Karp. "Even more routine would be a guy has information about a major felony, he walks down the block to the police station and gives his statement to a detective. It's a lot less routine when the guy retains a high-priced downtown lawyer and asks to talk directly to the district attorney. I assume he wanted to speak to Mr. Keegan?"

"Actually, no. He asked for you by name."

"Did he? Getting less routine by the minute, Bill. This fellow got a name?"

"Yes. He calls himself Willie Lie."

Karp waited and then said, "Well, I just checked my calendar, Bill, and I see it's not April Fool's Day, so . . ."

The booming laugh again, more nervous still. "Yeah, yeah, I know, what a name for a witness. But the man seems legit to me. He's an Asian gentleman."

"Is he? Well, you can tell Mr. Lie to walk over to the nearest precinct and make his statement—"

"Uh-uh, no, sir. That's out. Mr. Lie wishes to

deal directly with you on this matter. He will not be forthcoming absent that."

"And I assume you informed your client that all citizens have an obligation to help the police and that intentionally withholding information could be construed as hindering prosecution, which, given the underlying crime in question, would be a felony itself."

"Yes, I explained all that to Mr. Lie. He still insists on you."

"Any idea why?"

"Um, he says he doesn't trust the police, but that you have a reputation as a man of honor. That's almost a direct quote."

"Well, that's flattering," said Karp, "and I'll admit you've got me interested. Tell me one thing: What's the source of Mr. Lie's knowledge of the crime?"

A pause. "That's something I think we'll need to discuss face to face, Butch. Let me just say that my client has convinced me that his knowledge is comprehensive and authentic."

Karp suddenly recalled Guma's remark about all of the fine ethnic groups available as a supply of hit persons, and said, "Uh-huh. Bill, is there any chance that your guy is a participant in the crime in question?"

Another laugh, shorter and sharper. "Oh, I think when you meet him, you'll see why that's funny. But as far as any substantive information is concerned—"

"Yeah, right, you need to discuss it face to face. Okay, he wants to see me, I guess you know where the courthouse is. Why don't we say four today?"

• • •

William Fogel was a broad, well-set-up man some-what older than Karp, with fine yellow hair improved by an expensive hairpiece and a broad, friendly, ruddy face. He was wearing a double-breasted gray pinstripe, a yellow silk tie decorated with little scales of justice, and a gold Rolex set with diamond chips. He would have looked well in a courtroom, except that Bill Fogel had arranged his career so that he never had to go anywhere near a courtroom. His firm had guys who did that, in the rare cases when the Fogels of the bar did not arrange a mutually agreeable settlement.

His client would hardly have made half a Fogel. He sat on the edge of his chair like a child in the principal's office, an Asian man, thin, bone-faced, with the short-sided rooster-crest haircut of the recent immigrant. He wore a cheap white shirt buttoned to the neck, dark pants, and black loafers. They were sitting around the round table in Karp's office, and each of them had a yellow pad in front of them. Karp thought it significant that Lie was taking notes, too. They had covered the preliminary introductions, and Karp now said, "Let me first say what we're about here. I'll take the lead because it's fair to say that I have the most experience with matters of this nature." He glanced at Fogel, who gave him a grateful smile, and at Lie, who returned a noncommittal stare. "My only concern right now is to make it possible for Mr. Lie to convey whatever testimony he has in a way that will serve justice. No record is being made of the conversation we're about to have, and at this point we can take it as being off the record. Agreeable?" They both nodded, and Karp was interested to see Fogel glance toward Lie before he gave his nod.

"That being the case, Mr. Lie, let's hear what you have to say."

Lie addressed his yellow pad, eyes downcast. "I come here, New York, in 1980. From Hong Kong. I very poor at this time. I—"

Karp said, "Excuse me, Mr. Lie, are you a legal immigrant?"

"No, smuggled. Mexico, Houston, Seattle, here. So, 1980, I poor, I have no job, no family, so start in gang. White Dragon gang. Very big gang in Chinatown. I work protect gambling, massage girls, fight other gangs, also what you call, get money from storekeeper, *lei shi* . . ."

"Lucky money," said Karp. "Extortion."

"Yes, extortion." He said the word carefully, as if it was one he really wanted to remember. Fogel gave Karp a curious look but said nothing.

"So I work this way, some year, then, what we call big brother in tong, make me *dai ma*, big horse, boss, yes? Of other gang people. I have territory, some streets, I make sure all money collected, other gang stay out."

"Excuse me," said Karp, "this is how you earn your livelihood, Mr. Lie? You have no other employment?"

"Yes, livelihood is all this what I am saying," Lie said, and resumed. "So one my streets, Elizabeth

Street, north of Canal Street, one end Chinese people, other end Italian people. So I meet Italian people, they say wise guys, Mafia guys. But we, they not do business, we stay separate all the time, separate, so I am surprised, one day, Italian man come to me, say, want to make some money? So I go have drink with him. So he say to me—"

"Just a second, Mr. Lie—this man, what was his name?"

"Ah, name Scarpi. Gino Scarpi. So he say, you want to work for us distribute product in China-town? This surprise me, because, ah, most times Chinese man is selling product to Italian. Bulk shipping."

"This is drugs you're referring to?"

"Yes, drugs. So I say to him, okay. I don't tell big brother in tong, I figure, work for myself, you know? And we do business, Asian heroin, very pure. This is for year, year and a half, all going good, no problem. Then one month ago, something like that, Scarpi say to me, Willie, you know where I can get shooter, I have job for shooter. So, you know, I must laugh because, I say to him, why you need me, huh? You *Mob*! You don't have shooters? He say, yeah, we got, but can't use them, he don't say why not. Hundred thousand dollar, he say, you pay shooter. So, I say know guys, I give them a call, but no more, I don't set it up, he must set it up. Scarpi. He don't like that. He say, I pay you money, you do job. I say no thanks, I say, what you think, this Chinese restaurant?"

To Karp's surprise Lie giggled then. "You understand? I not crazy man, I *gangster*, but *Chinese* gangster, not want shoot some Italian, get killed that way. So I go away. Two day later, at night, car comes, two men tell me, get in. So I go. Take me to apartment house, go up back way. Fancy apartment. There is Scarpi, there is another man, they say, this Joe Pigetti, big boss, I never meet him before. Pigetti say, once we ask you nice, now we don't ask, we *tell* you, you get shooter, you take out Eddie Catalano. So what could I do, I say, yes, boss. Then he say got to happen a special night, a special time, nine of June, around three in morning. This two days later now. So I say, yes, boss. So two days, I get boys for this, tell them it must be so, it must be this way. Don't use my own boys, get Viet boy, I know this shooter, he kill like it nothing, crush of fly, also another boy to help him. So they do it. Scarpi give me envelope, I give to them, I don't touch, don't count. Don't want it. They take it, I don't get no complaint. That's all." He looked blankly out at them, as if he had just told a joke without a punch line.

"Mr. Lie," said Karp, "how come you're here? I mean, why did you call a lawyer and come in here with this story?"

"Is not story, is true!"

"Yes, of course, but what was the reason that *made* you want to tell this true story to me?"

"Oh, yeah. Well, I scared they try to kill me, you know shut me up. So I tell, ah, Mr. Fogel this story, maybe I get some, what you call, witness protection." He looked over at Fogel, whose smooth face was professionally neutral, with perhaps a hint of discomfort around the eyes.

"That's an interesting story, Mr. Lie. Would you be able to provide corroboration?"

Fogel said, "Mr. Lie, what he means is he needs something to back up your story, some other witness, some—"

A look of what seemed like impatience seemed to flash from Lie to the lawyer, and he said, "I know what is corroboration. Yes, I have this. I have boys who did job, names, places you find them, and, have gun they used. They use, they give it to me to get rid of, but I don't do it. So, yes. But I must have immunity. Transactional immunity."

Karp shot an inquiring glance at Fogel, but the man seemed bemused by his client's statement.

"Well, Mr. Lie," said Karp, "as your lawyer may have informed you, all witnesses before New York state grand juries receive automatic transactional immunity. That is, a witness is immune from prosecution connected to any transaction arising from anything covered in his testimony, a very broad immunity."

"Yes, is what I want," said Lie.

"Right, I understand that, Mr. Lie. But here's my problem. I don't know you, I don't know who you are or what you've done. Until you've made a formal statement and provided us with the means to corroborate it, I can't actually guarantee you anything."

Lie shook his head. "Is not good, not for me. Look, I admit I am gangster, I admit I sell drugs, I set up murder. When you have this all signed, you can say, Mr. Lie, you talk, you testify or you go to jail."

Karp pushed his chair back and said, "Bill, I'm going to step outside for a few minutes, and in that time I'd like you to explain to your client how a proffer works and how we're really not interested in pulling any fast ones on him." He stood up. "While I'm out, would anyone like a soft drink? We have Coke and Diet Coke and Sprite, I think." Fogel declined; Lie asked for a Coke.

Karp went into the outer office and used the phone to call the desk man at the D.A. squad, the small group of police officers assigned permanently to the district attorney's office for various cop-type chores, and said, "Mel, get on to CATCH and find out if there's a record on a mutt named Willie Lie, el-eye, or el-eye-ee, Asian male, age about thirty, five-five, around one-forty. Also, get a couple of the guys posted outside the courthouse. The mutt's in my office now, and when he leaves I want him followed. He's wearing a white shirt, dark pants, loafers. And tell Captain Fulton to call me as soon as he can. I may need full surveillance on this character. Got that?"

The officer said he had. "Is that it?"

"No, send a CSU tech up here in about fifteen. I'll have something for him."

Karp hung up and went to the coffee room behind the secretary's office and, after killing five minutes with a newspaper he found in the trash can, he took a couple of Cokes from the refrigerator, wrapped them both in paper napkins, and went back into his office.

"Any progress?" Karp asked, handing a can to Lie, who picked it up, popped it, and took a swig. It was clear to Karp that lawyer and client were at odds. Lie had a cast to his face that made him look a lot less like a Chinese waiter and a lot more like what he said he was. Fogel looked confused and out of his depth, no surprise there.

"Butch, I'm afraid we're at something of an impasse. Mr. Lie is not willing to proffer more than a version of what he has already related unless he is guaranteed protection and full transactional immunity."

"Well, then, Bill, I'm afraid I can't deal. No offense intended to your client, but somebody could walk in off the street, say he just shot the mayor and say that your grandmother set up the hit, and ask me to let him skate on it in return for his testimony against granny."

"That's not a relevant analogy, Butch," Fogel objected. "Mr. Lie had a very minor role in the Catalano killing. He's giving you a major organized-crime figure."

"He's giving me nothing but smoke, Bill. I need the shooters, the weapon, and a detailed account of how it was ordered, paid for, and carried out. With that, and after due investigation to see if the story checks out, I would be glad to place your client before the grand jury with the routine transactional immunity. Alternatively, I can offer him use immunity on his testimony, and offer him protection as a material witness. But other than that . . ." He opened his hands palm up, the gesture of helplessness.

Lie placed his Coke back on the table and rose.

"Now this over. Now we go to see United States attorney." He waited to see what effect this would have on Karp, and Karp was surprised that a Chinese gangster, a relative newcomer, had grasped the fact of rivalry between two prosecutorial organizations enough to expect that there might be such an effect. He did not think a malpractice lawyer like Fogel had the balls to play that high-stakes game. There was more to Mr. Lie than was first apparent, it seemed, and it seemed to Karp that he, rather than Fogel, was calling the shots.

Karp smiled and gestured in the direction of the federal building, and they left. Shortly thereafter, the crime-scene-unit tech, a small, dark man in civilian clothes, came in and took away Mr. Lie's Coke can, carefully ensconced in a plastic bag. Then it was time for Karp's four-thirty meeting with the administrative judge's staff, and when that was done he fielded some phone calls, and did not break free until nearly six.

There was a message waiting from the D.A. squad desk man. Karp called him back and received the news that Willie Lie had no criminal record, no driver's license, no Social Security number.

"This guy an illegal?" the man asked.

"He says. I got the lab guys working on pulling some prints he left here."

"That could help if he has a sheet in another state and the locals bothered forwarding them to the NCIS. Meanwhile, you got a nobody."

Not a nobody, Karp thought. A somebody, and a dangerous one at that. For in the last moment of the meeting, when Bill Fogel had gone out the door, Karp had used his splendid peripheral vision to observe Mr. Lie pause on the threshold and shoot back at him a look full of assessing intelligence, guile, and impersonal hatred.

9

AFTER CHINESE SCHOOL LUCY USU-
ally went to get something to eat with Janice and a
group of friends, but today she had promised to go
up to the lab and have lunch with Ronnie Chau
before going to the lab. Chau had invited her several times in the past weeks, when Lucy had been
too depressed to go, but the new Lucy had made
a cheery call from a pagoda-tipped phone booth
after class and set it up.

She boarded an uptown Broadway train at Canal, found a corner seat in the first car, and reached
into her bag for a copy of *Sing Tao Jih Pao*, the Chinese newspaper. It amused her to observe the reac-
tions of the passengers to a white girl reading it.
But as she reached into the bag, her hand touched
an unfamiliar object, and she drew out, wonder-
ingly, Tran's copy of *The Tale of Kieu*.

Her eyes stung and she had to take several deep
breaths of ozone-rich subway air before her emo-
tions were back under control. She inspected the
book closely. It was stained on the edges and end-
papers with water and earth, and on the leather of
the back cover there was a large dark brown blot of

what was surely blood. She stared at it, jogging on her lap in the train's motion, a holy thing, she thought, a relic of romance, of war, of horror, of courage, of desperate flight, and she felt honored beyond endurance that Tran had slipped it (she could not imagine how) in with her possessions.

She turned past the title page, her fingers caressing the blurred memento of the dead wife, and began to read. It was slow going, for the orthography of Vietnamese is complex and the language was poetic and refined and, in the fashion of classical Asian poetry, the poet made use of compressed references that would be familiar to any Vietnamese, whose meaning she had to guess at. The train was rushing out of 72nd Street before she had the first verse clear.

A century. In a span that long of life on earth
Talent and destiny will often war,
Sea becomes mulberry field and returns to sea
And you must watch things that sicken
    the heart.
Yet, is it so strange that loss and gain balance,
    although
Blue Heaven, in spite, strikes down the
    rosy-cheeked girl?

She shuddered with pleasure as the meaning revealed itself, and attacked the next verse at once. She was so absorbed in this difficult work that she forgot where she was. She did not notice the gradual emptying of the car as the train moved farther north on its route, nor did she notice the three young oriental men in black clothes and sunglasses sitting together at the car's other end, did not even notice when the train stopped at and departed from 168th Street. Three minutes too late, in the irrational spasm well known to subway riders, she yelped and leaped to her feet, hurriedly stuffing the book back into her shoulder bag, and went and stood swinging from a strap in front of the door, cursing silently to herself and watching the columns whiz by in the dark.

Lucy exited at 181st Street and made for the crossover to get back on the southbound line, and that was when she noticed the three oriental youths for the first time. They had followed her off the train. A pulse of fear, a flush of embarrassment: How could she have been so stupid . . . !

She kept walking, searching for people, but the crossover and the adjoining stairways were deserted. One of the youths moved past her, to the stairs that led to the southbound platform, and turned, grinning up at her. The other two closed in from behind. Lucy bolted down the stairs, faked past the guy below, and dashed toward the stairs to the platform. With relief she saw that there were a half dozen people waiting for the southbound Broadway express.

Then she was falling, jerked off her feet by a hand gripping her shoulder bag. She landed painfully on her hands and knees, rolled down three steps, and staggered to her feet. She saw the backs of the three men retreating, heard their running footsteps echoing off the tile walls. Her heart jerked as she realized they had taken the bag with Tran's book inside it. Without further thought she raced after them.

On the street, out in the sunlight, she looked around wildly, spotted the three of them crossing Broadway, and headed toward them. She had no idea how she was going to get the bag away from three men. If there was anything at all rational lurking under the stew of fear and rage that occupied her mind, it was the belief that, having taken the few dollars she had in there, they would toss the bag in the gutter and she would get the book back. She was not going to leave without Tran's *Tale of Kieu*.

The youths were about twenty yards ahead of her, laughing and tossing the bag back and forth. Every so often one of them would glance over his shoulder to see if she was still following. This should have tipped her off that something was up, but her usual instincts were in suspension. All she could think about was the book, and losing it, and what it would mean.

They went east on 182nd Street, Lucy following. They hadn't looked in the bag yet. Vaguely she wondered why. They should rifle the bag, take the cash, and dump it. She prayed for a cop car to come along. It was not the sort of neighborhood where a little white girl could ask a stranger to go up against three Asian toughs over a grungy-looking canvas bag.

They stopped and conferred, the three dark heads

close together, and then they headed for an abandoned building, a sooty former tenement with weathered plywood over its doors and windows. One of them found a way in, clearly much used from the evidence of the trash and crack vials scattered around it, and the three of them disappeared inside. Hopelessly, Lucy followed them in, as if drawn by an unbreakable wire. Her sneakers crunched thin glass, she ducked under a plank, entered darkness, and immediately, as she had half expected, was grabbed in a bear hug from behind, with the hand of her captor jammed across her mouth. The man holding her said nothing as he hustled her along the ruined corridor. She didn't bother to struggle, but went dead in his arms, making him carry her weight. He was a slightly built but muscular man, smelling of acrid sweat, a lilac hair oil, and, strongest of all, a smell she knew very well. It was *nuoc mam*, a pungent sauce made from fermented fish, and it told her that she had been captured by Vietnamese.

"Why does this make me want to grumble?" said the district attorney. It was the morning after Karp's interview with Fogel, and Karp was in the D.A.'s office, filling him in on the abortive negotiation.

"Because you want it to have been a break for us, and it may *be* a break, but not in the form it was offered. Lie thinks he's being smart. Okay, he *is* smart, the little fucker. You know what they say,

Jack, we only think criminals are stupid because we never meet the smart ones. Here's a mutt who's been selling dope and doing all kinds of evil for four or so years, and he's got no sheet at all. If I took his bait, we could've found ourselves committing to look the other way on God knows what kind of mass destruction."

"Somehow I doubt Tommy Colombo is going to have those kind of scruples," said Keegan sourly. His immaculate cigar drooped below a lower lip petulantly protruding.

"I agree, and that's the difference between a cheap grandstander like Tommy Colombo and us. What's the matter, Jack? You don't look happy."

"I'm struggling to keep my joy under control. You know we're going to get raped in the press on this. Colombo's going to have a field day."

"True, but meanwhile it's over three years to the next election. Let him have his thrill. Meanwhile, we still have our ace in the hole."

"Which is what?"

"Murder," said Karp. "The feds can't offer immunity against a crime that's not on their books. So sooner or later we'll have our crack at Mr. Lie and whoever really did Eddie Cat. Even assuming that's not saying the same thing."

"You think Lie was more involved than he's letting on?"

"It wouldn't knock me off my chair. Priority one is finding out more about this guy. Especially where he was on the night of, although I'd lay money he's alibied to the hairline."

Keegan considered for a moment, then nodded, and placed his cigar on his desk. "Okay, go do it, and keep me informed. And fill in Roland, too. He's going to be even more delighted than I am."

"He'll get over it," said Karp.

"Oh, yeah. Especially since he's going to have to field the press questions, him or you, buddy, because this is one I'm happy to delegate to my loyal staff. What about the Colombo front?"

"Oh, I think he'll give Mr. Lie a big, sloppy kiss. He'll buy whatever he has to say and put him in front of the federal grand jury and use his testimony to indict Pigetti under any number of federal statutes. Conspiracy, interfering with a federal prosecution, witness intimidation, depriving Mr. Catalano of his civil rights. There's a grab bag for him there."

"And what does Lie get out of all this?"

"Oh, he'll get federal immunity, of course, but what he mainly wants out of the feds is the witness-protection program. Mr. Lie is what they used to call a shadowy figure, Jack. He tried to set it up with us so that he'd start with a clean slate regarding any state crimes he's committed. I wouldn't roll on that, so he's dropped back to his second choice. I have the feeling that he wants to fade away entirely about now, and Colombo is going to help him."

"And we're going to stop him, I hope you're going to say."

"Oh, yeah," said Karp. "If we can."

[NYT 12 JUN 60]

GANGLAND LAWYER IN SUICIDE
LEAP FROM EMPIRE STATE

By Joseph P. Huntington

Police sources revealed today that the man who threw himself from the observation deck of the Empire State Building at 9:30 yesterday morning was Gerald S. Fein, of Brooklyn, a disbarred criminal lawyer well known for his defense of reputed organized-crime figures. According to police, Mr. Fein left his home at 1320 Avenue M in the Flatbush section of Brooklyn at the usual time, about eight o'clock, and arrived at his parking garage at 8:45. He then walked to the Empire State Building, where his law firm, Kusher, Fein and Panofsky, had offices on the fifty-seventh floor. Witnesses, including Dennis Horgan, 32, a ticket taker at the Empire State's observation deck, stated that Mr. Fein entered the deck at about nine, purchased a ticket, and strolled around the deck for a few minutes. The deck was relatively empty at that time of day, Mr. Horgan recalled, and Mr. Fein did not seem to be particularly distraught. Some minutes later, in a manner still under investigation by police, Mr. Fein made his way past a normally locked door to a service area, and then through another door to the parapet above the observation windows, where he threw himself off. He landed in the roadway of Fifth Avenue, ten yards from its intersection with 34th Street, causing several minor traffic accidents. No injuries were reported.

Because of Mr. Fein's ties to reputed organized-crime figures, a police investigation has been authorized under the command of Detective Lieutenant Arnold D. Mulhausen of the 14th Precinct, but at present the police have no evidence of any foul play. Mr. Fein's family remains in seclusion and was unavailable for comment, but Mr. Herschel Panofsky, Mr. Fein's law partner, was reported as saying that Mr. Fein had been despondent in recent weeks after losing his appeal against the New York Bar Association's decision on April 18, 1959, revoking his license to practice law. Mr. Fein was convicted of jury tampering in the trial of alleged racketeer Salvatore Bollano for the murder of an associate, John Gravellotti. Mr. Fein had won an acquittal for Mr. Bollano in that case, but his victory was immediately marred by accusations that several jurors had received bribes. In the jury-tampering case against him, Mr. Fein had accepted a plea bargain, resulting in a fine and a suspended sentence. Mr. Panofsky said, "Jerry expected a censure from the Bar Association, but not the loss of his livelihood. He just couldn't handle it. The law was his whole life."

See obituary on Page A30

Marlene declined to read another obituary just now, although she thought the one in the *Times* would be the most complete. There had been seven daily newspapers in New York when Jumping Jerry had gone off that parapet, and each had given the suicide a big play. Marlene's secretary and factotum, Sym McCabe, had been set to gathering Xeroxes of these reports for the past week or so, and doing other research tasks. The young woman sat across the cluttered table from her, poring over phone books, trying to locate various people who might be useful to the investigation. Sym was a small tan woman of twenty-odd, with large, suspicious eyes and an intense, hungry look, like an osprey nestling. She was another of Marlene's brands from the burning: taken in at seventeen, illiterate, addicted, and carrying an unspeakable family and sexual history, taught, encouraged, nurtured, and converted into a useful citizen with a GED and twenty credits already at Manhattan Community College. This was the first time Marlene had sent her out to do research. Sym had found that while scoring facts was not as easy as scoring dope, many of the same skills were required.

"I got six John J. Dohertys in the five boroughs," she said. "You want me to look on the Island, too?"

"No, call those first, maybe we'll get lucky."

Sym went into the front room to call, and Marlene shoveled through the piles of folders and clipped copies on the table, looking for a place to start spending Vivian Fein's money in a useful way. There was plenty of it. Two days before, Marlene had walked out of a cubbyhole in the diamond center on 47th Street, minus Vivian's gaudy ring, and holding a certified check for $108,750, after which, armed with a power of attorney from Ms. Fein (or Mrs. Bollano, as she would have been called in certain circles), she had opened a checking account for the woman, plus an escrow account upon which Osborne Group Security, Inc., was entitled to draw for the purposes of conducting an investigation into the death of Gerald Fein.

Her hand fell on a thick folder containing a stack of glossy photos. Sym had found a photo essay in *Life* and then tracked down the photographer's agency and paid them to generate prints, not only of the shots *Life* had used, but all the relevant shots in their negative files. She'd been sent to do the same at most of the other prominent photo agencies, because Marlene believed that almost everything you wanted to know about had been photographed by somebody, somewhere, and this was especially important in a situation where she didn't really understand what she was searching for. Again, the two big questions: First, why now? The man had been dead twenty-three years, the daughter had let it lie all that time, and then it had become desperately important. Marlene had asked, and been given the answer, not very satisfactory, that Ms. Fein had decided it was time. Clearly something to do with leaving the hubbie, divorcing in a sense from the Mob. That made some sense, but Marlene thirsted after details. The second was, why had a supreme courtroom master copped a plea to something he hadn't done? Or maybe he had done it. Something to explore with the old-timers.

She thumbed through the stack of glossies. A set of Gerald Fein in happier days: here was one of him entering a nightclub (El Morocco) with a blond woman on his arm, a beefy guy on the other side, smiling. The woman was Celia Fein, the wife, a looker, circa 1955; the guy was Charlie Tuna. Fein hung out with very bad people, and he also took his wife to nightclubs. The lady on Charlie Tuna's arm was not his wife. Other nightclub shots, Fein at a long banquette table, laughing with the scum of the earth, dancing with the wife, talking earnestly with Sal Bollano. Where was Panofsky? Not a night-clubber? Maybe he didn't like to get his picture taken. Next, some domestic shots, Fein and Celia, with little Vivian, not so little in this one, pretty like her mother, blond and delicate. It was a series of shots taken at some civic affair, all of them dressed in late-fifties high style, Fein himself in a double-breasted suit and topcoat, Celia in a fur coat, Vivian in a white fur jacket and matching hat. About fourteen, Marlene estimated, smiling shyly at the lens, while her daddy radiated love and bonhomie around him. Marlene studied the man's smiling face. Energy, was the first impression, boiling spirit, barely contained behind the smile, the glinting eyes, the jutting jaw. One of the generation impressed by the fabled insouciance of FDR, Fein had adopted the lifted chin, the upward-pointing smoking apparatus, in Fein's case a panatela rather than a cigarette holder, and he was able to bring it off too, because he was smoothly handsome in that tailored, buffed, 1940s way: wavy dark hair, large pale eyes, a noble nose, terrific even white teeth, a solid chin with a Clark Gable dimple in the center of it. Good-sized man, too, athletic, broad-shouldered. Must have been a terror with the ladies, Marlene thought, but it turns out he takes his wife to El Morocco with the bad boys. Flip to the next one. Same civic event: Dad and Vivian watching something, a theatrical act maybe, part of a well-dressed audience, but Dad isn't watching the act, he's watching Vivian, with oceans of love in his eyes. Marlene didn't think that could be faked, not in a candid shot like this. The guy loved his family, no question. So why did he do it? He killed himself for the insurance? Make a note, check the policy value.

Another set, this one of the funeral, a big one, a mob affair, all the big guys sent flowers, both Bollanos, Big and Little Sallies carrying the coffin, and was that Abe Lapidus standing there, a stricken expression making his sad face sadder? Yes, it was, and who was that short, pear-shaped man, struggling to hold up the end of the casket? Marlene rooted around and found a hand lens. Yeah, unmistakable, although she had only ever seen the man garbed in black, on the bench: Herschel Panofsky, now H. R. Paine, His Honor. The ugly little fucker, as he was often called down at the courthouse, often by the current crop of Mob lawyers, and he was, his head too large for his ass-heavy soft body, a bulging forehead fringed by sparse, crisp curls, armpit-style hair (another nickname, The Armpit), a little parakeet beak of a nose, a sloppy mouth, not much chin. No Gableoid dimple there. Another shot: the ugly little fucker comforting the grieving widow and the daughter graveside, the daughter not being all that comforted, Marlene thought, a look of actual repugnance there through the tears, which just went to show, a picture worth a thousand words—she would have to ask Vivian about that when next they saw one another, maybe this very evening.

Then a thinner sheaf, these in color, the worst ones, and who knows how Sym had wormed them out of the official files, probably the same way she had procured drugs, whining and money, but here they were, what happened when a body fell nearly a thousand feet and reached terminal velocity before striking asphalt. He'd landed facedown, although it was hard to tell from the photograph; no, there was a black patch that had been the back of a well-tailored lawyer's pinstripe, relatively untouched by the wide pool of horrors that surrounded it. Marlene made herself look, even wielded the hand lens, identifying the bits. Fein had gone out without any identification that morning—that could be a significant detail—which was why it had taken the cops some twenty-four hours to discover who the jumper had been. He'd left no note. Marlene put the lens down and gasped in some air. She'd spotted the dimpled chin, curiously blood-free, attached to a long, twisted piece of disassembled face. Well, enough of that! She put all the photographs away in their folders. She could make no connection between the robust, dashing man in the earlier photographs and the offal on Fifth Avenue. Sure, in literature they had them, Gatsby and Richard Cory, the shiny front with nothing behind it, but she doubted that Gerald Fein had been such a man. On what evidence? That look at the daughter, maybe? Panofsky was wrong; the law hadn't been his whole life. Gerald Fein had a family.

Sym stuck her head in. "Phone for you. Some woman named Chau. Wants to know where Lucy's at."

"I'll take it in back." Marlene got up, stretched, yawned, and went back to her desk, located behind a bookcase full of potted plants in the rear of the big room.

Dr. Chau introduced herself and informed Marlene that Lucy had not shown for their noon lunch date; nor had she arrived at one-thirty for her regular lab session. She had never missed one before.

"Maybe she just forgot," said Marlene, not believing this at all. "I mean, she's a genius, but she's twelve."

Chau seemed satisfied with this, and Marlene got rid of her as soon as she could, pressed the disconnect, and immediately dialed Tran's pager. She waited. The torment lasted ten minutes, and then Tran was on the phone.

"Is Lucy with you?"

A rather long pause. "I presume she is not at the laboratory, then."

"No, they just called. Tran, you don't think . . . ? I mean, those men who bothered them before . . ."

"I very much doubt it, Marie-Hélène. However, I will find her."

"Where? Where is she?"

"Do not become upset, my friend. There is no one who wishes to hurt Lucy at present. She is an impulsive child and may have gone off somewhere. I will inspect her usual haunts." In English he added, "No sweat it."

"Don't sweat it, you mean. 'No sweat' means a trivial problem."

"This is also apt," said Tran in French. "I will call. Until later."

It had to be Leung, Tran thought, one of those phone calls from Li's Restaurant had set up a lift, and they would have had to be good to have netted Lucy in daylight, in the city. The other day Leung had used his own boys, Chinese, and they had been foiled easily. He would not do that again. He would use . . . who? Local people, certainly—you wouldn't import a group from Hong Kong to lift a little girl; they might get lost or make some stupid error out of mere . . . what was the word? Disorientation? Disoccidentation? There was no such word in any language, attesting to the cultural hegemony of the West. They would be Asian, probably; Tran couldn't see a tong man hiring long-noses for such a job. That narrowed the field. Kidnap-capable gangs were not exactly common, even in Chinatown. Tran knew several, and he decided to start with the one he used himself, when he had need of such services.

The business offices of the Hoi Do an-truong were located above a Vietnamese grocery on Lafayette, just off Canal, in the heart of the area that Vietnamese gangs had recently claimed for their own. Vietnamese gangs are not squeamish in their choice of names, unlike the Chinese, who prefer flowery vagueness with a "harmonious" or "benevolent" tossed in. One Viet gang of the period was called Born to Kill; Hoi Do an-truong means "the society of those with severed entrails," aka "The Sorrow League." In Vietnamese folklore that name refers to an association of men and women of talent doomed to a life of woe by cruel fate.

When Tran approached the building, its doorway was decorated with the usual gaggle of black-shirted, sunglassed young thugs. Others leaned against late-model Lexus or Maxima cars, also black, parked and double-parked in the street outside. These young men had all been children during the war; most were orphans and the Hoi Do an-truong was the closest thing they had ever known to a family. Tran did not exactly approve of them, but he understood the wounds they had experienced and did not condemn their predation on the Vietnamese refugee community, many of whom had spent a good deal of energy trying to kill him back in their native land.

Tran passed through these youths without challenge and entered the building. They looked at one another through their sunglasses and laughed nervously. There was some debate among them as to who the old guy really was. Some thought their *dai lo* called the man Major Pham as a nickname, as an American gangster might call an associate King Kong or Terminator. Others thought he actually *was* Major Pham, the unkillable terror of the Iron Triangle, whose name was used to frighten children at a time and in a place where children were not easy to frighten. In any case, they treated him, as their leader did, with vast and wary respect.

The *dai lo*, or big brother, of the Hoi Do antruong, called himself Freddie Phat. He was thirty-five, tall for a Vietnamese, and had a handsome, intelligent face. He wore fashionable tinted aviator glasses, a gray silk suit, and a dark blue shirt with a pale blue tie, open at the collar. His office was the kitchen of a tenement apartment in which many of his associates dwelt. When Tran barged in, he immediately dismissed the two men with whom he was talking and offered Tran a chair at the chrome and formica kitchen table that served as his desk. Tran remained standing. He said, "Tell me you didn't take her."

Freddie Phat swallowed the insult represented by Tran's tone of voice, and his refusal of a seat, and the implied refusal of tea and snacks and a civilized conversation before getting to business. Phat was one of four people in the United States who knew who Tran really was (the others being Lucy Karp, Marlene Ciampi, and a woman who worked in a fish-packing plant in Texas) and so he did this out of respect, rather than because he was afraid of him (although he was afraid of him, too), respect for what Tran had been through in the service of his ungrateful country.

It did not occur to him, although he was an excellent liar, to lie in this instance. He said, "No, naturally not, although I was approached with the contract."

"Leung?"

"One of his people came, a little before noon. I

said no, and I suggested it was not a good idea to annoy that particular girl."

"Who?"

"The word I have is that they went to the Vo brothers. The Vo would do it. The Vo will do anything, as you know."

Tran paused and waited for his heart to slow to its normal rhythm. It was somewhat of an effort to control his voice as he asked, "It was not a . . . water contract, was it?"

Phat shook his head. "Not that they said, only a simple lift and hold. I believe they wished to frighten rather than harm and also to find out what she knows about certain events."

"I see." Tran pulled out a chair and sat down. Phat thought he looked older than he had a few minutes ago. Tran looked across the table at the *dai lo*. "I will need your help to find her, all of your people, and immediately." When he saw Phat hesitate, he added, "The usual rates, of course."

Phat made a dismissive gesture. "No, it is not that. We would be happy to be of service. But this is, as I understand it, a tong matter. The Da Qan Zi has been mentioned."

"And so you are afraid."

"I am prudent. We are very small here, and the Chinese are very large. We do business with our own people and so they allow it, but if we intruded in a tong matter . . ."

"You already have, the other day. Have you forgotten?"

"No, but at that time I didn't know what I know now." Phat was conscious of Tran's gaze, that famous gun-barrel stare. He felt the first prickles of sweat start on his forehead. He said, "Let me do this. I will set my boys to watch their house in Brooklyn and that place they use on Hester Street and other places where they are known. If we see the Vo boys or the cousin, we will follow. I will call you as soon as the girl turns up."

After a pause, Tran nodded sharply and stood up. At the door he turned and said, "If she is found safely in this way, I will owe you a debt."

And what if not? wondered Freddie Phat, and shuddered, as a miasma of the old war seemed to drift through the room, and he recalled some of the stories about Major Pham and the fate of those he disliked.

Lucy surprised herself by not being more frightened. The worst thing really about the abandoned building was when she had to go to the bathroom, and they took her to what used to be one, but there were no fixtures in it and she had to go in a smelly hole in the floor where the toilet had been.

Being kidnapped by Vietnamese gangsters was no joke, of course, but it was also the most interesting thing that had happened to her recently, and she was fascinated with her captors. They did not know that she could understand Vietnamese and therefore spoke freely among themselves in her presence, there in the ruined room. Early on she had learned that they were not going to harm her, but had been hired to hold her for a man they called "the Chinese." Lucy knew whom they meant, and the knowledge buoyed her, for she also knew that Tran was watching Leung and that he would very shortly learn what had happened to her and take appropriate measures. Lucy's faith in Tran's powers was in the same ballpark as her faith in the Deity; in Heaven, God disposed, in New York, Tran. With respect to the former power, she had a fine sense of what sort of prayers would be most effective, and so she did not pray for release from her captivity but for courage and endurance and also that when Tran found her, he would not be too awful to her captors.

These were two brothers, surnamed Vo and a cousin, surnamed Nguyen, and they all had adopted, in the usual way, gang nicknames. The smaller of the two brothers, a rat-face with brown teeth, was called Needlenose. The larger, beefy for a Vietnamese, and with coarse long hair and dark skin, was Sharkmeat. The cousin was Cowboy, hardly more than a boy, delicate-boned, wiry and nervous. Lucy gathered that he had been in the country for less time than the others had, and they bossed him around roughly.

"Hey, Cowboy, we're going to call Kenny again," said Sharkmeat. "You watch her."

"Yeah," said Needlenose, "watch, but don't touch. We know you go for hairless pussy."

"He *is* a hairless pussy," said Sharkmeat, and laughing, they stomped out.

Some minutes passed. Nguyen spent the waiting time ripping a hole in the plaster wall with a large, heavy butterfly knife, but Lucy felt his eyes on her and when she turned her head, he was staring at her. She returned his gaze. Nguyen stopped his hacking at the wall and picked up Lucy's bag. He examined her wallet, her notebook, the various odds and ends she had accumulated. He riffled through a French-English and a Vietnamese-English dictionary, and a paperback of *Kim*. He picked up *The Tale of Kieu*, studied it briefly, and then stared again at Lucy. He walked over to her, holding the book.

"You read this book?" he asked in English.

"No," she answered, "I only look at the pictures."

"But the book has no pictures," he replied in Vietnamese, and then did a double-take when he realized that the girl had also spoken in that language.

"You speak Vietnamese!" he exclaimed.

"All Americans speak a little Vietnamese."

He gaped at her. She said, "That was a joke."

"But where did you learn it?"

"From a friend." She indicated the book. "Have you read this?"

He looked down, flushing. "No, I had to leave school. To work, and then . . . but I know this . . ." and here he declaimed in a singsong voice, "'The breeze blows cool, the moon shines clear, but in my heart still burns a thirst unquenched.'"

"Yes, that's from where Kieu and Kim are on their first date and she plays her lute for him. It's so beautiful. I wish I could read it better, it's still hard for me. How old are you?"

"Seventeen. How old are you?"

"Fourteen," she lied. "How long have you been in America?"

"Oh, six months, something like that."

"And do you like this kind of work? Kidnapping people?"

He shrugged. "I have no choice. My family brought me over here, and I have to do what they say."

They heard footsteps approaching. Lucy put her hand on his arm, which was warm and smooth. "Brother," she said urgently, "please don't tell them I speak your language. I think they would get angry if they knew."

Cowboy stared at the little white hand on his arm. He nodded sharply and moved away as the other two men came back into the room. Kenny Vo, their leader, had apparently been contacted and was on his way. They sat back against the wall, chain-smoking, and talking about women and gambling and teasing Cowboy. Lucy shut her ears to that and returned to her translating, turning, as the poem recommends, the "scented leaves by lamplight to read the tale of love recorded upon green chronicles." She had progressed to where the sisters Van and Kieu (both beauties, but Lucy decided to forgive them that, and besides, Kieu was possessed of a deeper charm and talented as well) were lamenting over the grave of a famous beauty of the past who had been betrayed and died of it, when Kenny Vo walked in and started barking orders. Vo had a family resemblance to his brothers, bearing a version both of Needlenose's sharp features and Sharkmeat's muscular bulk. He moved and spoke with casual brutality, and when he looked at Lucy it was as if he were looking at some inanimate and unappealing package, a sack of elderly chicken parts in need of rapid disposal, for example.

"Get her in the trunk," he ordered. "Cowboy, watch the street."

This *was* frightening. Lucy had always disliked enclosed places, and the dark, and being constrained, and so her control gave way, and she fought, and having been trained in boxing from an early age, she got a few good shots in before she was slapped silly by Sharkmeat and stuffed in the trunk of a Lincoln. Her bag was gone, but she had Tran's book shoved down her waistband. An interminable, painful ride over New York's infamously ragged paving, and then they popped the lid and threw a stinking blanket over her and hauled her indoors. She ended up on a mattress in what looked like the finished basement of a suburban house, a window-less room, panelled in cheap pine-look sheeting, with red and black linoleum on the floors. There were two doors, one locked, the other leading, de-lightfully, to a tiny bathroom. She used the toilet and then checked herself out in the medicine-cabinet mirror. Bruises on cheek and jawline, and a big smear of blood down her chin and spattered on her T-shirt from where her nose had bled: a mess. She washed her face gingerly and dried off with wads of toilet paper.

She went back into the other room, sat on the mattress, and listened. She heard the sounds of sev-eral men walking and speaking some tonal lan-guage, but could not make out what was being said. The Vo boys, she presumed, and maybe the Chi-nese guy. The talking became louder, turned into an argument. She heard stomping, slammed doors. From outside came the sound of car doors. A car started up and pulled away. Could they have left her here alone? No, she heard steps above. Sighing, she drew out the book and rolled over onto her belly. She translated:

> Since time out of mind, cried Kieu,
> harsh fate has cursed all rosy faces, sparing none.
> As I see her lie there, it hurts to think
> Of what will come to me hereafter

An unpleasant thought; she wished Tran would hurry the hell up.

10

KARP WAS DINING IN COLUMBUS PARK behind the Criminal Courts Building, using the twenty minutes he had to spare between his briefing of Jack Keegan and his appointment to address the incoming class of ADAs. He sat on the edge of a park bench, leaning over his spread knees, head down and slurping noisily, a position necessary if one wished to eat a sausage, fried onion and pepper hero laden with hot sauce and oozing grease without collecting souvenirs of the meal all over one's immaculately pressed suit. An occasional pigeon darted in between his shoes to sample the dropped bits. Karp noted that the birds always dropped these after a taste, and took an odd comfort in the fact that his normal lunchtime diet would gag a New York pigeon. There appeared now in his restricted field of view a pair of gleaming faux crocodile loafers decorated with gold-colored clasps, above which were black silk socks, above which were the legs of a brown pinstripe on tan wool suit. A deep voice said, "Nice day for a picnic, Stretch. They said I'd find you out here, and here you are."

Karp carefully deposited the ragged and soggy

sandwich on a square of waxed paper and looked up. He saw a smiling solid man in his early fifties, broad-shouldered and half a foot shorter than Karp himself, with a brush mustache and graying sideburns on his mahogany face. Captain Clay Fulton was Karp's first and best friend on the police force. A dozen years his senior, Fulton was the first black college-educated detective captain in the department's history, highly decorated, feared and mistrusted by the department grandees, and hence left pretty much on his own. Officially, he ran the D.A. squad; unofficially, he was more or less Karp's private police force, which amused him, and kept him virtually free of the cop bureaucracy he despised.

"It is," Karp agreed. "Get yourself something from the wagons and sit."

Fulton made a face and sat down. "I used to eat like that when I still had a stomach. You know, Stretch, when you're a big shot you're supposed to have lunch in a restaurant, the waiter brings you the food, the kitchen got a health permit, you bask in the admiring glances of lovely women . . ."

"I'm practicing for when I get fired. You got any good news for me?"

"About this Lie character? Not to speak of. The prints came back zilch. Not known on NCIS. We're trying Interpol, but that'll take awhile."

"Try the Hong Kong police."

"You think he's from there?"

"It's a good guess. All these Chinese bad boys check in there sooner or later. Where did he go after I threw him out?"

"Downtown, an office building. His lawyer's place, but they didn't stay there long. They hopped a cab back up there." Here he jerked a thumb over his shoulder in the direction of the federal building. "They went in, and about an hour later the lawyer came out alone."

Karp nodded. "So they did a deal. Lie probably went out of the garage in one of those black-window vans with a couple of FBI guys to keep him company. He's eating his chow mein in a U.S. government safe house as we speak."

"They definitely did a deal. The feds rousted Joe Pigetti out of the La Roma restaurant twenty minutes ago."

"See, that's what we get for being honest guys. We get to finish our lunch."

Fulton said, "You thinking now you should've grabbed him when you had him, maybe."

"Not on the terms he was offering. Next time I grab him, he won't be doing the bargaining."

"You're mighty sure of that, considering you got jack shit solid on the man."

Karp resumed his lunch, leaning forward, saying between bites, "Clay, the guy's dirty. All you got to do is find the dirt."

"Oh, we'll look, all right, but it's Chinatown. And I thought I taught you to avoid betting on the come."

"I have perfect faith in your talents," said Karp, balling up his waxed paper and napkin and tossing it ten feet into a trash basket.

A shadow fell on them, and they both looked up to see a ragged, ashy black man pushing a shopping cart full of stuffed plastic bags. "Spare some change, brother," the man said to Clay.

Fulton pulled a money clip out of his pocket, peeled a single off, and gave it to the man. "Take care, pop," he said.

"Pop yourself," said the man. "You old enough to be *my* daddy." He rolled his establishment away, grumbling.

"No good deed goes unpunished," said Karp.

"You said it, man, and to think that at one time that guy was an assistant district attorney. The man just wouldn't stop betting on the come."

Karp laughed and pointed with his chin across the park. "No, *there's* the lawyer. See her legal pad?" It was the old woman Karp had met previously, sitting in the shade of a tree, scratching away with her pencil. She raised her head, peered across the dusty lawn, made getting-under-way motions, and waved to Karp. Who rose hastily and said, "Clay, I got to go before she comes over here and starts bending my ear. She's got me confused with the court of appeals. Keep in touch."

The call from Freddie Phat's watcher came in at a little past three, and about five minutes later Tran got the word that the Vo gang had dragged a blanket-wrapped bundle into their Brooklyn house. It took him forty minutes to drive his motorcycle from Manhattan to Avenue J in Brooklyn, via the Battery Tunnel and Ocean Parkway. He parked across the broad boulevard, crossed it, and walked up to the door of the modest two-story semidetached house.

He rang. He saw part of a face looking out through the slats of a venetian blind in the front window. The door opened, and the large Vietnamese who opened it scowled and said in halting Cantonese, "Fuck! Where you been, man? They went looking for you."

"The girl is here?" asked Tran.

"Yes. I must go page my brother now. Wait here."

He turned to go, but Tran did not wait. Instead Tran slid his great big Colt .45 Commander out of his waistband and slugged Sharkmeat over the head with it. The man grunted and dropped to his hands and knees. Tran kicked him hard in the short ribs, and he fell over onto his side.

Tran quickly knelt and jammed the muzzle of his pistol into Sharkmeat's ear.

"Where is she?" he asked in Vietnamese. Blood seeped up around the grinding muzzle, covered the front sight blade, and filled the little channels of Sharkmeat's ear.

In a while, Sharkmeat told him where, and also that he was alone, even volunteering that the door was locked with a padlock, the key for which was hanging on a nail by the basement door. Tran whipped out a pair of heavy-duty plastic cable ties and trussed the man up hand and foot.

"What took you so long?" asked Lucy, who was waiting at the door when Tran burst through, she having heard and interpreted the unpleasant noises that had lately come from above.

He looked at her face a moment and said, "Who did this to you?"

"It's nothing, Uncle Tran, really. Let's just go."

He grabbed her by the wrist and yanked her roughly behind him, up the stairs and to where the Vietnamese lay bound.

"Him?"

"They all did, come *on*, Uncle . . . no, *don't* do that, please, *please!*" Struggling, she managed to get between Tran and the bleeding man, so that Tran had to stop hitting him with his pistol, and knelt, breathing hard, like a blown horse.

Tran wiped blood and bits of broken tooth from his pistol barrel on Sharkmeat's shirt front, and then he stood up, grabbed Lucy's wrist again, and pulled her out of the house and across Ocean Parkway, Lucy protesting and demanding to be released all the way. Tran lifted her onto the pillion seat, cranked the motorcycle, and sped northwest to the Battery Tunnel. After reaching the Manhattan side, Tran turned into a narrow side street and stopped. He reversed himself on the seat and faced Lucy, his eyes terrible.

"How?" he demanded in Vietnamese. "How were you captured, and by the Vo brothers, too, who are turtle heads, crude thugs—how?"

"I found the book, Uncle Tran. And I was reading it, translating it, on the subway, and I got too caught up in it, I guess. . . ."

"On the subway? You were reading on the *subway*? You are supposed to watch on the subway. You read behind locked doors. How did they take you on the subway?"

"They didn't. I mean, I spotted them after I missed my stop, and then I ran but they grabbed my bag and I followed them out . . ."

"You *followed* them? Did I understand that you *followed* them?"

"Yes, see, they took my bag. With your *Tale of Kieu* in it . . ."

Tran grimaced and stuck all his fingers in his mouth and chewed them, growling.

When this fit concluded, he shouted at her, "Imbecile child! For a book? You put your life in danger for a *book*? Are you *insane*!"

And then, of course, Lucy did what she hadn't done yet, which was break down and blubber like a three-year-old, the deadly fear boiling up now that she was safe, but also because of the unfairness of Tran, to be angry with her when she had saved his relic, and so he had to comfort her, dragging her down the seat and pressing her against his small, iron-hard chest, and stroking her dirty, damp curls until she was calm again. He gave her a clean handkerchief to mop herself up, and he said, in gentler tones, "My very dear idiot child, we must decide what we are to do now. The Vo will be angry about this, and they are as relentless as hungry dogs. I cannot guard you every minute of every day. Therefore, we must remove the Vo."

"You intend to kill them?" she asked, a mixture of awe and disgust in her tone.

Tran rolled his eyes. "Of course I don't intend any such thing. Where do you get these ideas? No, we must go to the police and they will arrest them. They committed very serious crimes, and it will be better for us if they are in prison."

Lucy gaped, astounded. It was like hearing that the president of Pepsi was thinking about putting

Coke machines in the corporate headquarters snack bar. "The *police*! We never go to the police."

"Well, yes, as a matter of fact we do. Your mother has made it a principle never to engage in any activity that the police and the courts can do better—"

"My *mother*!" cried Lucy in an unpleasant sneering voice.

"Yes, your mother, who will, of course, have to be told of this. And your father also."

"You would *tell* them!" she cried, tears welling once more. "Traitor! I will never speak to you again as long as I live." She jumped off the pillion seat and flounced away, in the direction of Broadway. Tran cursed and called after her, but she didn't stop. He kicked his motor into life and followed her down the street.

She walked on, ignoring him, her back stiff and straight as a mast. Tran found himself quite baffled; his long career as a terrorist and guerrilla leader had not prepared him for combat with an American teenager in a snit. In time they reached Broadway, at which point Lucy stopped, turned, and came up to him.

"Go away!" she commanded.

"Lucy, have some sense," Tran said. "Get on the motorcycle and we will go someplace quiet and talk. You must be hungry—"

"No! You see that policeman over there?" She pointed to where a blue-and-white was parked, its occupant out ticketing cars. "If you don't go away, I will tell him I am a frightened little girl and you are the bad old man who has been following me and that you hit my face."

Tran took in a startled breath, so long and deep that his nostrils pinched and whitened. Without another word he swung the machine away and roared off back the way they had come. Lucy watched him disappear, feeling empty. Really empty, for she was starving as well as spiritually desolate. She had no money for food, but she did have a subway token. She never left the house without one secreted in the little change pocket of her jeans. She walked to Wall Street and took a northbound train, intending to go to Canal Street and home, but at the Chambers/Centre Street stop, she jumped to her feet, impelled by a pressure she could not have described, but which could not be resisted, and left the train.

"So much for the organization of the office and what you can expect to be doing in your first months here," said Karp. "I want to finish by telling you some stuff I wish someone had told me back when I started here, way back in the second Roosevelt administration." This raised a polite titter from the fifteen young lawyers assembled in the jury box of a temporarily vacant courtroom. Karp stood in the well of the court facing them, incidentally demonstrating how to stand in the well of a court and talk to a jury, which it seemed to him some of these kids might not know how to do, so green were they.

"First of all, you all have something in common, besides being lawyers. Can anybody guess what that is?"

The group looked around at one another speculatively. Eight men, seven women, four black, two Hispanic, one Asian, the rest white, or white-ish. Nobody had a clue.

"I'll tell you," said Karp. "Every one of you participated in a competitive sport. Most of you are team athletes, but we have a varsity sprinter, a couple of state-level tennis players, two women's varsity crew oars, and a junior chess master. This is not an accident. Prosecuting in an adversarial system requires the same kind of competitiveness, endurance, guts, mercilessness, and ability to play when hurt that're necessary to succeed in sports. Just like sports, this game is about winning under a set of rules, but it's not all about winning. It's mainly about doing the right thing. Just do the right thing and don't get all concerned about your won and lost record. Doing the right thing and keeping your integrity is important because you're probably not going to contribute much to making the world a better place, not that you're going to be able to see at any rate." Here he paused and looked a selection of them in the eye, using his ever useful Severe yet Compassionate Look.

"This is a *hopeless* job," he said vehemently. "Your work will not help make things better, because we don't understand what causes crime, and it's not entirely clear that punishment, which is what we mostly do here, helps the problem. It may even make it worse. This society, this city, is like a ship that's hit a rock. We don't get to steer it to safety and we don't get to plot the course to avoid more rocks and we don't get to evacuate the women and children.

What we do get is a crummy little office in the bilge of the ship, where we work the pumps, keep the water level down, and prevent the ship from going under entirely. Right now the water's coming in a little faster than we're pumping it out, which sucks, so to speak, but on the other hand, if we stopped pumping, it'd be all over in a pretty short time. What I've just described is damned near the full extent of the job satisfaction: pump, pump, pump, and listen to that water slosh out. That's the *good* part. The downside . . ."—here he waited for the laughter to subside—"the downside is you may screw up and let someone out who should've been in the can, and he does something bad again, and it's on you, he kills someone, say, and it's on *you*." He waited for that to sink in.

"Fortunately, there are ways around both these problems. It turns out there are some objective standards for doing this job, about how to prepare a case for prosecution, and you will find that preparing a case in this way is a source of real satisfaction. Once again, sports: it's great to win, but sometimes the other guys are just better, so you have to be content with just playing your best. Justice and success are not defined by the vagaries of jury deliberations. The only issue for you is whether each case is a legitimate case to prosecute. Are you convinced a thousand percent that the defendant is guilty and that you had legally admissible evidence to prove guilt beyond a reasonable doubt? It's a gem of a system, folks, but it can be corrupted by the people in it. Don't become one of those people! Now, we will ensure that you prepare cases in the proper manner, and that you play your best, by yelling at you when you don't. We have a large number of expert yellers on staff, and you'll meet all of them as time goes on. If you really push at it, and you can take the yelling, you will learn how to prepare cases in such a way that the likelihood of screwing up is reduced to near zero. One final thing: it's never personal. You're doing the law, you're not trying to *get* some guy. You start eating your liver on these cases, in a month you won't have enough liver to make a decent chopped-liver sandwich. Oh, yeah, one final, final thing. You think what I just said is cynical. It's not, it's just hard-boiled. This is a hard-boiled outfit here. It's also the best prosecutorial organization in the free world, because, by and large, it's *not* cynical. I'll tell you what cynical is. Cynical is saying, rules are made to be broken, and then breaking them. Cynical is drilling some poor bastard because you think it looks good in the press. Cynical is letting politics into your legal decisions. Cynical is rolling over for the cops because it's popular and it makes your job nicer if the cops like you. Cynical is not trying because the Supreme Court has tied your hands with all these crime-coddling decisions. Don't be cynical, guys. It's not part of the job, and it's not nice."

Karp looked up as a short brown woman in a dark blue suit came through the door.

"Ah, here she is," said Karp. "Folks, this is Rita Mehta, one of our fine assistant bureau chiefs. Rita helps run the Criminal Courts Bureau, where you'll start your work here at the D.A. Criminal Courts handles the misdemeanors we cop felonies down to when we're feeling cranky, and Rita here is going to teach you how to slap the wrists of hardened criminals."

"Softened criminals, too, don't forget those, Butch," said Ms. Mehta.

The usual relief of nervous laughter. He had noticed some of the kids really listening, not being embarrassed, or just taking notes, as in law school. He turned the group over to Ms. Mehta, got the (also usual) nice round of applause, some worshipful stares, most of them from the women, and left the courtroom.

She was curled up on a couch in his office, reading a small blue book, and when he saw her face, he cried out, "Good God!" and felt a clench around his heart. He knelt down beside her, his face close, examining the bruises. "Lucy, what happened to you?"

"Nothing, I, like, got mugged," said the daughter blandly.

"Mugged? Where? Did you report it? Did the cops bring you here? What—"

"Dad, settle down. I'm not hurt. It looks a lot worse than it is. But I have to talk to you, *now*. I think I'm in trouble."

Karp drew up a straight chair and sat down on it, his heart pounding. There was an instant of ice-cold, ignoble rage against his wife (why isn't she *watching* this child?), which he suppressed, and a cacophony of head voices suggesting modes of trouble—drugs, thefts, sex, diseases—which he could not. He swallowed hard and asked, "Felony or misdemeanor trouble?"

"Um, well, *I* didn't do anything bad, but there's like a big felony *involved*."

"You want to tell me about it?"

She looked away from him. "I can't, Daddy, that's the problem. I swore an oath I wouldn't and there are other people involved, and they'd get in giant trouble if I told and they didn't do anything wrong either."

Karp resisted the impulse to switch from Daddy mode into interrogator mode. This was hard on him because he had no doubts about his skills in the latter and considerable doubts about his skills in the former. He made himself say, gently, "That's quite a problem, Luce. How are you going to handle it?"

"I don't kno-o-o-w," she wailed, and started to cry. Karp moved next to her on the couch and swept her into his arms. Lucy was startled by the difference between being hugged by her father and being hugged by Tran, so much so that she stopped crying. She totted up the differences, fascinated. The smell. Daddy was regular American, like the air, a little soap, a little aftershave, clean cotton and wool, Home. Tran was fish sauce, lilac hair oil, motorcycle oil, leather, foreign, Other. The feel. Daddy was large, comforting, deep, summoning thoughts of babyhood, absolute security, the moments before sleep. Tran was hard, protective, too, but like an iron shield, something you had to use, not just sink into, and a wild heat came off him, in her imagination like hugging a leopard. It then occurred to her that once Tran had hugged his own daughter, and that he had not been like that to her, no, he must have been to that girl the same as her father was to her. She tried to imagine Tran different, softer, and then the Asian thing struck her again, the suffering. She was sobbed out by now; still, thick tears trickled down her cheeks. And a last thought, more of a wordless feeling: this sinking safety, delightful as it was, belonged to her past, she was going away from it even now, but Tran, or something Tran-like, was her future. She recalled how she had acted the spoiled baby and threatened him and felt deep, blushing shame.

Karp held his daughter away from him, at arm's length, saw the agony in her face, said as gently as he could, "Lucy, listen to me. You are a kid. This is over your head. You can't handle this yourself. You have to tell me about this, now, the whole story."

"I can't, Daddy."

"Well, then let me tell you what I think I know already," he said, his voice growing sterner. "You witnessed a crime. What crime? A good guess would be the double murder at the Asia Mall. Why? It went down in a place you hang out in all the time. I know you and your pals like to play hide in that storeroom; maybe you were there when it happened and saw who did it. I know you got beat up today, and I doubt it was a random mugging. Somebody was sending you a message. They were telling you to keep your mouth shut. And you're doing just what they want, just what the bad guys want."

"That's not why I'm not telling. I told you, I swore I wouldn't."

"Lucy! Listen to me! This isn't a kid thing anymore. You *have* to tell me."

As soon as this was out, he knew it was the wrong thing to say. She stiffened, and on her face appeared the very tintype of her mother's mulish expression. He changed tack.

"All right, Lucy. You came to me for help. What do you expect me to do? Huh? Hey, great, you're concealing evidence of a felony, here's a dollar for ice cream, run along and play? You know, I swore an oath, too, to uphold the law. I'm not allowed to ignore stuff like this. If you weren't my daughter, I could get a judge to hold you as a material witness, and then you'd be put under guard, and when it came to a trial you would *have* to tell what you knew and if you didn't you could be jailed for contempt and kept in jail until you talked. That's the law."

"Okay, arrest me, then! Go ahead! I don't care."

Karp sighed. "Oh, sh . . . I'm not going to arrest you, okay? I'm in the same fix you're in, kid. I'm your father, you come first, no question. But as of now, I'm breaking the law. So we're both in a pickle."

"Could you, like, lose your job?" she asked. This aspect of the situation had not occurred to her before. Indeed, she *was* over her head.

"I could, if anyone found out about this conversation," answered Karp, feeling horribly guilty at putting this kind of pressure on the girl, but what else could he do?

Lucy wrapped her arms around her head to shut out the tormented choices and buried her face in the cool, smelly leather of the couch. Karp waited. She said something he didn't catch.

"What was that, honey?"

"Kenny Vo," she whimpered.

"Who's Kenny Vo?"

"The guy who beat me up. He's a Vietnamese gangster." She described what had happened to her, and he took notes. His throat and nose ached with stalled weeping. When she ran down, and had another cry, he asked, "Did he do the murders, too?"

She blinked away the silvery tears, and her pale brown eyes stared levelly into his. "I don't know anything about any murders," she said.

"Okay," said Karp, knowing when he was beaten. "Here's what we're going to do. I'm going to get Ed Morris to take you back home, and I'm going to arrange for a policeman to watch the loft. I don't want you going out by yourself until we get this thing cleared up. Do you understand that? Not even down to the store, or to Mott Street, or Janice's. If you can't promise me that, then you really will have to go into protective custody."

"Okay, Daddy," she said meekly, carefully not promising, and to her immense relief, he turned to the phone and did not press her on it.

When Morris, Karp's driver and also a D.A. squad detective specially trained not to ask questions, had taken Lucy away, Karp went to the men's room, splashed cold water on his face, dried it with a towel, and looked deep into the mirror to see if the monster he had become showed much yet. No, not much, which said something for clean living and an absence of cynicism. Karp had been perfectly sincere in his lecture. He was not cynical about the law, was in truth as deeply in love with it as he had been when as a young, dewy bride he had first stepped across the threshold of 100 Centre Street long ago, and was continually amazed at how a system so inherently stupid and run, by and large, by moral imbeciles, kept cranking along, doing as well as it in fact did. What had not come up in the lecture was what to do when dedication to the law ran up against love of family. Marlene's shenanigans were bad enough, but Marlene was at least an adult, and Karp truly believed that if he caught his wife in a conscious felony, he would turn her in. It was different, he discovered, when his child was involved, a child who was turning out more like her mother than Daddy felt comfortable about.

Yes, the mother. Karp went back to his office and placed a furious call to the mother, and, fortunately for his marriage, did not get through. He was too old-fashioned a man to allow himself to express anger to an anwering machine, so he left a mere urgent message. He did the same at her office, and then tried the car phone (nothing) and then left another message at her paging service. He then put his notes into shape for a warrant and called Mimi Vasquez, who was in, and available at that very moment.

Nor was that the only favorable contrast with his wife. Mimi Vasquez was in her fifth year with the D.A. and her second in Homicide, and clearly a rising star, quite apart from her status as a Hispanic woman and thus an affirmative action two-fer. Karp had spotted her as a comer early on, and nudged her career helpfully when needed. Vasquez had the broad shoulders, solid build, and narrow hips of a distance swimmer, which she was, a neat round head, and short thick straight hair, cut close. With her round face, huge dark eyes, flat nose, and tawny skin, she presented the appearance of a not entirely terrestrial creature, a seal perhaps, recruited into the legal profession in exchange for those shiploads of lawyers the jokes are always drowning. She and Karp agreed perfectly on what was important; she was one of those who had instinctively understood his corny lecture and gone on to put principle to the test of action. Not in the least frightened of trials, she'd won a couple of nice ones recently, without becoming obnoxious about it as so many of her male peers did after similar victories. She reminded Karp strongly (and sadly) of his wife, when his wife had been a respectable colleague rather than a loose cannon with a short fuse.

For her part, Vasquez was always delighted when Karp took an interest in her work. Not only did he know a lot, but he was not, like Roland Hrcany, her immediate boss, trying tediously to get into her pants. As to that aspect, should anything unfortunate and permanent befall Mrs. Karp, Mimi Vasquez was perfectly willing to dispense entirely with pants *in re:* Butch Karp, a willingness she shared with any number of women at 100 Centre Street, and of which the object was entirely oblivious.

Upon receiving Karp's call, Vasquez had spent three minutes in front of the glass in the sixth-floor ladies' getting herself into perfect court-appearance order and two minutes after that was sitting in Karp's side chair, legs neatly crossed, ears perked, pad on lap.

"How's the Sing double going?" asked Karp.

"Nothing new since the last time you asked," replied Vasquez, and seeing his frown added, "I realize that's not the right answer, but it's always like that down there, especially in this case, where it looks like an out-of-town job. You know the story: a couple Ghost Shadows hit a Flying Dragon one night on Canal Street, at least there's talk on the block, some history behind the crime, and we can bring in the snitches, not that Chinatown is full of snitches, but the cops hear stuff. Here . . . it's like it never happened. A couple out-of-towners with heavy triad connections in Hong Kong walk into a stockroom, followed by person or persons unknown, and wind up dead. Nobody the cops talked to will admit to seeing anything unusual."

"Who caught it in the Five?"

"Phil Wu."

He waited, but she did not elaborate. "And . . . ?"

"I never worked with him before, but Roland says he's okay. Smart, speaks Cantonese and Mandarin. He had the collar on that pool hall shooting in '81, Bayard Street. He seems to be doing the right things, but . . ."

"Uh-huh. He talk to the Chen family, do you know?"

"They own the place? Yeah, in the original canvass at the crime scene."

"But not afterward?"

"Not that I know of." She gave him an interested

look, scenting something. "Why? You think they're connected?"

"The vics got in through the back door and so did the killer. That back door is always locked. Somebody opened it from the inside. Also, there are always people in and out of that stockroom. If nobody saw anything, then either they're lying or they were pulled away from there."

She was frankly staring at him now, as if he had just produced a live chicken out of thin air. "Jesus, Butch! How the hell do you know all that?"

Karp glanced away, as if embarrassed. "We've known the Chens for a long time. That door is on Howard Street right down from where we live. I've seen delivery guys ringing the bell back there or pounding on the door a million times. It's never unlocked except when they're taking in merchandise."

Vasquez waited a moment and then asked, "So . . . what? You want me to bring in the Chens or . . ."

"Yeah, bring them in. Nothing heavy, but you need to find out whether there've been any threats, keep your mouth shut or else. Re-interview the whole staff there too. Explain to everyone that keeping information from the authorities is a serious crime, and so is threatening people who have information about a crime. Get Wu to explain things in Chinese just to make sure they understand."

She wrote rapidly on her pad and then looked up again. He asked, "You ever hear of a Kenny Vo? Some kind of Vietnamese thug?"

"Doesn't ring a bell. Is he involved in the Sing double?"

"It's possible. Swear out a warrant and have him picked up. He's got an associate with a busted face, so have them check the emergency rooms. The charges are kidnapping one and assault two. Here are the details." He passed a sheet of yellow bond across the desk. She read it and gaped.

"Your *daughter*?"

"Don't ask, Vasquez," he said. "Just do it, and when you've got the son of a bitch I want to see him. And make sure Roland's in the loop on this. Go ahead," he ordered, blocking the questions he could see forming in her eyes. "Do it now!"

After Vasquez left, he stared at the door that closed behind her, his ordinary impulse to action quite overcome by confusion and dull despair. Over the years he had become used to Marlene's quasi-legal and perilous lifestyle and had even accepted that it might involve some danger to their children—Manhattan was in any case a risky place to raise kids. Karp was good at accepting things he couldn't change. But the idea that Lucy was *on her own hook* getting into Marlene-style trouble had struck him like a clout on the ear. It was not to be borne. It wasn't fair. He didn't deserve this.

Karp was several leagues into the sere and unfamiliar country of self-pity when the phone rang. Listlessly he raised it to his face and spoke his name.

"Butch? It's me. What's so urgent?"

"Where are you?"

"At Mattie's. What is it?"

"Oh, not much. Your daughter was kidnapped and beat up today while you were out solving everybody else's problems." He heard a quick gasp over the wires, and then Marlene asked in an over-controlled, even voice, "Is she all right?"

"Yeah, she got out of it with a shiner and a bloody nose. She's home and I got a cop watching the place. Marlene, what the *fuck* is going on? Will you please *tell* me before you get our kid killed?"

"*I* get . . . ? What the hell are you talking about? You think *I* was involved in getting her . . ."

"No," he shouted, "*I'm* the one who's modeling semi-criminal behavior, and sometimes not so semi either. Jesus, Marlene, she's up to her little ears in a double murder, and those fucking Chinese pals of yours are in on it, too. You better tell me what the hell is going on, because if I don't get some straight answers right away—"

"Oh, *shut up*! How dare you accuse me of endangering my child!"

"No reason, except you've done it about a *dozen* times that I *know* of."

"I'm not going to talk to you when you're like this. I'm hanging up."

"Marlene, don't you dare put down that phone! Marlene . . . ?"

He heard a scream over the phone, coming as from far away, and then a loud bang, and then more screams, and a string of pops that sounded like firecrackers, but which Karp doubted very much were firecrackers.

"Marlene, what the hell. . . ."

"Oh, Jesus!" said Marlene, and then, "Butch, I got to go now."

He yelled her name a couple of times into an instrument unmistakably dead and, slamming it down, cursed fervently to the unsympathetic heavens. Then, being a good, even a model, citizen he dialed 911 and called in the shots fired and gave the address of the East Village Women's Shelter.

11

MARLENE DROPPED THE PHONE, LEAPED up, and made for the door of Mattie Duran's tiny office, where she was knocked back against a filing cabinet by the incoming proprietor, who did not interrupt her violent Spanish cursing to make an apology. The woman raced to her desk, leaned over it, jerked open a drawer, and came away with her family heirloom, a Colt Peacemaker .44 caliber revolver, like the ones cowboys shoot in the movies, but this one was real and it worked. More shots sounded; above, a child began to shriek in terror. Marlene got out a feeble "Hey, wha—" but Mattie had already gone off at a run, the sound of her steps echoing in the narrow hallway. Marlene ran after her, unlimbering her own weapon, yelling for Mattie to for chrissake wait up.

A nice little firefight was under way in the shelter's reception room. Marlene could not see anything much because Mattie had halted in the doorway, but she could hear the sound of a heavy pistol firing and the snap and thunk of bullets flying and striking the walls and floors and furniture. A man was yelling obscenities in the entrance hallway, beyond the door with the glass window, now shattered. Mattie raised the big Colt and took aim.

Marlene felt the rage rise in her; these *morons*, and Mattie Duran not the least of them, were going to keep shooting until someone was dead or a stray round traveled up into the building and struck some kid. Unlike most people, Marlene when enraged did not start shaking and doing irrational things. Instead she became preternaturally cool, steady, and calculating. Scholars who study men in combat have discovered that this anomalous condition is present in about two percent of soldiers, who make up the vast majority of both heroes and the perpetrators of atrocity. An odd gift to bestow on a Sacred Heart girl from Queens, but there it was, and Marlene used it now, first throwing a solid body check into Mattie, knocking her against the door frame and, not incidentally, ruining her aim. The Colt boomed in Marlene's ear, deafening her. Then she was past Mattie and into the anteroom. Vonda the guard, she noted in passing, was crouched behind the thin protection of her steel desk, her face a ghastly greenish-tan, trying to clear the round jammed in her shotgun, while confronting her from the doorway were two obvious Mafiosi, one shooting, the other crouched low, changing magazines on a large chromed pistol. Marlene strode directly up to the two amazed men, firing rapidly, every shot finding its mark in a disabling but non-lethal place, the guy on the left going down with two through the shoulder and one through the other bicep (his gun rattling onto the floor) and the second taking a bullet through his raised kneecap; he went over like a ninepin, howling. Marlene kept moving, kicking their guns out of reach, passing the shattered inner door and up to the shouting man in the hallway.

This, as she had expected, was Little Sally Bollano, singing an aria in which the words *cunt*, *fucking*, *stupid*, and *bitch* appeared repeatedly in uninteresting combinations. Little Sally was locked from behind in the embrace of an enormous neckless man who filled the hallway like a cork in a bottle. This was Lorenzo Mona, Larry Moon as he was known, the Bollanos' leg breaker and Little Sally's personal bodyguard. Marlene read confusion and dismay on the vast, lumpy face: he couldn't let the boss proceed farther toward what had become a free-fire zone, nor did he have the gumption to roll the little shit under one arm like a newspaper and carry him out of there. Marlene attempted to resolve his confusion by pointing her smoking nine at Little Sally's low forehead. "Out! Get him out of here!" she shouted. This had the effect of redirecting Little Sally's attention from the absent wife to the woman just in front of him, and he launched his signature *fucking*, *stupid*, *cunt*, and *bitch* at Marlene, together with a shower of fine spittle. He seemed not to notice the gun pointed at him, and on closer examination Marlene could see why: his dark pupils were contracted to the size of elementary particles. As per his rep, Little Sally had medicated himself before attempting a complex mission, with the usual result.

While Marlene considered her next move, whatever it would have been was preempted by the sound

of thumping feet and shouts of "Freeze! Freeze!"
Marlene looked around Lenny Moon's bulk to see
the face of a terrified young cop. He was pointing
his .38, perhaps for the first time in real life, at her
in the approved two-handed grip, and she saw with
remarkable clarity that it was cocked and that the
hands that held it were trembling. She would have
been happy to freeze, but the cop changed his tune
to "Drop that fucking gun! Now! Now!" She could
see his finger tightening on the trigger, the knuckle
turning white. Make up your mind, sonny, was her
thought, and also, oh fuck, what a stupid exit, shot
by an infant cop, at which moment Lenny Moon,
straining to look over his shoulder at this new
source of potential danger to his charge, relaxed
slightly his grip, whereupon Little Sally got an arm
free and sucker-punched Marlene in the jaw.

It was a good solid shot: Marlene saw the familiar blazing lights and fell to the floor, where Little
Sally connected with a couple of hard kicks to the
side of her skull. After that she saw through pain-
fed mists an impossible number of dark blue-clad
legs towering above black, thick-soled shoes, and
felt herself frisked and rolled, and cuffed. She heard
shouts and more rude language. She blacked out
momentarily, relaxing into the puddle of warm
blood that had gushed from her bitten lip and
tongue, and the next thing she was aware of was being hustled out by a couple of cops and tossed into
the rear of a blue-and-white (of which there seemed
to be unreasonably many on the street in front of
the shelter), the driver of same complaining that the

bitch was going to bleed all over his vehicle, until an authoritative voice told him to shut the fuck up, Chapman, and he got in and drove off. Marlene lay back in the cool, disinfectant-smelling plastic, and gladly abandoned all responsibility for herself and others, which is one of the very few pleasant features of being arrested.

When his wife got into violent-felony trouble in the County of New York, which she did more frequently than your regular Smith College, Yale Law grad, Karp naturally had to recuse himself from any involvement in the procedural aspects of the case. He interpreted this, however, as not forbidding the conveyance to him of information about her fate from various sources, for it is no fault to keep one's ears open; God, after all, did not provide us with earlids, and the criminal justice system was chock full of people in the know who wanted to do the chief assistant D.A. a favor. Thus he learned in short order what had gone down at the EVWS, that his spouse had shot two Mafia soldiers and had been written up for assault in the first degree, that she had been punched out, that Little Sally's wife, Vivian Fein Bollano, was a shelter resident, that Little Sally and his three fuglemen were in custody on a variety of serious charges, and that the bunch of them, including Mattie Duran, were in the cells at the Ninth Precinct waiting for transport to central booking.

Replacing the phone after the last of several informative phone calls, Karp swiveled around in his big leather chair and stared out the window. He placed a pencil in his mouth and tapped out the rhythm of "Yellow Rose of Texas" between his upper and lower teeth with plenty of grace notes, as his mind drifted like a hang glider through the twisted canyons of the present situation. After four choruses he re-swiveled, stuck the pencil behind his ear, and picked up the phone.

The words "urgent," "emergency," and "Marlene," got Harry Bello out of the meeting he was in and onto the phone. Karp explained what had happened at the shelter, and Harry listened without asking a lot of dumb questions. Karp and Bello were not friends, but Karp thought the guy was a pro, as he himself was, and they both agreed that Marlene was definitely *not* a pro in her chosen field of endeavor and was bound to fuck up big-time, as now, so they had a basis.

"I'll go bail her out," said Harry. "We're covered for this kind of thing."

"Yeah, she's got community ties and a job. It shouldn't be through the roof. By the way, Harry—this Bollano woman she was seeing, could you fill me in a little on that?"

"She's a client's about all I can tell you, Butch," said Harry after a judicious pause.

"You think she might know something about the Catalano hit, that's why she took off from the happy home?"

"I couldn't say, although, considering the husband, she wouldn't need that much of an excuse."

"You think *Marlene* has any information about that, the Catalano thing?"

"I couldn't say. Marlene knows all kinds of stuff. As you know."

Karp laughed. "Okay, Harry, go get her. Tell her there'll be a lamp in the window."

Karp hung up, rose, grabbed a pad and the pencil, and walked over to the D.A.'s office, where he consulted the printed daily schedule O'Malley kept available to staff. Keegan was booked solid all through the afternoon. Karp regarded the three suits waiting for the next appointment, leaned down, and said sotto voce to O'Malley, "I need five minutes before these guys go in."

"It better be something," said the secretary. "These are the boys from Albany on the budget bill."

"He'd want to know," said Karp. "I guarantee it."

She nodded assent. Karp waited, and in ten minutes the door to the inner office opened and Keegan came out with a monsignor, a priest, and a nun. He shook their hands warmly, his eyes at the same time darting over the Albany group and then alighting on Karp, who discreetly extended five fingers. Keegan passed the religious party through, shook hands all around with Albany, made a graceful excuse, and motioned Karp to follow him in.

"Christ on a crutch!" he exclaimed when Karp had given him a telegraphic version of the recent events in the East Village. "That woman doesn't have the sense God gave a cat."

"She has her little ways," Karp allowed.

"At least she didn't kill them, that's something. All right, I'll get Sullivan to handle it. That all?"

"No. You notice who was conspicuously absent from the business at the shelter?"

Keegan wrinkled his brow. "Joe Pigetti?"

"Uh-huh. Who's supposed to mind Little Sally so he doesn't shoot up speed and pull shit like this? He's not there because the federales picked him up today on the say-so of our Chinese friend. So it appears that in one, as they say, fell swoop, the Bollano main guys have been put out of action. One killed, one arrested for various federal crimes connected with the murder of same, and one led to commit a variety of violent acts—and who tipped him off to where his wife was hiding out, I wonder? If Marlene hadn't stepped in, we could've had a couple killings, maybe more, all on Little Sally."

"So?"

Here Karp paused, wrinkled his nose, and took a long, noisy breath, as if checking the age of a suspect mackerel.

Keegan nodded a couple of times and said, "You're saying that someone has a hard-on for the Bollanos and they're, what? Using us to take them out?"

"If so, it's a subtle play. At the risk of political incorrectness, you might even say *oriental* subtlety."

"Our Chinaman."

"It wouldn't surprise me," said Karp. "I've already got Fulton on the case, and I'm going to V. T. Newbury from Fraud and put him on it. He's the best paper guy in the business. This Lie has to be connected to something bigger than a Chinatown gang and a mob shooting."

"Okay, make it happen and keep me posted.

Now, scram! I got to talk about money with these apple knockers."

"I'm gone. I'm taking off the rest of the day, by the way. Besides Marlene, my daughter got mugged this morning."

"Jesus! Is she okay?"

"A little shaky, maybe," said Karp, rising to go. "I'm going to complain to the D.A. about crime in the streets."

"You look like shit, Marlene," said Harry Bello.

"I *feel* like shit, Harry," said Marlene glumly, which came out, "I seel ike sit, Ahee," because of the swelling of her lips and tongue. They were in an interview room at the Ninth, an irregular meeting, but Harry still retained some clout from his years on the cops and, of course, everyone knew who the husband was. Harry wanted to hear the story before the Osborne Group lawyer got there.

"Besides that, how was your day?"

She had to laugh, a high sound that lasted a little too long. "Actually, until Butch called and said Lucy got beat up, I was having a pretty good one."

His eyes widened. "Lucy got beat up?"

She placed a calming hand on his arm. "It's okay, Harry, she's okay. I'll take care of it."

"Bullshit, you'll take care of it. You can't take care of yourself. Who did it?"

She took her hand away and her look hardened. "Don't get involved, Harry, all right? It's got nothing to do with you."

"I'm her godfather, Marlene."

"Good, so protect her from the flesh and the devil, but don't butt into this. You want to hear the story or should I go back to the cells? It hurts when I talk."

He relented, nodding. "Okay, go ahead. You had this great day."

"Yeah, this morning I was at the abortion clinic in Chelsea, to check on the security construction. It's going good, Ms. Reiss-Kessler is very pleased. My views on abortion did not come up, I'm back in the club. Like you said, you never know. The cops got the guys who did it, some sect in Jersey. All but one of them. You heard about this? The actual shooter got away, name of Reginald P. Burford. Blasted his way through a roadblock and escaped to the wilds of New Jersey. I didn't know Jersey had any wilds, but apparently they do, down there in the Pine Barrens, lots of little villages full of skinny blond people with their eyes too close together. Reginald is from there. It's like looking for a Mafioso in Sicily. Anyway, me and Ms. Reiss-Kessler had a nice chat, she wanted to know if we could arrange firearms training for her staff, maybe she could branch out into making non-flushable corpses. I managed to dissuade her from this. Then lunch. I fed the dog . . ." She stiffened. "Jesus, Harry, the dog's still in the back of the car. He'll be frantic!"

"He'll be sleeping. Don't worry about the dog, I'll take care of the car and the dog. What happened after lunch?"

"Oh. Right, so then I came here—I mean, I went to the shelter to talk to Vivian, tell her what I'd found out already, and get her take on it. And I was holding the big questions in reserve, hey, Viv, how come a nice Jewish girl marries a psychotic mobster? Also what happened? How come out of nowhere you just *have* to investigate dad's death after twenty years? You know, see if I could develop enough report to drop that kind of stuff on her."

"Rapport, you mean."

"Huh? Oh, right, rapport. So, anyway . . ." She seemed to go blank for a moment. Then she blinked and asked, "Sorry. Where was I?"

"You were going to tell her what you learned already. Marlene, are you feeling okay?"

"Yeah, I'm fine. Well, so I go in there, she's looking rocky, antsy, not a stay-at-home, our girl, maybe she misses shopping, getting in the Jag and driving the roads. A little cabin fever. She does pills, too. I tell her I went over the press reports, the background, the trials, disbarment proceedings, transcripts, and all that, and the story is that he was despondent over the loss of his livelihood and that's why he did it, and did she agree, was he depressed in the days before he did it or not? And she said, in effect, horseshit, my father wasn't down, he was always up, full of life, he had money stashed, he had plans for moving to California, starting over. Very passionate. She thinks he got whacked."

"What do you think?"

"No evidence for it. No other parties seen in the area. On the other hand, no suicide note either. The police instigation, from the press reports, looks serious, no editorial suggestion it was anything more than a regular whatchamacallit, a . . . I mean, that he killed himself. I need to talk to your pal Black Jack, though."

"Uh-huh, and what about your big questions? I mean, does she even know you know she's Bollano's wife?" Harry was watching Marlene very carefully, his stomach fluttering, his hands damp.

"No, we didn't get to that yet. I was trying to get her to list all the people involved in the cast then, who were still around and who might know something, and I mentioned her mother and she got upset, no, my mother doesn't know anything I don't, and we fenced around about that for a while, and then my paginator rang and I went down to call Butch, and while I was on the phone the bastards broke in. They must have jimmied the front door, and they used a . . . you know, a thing, a wrecking bar to break through the glass, and she, Vonda, shot at them but missed, and they started shooting at her and then . . . and then I . . ."

She looked up at him, her brows knotted, her thick eyebrows nearly touching. "I can't remember. First they broke the door down with the iron, and then I threw it at my mother."

Harry's reflexes were not what they had been, not after the years of boozing, but he started moving when he saw her good eye roll up in her head, and so he was able to catch her before she fell off her chair.

Karp had himself driven home in a police car, a privilege he rarely exercised, except in direct line of duty, which, he now observed sourly to himself, home had very nearly become, with his daughter a possible witness to murder and his wife behind bars.

The little boys, at least, remained uninvolved in any crime more serious than Deliberate Spill of Apple Juice, two counts (Zik), and Assault With Plastic Brontosaurus (Zak). Karp held court on his lap in the living room, and let both of them off with a warning. Where's Mommy? they wanted to know. Mommy's still at work, he lied. He asked Posie to go ahead and feed the monsters, and asked, "How's Lucy?"

Posie rolled her eyes and pointed her chin in the direction of the girl's bedroom.

"She got home, went in there, locked the door, and hasn't been out once. She's grounded, huh?"

"In a way," said Karp. He went to the bedroom and got out of his suit and into chinos and a faded sleeveless sweatshirt and, sighing, went down the hall to knock at the prison door.

"Lucy, it's me, open up."

Steps, the click of the lock, more steps. He went in. A cassette recorder was playing some sort of odd music, a throbbing, low electronic droning, with a voice over it, husky, insistent, seductive, not singing but speaking in precise short sentences. Lucy had returned to her bed and picked up a small blue book. Karp sat on Lucy's wooden swivel chair and took in his surroundings, as always, with some wonder at the mysteries of how kids turned out. Unlike most children her age, Lucy was neat, almost compulsively so. Her room resembled the habitation of a scholarly nun: a simple narrow bed, with a duvet in the form of the flag of Italy, above it a colorful, rough, gory Haitian crucifix, low bookcases along one wall, the books lined up and arranged by subject and author, on the other wall a desk, excruciatingly neat, sporting a little row of dictionaries between plaster gargoyle bookends, above which a large cork board displayed calligraphy samples, a chart of the 209 common radicals used in Chinese characters, a print of a portrait of an elderly gentleman in ecclesiastic garb (Cardinal Mezzofanti, 1774–1849, once the Vatican librarian and, Karp had been informed, a linguist quite in Lucy's class), a school picture of her eighth-grade class, matted in cardboard, a poster of Bob Marley singing, a glossy photograph of a woman with short blond hair wearing sunglasses and a man's suit and tie all in white, and a colored map of the world, showing in color-coded boxes the languages spoken thereupon, with a scatter of red map pins indicating those Lucy Karp had already mastered.

"Who's the singer?" Karp asked.

"Laurie Anderson," said Lucy shortly, not looking up.

"She's not exactly singing, is she? Not the kind of thing you can dance to."

"I like it. I like the words." Silence afterward.

"Put the book down, Lucy," said Karp after a minute of waiting. "We need to talk."

She huffed and snapped it down on the bed, and sat up against the wall, looking at him with that angry, bored expression every parent of an adolescent dreads to see. She had scrubbed her face and pulled her hair back severely and had changed into baggy black shorts and a white T-shirt printed with the photograph of a professorial-looking man with bushy hair, underneath which was the text COLORLESS GREEN IDEAS SLEEP FURIOUSLY.

"Your mom's in jail again," he said, thinking once more that this was not a sentence he had ever imagined speaking in former years.

"What did she do?"

"Allegedly shot a couple of gangsters trying to bust into the shelter and grab some woman."

"She kill them?"

"No, as a matter of fact, she did not. As I understand it, she waded into a hail of bullets, disabled the two bad guys with four shots, and got punched out in the scuffle when the cops got there. A pretty heroic deed, it seems. Uncle Harry's down with her to help get her through and bail her out. She should be home later tonight."

"Uh-huh."

"Thank you for your concern," said Karp, and was immediately ashamed of the sarcasm. Sarcasm had been a major tool in his own upbringing, and he had resolved never to use it with his own children. It was worry, and tension, and suppressed anger, he supposed. He went and sat down next to her on the bed and placed an arm over her thin shoulders. She was stiff as a tailor's dummy. The Laurie Anderson tape came to an end. Off in the loft they could hear the sound of the TV and the ringing of the phone.

"Lucy, are you okay?"

"I'm fine, Dad."

"You're not fine. You were kidnapped and beat

up today. It's okay to feel a little stunned. Maybe a couple of days at home will do you some good. It shouldn't take longer than that to pick up those guys." No response. He said, "Have you thought of anything else you'd like to tell me?"

"No," said Lucy, and then the door to her room burst open and there was Posie, looking distraught. "Butch! Harry Bello's on the phone, he says it's an emergency."

So it had been. Harry was calling from Beth Israel Hospital. Something was wrong with Marlene's brain, which Karp already knew, but this was different, she was in surgery. This announced, shrieks and wails from Posie, sympathetic crying from the two boys, from Lucy, to Karp's surprise and bemused relief, a cool efficiency. The girl got Posie on an even keel again, comforted the babes, organized cocoa and cookies, dialed the TV to an anodyne program involving space creatures. Karp grabbed his wallet and a jacket, made a call, and headed for the door. Lucy had her sneakers on and joined him.

"I'm coming," she announced.

"You're sure you're up for this, Luce?"

"She's my mother." Looking down at her, Karp saw this fact reflected in the set of her pale little face and the look in her yellow-brown eyes. He grasped her hand, and they walked out together.

They went uptown in an unmarked, siren and lights. Harry met them at the neuro ward. Still in, no news.

"How long has he been here?" asked Karp.

Harry looked over at the corner of the waiting room, where Tran sat, motionless in a green plastic chair.

"About ten minutes after we got in. How did he find out? You got me. He hasn't moved, hasn't gone out for a smoke, and I know the little fucker smokes like a chimney." Harry shook his head and did a sort of shuddering shrug, expressing a desire that such things not be: Italian mommies shooting and getting kicked in the head by Mafiosi and being friends with weird Asian bad guys. As he did this, his goddaughter (and that was *another* incomprehensible thing!) sat down in a plastic chair as far as the room allowed from Tran. Harry and Karp exchanged a glance and afterward looked elsewhere.

Something over an hour later, a small sandy man in green surgical scrubs came into the waiting room and asked for Mr. Ciampi and was surprised when three men and a girl leaped up. When he had got everyone sorted out, the surgeon, a Dr. Nagel, informed them all that Ms. Ciampi was in recovery, that the procedure had gone routinely well, and they could visit with her in about a half hour. He was under the impression that this was a sufficient interaction with the family and was about to toddle off when Karp and Bello both apprised him forcefully of the need to render more information, after which both of them shot questions at him as only a pair of consummately skilled questioners could. So they chatted about transient ischemic episodes and subdural hematomas for some time, the two men standing uncomfortably close, and when they got to the part about possible linguistic impairment, Dr. Nagel was startled to find that the skinny little girl was very nearly as well informed about the neurological basis of speech as he himself was, and he was extremely grateful that the surgery had been a fast drill and drain job and that the woman seemed to be perfectly healthy, because he would not have wanted to explain away any of neurosurgery's innumerable possible fuck-ups to this gang, no, not at all.

Lucy was shocked at how her mother looked when they rolled her into the room. They had cut off her hair and wrapped a turban of bandages around her head, and the big, nasty bruises around her mouth added nothing to her allure. Lucy had in her darkest, most secret, never-to-be-confessed thoughts occasionally wished for her mother not to be so damned gorgeous, and now here it was (if only temporarily), and the eruption of guilt and shame it occasioned overwhelmed the child and she gave a piteous wail and ran from the room. Tran hesitated a moment and then followed in her wake.

Karp cursed softly and pulled a chair up next to Marlene's bedside.

"How are you?"

She gave the inevitable reply, a slurred "Honey, I forgot to duck," and then asked, "What's with the kid?"

"She had a rough day. She'll be okay."

"I look like hell, huh?"

"Heaven," he said. Behind him Harry Bello murmured, "Take care, Marlene. I just wanted to see if you were all right."

"Thanks, Harry."

"You're covered on this; the firm will take care of everything," he said, and left.

"That's a relief," she said. She grasped her husband's hand, hard. "I can't remember anything after I talked to you, about Lucy, except a little at the cells there, with Harry. I knew something was wrong with my brain, but I didn't know how to say it. I couldn't find the words. Would you still love me if I couldn't talk?"

"Somewhat more, maybe," he said, and got a smile. "We have to stop meeting in hospital rooms, Marlene. Marlene?" She had drifted off, the smile still in place. He stayed there, holding her hand, also unable to find the words.

Lucy, meanwhile, had run through a teary blur to an exit door, gone down a flight, and collapsed on a stair, sobbing, her face against the unyielding cold steel of the railing.

"I want to die," she cried, in French, as soon as Tran was seated next to her.

"Yes, I know the feeling," he said, "and yet remarkably, at the times I most wanted death—I was presented with the opportunity to die in a very large number of convenient and glorious ways—I never took them. Also, I observed that death came to people who very much wished to live. So after that I was impressed with the idea that my life might have an interesting purpose, after all, not one I might ever have thought of either. This seemed enough reason to go on, until death should make up its mind to take me."

Lucy snuffled, received one of Tran's infinite

supply of clean hankies, blew, asked croakingly, "What was the purpose?"

"I don't know yet. Maybe it is you. Perhaps I am to teach you how to manage your gifts. Perhaps the fates that gave them to you, in a moment of hilarity, decided that a horrible old Asiatic person would be just the one to make sure you became the sort of woman who could put them to good use."

"I detest my gifts!"

"Allow me to doubt that," Tran said dryly. "In fact, not only do you treasure your gifts but, greedy little thing that you are, you desire those that belong to others. Those of your beautiful mother, for example. How many times have I seen you look at your reflection and recoil, appalled. The envy is, I assure you, quite palpable."

Lucy felt hot bars spring onto her cheeks. "You are disgusting," she snarled, and burst again into tears.

After an interval of silence he said, more gently, "My dear, in the end you are still only a little girl, and greatly loved. Much may be forgiven you."

She fell against his hard chest, sobbing. "It's the *guilt*, Uncle. I can't stand it!"

"Ah, as to that: I know very little of guilt. It strikes me as a useless emotion, since it does the bearer no good and yet does nothing for the person about whom one feels guilty. Shame, on the other hand, is of some value. It can be easily discharged by humble apology and by sincere rededication to one's duty."

This hung in the air for a long moment, during which Lucy stopped weeping, uttered a long, shuddering sigh, wiped her face, blew her nose, drew away, and straightened her back. She said, "I am sorry, Uncle Tran, that I was stupid, and threatened you with the police. I never would have done such a thing. I ask you to forgive me."

"You are forgiven," said Tran. "Now, perhaps we may go and visit your mother."

Karp sat and watched Marlene breathe for a few minutes, assuring himself that she was merely resting, and then he slipped out and went to a pay phone, where he made several calls, one to a court clerk, one to Roland Hrcany, one to the captain of the Ninth Precinct, and one to Clay Fulton. For Marlene was still officially a prisoner in custody, who, when stricken, should have by rights been placed in the prison ward at Bellevue, a concern not noted for its expertise in brain surgery, but those who have deep connections in the criminal justice system often receive special treatment, and Karp, who ordinarily did not approve of special treatment, felt only the faintest blush of shame as he called in chips and arranged it for his wife. Records were jiggered, papers were misplaced. Marlene Ciampi was made to vanish for a time from the cognizance of the law.

Karp walked out of the hospital and hung around in the balmy evening on the corner of 16th and First Avenue for a quarter of an hour until a dark Chevrolet Caprice rolled up to the curb and he got in.

"How is she?" asked Clay Fulton, switching off the engine and the lights.

"Pretty good, considering," answered Karp. "Thanks for coming."

"You had a rough one, Stretch," Fulton said. "What can I do?"

"For starters, listen," Karp replied, and he related the theory about the recent troubles of the Bollano family he had outlined earlier to Keegan.

"And . . . ?" was Fulton's comments when Karp finished.

"What, you don't think that's suspicious, the whole top of the order getting knocked out that way?"

"It happens all the time. Some of the other goombahs figured Big Sally's day was over, the kid is a loser, the capos are snapping at each other, the outfit was ripe for takeover."

"And the Chinese connection, Willie Lie?"

Fulton laughed. "Yeah, Willie. Willie is a card, all right. No flies on Willie."

"How do you figure the connection?"

"Here's how it plays. Pigetti sees the Bollanos are fucked and they're drawing all kinds of heat. He makes a deal with another family, the Gambinos, the Luchese, who knows? To the effect, I'll take care of our guys in a way that will never get back to you, and when I end up on top, you'll accept it. Go ahead, Joe, good luck, they say. Joe gets the Chinese fella to whack Eddie Cat. That's one down. Then he's got to get rid of the Chinese fella, but he misses, and Willie gets spooked and runs to the law, and Joe gets the shaft. The best-laid plans."

"What about Little Sal, and his wife running off just at the right time?"

Fulton shrugged. "Fuck him, the little shithead is crazy. We knew that already. If not that, then something else."

"You think it's all in my head?" Karp asked.

"No, I think what's in your head is you're worried about the kid and this Chinatown business and about Marlene. Jesus, Butch! Your kid gets kidnapped and beat up, your wife's in a gunfight and almost dies from a kick in the head. You expect to be thinking clearly?"

Karp thought about this. He thought he *was* thinking clearly, but, of course, one always did, even in the throes of mania. This is why one needed sensible pals. He made a silly, shuddering sound and rubbed his face vigorously. Fulton chuckled and laid a heavy arm over Karp's shoulder.

"Listen to your Uncle Clay, Stretch. Just focus on taking care of your crazy lady and that kid. I'll take care of the bad guys."

"How is that going, by the way?"

"Fair, so far. Nothing on Willie, but we picked up one of the Vo boys at Kings County, face all beat to shit. We'll need Lucy to look at a lineup when the guy's back in shape. As far as the other three bad boys, we're looking, but . . . you know how it is. Asians: we don't speak the language, they don't talk to cops. These Viet boys travel around a lot, too. Show up in Bridgeport, pull a home invasion, next week they're in Richmond knocking over a jewelry store. I got them out on the wire. We'll see."

Karp popped the door and got out. All of a sudden he felt deeply tired, wobbly in the knees, his head dull, eyes grainy. He leaned in at the window.

"Okay, Clay, thanks. Keep in touch."

The car drove off. Karp walked back to the entrance and met his daughter coming out, accompanied by Tran.

"You all right now?" Karp asked, caressing her hair.

"Yes, I think so. I saw Mom. And I apologized. Tran's taking me home."

An objection hung on Karp's tongue. He'd get a police escort, he was about to say, and then thought better of it, realizing that he had unexpectedly become someone who sends his little girl home with some kind of weird Asian professional assassin or whatever Tran was, not what he had started out as at all, or even imagined. He looked Tran in the face—carved ivory, it looked like in the orange glow of the lights of the avenue. He held out his hand. After an instant's hesitation, Tran took it.

"Thanks for what you did for Lucy. I appreciate it," Karp said.

"No sweat," said Tran.

12

ON THE MONDAY AFTER THE EVENTS at the East Village Women's Shelter, Karp called Roland Hrcany.

"Doing anything for the next hour or so?"

"Why?"

"Tommy Colombo's holding a press conference in ten minutes. He's got his federal grand jury indictments. I want to hear what he's going to do about the Pigetti business."

They walked across Foley Square to the Federal Building and went to the press room on the eighth floor. They got in without difficulty, using their D.A. identification, and stood at the back of the room behind the TV cameras. Inside the miniature auditorium was the usual bedlam—cursing of technicians, the sounds of marshaling and testing media gear, the low, dull roar of the jackal press. Roland was smiles, Karp glum. He hated this, while Roland had the politician's instinct: he understood that in the present age it was not what you were that counted but how you appeared, which was controlled by the fifty or so ladies and gentlemen seated and standing in the hot, bright room.

Nine-thirty came. Karp checked his watch irritably. Colombo was making them wait, just like the president. Roland was trading wisecracks with a couple of print guys. Karp heard him say, "Ah, the lovely and talented!" and turned to see Gloria Eng approaching, trailed by her crew. She gave Roland a professional dismissive smile and focused on Karp.

"How's Marlene, Butch?" she asked.

"Recovering," said Karp.

"Good. No impairment, then?"

"No."

"That's great. I'd really like to do a piece on the raid. Any chance of setting that up?"

"Ask her," said Karp, continuing his well-known tradition of restricting all his conversation with the press to phrases of two words or less, a habit that had earned him among journalists the nickname "No Komment Karp."

Eng made a gesture, and the camera light behind her shoulder went on, blinding Karp as she brought her microphone up to attack position.

"You know, Sal Bollano's lawyer is claiming it was a setup. The story is he and his bodyguards were lured to the shelter so he could be assassinated in so-called self-defense. They claim Marlene was in on it. What about that, Butch?"

"No comment," said Karp.

Eng rolled her eyes and turned to Roland. "Do you have anything on that, Roland? Is the D.A. going to look at this as an attempted murder?"

Roland flashed his perfect set of caps. "Well, Gloria, it's far too early for any speculation on that score. The police investigation is still ongoing."

"But Marlene Ciampi remains in police custody, is that right?"

"As far as I am aware," Roland lied.

"And what about the Catalano murder?"

"That investigation is still ongoing."

"You don't intend to charge Joe Pigetti with that homicide?"

"As I said, Gloria—"

"Is it true that a witness to that murder presented himself to the district attorney's office and you turned him away?"

The smile vanished from Roland's eyes, and involuntarily they flicked over to meet Karp's. Gloria Eng's smile broadened, because she now had tape of the Homicide Bureau chief looking shifty in response to her questioning. Roland cleared his throat. "Gloria, we, ah, get any number of people coming in and claiming to be witnesses to crimes. There's an assessment procedure that we go through, and I would venture to say . . ."

A venture aborted, for Roland was saved from having to concoct a load of nonsense by a stir at the front of the room. The man himself walked across the little stage and took up position at the podium behind the Justice Department seal and a bouquet of microphones. The room settled, the lights flared, the cameras hummed. Thomas Colombo looked at what he had wrought and apparently found it good, for the small man seemed to inflate under the focused attention of the onlookers.

"As many of you are aware," he said without preamble, "for the past three months a federal grand jury has been hearing evidence concerning the influence of organized crime on various businesses in this city. I am pleased to inform you that the grand jury has issued twenty-four indictments under the so-called RICO law, that is, the federal Racketeer Influenced and Corrupt Organization statute. This statute is our major weapon against the ability of organized crime to infiltrate and corrupt legitimate enterprise and to launder its ill-gotten revenues. Among the criminal organizations of this city, it is the crime family run by Salvatore G. Bollano that has been most famous for the extent and subtlety of its infiltration. It has sent its grimy tentacles into commercial laundries, food importing, meat cutting, trucking, restaurants, construction, and waste hauling. To cover up these infiltrations, it has bribed and corrupted public officials at all levels, including those in the criminal justice system itself. It has threatened, beaten, kidnapped, and murdered, without mercy, without the smallest shred of human decency. For over thirty years it has operated with impunity, garnering astronomical profits, and hanging like a bloated parasite on the economic life of New York. The head of this organization, Salvatore G. Bollano, and his henchmen have considered themselves immune from the law and from the legitimate anger of the people. I'm here to tell you that as of today, that immunity is at an end."

"He's in rare form," said Roland. "I like grimy tentacles."

"Bloated parasite isn't bad either," said Karp. "But twenty-four RICO indictments seems kind of slim for how long he's been hacking at this."

"All you need is one good one," said Roland.

"Ah, here's the charts and the pointer. I always like the way he snaps his little car aerial out. Do you think it has sexual connotations, these guys and the pointers?"

Colombo had gestured to one of his minions, who had thrown back the cover from a stack of large charts on an easel, and Colombo was indeed probing it with a gleaming extensible steel pointer. First he poked a chart depicting the organization of the Bollano family, then one showing the various businesses it controlled, then a chart summarizing various pieces of paper evidence, phone taps, and grand jury testimony, tying reputed members of the Bollanos to this or that restaurant, laundry, or trucker. It went on, and grew tedious. It seemed that a large number of people with Italian surnames (many bearing colorful sobriquets pronounced by the U.S. attorney with obvious relish) had indeed been very naughty. They had bribed platoons of petty officials and had made threatening calls to good citizens and hadn't paid their taxes and had lied like bandits under oath. Not much juice here yet. The TV people began looking at their watches. Colombo appeared to sense this and moved toward his punch line, snapping his pointer in with a sharp click and turning back to face his audience.

"How did Salvatore Bollano assemble this vast empire of crime?" he demanded rhetorically. "By violence, by murder, and the credible threat of violence and murder. Now murder, as you know, is not a federal crime. But ordering murder to prevent testimony to a federal grand jury *is* a federal crime. Three weeks ago Edward Catalano was scheduled to appear before a federal grand jury. As noted in the chart I just showed you, Mr. Catalano, street name Eddie Cat, was one of Salvatore G. Bollano's closest associates. He knew where the bodies were buried, and I mean that literally, and he was going to tell what he knew. He never got the chance because he wound up with five bullets in his head on the night before his scheduled appearance. Recently, however, a witness has emerged, a witness who will lay the murder of Eddie Cat at the doorstep of none other than Salvatore G. Bollano. This witness is a Chinese illegal alien named Willie Lie . . ." This stirred up a murmur of nervous laughter, and Colombo waited, unsmiling, for it to die away, before continuing.

"Mr. Lie has testified before the federal grand jury, and on the basis of that testimony we issued indictments and have arrested Mr. Joseph Pigetti on charges of conspiracy, interference with a federal prosecution, witness intimidation, and kidnapping in connection with the abduction and murder of Edward Catalano. That concludes my presentation, and I am open for questions at this time."

"Oh, shit, it's going to be a feeding frenzy," said Roland as a forest of hands shot up from the ranks of the press.

No one asked about the various indictments, the ostensible purpose of the press conference. What they wanted to know about was the murder and the mysterious witness. Where was this witness? In protective custody. Why wasn't Pigetti being charged with murder? Colombo was happy to explain that murder was not a federal crime. Murder was, of course, a crime under state law, and the witness, Mr. Lie, had approached the district attorney's office with his information, but the district attorney had refused to act on it. Pandemonium, shouts, urgent wavings. Colombo picked one and got the obvious: why did the district attorney not act?

"I have no idea," said Colombo, his expression indicating that he had a very good idea. "In general, federal investigations enjoy excellent cooperation with local law enforcement, using both state and federal statutes against defendants of this type. After all, we're all on the same side. There are exceptions, of course, in cases where organized crime has compromised local law enforcement organizations."

"Son of a *bitch*!" said Roland, loud enough to draw curious stares from several journalists.

The follow-up question was a no-brainer. Are you implying that this is the case with the New York D.A.? Through a half smirk Mr. Colombo declined to imply anything, asserting that he was interested only in evidence, but that the D.A.'s investigation of the Catalano murder seemed to be in some disarray. The police had come up with a good suspect for the trigger man, but the D.A. had declined to arrest this person. Was there an active federal investigation of the New York D.A.? Mr. Colombo reminded the assembly that grand jury procedures, especially as regards investigations in progress, were closely sealed, but that he intended to vigorously pursue any and all lines of inquiry, no matter where they led, and that was all the time he had for questions, thank you.

"I guess we saw how the pros do it," was Karp's comment as they weaved through mobs of rushing journalists.

"Yeah, a truly brilliant job, the little fuck. He just about accused us of sleeping with the Mob. Jack's going to have twins. And he knew about the Marky Moron business, too. Shit!"

"Hey, we did the right thing there. Cops talk, and Tommy's always got his ears open for bitching about his colleagues," said Karp as they passed through the lobby of the Federal Building. "The story is the putatively mobbed-up D.A. won't get tough with the Bollanos, so the feds have to step in."

"Yeah, and he's going to pressure us to give state grand jury immunity on the Eddie Cat hit. And not just for the Chinaman. He's going to want us to walk Joe P. on it, too. He'll be glad to forget a murder or two or three provided someone drops a dime on the Sallys."

They paused outside the building, before the long, rusted steel Serra sculpture, another federal creation that no one liked but everyone had to live with.

"Don't worry, Roland," said Karp soothingly.

"Easy for you to say. Frank Anselmo is flashing his famous I-told-you-so smile and telling everyone you fucked us up."

"Time is on our side," said Karp.

"Is it? You mean, if we find this Lie is dirty in a previous life. I wish I was as sure as you."

"I met him."

"You did. What are you going on, your famous instinct?"

"That, and the fact that the guy asked for me. Why me?"

"You're in the papers, on TV."

"Yeah, but so are you, so's Jack, for that matter. No, the connection has to be Chinatown, the Chens, Marlene, Lucy . . . something. I live around there, so I'll be more . . . what? More sensitive to the plight of a poor illegal immigrant gangster? Easy to get to if I don't do what they say? Anyway, the guy's not what he seems, and it's just too damn convenient him turning up to pin it all on Joe P."

"I'd like to get my hands on the shooter. By the way, Lie has got a solid alibi. On the night of he was gambling. A couple dozen great and near great of Chinatown saw him."

"So we're looking for two *other* guys. I assume the cops are on it?"

"Balls to the wall, or what passes for it nowadays, but no real leads," said Roland glumly. "How's V.T. coming on the paper?"

"I was just going to go see him," said Karp as the two men entered the courthouse via the special D.A.'s entrance on Leonard Street. "Come on along."

Roland checked his watch. "I'd love to, but I got to see Judge Paine on something. Be nice to have him up there if we ever get a defendant on Catalano."

Karp made a sour face.

"What, you don't like Paine? Heshy Paine? He's got the world's biggest hard-on for the Mob."

"I know that. The problem with prosecutor's judges, as you well know, Roland, is that they're so eager to please that they leave a trail of reversible errors the size of the Thomas E. Dewey Thruway. Give me fair any day."

Roland ignored this last, waved, and went off to his date, leaving Karp feeling like a tendentious jerk. Having someone like Paine in there meant that you'd win your case, and two or three years later the guy would walk on appeal, which did not, if you were Roland and his many epigones, count on your scorecard. When Karp put them away, he wanted them to stay put for a decent interval, just as they had back in the golden age under Garrahy, but he understood that this was a minority opinion in the current age of brass.

Karp went back to his office, checked his messages, found one from his daughter and one from V. T. Newbury. Feeling only somewhat guilty, he called Newbury back first, had a brief conversation arranging for an immediate meeting, and then called Lucy.

"I have to go to the lab," the girl said. "You still have that cop outside."

"Lucy, we haven't got those guys yet. I don't want to take a chance on them trying anything again."

"Tran will be with me. He'll stay with me the whole time. Please, Daddy dear?"

She hadn't called him "daddy dear" in a while, so he adopted a milder tone. What he wanted to say was, okay, Lucy, I know you think Tran is some kind of superhero, but we can't take the chance, et cetera, et cetera, and more paternal bumf as needed, but all he managed to get out was, "Okay, Lucy—"

At which point she shrilled, "Oh, great! Bye," and the phone went dead.

Karp yelled out a curse and redialed. Four rings and the machine picked up. He slammed down the receiver and dialed the first four digits of Marlene's car phone before he recalled that his wife was still in the hospital. Uttering foul language, he then called Columbia information, got Shadkin's lab number, called it. A woman answered and informed him that Lucy Karp had not yet arrived but they were expecting her. And who was she speaking to?

"Oh, never mind . . . her father, tell her her father called and have her call . . . oh, hell, just forget it!"

Who to call? He sat there for a minute, fuming. Call the cops? For what? They were doing what they should, looking for Kenny Vo and company. That damn kid! And what was he going to do when he caught up with her? Give her a *spanking*?

"Should I come back?" V. T. Newbury asked from the doorway.

"Huh? Oh, no, I was just thinking of something." Embarrassed, Karp put the phone down in its cradle.

"I'll say. You were sitting there like a waxwork. I was thinking alien abduction."

Vernon Talcott Newbury came in and sat down in Karp's side chair, crossed his elegantly flanneled legs, and plunked a thick folder on the desk. Newbury was a short, slight, beautifully sculptured man, somewhat younger than Karp, the scion of a family that had helped give Peter Stuyvesant the boot back in 1667, and had been prominent in the

financial life of the city ever since. That such a refined creature should have chosen to labor in the
deep slime pits of the criminal courts was unusual;
that he had stayed made him unique. Karp thought
V.T. was the smartest person currently thus em-
ployed and considered him his best friend. He was
an ornament at the Fraud Bureau, where it was
agreed that when it came to tracking dirty money
and bad paper, the perfect little gentleman (as he
called himself) had no peer.

V.T. looked at Karp closely, a smile hesitating on
his face. "You okay, Butch?"

"Yeah. No, my life is collapsing, but never mind.
What've you got?"

"Marlene all right?"

"Yeah, recovering is what they say. Head trauma,
they like to keep them in there for a while. So, you
find out our guy's secrets?"

"A few. Given the guy, I'd have to say I'm just
penetrating the dew on the apple." He opened his
folder. "Okay, some background. This was explained to me by the nice Mr. Yat over at Citicorp.
The first thing you start with when you want to
trace someone's movements or money is, naturally, his name. With Chinese persons this is not
straightforward. The Chinese character that repre-
sents the name is unchanging, but the way we bar-
barians transliterate it into something we can read
varies wildly, and not just because of the different
systems we use, but because the way a character is
pronounced varies depending on the speaker.
When I say 'varies,' think, oh, English and Portuguese."

"You mean the Mandarin and Cantonese business?"

"For starters. There are *lots* of dialects in China, really they're independent languages, and so in the nineteenth century when they brought the telegraph in, they concocted a standard code for every character, and that's the only way you can figure out someone's real name, by getting him to write down the character and using a code book to look up the STC number, the standard telegraphic code. That's what the Hong Kong cops use to keep track of people. Anyway, we obtained from Mr. Lie's landlord a signature in characters—he says he's Lie Tan Wo—and we faxed it to Hong Kong. His surname came up 2621, fine, but not much help. It's like Smith, only worse, because that particular name is the third most common name in China. It means 'plum.' There are probably sixty million people named Li, or Loei, or Looey. Now, besides those, there are regional variations of any particular name that might not sound anything like Li. For example . . ."

One thing about V.T., Karp now recalled, was that when he got his teeth into something, he went on about it, telling you more than you wanted to know. Besides, the conversation was reminding him uncomfortably of his daughter, sinking perhaps even now into some new oriental miasma.

"Cut to the chase, V.T.," Karp interrupted. "Did you find the guy or not?"

"But this stuff is *interesting*. Jeez, what a grouch! Okay, we also faxed fingerprints and a snap one of Fulton's guys took on the street. I spoke to a Captain Chui over there, and his people ID'd him as Nia Tu Wah. They were very surprised to learn Mr. Nia, that's the surname first here, had shown up in New York. They thought he'd gone to the Yellow Springs."

"Where's that?"

"The land of the dead. He was, or maybe we should say *is*, a hot prospect in a triad called . . . let's see here, Da Qan Zi. It means 'big circle gang' or 'big circle boys.' "

"And who are they?"

"Mainlanders. Big Circle was a Red Guard camp back during the Cultural Revolution. These people are all former Red Guards who got to like kicking in teeth back then and kept up the practice, except now they do it for money instead of for the Great Helmsman. Recently they've been expanding outside of the People's Republic—Taiwan, Macao, Indonesia, and Hong Kong itself—leaning on the local triads. They do drugs, immigrant smuggling, prostitution, plus extortion. Very upsetting to the old-line triads is what I hear. Mr. Nia worked out of Macao."

"Upsetting as in tong war?"

"Triads aren't tongs, but yeah, there's been violence. For example, in Jakarta last month . . ." He stopped and looked at Karp, on whose face he recognized the lineaments of deep thought. Karp was off line, and V.T. waited while the processor hummed. "Yes?" he said when Karp's eyes had unglazed.

"Oh, just something else. You know, we had a double murder in Chinatown the other week.

Apparently a couple of big triad honchos from Hong Kong, father and son. Isn't Macao near Hong Kong?"

"Like the Bronx and Brooklyn. You think there's a connection with Lie? Or Nia?"

"I don't know. I'm worried about Lucy. She's involved in some way in it. Some heavy guys went after her the other day. No, she's okay, but my mind keeps going back to it. She won't tell me anything about it, apparently because she doesn't want to get her pals in trouble, which leads me to believe some of the pals' parents are embroiled in it. It's just one more damn thing."

"Interesting, though. How many triad guys from Hong Kong are in New York at any one time?"

"Fourteen hundred and two, for all we know," said Karp sourly. "There's not a lot of intelligence coming from that sector."

"True, but it strikes me as funny anyway that two of them get whacked and another claims he arranged a murder for the Mob. Maybe that's his regular line of work."

Karp shrugged. This was speculation, and V.T. knew that speculation in advance of any evidence was to Karp the next thing to an indictable offense. It always amazed V.T., who loved speculation himself, that his friend had no interest at all in whodunit, but only cared about how-you-got-'em.

After a vaguely embarrassing pause Karp said, "So what else do you have besides this ID?"

"Not a lot," V.T. admitted. "The guy's illegal, so he has no decent paper and we have no record of entry. He lives in a two-room, third-floor walk-up on Bayard Street, pays cash, no phone, no car, no bank account that anyone can find. The feds, of course, tossed the place pretty thoroughly by the time we got our warrant, so no great finds there. He hangs out in little restaurants, uses pay phones. He's connected with a Chinatown gang called the White Dragons, runs the usual extortion business, supplies guards for illegal gambling games, provides girls for Chinatown big shots. A typical small-time gangster, just like he says he is. Or so it seems."

"Why 'or so it seems'?"

"Because why would a major Hong Kong triad hood come to New York with just the clothes he's walking around in to shake down Chinese restaurants for lucky money?"

"He was a major drug trafficker."

"So he says, but still, it doesn't answer the question why, of all the hoods in Chinatown, he gets picked to whack a heavy wise guy. Then, instead of splitting to Hong Kong or some other Chinese neighborhood where there isn't a chance in hell the Mob would ever find him, he walks in out of nowhere and asks for Butch Karp and spills his guts in return for immunity and protection. Which, when he doesn't get it, he waltzes over to the feds and slips into a federal witness-protection program. This is a guy from a criminal subculture that *never* deals with the authorities. These guys make the Mob look like a flock of canaries. It doesn't make sense."

Karp made once again the deep sniffing noise he

had used with Keegan earlier. V.T. grinned and nodded. Karp related the same suspicions to him.

V.T. said, "So you think somebody is knocking off the Bollano family in a very subtle way, so as not to engage the attention of the other families. The Bollanos are having a little trouble, we'll wait and see what happens. The Gambinos, the Lucheses et al. are watching each other, nobody's making a grab for the territory like they would if it was a full-scale intra-family struggle. And you think the Chinese might be involved?"

"It wouldn't exactly surprise me. I wish to hell, though, I could figure out his game. The guy's on ice. When he gets out, he's not going to be a gangster anymore, he's going to be a protected witness. Where's his win, except staying alive, and you already pointed out the flaw there. All he needs is a ticket to some other Chinatown. Can you see some low-hairline Italians trying to find this guy in, say, Panama City? Or Manila?"

"It'd be nice if we had the actual trigger man in Catalano," said V.T.

"Yeah, it would, but my suspicion is he is never going to give them up unless and until he gets full transactional immunity from all state prosecution on the evidence he presents. Which I am not going to offer. We have to come up with physical evidence, or another witness, or the trigger man or men, so we can put the squeeze on him. I might cut a deal to get the guys who ordered the hit, but I'm not giving this mutt a free ride with as little solid information as we have now. Colombo can play that game, not me. Frankly, I was hoping you'd find a stash of money with Joe's prints all over it or a pocket diary with an entry 'three A.M., commit murder, pick up milk and corn flakes.' You let me down *again*, V.T."

"What can I say, I'm a sack of shit. Talking about games, we don't know what game Hong Kong is playing. We don't know this Captain Chui from a hole in the wall. He could be bent. The real Nia wants to disappear, the cops there get this call from New York, who is this guy? Captain Chui, who's been on the triad payroll for years, says to himself, oh, great, we'll say it's Mr. Nia. That way there's a record of the guy in custody in New York, case closed in Hong Kong."

"Yes, and they all lived happily ever after. It could be *anything*, V.T. This whole thing reeks of fanciness, from the bullet through the clock to Little Sally's old lady in that goddamn shelter. Shit!" Karp rubbed his face, a characteristic gesture of terminal frustration. "I *hate* this crap. It's *wrong*. There's a mind behind this, fucking with us, and I think Mr. Lie knows who it is."

"Maybe, but in any case, the fucking is succeeding. We are fucked. So what's next, boss?"

"The usual. Keep poking. I don't believe in criminal masterminds. Fu Manchu has left the building. There's always something they miss. For example, where's the money?"

"I told you, the guy doesn't have a bank anywhere that I could find."

"Bullshit! I can't believe some of that murder contract didn't stick to his fingers, and besides, the guy's a gangster. A fucking drug lord, to quote our colorful press. Gangsters have cash money, lots of it. It's not in his apartment, so where is it? Known associates? Girlfriends? Like the man said, follow the money. Get the cops to shake and bake down on Mott Street. And don't take any of this oh, it's Chinatown crap. They want to come out of there and play on our court, then they got to play by our rules. Who're you working with in the Five?"

"Phil Wu."

"What's your take?"

"Good. Professional. Speaks the language. Besides that, what can I say—opaque."

"I want to meet him. He's got this double murder, too."

"So you do see a connection. I thought you didn't want to speculate."

"I don't," said Karp. "But I would like to explore the issue with Detective Wu."

After V.T. left, Karp explored the issue some more by himself and decided he needed some information from a source unconnected with the mysterious east, but mysterious enough for all that. He called Ray Guma and got him on the line, and came quickly to the point.

"You know Gino Scarpi, Goom?"

"I know all the Scarpis. I know his older brothers better, but I know Gino, too."

"Have you visited him in the hospital yet?"

"I have not. Gino and I have drifted apart in recent years. You think I should?"

"It'd be a gesture. Go, converse, make him an offer. He's looking at attempted murder, assault one, discharge firearms, reckless endangerment, B and E, attempted kidnap. That can't be pleasant."

A pause on the line. "The Scarpis tend to be stand-up fellas, Butch, I don't know if—"

"Uh-uh, you misunderstand me, Goom. What I'm interested in is off the record, a sidebar. I need to know how they picked our Chinese guy for the hit on Eddie Cat. I mean, do you believe that they just grabbed one of their dope dealers and pressured him to whack a *capo regime*?"

"So you want the background on Willie, nothing you're going to use in court?"

"Deep background. I also want to know how come it was just now that the wife left Little Sal. And how he knew where she was. And between you and me, if he plays nice on that, when it comes to it, we won't drop the courthouse on Gino."

"I'll bring him some cannoli," said Guma.

Karp hung up and, sighing, began work on one of his most tedious jobs, which was his monthly inspection of the various manning charts that attempted to ensure that whenever the criminal justice system required a representative of the People, a live and presumably competent human body would occupy a particular volume of space at a particular instant of time. This was difficult enough during three seasons of the years, but it was well-nigh impossible in summer, when people, including those who worked as ADAs, wished to take vacations. These charts were prepared by a team of trolls down on the fourth floor, but Karp had to look them over to ensure that the hardest workers were not being screwed and that the absolute power of judges to hold court when they pleased (or not, as was more common) did not become too onerous, and also that the various legal constraints on judicial delay were not being violated. He hacked away at this for an hour or so, making notes on a yellow legal pad. He reached the last page of the pad and reached for a new one from the stack on the side of his desk. The top sheet of the one on top had been scribbled on, so he ripped it off, crumpled it, and was about to shoot the paper ball into the waste can that stood on top of a bookcase at the far end of the room, as was his wont, when he paused and uncrumpled the paper. It was, in fact, the sheet that Mr. Lie had been doodling on during his interview. Doodles, yes, and what looked like Chinese characters. He smoothed the sheet out, folded it, put it in his shirt pocket, and then tried to resume work on the charts, but after a few minutes he tossed his pencil against the wall, grabbed the phone and called home.

Lucy answered, as he had hoped.

"How was the lab?" he asked.

"Labbish. What's wrong?"

"Nothing's wrong. I'm bored. Want to go out somewhere?"

"Like where?"

"Where you choose."

"There's a Chinese calligraphy exhibition at the Metropolitan Museum."

"Perfect," said Karp with, to his credit, barely an inward groan. "You can impress me with your brilliance."

"Can Mary come?"

"No, she can't."

"Why not?"

"Because you're my darling and I want to spend a couple of hours alone with you before you get married." There was silence in response to this. Karp continued, "Is your guy around?"

"Tran? He's in and out."

"Tell him he's got the afternoon off. I'm sending a heavily armed policeman to pick you up. Be ready in fifteen minutes."

Karp rang off and pushed a speed-dial button, connecting him with Ed Morris, his driver.

"You need to pick up a witness for me, Ed," said Karp, and gave an address.

"That's your place," said Morris.

"Right. My daughter."

"Uh-oh. Will I need backup?"

"Alert the tacticals just in case."

In the unmarked, driving uptown, Lucy asked grumpily, "Isn't this corruption? Taking your kid out in a cop car?"

"Not in the least," said Karp. "After this we're going to go to the hospital to see your mother, who is a witness in a major crime. As are you. Believe me, this is official; right, Ed?"

"Extremely." He goosed the car's siren, moving a cab slightly out of their way. "See?"

"Then why are we going to the Met?"

"To see the Chinese stuff, and you're entitled to police protection while we do it. Afterward, if you're not satisfied, it's your right as a citizen to lodge a complaint against the two of us. Meanwhile, let me see you smile. Go ahead, it won't break your face."

Lucy managed a thin one, with which the dad had to be content, but somewhat later, in the Asian gallery, the girl's mood lifted. They walked together down the halls of lit glass cases containing scrolls of calligraphy, Lucy occasionally stopping to translate a poem or stopping to stare, transfixed, at one of the cases. Karp spent his time staring not at the meaningless squiggles on brown silk but at his daughter, thinking about paternal love, and fate, and genetics, and about how he, being who he was, should have been landed with this particular child.

After an hour of this, he found her looking back at him. "You hate this, don't you?"

"Hate is too strong a word. But I'll admit that to me it compares unfavorably to an afternoon at Yankee Stadium, Ron Guidry against Roger Clemens."

She laughed. "We could do that, too. But it was *really* nice of you to make the sacrifice. I'm really glad I got to see this."

"My pleasure. Want to see more, or go down to the cafeteria and get something to eat?"

"Eat. I'm calligraphied out."

Seated in the cavernous eatery in the museum's basement, the two chatted amiably about Lucy's experiences at Columbia, the scientists who worked with her, and what they were discovering, about the doings of her friends, movies she wanted to see, her reading, her recent work at the Chinese school, exactly as if she were a regular kid, and he a regular dad. The avoidance of certain topics was hardly any strain, and it did both of their hearts good. Mention of the Chinese school triggered something in his mind, and it niggled at him until, just as they were about to leave, he recalled the yellow sheet in his pocket. He pulled it forth and spread it out in front of his daughter.

She looked at it and frowned. "Terrible characters. Very badly formed. Where is this from?"

"Someone left it in my office. Can you read them?"

"Uh-huh. This is *liang*. It means a roof beam. This is *jí*, which means rank, but it's pronounced *kàp* in Cantonese."

"What does it mean in Cantonese?"

"The same thing, but around Chinatown it's also us. I mean, it's the way our family name comes out. It sounds the same and it's an auspicious character. This one I don't know, this one, *yù*, I know from restaurants, it's 'clam,' these two mean 'each other,' I don't know this one, don't know, don't know, this is 'gain' and this is *lì*, 'profits.'" She frowned at the line of characters, then her face brightened. "Oh, I get it! It's a saying: *yù bùng xiang zheng yú weng dé lì*. Okay, down lower, this here is *yú*, which means fool or foolish . . ."

"Wait a second, I thought it meant clam."

"No, Daddy, *yù* means clam; *yú* means fool. Can't you hear the difference?"

"Nope. What does the saying mean?"

"Oh, something like, when the snipe and the clam wrestle, the fisherman benefits."

"Ah, so," said Karp.

She gave him an interested look, then returned to the page. "All this scraggly stuff I can't make out. This at the bottom is . . . oh!"

"What?"

She was blushing. "It's sort of, like, nasty."

"I'll forgive you. What does it say?"

"Literally? Prick hairs sautéed with Chinese chives."

"Good God!" said Karp, laughing. "What's *that* all about?"

"It's Hong Kong slang," Lucy explained, laughing, too. "It means, like, a total mess you can't get out of."

"Do you know what Stendahl said was the worst thing about being jailed?" Tran asked.

From her bed Marlene replied grumpily, "No, but I'm sure you're about to tell me."

"You are correct. He said that it was that one could not avoid unwelcome visitors. Do you feel so?"

"No. I welcome all visitors, except those that wish to probe and manipulate my body. Those I detest. The others are useful for ridding myself of accumulated frustration through a display of ill temper. If I am here long enough, I will have no friends left."

"On the contrary, my dear: any friend who was liable to be put off by rudeness and ill temper has long since abandoned you."

Marlene threw a pillow at him, which he caught, and returned tenderly to its place behind her turbaned head. She said, "This is driving me crazy. I have all these people depending on me, the clients . . . God knows what's happening to them."

"So far, nothing, I can assure you. I, rather than God, have been keeping track of them all while you lie at your ease like a duchess. Nothing has been let slip in the past three days."

"What? How have you done that?"

"Operatives have been hired and assigned, schedules have been made, checks have been issued. The world goes on quite well without you, Marie-Hélène. You are perfectly dispensable."

"I am astounded. I had no idea you were such a genius at organization."

The man who had planned the 1968 Tet offensive in Tay Ninh province accepted the compliment with a sweet smile, saying nothing. Marlene glanced at the room's door, for the third time in as many minutes, a concerned look blooming on her face.

"And what about Lucy?" she asked.

"I would say she seems well, despite the burden she carries," said Tran after a moment's consideration. "She is pinched by always having me with her when she is not at home. She spends much of her time at the laboratory, and at home Mary Ma visits her often. Today, I am happy to say, she is off with her father. I would like to see her light again, as she was, but that will not happen until this business is resolved, or until she tells what she knows."

"They still haven't caught those bastards?"

"No, only the one I interviewed. The Vo are elusive. I have my own inquiries out. But even if the Vo are taken off the board, Leung will still have an interest."

"Leung set up the kidnap?"

"Without question. I was able to overhear a conversation between Leung and Mr. Yee, the leader of the Hap Tai business association. He told Yee that the Italians had killed the Sings."

"Do you believe that, Tran?"

"Perhaps. But even if true, Leung was involved as an emissary or master of ceremonies, even if he did not pull the trigger. Then they spoke of Lucy and how she might compromise the silence of the Chen family in this matter. Leung is clearly very concerned to remain free of any taint of this assassination. Afterward, he made a phone call which, as I surmise now, could only have been to the Vo. But there are many other bastards for hire besides the Vo. Leung seems to have disappeared, by the way."

"And this means . . . ?"

"Who can tell? Perhaps he went back to Hong Kong, where he belongs. Perhaps . . ."

This thought was lost as a rapid knock sounded on the door, and it opened to reveal Sophie Leontoff in a wheelchair, with Abe Lapidus behind her, pushing.

Cries of amazement, commiserations, imprecations (Marlene, dolling, what are you, nuts?), introductions. When the old lady learned that Tran not only spoke French but had been a resident in Paris, she began to rattle away in that language with Tran, leaving Marlene to listen with one ear, while explaining choice bits to the bemused Abe.

"Sophie told me about that kid of yours with the languages—amazing, just unbelievable," he said, shaking his head.

Marlene acknowledged this and added, "It's funny, we were here last time talking about Jerry Fein, and now I'm in the hospital myself because of his daughter." She explained what had happened the other day at the shelter. "Small world, huh?"

"Yeah, that's some story. But I got news for you, honey: it's smaller than you think. Jerry Fein was also Morris Leontoff's attorney, may he rest in peace. You didn't know this? Of course, how could you? Sophie, you remember Jerry Fein?"

Sophie interrupted a description of what used to go on at a certain joint in Montparnasse, served up for comparison with Tran's description of same (not too different) and said, "Of course I remember Jerry Fein. He jumped off the Empire State, I should forget that?"

"I mean before, when he worked for Morris."

"Of course. Him and Ceil. We were at the beach together, also—years. What a nice man, so good-looking. And such a dresser! A tragedy he should go kill himself like that! How come you're asking?"

"Marlene has his daughter for a client," said Abe. "That *momser* she married attacked her, and Marlene got in the way."

"That girl," said Sophie darkly, and a look passed from her to Abe, which Marlene saw, and which popped her curiosity up a gear.

"What about her?" Marlene asked.

"Nothing," replied Sophie, falsely bright. "A beautiful girl. All the boys were after her, at the beach, at school. She went to Erasmus. She was the queen of the, what is this, the dance . . . ?"

"The prom," supplied Marlene.

"Right, the prom queen. Gorgeous. Jerry was so proud of her . . ." Another of those looks. What was going on here? Marlene took a plunge.

"Aunt Sophie, why do you think Jerry Fein killed himself?"

But too great a plunge, it seemed. "Oh, listen, dolling, why do you want to talk about sad old stuff? Talk about the happy. I had too much sad old stuff, dolling, believe me."

There was a moment of embarrassed silence, and then Tran, bless his heart, launched into an innocent question about old Paris, and the French chatter cranked up again.

Abe Lapidus looked at Marlene. There was a shadow in his eyes that hadn't been there before. He leaned over her and said, in the manner of a lawyer counseling a client at trial, "You want to know about Jerry? The whole *megilla*?"

"I think I have to, Abe."

"You don't believe let sleeping dogs lie?"

Marlene said, "You know, Abe, as a matter of fact, I do. Unfortunately, this dog is up, awake, and tearing around growling and biting. People have been hurt already, including me, and more people are going to get hurt. That's what I think. What do you think, Abe?"

Abe sighed and said, "You get out of here, you call me. We'll have lunch, I'll give you some names."

13

THEY KEPT MARLENE IN THE HOSPITAL for eight days, which in her opinion was at least three days too long. She felt fine, she told them, but they continued to probe her with the wonderful and expensive machinery of the modern neurological suite until they were satisfied that they were more or less tort proof, should she begin to imagine herself the Empress Josephine upon her release.

Karp came to take her home, and found her in her room, sitting on the edge of the bed, dressed in the clothes he had brought in the previous day, a black cotton shirt and trousers and a long, smoky silk scarf, which she had made into a turban around her cropped head. Marlene did not look good in a turban, or in the yellowing bruises that covered one side of her face, and, as her false eye was no longer shielded by a strategic fall of hair, her glance was curiously lopsided. And glum. It tormented Karp's heart to contemplate what he was about to do, but he chilled it down and said, "We have to talk about this business, Marlene."

"What, now?" she asked, scowling.

"Yeah, now." He drew a deep breath, released it,

as before taking an important foul shot. "I need you to give me the whole story. On Vivian Bollano. And on whatever's happening out there in connection with the Chinatown murders. Whatever you know."

She stared angrily at him, but his glance didn't falter, and after a moment her eyes fell and she asked coldly, "To whom am I speaking now? My husband, or the chief assistant district attorney?"

"Well, Marlene, the answer to that is 'both,' and the fact that this creates problems for us is not my doing."

"What are you going to do? *Interrogate* me? Maybe I should have my attorney present."

In one part of his mind, Karp saw himself pointing to the telephone and heard himself saying, "Maybe you should," but what he did instead was to slump into a chair, catch her eye with his again, and say, "Marlene! Look at me! Listen to me! This is tearing me up. It's breaking my heart. I've already compromised myself six ways to Sunday getting you in here instead of the lock-up ward at Bellevue, but I can't just give you a free ride if I think you have knowledge constructive to three homicides. Which I do. God, I don't *want* to put legal pressure on you. *Legal pressure!* We're *married*, for crying out loud! I want you to tell me because you love me, because you trust me, and because I'm worried nauseous about our daughter, who's in danger because of something I think she saw and won't tell me about. Now, come on, Marlene! Talk to me!"

"And if not, what?" she asked, her voice neutral.

"Oh, shit! That's *not* the right answer, Marlene."

She repeated it. He looked at her, closed his eyes, shook his head, sighed, and said, "Okay, if not, then there are a pair of cops down the hall who will take you in and process you just like any other person charged with assault. I'm out of the loop officially in any case; Tim Sullivan will handle the whole thing out of Felony. He's going to ask Roland what the story is, and Roland is going to say, because it's the truth, that you're hiding something, and Tim's people will bring that to the attention of the judge. Roland could also buy, or pretend to buy, the story that Bollano's people are putting out, that it was an assassination attempt on him—"

"Do you believe that?"

"Oh, crap, of *course* I don't believe that, Marlene. That's the point, it doesn't matter what *I* believe. I'm supposed to be out of it."

"But if I spill my guts here, then you're *in* it again, you smooth the way, get me through arraignment and bail, and I'm home all cozy and safe. Is that the deal?"

She was perfectly right. The thing stunk, a spaghetti tangle of legal and domestic business, an archetypal Karp family katzenjammer. Flat-voiced, he said, "Yeah, that's the deal."

She nodded. "Okay, then here's my response to that deal. About Vivian Fein Bollano, I will say absolutely nothing. Everything that has passed between us is protected by attorney-client privilege, and I will so maintain to a judge when the time comes. About the other thing: you've probably come to the same conclusion I have, that either Lucy witnessed the Asia Mall killings or some of her friends did, or they all did. Lucy was out of circulation for a couple, three hours that afternoon at just the right time. You know about Lucy and Janice getting rousted by a couple of gangsters. Then she gets snatched last week. Tran believes that on both occasions the people involved were mainly interested in finding out what the girls knew and whether they'd told anyone else about it. He's turned up a name, Leung, a local hard boy, but clearly just a go-between—"

"Why? Why just a go-between?"

"Because the Sings were big shots, triad guys. Somebody wanted them hit would have to have some serious muscle to back up the play. Leung's a small-timer. Tran says." She summarized Tran's information about the Yee-Leung connection.

"But the cops say they sent in people from out of town," Karp objected. "Why would they care if the girls saw who did it?"

"They shouldn't," said Marlene. "The fact that they do argues against the foreign hit-team story." She reminded him what Tran had told her earlier about triad politics and the likely results of the killings at the Asia Mall.

"In any case," she went on, "neither Lucy nor Janice nor Mary is going to come forward as a witness because Janice and Mary are too vulnerable and Lucy is too loyal. The cops and Tran are looking for the Vietnamese who snatched Lucy, and when they're caught, we'll know a little more. Meanwhile, I don't judge that any of them is in serious danger, as long as none of them come forward as a witness."

"You're *encouraging* Lucy to keep quiet here? You approve of this?" Karp could not keep the outrage out of his voice.

"Yeah, not approve exactly," said Marlene forcefully, "but understand, appreciate where she is, where they all are. Like it or not, they come from a different culture, and our little honey has roots in that culture, at least partially. Given a choice, I'd rather keep her roots intact than tear them up in the interests of a judicial process. I respect your parental interest, believe me, but right now, with Tran watching her, she's as safe as we can make her, safe as the child she is is going to be. You understand what I mean, Butch? As the child she *is*, not the child you'd like her to be. I know you think I *designed* her to be this way and I'm a terrible mother and all—"

"I don't—"

"You do, but believe me when I say I didn't do anything like that. I wish to God she collected stuffed animals and went to the Girl Scouts, but she's never going to be that kid. Deadly genes, and not only from me, by the way, darling, plus the usual shake of the dice, thank you, God. I love her to pieces and I know you do, too, and the chance that she's going to break both our hearts is very high."

For a long while he sat there, saying nothing. He was reflecting on how much he had changed since he met this woman, how he would have reacted in former years, with his first wife, for example, had such a situation come up. There would have been broken furniture.

He said, "You know, it's funny: it goes against my every instinct, but I think you're right. But there's something else . . . I can put myself behind your eyes and see things the way you see them. It took awhile, but I can do it, because I really love you. I wonder if you can do that for me, see what this, this life we all lead, costs me, being who I am."

"Oh, yeah," she said. "That's what women do, and they do it so unthinking that everybody takes it for granted, they'll see the man's point of view. I'll give you an example. When I waded into that gunfight, what I was thinking, besides that I had to stop it before some innocent schmuck caught one, was you, that I didn't, I couldn't *kill* anyone in New York County because of what it would mean to you, and so, you know they teach you to aim for the center of mass and keep firing until they go down, but I'm a good enough snap shot that I could have popped both assholes in the face and moved on and even taken out Sally and his baby-sitter, and I would have walked on it, too, but what I did was I risked my life to disable those guys instead, and got my brains kicked in. That was very largely for you."

"I don't know what to say," said Karp after a hard swallow.

"I do. Let's get the fuck out of here before we both start sniveling." She stood up straight, lifted her chin, and said, "Bring on your cops. I'm ready."

"Lose the Joan of Arc routine, kid, it's only calendar court," said Karp. "And I think I'll take you in myself."

She smiled for the first time and said, "Oh, yeah? Think you can handle me, big boy?"

"As long as you're unarmed," said Karp.

He turned his wife over to Clay Fulton at the courthouse, the detective having accumulated the necessary paper to bring Marlene back into the system, and then he switched his mind away from her and her fate and directed it to the problem of the Asia Mall killings, because Mimi Vasquez was supposed to be waiting for him at his office with Detective Wu in tow.

They were there as promised. Karp got them arranged around his small, round conference table and took a moment to examine the cop while the man chatted with Vasquez. A little under forty was his estimate, maybe five-eight and well proportioned, with a square, fleshy face that bore a genial expression. Detective Second Grade Wu was clearly satisfied with himself and with the world.

They talked casually for a while, making the easy comments about events and mutual acquaintances that must precede every business meeting between strangers. Karp learned that the detective was a first-generation Chinese American, whose father had done some service for the Allied cause in World War II and had thereafter been granted access to America. Wu had been born in Chinatown, educated in public schools, and having discovered no talent in himself for either scholarship or trade, had joined the cops fifteen years ago, to the lamentations of both parents.

"Why is that?" Karp asked, the thought of Lucy and what Marlene had said about culture popping unbidden into his mind.

"Old country Chinese and the police . . . the cops there were less than dogs, not just corrupt and brutal, but a matter of status, like caste. They're down there with the butchers and shit carriers."

"Just like here," said Karp, and they all laughed and, having gotten the man relaxed enough to laugh, Karp slid into the interview with, "So, Phil, when did you decide the Sing murders weren't worth serious effort?"

Wu's laugh turned to a kind of scowling snort. "Hey, wait a second, I put in as much effort as I could under the circumstances," he said. "Ask Mimi here. The vics were strangers, it wasn't a robbery, we traced the whole thing back to Hong Kong. There were absolutely no leads locally."

"You talked to Mr. and Mrs. Chen?"

"Yeah, sure," said Wu warily. "What about them?"

"What about them? You think two big-time triad tough guys could hold a meeting in their storeroom back there without the Chens or their employees knowing about it? What did you get out of them?"

Wu shrugged. "The usual. I told you what Chinese people think about the police. Nobody saw nothing."

"But somebody unlocked that door back there so the Sings and whoever shot them could get in. So somebody in there must have set it up."

Wu looked uncomfortable. He hunched his shoulders and uttered what might have been a laugh if there had been anything amusing going on. "Okay, look. Here's the situation. You know about tongs? Okay, you know what *guanxi* is, connections? Okay, I know what went down, the Chens know I know, but it doesn't do us any good to rub their faces in it, you understand? I got to work that community every day. If I make the Chens lose face over something where I'm never going to get these guys, then when I catch a case where I got a fighting chance to nail the perp, I'm fucked . . . sorry, Mimi, I meant . . ."

The man was actually blushing. Vasquez said, "I've heard the word before, Phil. What you're telling us is that you think Chen set up the meeting as a favor for his tong, the tong doing a favor for these Hong Kong triad guys, *guanxi*, right?"

"Right. Happens all the time. But something went wrong. Instead of a meeting the guys got murdered. I asked Chen did he know that it was going to be a hit, and he said, no. I mean, what the hell else was he going to say?"

"So, naturally, you asked him who set up the meeting, and he says . . . ?"

"The head of his business association, Benny Yee."

"And Mr. Yee said . . . ?"

"He got a call from Hong Kong."

"And when you checked his phone records, you found what?"

The detective hesitated, licked his lips. Karp snapped his knuckles once on the table, a loud, startling sound, and spoke angrily. "Oh, come on, Phil, tell me a goddamn *story* here! Why do I have to drag stuff out of you? What's going on?"

Wu's golden skin darkened as if it were being toasted, except around the nostrils, where little patches turned white as parchment. Oddly his mouth still retained the dead ghost of his original smile. "Well, Butch, I'll tell you what's going on," said Wu in a tight voice. "Mr. Yee is an important guy in Chinatown. He's extremely helpful to the police. We get any serious violence in Chinatown, we ask Mr. Yee about it, and a couple days later the perp knocks on the door of the precinct and hands over a neatly typed signed confession. So when Mr. Yee tells me something, I take his word for it, unless I got independent evidence he's lying, which I don't. You know what face is? If I call Mr. Yee a liar, like if I start to check his phone records, I guarantee you, I will not clear another case out of there as long as I'm alive. That's what's going on."

"He *is* a liar," said Karp. "That meeting was set up by a man named Leung, right here in the city."

"Leung?" cried Wu, the name exploding into the air like a firecracker. "Leung? What're you, running your own investigation without telling me?"

"No, but it looks like it would've been a good idea," snapped Karp.

Wu stood up so fast his chair fell over backward. "I don't have to listen to this shit."

"Sit down, Phil," said Vasquez. "Butch didn't mean it. Nobody's telling you how to run your job. He's pissed because his little girl looks like she's caught in the cross fire here."

Wu picked up his chair and sat down. The conventional smile was gone, replaced by a look of absolute neutrality. Karp realized he had violated some rule involving face, but he did not care in the least. He held his tongue, making Wu ask the obvious question, "What happened to your kid?"

"She's the one the Vo boys kidnapped. There's a bulletin out on it."

"She's *your* daughter? Jesus!" Wu looked genuinely shaken for the first time in the interview. Karp warmed slightly toward him. Wu asked, "And this . . . kidnapping, you think it's connected to the Sing double?"

"I'm practically positive. My daughter and a friend were molested by some Chinese punks a couple days before that, and the punks said this Leung sent them."

"Who did they tell?"

"An informant working for my wife."

"What's his name?"

"That's not important just now, but the same informant told us that he overheard Mr. Yee and Mr. Leung in conversation, in which it was made perfectly clear that Leung had asked Mr. Yee to arrange the use of the stockroom. Basically, Leung was apologizing to Yee for the fact that the Hong Kong people were capped and telling him to make sure that nobody talked about any of it. So, tell me about Leung. What's his story?"

"If it's the Leung I know, he's nothing. A Chinatown skell, does odd jobs for the Háp Tài, runs some rackets. I never heard he was big with the triads. I'd guess he's some kind of messenger boy."

"He have a sheet?" Vasquez asked.

"I'll run him," said Wu, pulling a notebook

from his jacket pocket and making a note with a ballpoint. "Look," he continued, the smile returning, "I'm sorry I blew up like that, but, you know, Chinatown, no offense, but if you don't know what you're doing or who you're dealing with, you could screw up stuff you don't even know about."

"I appreciate that," said Karp. "No offense taken." He watched the detective closely as he asked, "What about Willie Lie? Know him?"

The man seemed genuinely confused. "Lie? It's a common name." He frowned. "Oh, yeah, that's the guy dropped a dime to the feds on Pigetti. What's he got to do with this case?"

"Maybe nothing, just a thought. Anyway, do you know him?"

"I probably do. There's a shitload of Lies and Lees and Louies in Chinatown, and I guess the usual percent of them is bent."

"How about the name Nia Tu Wah? Ring a bell?"

"No. Should it?"

"I don't know. It's supposed to be Willie Lie's real name."

"Who told you that?" Smiling.

"We got it from the Hong Kong police."

"You got a Cantonese speaker in the D.A.?"

"No, my guy talked in English. To a Captain Chui."

Wu was grinning now. "Then you got bullshit. We hardly even bother talking to Hong Kong anymore. They're so infiltrated with the triads it's not even worth it. It's bad enough if you're speaking

Cantonese, but in English, forget it. They're shining you on, boss."

"Uh-huh. Well, thanks for that information, Detective Wu. I appreciate your help. Sorry again about that little misunderstanding."

Wu said, "Oh, no problem," and he got up and they all shook hands again. Wu said, "Take care, Vasquez, and I'm going to keep you more in the loop on this, whatever turns up, okay?"

When he was gone, Karp said, "So? What was your take on that?"

"Nice guy, not that sharp. He's gotten lazy because the tong guys hand things to him in return for not getting hassled. He was pretty open about it."

"Yeah. Nice guy, but I don't much like getting bullshitted by cops. What's the lesson here, Vasquez?"

"Be more suspicious? Isn't that always the lesson?" She did not look happy about it.

He smiled. "You got it, Vasquez. Meanwhile, until Leung turns up or we grab the Vo gang, we're more or less back to square one."

"Square two," said Vasquez. "Square one was before you squeezed the shit out of Phil Wu, like I should've done already."

After she left, Karp called Ray Guma to see if he had anything yet on Gino Scarpi, and learned from the bureau secretary that he was still out at Bellevue Hospital. Karp hung up the phone, swiveled around in his chair, gazed out the window, sucked softly on the eraser end of a new pencil, and tried to think whether he had left anything undone. He tapped out the rhythm of the Radetski March on his molars; nothing important came to mind. Guma dispatched to the Mob, V.T. mobilized and looking for the stain of dirty cash, Wu braced and put on notice, Marlene questioned and released. (She might even be home by now. He thought of calling but did not.) Lucy reasonably safe if their theories were correct. Okay, but what was nagging him? Oh, right, Willie Lie. Or Mr. Nia, as he might be. He stared at the phone, willing it to ring and convey to him some new piece of information about the Chinese. But it was silent. Karp slammed down the pencil, got up, and stalked out of the office and down to a courtroom, looking to make someone else's life hell.

Ray Guma, like most people, did not like hospitals, but he had necessarily spent a good deal of time in this one, Bellevue Hospital, where Manhattan keeps its morgue and its medical examiner and its prison ward, and he knew his way around.

He found Gino Scarpi lying in a small, locked, windowless room with three other damaged felons, looking drawn and pale. A good deal of the tough had been blown out of Gino, which is what three 9mm hollow-points will often do, even if they do not hit a vital organ. Both of his arms were in casts, and he had his bed cranked up the better to watch *Jeopardy!* on the TV when Guma walked in holding a small white cardboard box.

Scarpi looked up with an expectant expression, which faded somewhat when he saw who it was. "Ray Guma," he said. "Well, what do you know!"

"I brought you some cannoli, Scooter."

Scarpi moved one of his arms. "How the fuck am I gonna eat cannoli, Ray, what that fucking cunt did to me?" He was a square-faced man of twenty-six, with a thick head of curls that took up most of a low forehead. He had a lot of teeth also, and the beginnings of a respectable set of jowls, which he had set off nicely with a dense mat of black chest hair. The half dozen golden neck chains he usually wore were absent.

Guma placed the package on the side table and sat down in a straight chair by the bed. He said, "When your girlfriend gets here, she can slide it in your mouth and you can suck the filling out, kind of turnabout is fair play. She might get a kick out of it."

Scarpi started to glower in case he was being made fun of and then saw the humor in it and the sexual possibilities and decided to laugh instead. "Fuckin' Guma! So, what're you here about? I ain't supposed to say shit without fuckin' Kronsky holding my hand."

"Kronsky must be a busy man these days, what with Joey P. in the federal slams," said Guma. Marvin P. Kronsky was the Bollanos' chief lawyer.

"I ain't saying anything about that either."

"No problem. Tell you the honest truth, Scooter, I figured you could use some cheering up, and I also thought I could do you some good."

"The only thing's gonna do me any good, Guma, I swear to God, is getting my arms back and shoving that bitch's gun up her cunt and squeezing off ten rounds."

"That's not the way to be thinking, man. What you should be thinking is how do I get to spend my recuperation at home and not in a cell. What I hear is you're looking at about a third of the New York penal code: attempted murder, attempted kidnap. . . ."

Suspicion lit in Scarpi's small, dark eyes. "Ray, I told you already, you want to deal, go see Kronsky. That's all I got to say to you."

"Hey, what're you talking deal? They don't send *me* out to deal," said Guma in an aggrieved tone. "This is Raymond here, Scoot. I knew your parents, God rest them, I know your brothers, I knew you from when you couldn't wipe your ass. This is not about a deal. We don't need fucking lawyers. You know me, I'm in the *famiglia*, for chrissake. This is completely off the record here. I mean, when I heard what went down over by that fucking shelter, and I heard it was you, I couldn't believe it. You were always a sensible kid, you know? Not a crazy-ass guinea. So I figured, out of the goodness of my heart, I'd come down here, talk to the kid, find out the real story, and, you know how it is, if I could put some words in people's ears, off the record, you could maybe catch a break."

Scarpi was nodding. This was how it worked. He said, carefully, "Off the record?"

"Yeah. Just between us. What I want to know is something's got nothing to do with you, legally."

"Take off your coat and empty your pockets."

"Scooter! What the fuck, man! You think I would wear a wire?"

"Hey, it's my ass, man. And they don't call me

Scooter for years. It's Gino. Okay, I'm waiting, Ray."

Guma took off his suit jacket and shook it upside down, grumbling, and emptied his pockets on the bed. He pirouetted slowly and pulled his shirt tight against his body so that Scarpi could see that no little Nagra recorder nestled in his armpit or the small of his back.

"Satisfied? Because if you want to look up my asshole, it's no deal."

"Sit down, Ray. What do you want to talk about?"

Guma sat. "The wife, Vivian. What's the story there? Why she all of a sudden broke out."

Scarpi's thick eyebrows came together. "What the fuck you want to know for?"

"Hey, I told you. It's something else. Got nothing to do with you."

"Okay, you want to know about Vivian?" Scarpi leaned back on his pillows, considering. "What can I say. A cunt is a cunt, and as far as that goes, Jews are for lawyers, for accountants, not for in the rack. A piece of ass maybe, a change of pace, but for marrying, you should stick to your own, you know what I mean? But Little Sally, he's got to have this Jew bitch. This was all before my time, you understand, I'm just saying what I heard. I hear that they fight, he raps her around, she fights more. The way I figure, that's part of the deal—she likes getting hit, he likes to dish it out."

"Okay, but this is going on years, why does she split just then?"

"This I don't know. I'm not hiding under the

fucking marital bed, am I? Maybe she found another guy. Sally sure as shit had other women."

"Was she giving it to Eddie Cat?"

Scarpi let out a surprised snorting laugh. "Oh, *there's* a fucking theory."

"What, the Cat wouldn't have done it?"

"Eddie? Eddie would fuck a Froot Loop rolling down Broadway. But he'd have to be crazy to jump Vivian B. If Sally didn't whack him, the don would. You know how that shit works, Guma."

Guma smiled. "I rest my case."

For an instant Scarpi's eyes widened and his jaw actually dropped, but then he grinned slyly and shook his head. Laughing, he said, "Eh, Raymond, you old fucker, you almost had me there. Uh-uh, nah, no way, man. No way, if that was what it was."

"Why not?"

"Because if it was that, it wouldn't've been a couple in the head in a car. It would've been down by Sheepshead, out in an ice house, and Sally would've used a knife, and it would've lasted like three days. You know Sally."

"Yeah, I do, and that's why I thought, when this Chinaman came forward, this was like an insult to Eddie Cat; I mean, like they didn't even think he was worth getting whacked by a white man."

"Oh, yeah, well let me tell you about that chink fuck," Scarpi snarled. "No fuckin' way did Joey P. hire him to whack Eddie. The fucker's lying through his teeth."

"Gino, you hide under Joey's bed? Think about it. But forget that side of it for a second: the fact is you, personally, knew the guy, right? Because he named you specifically. I mean, what'd he do, pick your name out of the air? He read it in the Mob directory?"

"Oh, shit, yeah, I *knew* him. I even brung him up to Joe's place a couple times."

"What for?"

Scarpi dropped his eyes. "You know, like for business."

"Gino, what did we say?" said Guma, and pinched his lips together. "Off the record. Since when do you associate with those guys?"

Scarpi let out a bitter laugh. "Fuck, man, the way things're going, those're the only guys that'll be left. We're lucky we got four streets left downtown. No, this guy, Willie the Chink, he had contacts over the other side. You know, for product."

"Heroin."

"Yeah, and other stuff. And he could move cash, clean it up. Hey, what do I know about that shit? But Joe was like impressed. He treated the chink with respect."

"Uh-huh. So, Gino, if Willie's blowing smoke, who do *you* think whacked Eddie Cat?"

"Me? Fuck, Guma, I don't get paid to think shit like that. Like they say, it's not in my fuckin' job description. I tell you what, though: you find out who, you let me know."

Guma stood up, put his jacket back on, and collected his pocket contents from the bed. He smiled and said, "Believe me, Gino, when we find out, you'll be among the first to know."

A worried look crossed Scarpi's face as he said, "Yeah, but, Guma? Seriously, you think you can do me some good? I mean, I can take a jolt upstate but not cripped up like this."

Guma leaned over and patted Scarpi on the knee. "Hey, *paisan*, you know I'll do what I can do." He winked. "The fix is in."

"That's quite a story, Goom," said Karp later that afternoon when Guma had concluded the tale of his hospital visit. "What's your take?"

They were in Karp's office, Guma on the couch, Roland Hrcany on a side chair tilted precariously back against the wall, Karp in the big swivel chair behind the desk.

"What's my take? You're gonna laugh, but I think the mutt was leveling with me."

Hrcany did laugh, forced, hooting, unpleasant and overlong. "You're losing it, Goom. Too much time with the little birdies and fishies on the TV. You really expected the little fuckhead to tell you the *truth*?"

"Well, yeah, Roland, as a matter of fact. I realize he's just Mafia scum, but I made a living for years out of knowing when these guys are straight and when they're not, and he wasn't lying. Why should he? You honestly think he thought I was being cute? That I would double-cross him to make a case?"

Roland sniffed and picked up Karp's precious Mickey Mantle baseball. He tossed it up and caught it one-handed. "Okay, say you're right. Where does that put us? If Willie boy *is* lying, then why? What's in it for him?"

They thought. After some moments, Karp ventured, "He's moving smack, and it must be major weight if he's dealing directly with Joe P. He lied about being a dealer for the Bollanos. In fact, he's a supplier and a money launderer. And, let's say he rips them off on some delivery and the boys come after him and he panics and decides to go for protection. He figures that ratting out Joe P. for the Catalano hit . . . ah, shit, that doesn't work."

"Yeah, 'cause Gino would've mentioned that," said Roland, "and also, your point earlier, he's a chink. He doesn't really need protection. A ticket out of town and he's history as far as the Mob is concerned."

"Especially since he may not even be Willie Lie," said Karp. Then he told them what V.T. had told him about the ID from Hong Kong and the triad connection, to the accompaniment of muttered cursing and startled exclamations from the two other men.

"A fucking egg roll," was Guma's summation. "Looks simple on the outside, but who the fuck knows what's in it."

Gloomy silence for minutes thereafter, into which Karp put, "Okay, we could speculate all day and all night. What have we actually got?" He ticked the points off on his long fingers. "One, Lie's uncorroborated story about Pigetti. Two, the fact that someone or something is knocking off the big guns of the Bollano family. Three, Eddie Cat was killed in such a manner as to give Joe P. and his whole crew an alibi. Four, Little Sally's wife left him for a woman's shelter shortly after Eddie got killed. Five, the uncorroborated testimony comes from a Chinese gangster with possible triad connections who comes in voluntarily, asks for me personally, volunteers to be a grand jury witness, knows all about transactional immunity, and bolts when he doesn't get it. Okay, six: Willie Lie is for all intents and purposes nobody. He seems to have no money and no drugs we've been able to find. Have I left anything out?"

Roland said, "Yeah, Tommy Colombo."

"What do you mean? What's he got to do with anything?"

"He's got Lie. He's offered him what he wants on the federal side, but he'd love for us to play along, and nail both Joey and the Sals on murder charges. He'll keep the pressure up on Jack: why isn't the D.A. letting this little schmo skate in order to get these vicious kingpin killers? And if we put him in front of a grand jury without cutting him the deal he wants, he'll either clam or perjure himself—and that means that the only way we can hang on to him is on a pissant contempt or perjury charge, which will make Jack look like a prize ass, he's gumming up the crusade against the big bad Mob. Believe me, Butch, Jack's ready to roll on this, give the Chinaman his blind deal, anything to make the murder case against Pigetti. If Lie gets that, he'll give us the shooter, maybe the gun, the details, corroboration up the ass, the whole nine yards. So if that happens, all your points become moot. Joe P. goes down for the hit, case closed."

"That can't happen," said Karp. "Roland, I can feel it: there's an intelligence behind this, behind

Willie, and it's playing all of us, you, me, the Bollanos, Colombo. Something's going on here that's
bigger than putting one wise guy in jail for shooting another wise guy. Goom, if Pigetti and Lie were
together on the hit like Lie says, would Scarpi necessarily know about it? I mean, could Pigetti keep it
secret from the Bollano guys?"

"Hell, yeah, in principle. Joey'd be taking a big
chance, and Lie would have to be a major player to
set up Catalano on the basis of an eye wink from
Joe. But then why does he turn around and screw
Joey with this testimony bullshit? What's his
game?"

"He wants to squash the Bollano family?" Karp
suggested.

Roland let his chair rock down, and he tossed the
baseball to Karp. "That may be, Butch, but that's
not what they're buying today. Today the choices are
'D.A. convicts mobster' or 'D.A. fucks up big-time,
U.S. attorney convicts mobster.' Unless you can
come up with something with enough juice to give
Jack a third choice, I'm guessing he's sooner or later
going to roll over for Mr. Lie."

Mr. Leung was at that moment well content. Mobilizing Willie Lie had worked as he had expected.
Lie would keep the Italians confused, weakened,
and occupied, at little risk to the plan. The Chens
and their tong were neutralized for the time being.
Karp had proved a disappointment; he should have
leaped at the opportunity to bring a murder charge
against Pigetti, but he had not. Was it possible that

his daughter had been talking to him? But would a man like that heed a child, a girl child, no matter how skillful? It was hard to credit. He sensed from what he understood of the interaction between Lie and the federal prosecutor that there was an intense rivalry between Colombo and Karp. Clearly they were working for different political factions, just as in China. Perhaps money should be offered. Meanwhile, the snipe and the clam were still focused on one another, and Leung himself was perfectly safe, moving silently and steadily up the beach. It was just as the drunken American in Macao had predicted.

14

IT TOOK MARLENE AN HOUR ON THE Long Island Expressway to get to the Nassau County line and nearly another hour on feeder roads roaming the cloned streets of Great Neck Estates to find the colonial split-level house occupied by retired detective John (Black Jack) Doherty. As usual when making a cold call like this, she'd had Sym make a telephone contact to make sure the mark was still alive and not senile. (No, Mr. Doherty did not want to buy any aluminum siding from the young woman.)

The house was large and white and clean-looking, an American-dream kind of dwelling, set back on a broad, closely clipped lawn shaded by well-grown red maples. There was a gray Chrysler Le Baron, three years old and spotless, in the driveway. Over the doorway, fixed in the center of the triangular pediment, screamed a black iron eagle, below which was a small flagpole carrying the stars and stripes.

Marlene stood under the sluggishly moving banner and pushed the bell button, which was set into a brass plaque with another eagle on it. A brass eagle also served as a knocker on the shiny black door. As she waited, she could not help reflecting how much grander this house was than the one her parents lived in, although as far as earnings were concerned, a cop and a plumbing contractor had been about on a par back in the fifties. Maybe his wife worked, or his kids struck it rich and bought it for him, she thought, not really believing it.

The man who answered the door was in his mid sixties, stocky, with a dark, angular face, black hair going speckled gray on the sides, thick black eyebrows over dark eyes, a good example of the physiognomic style called Black Irish, supposedly representing gene lines dumped on the shamrock shore by the wreckage of the Armada. He was dressed for suburban comfort in a green cardigan, tan Lacoste shirt, pale blue Sansabelt trousers, and woven leather slip-ons. The fishing magazine he was holding completed the picture of a prosperous retiree, but his eyes were still cop eyes when he looked Marlene up and down. She was still something to see, with the face covered in yellowy-mauve blotches, but she had made the effort, having donned a blue linen suit, a crisp primrose blouse, heels, and a snappy panama hat to hide the Frankenstein stitches on her bristly skull. The cops still had her gun, and she was in no great hurry to get another one.

"Yes? Can I help you?"

"You can if you're John Doherty. Harry Bello suggested I look you up."

She could see him thinking. The NYPD has something over two thousand detectives, of whom only two hundred or so are detectives first grade. Bello had been one and Doherty had not, and even if their careers had not been exactly contemporary, Doherty would have heard of Bello as a rising hotshot.

"Harry Bello. In Brooklyn, yeah. I was in the city my whole career. He still with the force?"

"No, he retired and went private. I'm his partner, Marlene Ciampi." She held out a business card, one of the old Bello & Ciampi versions.

He read it, and when he looked up his gaze remained suspicious. They were still standing on the doorstep, and he had not yet made a gesture to invite her over his threshold. "What's this about, Miss Ciampi?"

"One of your old cases bears on an investigation we're running for a client. Harry thought you could be helpful, maybe supply some background that never got written into a DD-5."

"What case would that be?"

"Gerald Fein. You remember it?"

The big eyebrows rose a quarter inch. "Hard to forget that one." He looked at his watch. "I got an eleven o'clock tee-off at Fresh Meadows, but I could talk for a couple of minutes. Come on in."

He turned and led the way back into the house, through a small entrance hall past a living room demonstrating that the Dohertys must be among the very best customers of the Ethan Allen Company, down a hallway lined with family photographs (wife, four good-looking kids, an assortment of probable grandchildren), and into a pine-paneled room that was clearly the master's den. Doherty seated himself in a big maroon leather recliner and indicated a needlepoint-cushioned maple rocker for her to sit in. Marlene took in the unsurprising decor: framed photographs of Doherty in uniform and plainclothes with other smiling men, all Irish-looking, similarly dressed, awards, plaques, two stuffed fish of good size, a bass and a tarpon, an antique wooden eagle, hooked rugs on the floor, and the furniture, desk, chairs (except the man's recliner) impeccably early American maple and pine. Esthetic consistency was clearly a major value *chez* Doherty.

Settled, Doherty did not beat about the bush. "You want to know was the suicide legit?"

"Yeah, that'd be a good place to start."

He made a steeple of his fingers and looked out the window past beige drapes printed with flags and drums to a small stone patio and the yard beyond. "Officially, we found no evidence of foul play. The man went up to the observation deck, bought a ticket, opened a locked maintenance door, went out onto the overhang below the deck windows, and climbed over the parapet."

"And unofficially?"

"Unofficially . . . ? Well, I was the junior guy on the case. Arnie Mulhausen was running it, and he couldn't get rid of it fast enough. But I had some problems, yes."

"Like?"

"Okay, no note. Not unusual, but you have to figure, a lawyer, a man uses words every day . . . it made me itch a little. Arnie's take was, hey, the guy was nuts, right? Who else takes a header off of the Empire State? So I'm doing interviews, family, friends, associates—"

"Excuse me a second, Mr. Doherty, this kind of investigation for a jumper—it's not that usual either, is it?"

"Well, it's sad to say, it depends on the person. A cop eats the gun, hey, it's pretty cut and dried. Some guy gets out of Creedmore and jumps in front of a bus, same thing. Guy, a Mob lawyer, no history of depression, goes off a building, we look a little harder. So, my other problem, like I was saying, I couldn't get anyone to tell me Fein was depressed, despondent, whatever. The wife, the daughter, colleagues. He was laughing, he had plans to recover, he wasn't hurting that bad for money."

"Except for Herschel Panofsky," said Marlene.

"Yeah, except for him," said Doherty, giving her an interested cop look.

"That didn't make you suspicious?"

"Oh, suspicious, yeah. But, like Arnie said, who's to say the guy didn't have a great front, the only guy he leveled with was his partner? I checked up on Panofsky, just on my own, and he was alibied pretty tight on the day of. The guy became a judge later on. Changed his name. Anyway, I let it go."

"Anything else fishy?"

He frowned. "Fishy isn't the word I would use here. But, yeah, there was the key business. The door to the maintenance area was always locked. The management was real careful about that, for obvious reasons. Fein had a key. We found it in his pocket after he hit. Where'd he get it? We figured he bought it off one of the maintenance guys, and we sweated every one of them, every person who had access to a copy, and came up with zip." He paused and stared out the window again. From the yard came the liquid trilling of a robin, and they both listened to it for a while.

Doherty looked at his watch and leaned forward in his recliner. "I got to start moving," he said.

Marlene put away her notebook and stood. "You've been very helpful."

"I wish I had something else for you. You know, you have, detectives have, hundreds of cases, and most of the time you figure you gave it your best shot. Here, though . . ." He waggled a hand. "Nothing to go on, not really. And the family bought it, and that was it, case closed. Everybody bought it, as a matter of fact, except the secretary. She wasn't in any doubt."

"Secretary?"

"Uh-huh. Fein's personal secretary. She took it harder than the family, practically. She got to be something of a pain in the you-know-where after. She couldn't understand why we were treating it as a suicide when she knew for a fact that it wasn't."

"What was her evidence of that . . . oh, first, do you recall her name?"

"Yeah, as a matter of fact I do. A hard one to forget. Waldorf, like the hotel; first name . . . ?" He closed his eyes for a moment, opened them. "Jesus, it's gone! Sheila? Sharon? One of those. What she had was a bunch of letters, carbons, of stuff he'd sent out, all about relocating in California, applying for the bar there. Plans, you know? Therefore, not going to kill himself. Arnie looked at her stuff, didn't find anything definite. She kept coming by, here's more papers, Detective. After a while we didn't bother looking. I mean, the case was closed. Panofsky had to get rid of her. I guess she was an embarrassment."

Marlene made a note, shook hands, and they walked together to the front door, in her head asking the questions that couldn't be asked out loud, like how does an ex-cop on a pension afford a half-million-dollar house and a country club membership, tarpon fishing in Florida, and exactly how bent had Arnie Mulhausen been, and who else got paid off, and by whose money, for whisking Gerald Fein's murder under the rug back in 1960?

Ray Guma walked into Karp's office unannounced, slammed the door behind him, and flipped the thing onto Karp's desk. Karp looked at it, and then up at Guma, who was frowning so hard that his chin showed dimples and his thick eyebrows nearly met in the middle.

"That looks like a subpoena, Ray," said Karp. He picked it up with two fingers, like a dead fish, and snapped the folded document open. "Yep. I was right. It's a federal subpoena. When did you get it?"

"Just now. What the fuck is going on, Butch?"

"You got me," said Karp. He read through the document. "No indication of what they want you for, but there never is. The statute is 18 U.S.C.371, the good old criminal-conspiracy steamer trunk, could be anything. Got a guilty conscience, Goom?"

"Get out of here! Me?"

Karp laughed. He read the name of the issuing assistant U.S. attorney. "Douglas E. Eitenberg. You know him?"

"Never heard of the asshole. He must be new."

"Call him yet?"

"No, I was so pissed I didn't trust myself not to blow up on the phone there. I figured Jack's out of town, you're the man, I'd talk to you first."

"Wise. You want me to call him?"

"I want you to rip his lungs out."

"Maybe later. Okay, Goom, calm down, go back downstairs, give Roland a heads-up on it so he knows what's happening, and since I'm king for a day, I will call our colleagues and find out what the story is."

Keegan was at the Greenbriar in West Virginia at a big-time legal institute barbecue of the sort that he never offered to let Karp stand in at. Karp would be the district attorney for two whole days. As such, according to protocol, he should have called the U.S. attorney directly, or Eitenberg's boss in the organized crime and public corruption division, but he decided to let protocol go hang for once, and just penetrate through the bureaucracy in the hope that his temporary clout would blast some plain speaking loose from the lowly worker bee across the square.

He had O'Malley make the call (this is the office of the district attorney calling) and got the guy on hold and kept him there for a minute.

Eitenberg had a light voice, one that seemed only recently to have changed, and he spoke very carefully, with more than the usual number of ahs and ums.

After the briefest pleasantries, Karp said, "Yeah, Mr. Eitenberg, just checking out this subpoena you issued to one of our assistants, Mr. Raymond Guma. Do you recall that one?" Eitenberg did. "Well, here's the thing, Mr. Eitenberg, as a rule, we in the criminal justice business, being the good guys and all, we try to avoid this sort of thing, throwing subpoenas at one another. I mean, just as an example, if one of your fine federal law enforcement officers inadvertently violated the laws of New York state, we would not expect to find them in shackles walking the perp walk the next morning. No, a couple of phone calls, a friendly meeting or two, we'd straighten it all out. Unless there's some particular reason why Mr. Colombo doesn't want to go that way." Silence on the line.

"Is there?" Karp asked. Ums and mumbles, and Mr. Eitenberg would like to consult with his management.

Fifteen minutes later, that management called, in the person of Norton Peabody, the head of the organized crime division, a man Karp knew to say hello to, and by reputation. Buttoned down and intense was the rep. More pleasantries, after which Peabody said, "Doug Eitenberg tells me you have some issues on this subpoena we sent out to Raymond Guma."

"Issues, yeah. I didn't mean to get your boy all bent out of shape, but we were a little concerned. A subpoena? Why not a call? Or a visit? You look out your window, you could wave at my office."

"Well, the problem with that approach, Butch, is your guy showed up on surveillance saying some pretty disturbing things to a pretty bad wise guy. We thought it was best to keep the whole thing formal for now. You understand, given the sensitivity—"

"What wise guy was that, Norton?"

"Gino Scarpi. We have them taped in the prison ward at Bellevue."

"Oh, for crying out loud, Peabody! Ray was interviewing Scarpi at my direct request."

"That's interesting. It was clear from our tape that he had no recording device on him. Was there one in the room?"

"No, because he wasn't there to gather evidence. He was there to gather intelligence. It's not the same thing."

A pause. "Don't you think it's irregular to send an assistant district attorney to talk to a Mob gunman? Don't you have investigators for that?"

"Yes, of course, but so what? He wasn't sneaking off to conspire with a criminal, for God's sake. He was interviewing a prisoner at my direction. And for this he becomes subject to a subpoena? What is *wrong* with you guys?"

"You should see the tapes, Butch, before you go off half cocked. They look bad, real bad. Your boy sounds like he's a fully paid-up Mafiosi. He even says it out of his own mouth."

"Oh, Peabody, that is such *horseshit*!"

"Hey. I'm trying to be constructive, here. I tell you what: come over, we'll run the tape for you, and then look at me with a straight face and tell me you don't have a problem with it."

"I'll be right there," said Karp.

Marlene's next appointment was her lunch with Abe Lapidus, which had been scheduled for a restaurant in the Village, but on the way back from the Island Marlene decided that she was not up to facing stares in so public a place on her first day out, and so she called Lapidus from her car phone to cancel and he, sensing the problem, said, "Don't be ridiculous! You'll come up to our place. We got food, we got drinks, and later, if you want, you can visit Sophie." To this she readily agreed; she was accustomed to making light of her physical beauty, as a good feminist ought, but in fact, although she had learned over the years to deal with the missing eye, she found that the loss of hair and the marred face had proved too much for mere ideology. She didn't like being repulsive, and she was not going to expose herself to its consequences if she could help it, at least not before age seventy.

The apartment of Abe and Selma Lapidus was furnished in what Marlene always thought of as bad good taste: that is, they had paid a decorator to give them whatever look was fashionable at the moment, although in this case successive waves of fashion were in evidence, like tidemarks on a beach. The wall-to-wall was pale beige, the couch was Duncan Phyfe in pale blue silk, the coffee table was thick glass and chrome, the chairs were designish Scandinavian in teak and leather, the breakfront was massive mahogany from the current plutocratic era, and it was full of bits of pre-Columbiana and African fetish work to exhibit the right political sympathies with the oppressed. The wall art was expensive investment-grade abstract, plus one bright rya from the sixties decor, and a couple of original oils, pasty sad clowns by, Marlene would have bet a million, the chatelaine herself. The room was spotless, and smelled of Pledge and rug shampoo.

"Selma will be out," Abe had confided over the phone. "We won't be disturbed."

Nor were they. Abe served tuna fish salad on croissants, which they ate around the coffee table, with a big bottle of San Peligrino to wash it down, drunk out of cut-glass tumblers almost too heavy to lift to the mouth. A silent brown woman in a white uniform drifted in and served and quickly vanished.

They small-talked during the meal, and when the servant had removed the plates, Marlene got out her notebook. Before many minutes had passed, it was clear to her that Abe Lapidus liked to talk, that he regarded her as a captive audience, and that he considered himself free to ramble on about whatever interested him, something, she suspected, that was fairly rare in his life with Selma. He spun anecdotes of the New York bar of thirty years before, political perceptions, contacts with the famous of that era, general appreciations of the urban scene then and now, comparisons of same, to the detriment of the current era, and around and around the old barn until he was ready to discharge a useful nugget.

"I'm rambling," he confessed. "You wanted to know about Jerry Fein, and I'm rambling."

"That's okay," said Marlene. "Take your time."

He peered at her, tilting his head back to catch her image in his bifocals, and shook his head and tut-tutted. "What a shame! All your hair! And those bruises! That little son of a bitch, they should throw the key away, that . . ." He drew a breath. "Always, he was like that, a vicious, brutal piece of dirt. I don't know how many times Jerry pulled him out of trouble, starting from young, thirteen, fourteen. But what do you expect from that family?"

"You mean that they were gangsters, Mafia?"

"Oh, Mafia, schmafia! Darling, believe me, it doesn't matter what side of the law, it's the *character* I'm talking about. I knew Meyer Lansky quite well, and he was always a perfect gentleman. Lucky Luciano the same. Murderers, dope pushers, but also gentlemen. Can you understand that?"

Marlene could. "I know people like that," she said.

"Right. And there are distinguished citizens, businessmen, attorneys, never even dropped a piece of paper on the sidewalk, I wouldn't trust them alone with my daughter for five minutes. This one, the little Bollano, was a *momser* from the cradle, and the father was worse. If Jerry Fein had lived to see his daughter married to that piece of scum, he would have killed himself."

They both froze for an instant at this, and both then let out a burst of embarrassed laughter.

Abe took off his glasses and wiped his eyes with a handkerchief. "My God in heaven, some things are so tragic the only thing you can do is laugh."

"Yeah, about that: Why *did* Vivian Fein marry Sal Bollano? Any ideas?"

"Oh, well, you know, I only knew Jerry as a colleague, I wasn't intimate with the family. It's possible Sophie would have some thoughts on that, if you can get her to talk about it. She and Ceil were close for some years."

"Ceil is the mother?"

"Yes, and I believe she's still in their old house in Brooklyn. You think you'll talk to her? I hear she's not so good."

"If she'll talk to me. Vivian doesn't want me to."

"Ah, Vivian, what a shame, what a shame! Oy! A gorgeous girl, and he worshiped her, Jerry. For her sweet sixteen party he took over the Versailles ballroom, everything the best, fountains flowing with champagne, Lester Lanin orchestra, must have been five hundred people. Let me tell you, darling, if a bomb had gone off at that party, it would have wiped out organized crime in New York, *and* half of law enforcement. Jerry knew everyone, on both sides, and if you treated him with respect, he treated you with respect, he didn't care from what you made your money."

"Did he have any enemies that you know of?"

The man made a sour pickle face. "Enemies? What are you talking *enemies*? He was an attorney. He wasn't in politics, he didn't have the kind of practice where he would screw people. He represented defendants in court, that's what he did. If some of them were gangsters, then some of them were gangsters, big deal, the law says bad people are entitled to representation, too. This is not a life that makes enemies." He paused and looked at her more sharply. "So, how come you're asking 'enemies'?"

"The cop who investigated his suicide thinks there was something not right about it."

"Who, that what's-his-name, the big Nazi?"

"Mulhausen. No, he's dead. His partner, Doherty." She offered a summary of what she had learned from the former detective.

Lapidus waved a hand dismissively. "Ah, don't get me started on the cops. They do a perfunctory investigation, and then this guy gets a guilty conscience twenty-five years later. Phooey!"

"You think they were bent?"

"Think? No, they were all Abe Lincolns. Don't be ridiculous, the fifties? In New York? Sal Bollano had a bigger payroll in some precincts than the police department."

"Just a minute, Abe. You're suggesting that Sal Bollano had Fein killed and bribed the cops not to look so hard?"

"No, I'm suggesting look at the facts you just told me. One, no note. A man who loved his family? He wouldn't try to explain, say he loved them one last time? I can't believe it. Two, his appointment book was chock full for weeks after the death. A man makes dozens of appointments he knows he'll never keep because he's going to kill himself? Nah!"

"Were you interviewed by the police at the time?"

"Me? Nah, I told you, we weren't that close. But they did people I knew, and it was naturally, such a thing, a subject of discussion around the court-house. No one could believe it, no one!"

"Except Panofsky."

"Aha!" Abe raised a finger in the air, as if he had discovered something. "Smart girl. Except Panofsky."

"But eventually everyone went along with the suicide finding, nobody objected."

Abe sighed. "Darling, the family accepts it, the law partner accepts it, what can you do? We all fig-ured there was stuff, disgraceful things, we didn't know about. You know, back then some people wouldn't say the word 'cancer.' This other business, what you see on the talk shows, people wouldn't even confess to their closest friends."

"But his secretary didn't accept it, did she?"

"Oh, well, that was different, the poor woman! See, that was Jerry again, he would make people love him. Charming, even if you would have lunch with him, a casual thing, you would go away think-ing what a guy! And to tell the absolute truth, you would think you were closer to him than you really were. Anyway, Jerry took in this kid, Shirley, just out of high school, a nice girl, plain but nice, very efficient. She was with him years, never married, devoted, totally, you know? And, you know how it is, that kind of thing, she thought the sun shone out of his *tuchas*. So it was a killer for her when he died, she couldn't understand it. And she would go around with the appointment book, showing it to everyone, to *prove* that he couldn't have done what they all said he did, jump like that. Panofsky, the *momser*, threw her out right after the funeral. He didn't have the balls to do it himself even, is what I heard, he got Jimmy Nobile to do it."

"Who?"

"Nobile. They called him the office manager, but he was a, what they call a gofer, he did a little investigation work, collections, like that. If he's still alive, he'd know a thing or two."

"Any ideas on where to look for him?"

Abe shrugged. "No, no idea. You know, after I said to you, I mean there in the hospital, I could help you on this, I got to thinking, Who really knows the story? And it occurred to me, the people who know if there even *is* a story, they're either dead or they probably won't talk. Panofsky—"

"What's the book on him? I don't like that he was the only one who thought Fein was despondent."

Abe leaned back and rolled his eyes. "Oh, don't get me started on Heshy Panofsky! What can I say? You know the man from the bench. You know what he looks like, how he acts?"

"You mean arrogant?"

"Yeah, not unusual among judges, but Heshy was arrogant when he was a pissy little shyster with a walk-up office on Joralemon Street in Brooklyn. There was some family connection, in-laws or something, I don't know what, but in the early fifties it must have been, Jerry took him into the firm. And he found out—and you know, this was a litigating firm, pardon the expression, balls of brass, sue their ass, that kind—anyway, Jerry found out that Heshy was from hunger in the courtroom. It was all front with Heshy. It came time to put it on the line, he shut down. So, and this shows you what a decent guy Jerry was, he still kept him on. Him and Bernie Kusher took the court work, and Heshy became the fixer."

"What kind of fixer?"

"Oh, you know—traffic tickets, drunk driving, getting a contractor's license. He knew all the pols, all Tammany back then. The machine. Heshy moved a lot of fat brown envelopes around town, and a lot of the money wasn't so clean, if you catch my drift."

"Panofsky supplied Mob cash to politicians?"

Abe smiled. "You didn't hear it from me, darling. Which is why it was so ironic and so fishy that when somebody finally got caught moving one of those fat envelopes, it was Jerry and not Panofsky. Makes you think, don't it?"

"Panofsky framed Jerry?"

"Go and prove it."

"Jesus! How did he ever get to be a judge?"

Another smile, this one more patronizing. "Darling, listen to what you're saying. I told you he had the politicians by the you-know-whats. What, you think you get to be a judge because of your legal brilliance?"

"I stand corrected. Okay, forget Panofsky for now, who else besides this Nobile would know something?"

"Well, that's like I say, the problem. Mulhausen

the cop, but he's dead. The judge in the tampering case, Mohr, and the prosecutor, Currie, also both dead. Bernie Kusher, who knows? Probably dead already—"

"Tell me about Bernie. He was the third partner, right?"

"Right, Bernie Kusher, the third partner. He defended Jerry in the tampering case, or he would've if Jerry hadn't copped out. Another character. Bright, tough, a damn good lawyer. Very close to Jerry, very close: they went to Columbia Law together, started their practice together. I didn't know him well, but the pair of them were devastating in a courtroom. They won a lot of big cases back in the fifties. Sophie socialized with them more, the Feins and Bernie. He was divorced, I seem to recall. You could ask her. I don't have to tell you Panofsky hated him; they were poison together."

After that they talked desultorily about the tampering case, for Abe Lapidus recalled only the broad outlines of the plot, which centered upon the famous zippered bank envelope full of cash (the envelope itself amply stamped with Fein's prints) and a note typed on Fein's office typewriter, indicating that a vote for acquittal in the Gravellotti case would earn double what was inside.

Abe began to maunder again, supplying unwanted details about some peripheral courtroom figures.

"Oh, hell, Abe," Marlene broke in with heat. "You're telling me everything but what I want to know. Why didn't Jerry fight the thing? Why did he cop on it?"

Abe poured out some water, rattled the ice cubes, took a long drink. He gave her an odd look, compounded of assessment, affection, cynically exhausted humor.

"You're a smart cookie, Marlene. That's the big one. We all wondered about that too. Why did one of the sharpest courtroom jockeys around go into the tank when his own *tuchas* was on the line?" Another long pause.

"And? And?"

Lapidus chuckled dryly. "You remember the old Lamplighter? It was a saloon on Baxter. A courtroom hangout. It shut down."

"Yeah, in the early seventies. What about it?"

"This was the evening after Jerry pleaded. Bernie was there in the Lamplighter. He was falling down drunk, which we never saw before, believe me. All of us were what you would call hard drinkers in those days." He tapped his glass with a fingernail. "They didn't move much Italian seltzer in the Lamplighter. You drank scotch. Or martinis. But controlled. You got out of hand, they'd call a cab and stick you in it. Anyway, Bernie was there, buying rounds for anyone who'd yell, 'Fuck you, Panofsky!' And pouring Chivas down as fast as they could set it up, all the time raving about Heshy. How he wasn't going to let Heshy get away with it, he'd confess, he wasn't going to let his pal take the fall, cursing out Heshy and also Frank Currie . . ."

"He was the D.A. in the case?"

"Yeah. Not an ornament to the profession, if you want to know. Bernie was saying things like, 'I'll confess, and Frank Currie can kiss my ass!' People were looking at each other, you know, like when there's an embarrassing drunk. But trying to ignore it. The man was bellowing. And then Jerry walks in and goes right over to him. I figure Pete Demaris, who was behind the bar at the time, must've called him. They did stuff like that in the Lamplighter all the time. It was a club, like. So Jerry goes up to him and puts an arm around him and tries to lead him out, but Bernie won't go, he's holding onto the edge of the bar. He's saying things like, no, no, Jerry, you're not taking the fall for me, I'll confess, and Jerry, angry, telling him to shut the fuck up, excuse my French. Everybody pretending it wasn't happening, but ears flapping like Dumbo. And then Pete came around the bar, this was a real *bulvan*, if you know what that is, and he just tucked Bernie under his arm and they all walked out and stuffed Bernie into a cab and Jerry got in, too." He took another drink.

"So . . . what are you saying? That it was Bernie bribed the juror?"

"Oh, no. That was definitely Panofsky. I told you, he was the fixer. No, just when they were dragging him out the door, Bernie yelled something like, 'I did it!' and then some names—Mintzer, De Salerno, Maddux, and some others. Well, he was raving, so no one paid any attention. Later, they remembered."

"You've lost me, Abe."

"Yeah, it's complicated. I'm amazed *I* can remember it myself. They were names of trusts. The firm didn't have much of a trust business, mostly local guys who made a pile in the forties, wanted to protect their families. Maybe thirty million total. Bernie was in charge of the trust operation."

"And he was looting them."

"Looting is strong. He was doing floats, kiting checks, stripping a little interest. He never touched the principle. But definitely stuff that would not stand up to an audit. Heshy found out about it, needless to say. Not much got past Heshy. So, Heshy sets up the frame on Jerry, who practically laughs in their face when they indict him. He's gonna cram it up Currie's you-know-what. Now, Currie, like I mentioned, is a piece of work. He's desperate to get Bollano, he's got political ambitions, wants to be Tom Dewey number two fighting the mobsters. No ethics to speak of. He figures he squeezes Fein with this bribing a juror charge, it'll be like . . . what're those things the kids break and all the toys fall out? Mexican . . . ?"

"A piñata. But what about client privilege? Jerry was their lawyer."

"Hey, I said the guy was a nogoodnik. Fein knows all about the Bollanos, and Currie figures he's facing ruin, disbarment, he'll open up and spill goodies all around. He don't have to do it in the open. Crack the Bollano mob like that piñata. But Fein wouldn't play that game, no, he's ready to go to trial. Then Currie finds out about Bernie and the trusts, you can guess how. Now, from here it's speculation. I don't *know* any of this. You want to hear it?"

"Desperately."

He laughed. "Okay, cookie. Let's say Currie calls up Fein. We got the goods on your partner, he's going down unless you play ball. Jerry thinks fast. He says, here's the deal—I cop to misdemeanor tampering, you lay off Bernie, and don't *schtup* me with the bar. Currie says, what about the Bollanos? Nothing doing, says Fein, you don't like it, I'll see you in court, and Bernie can take his chances. So Currie, who's no dummy, he thinks, one way I got a good collar on a Mob jury tampering, the other way I got to go up against Jerry Fein and Bernie Kusher with a weak case, I could lose my ass. And what do I care about technical violations of the trust regs? No juice there. So they deal. But afterward Currie *does* put it to him with the bar, and Jerry gets the shaft. Besides the rest of it, Currie was a mean, vindictive son of a bitch."

"That's some story," said Marlene, "but it makes sense. Currie's dead, you said?"

"Yeah, Garrahy, the D.A., canned him when Bernie took off."

"Bernie took off where?"

"Oh, after Jerry died, he really did loot the trusts. Lifted over a million and disappeared. That's why I say that the people who were in the Lamplighter that night recalled the names. It was a big scandal, especially when it came out that Currie knew about the trust irregularities and did nothing as part of the deal with Fein. Bernie put that in a postcard he wrote from Papua or some South Pacific place—wrote it right to Garrahy. You know what Garrahy was like, what he'd do if he found out one of his people was blackmailing a lawyer by suppressing evidence of a crime. Fried Currie's shorts for him and gave him the boot. The man keeled over a couple of years after that. Heart. Bernie disappeared completely, lost in the Pacific."

"Like Amelia Earhart," said Marlene.

"Yeah, but believe me, darling, there were *more* people looking for Bernie." Abe smiled faintly, leaned back in his chair, and took his glasses off. He looked tired, as if this journey to the past had given him a kind of jet lag.

Marlene leafed through her notes. "What about the secretary, this Shirley Waldorf? I guess she's gone, too."

"Oh, no, she's still around. I see her from time to time on 34th Street. She lives there."

"Oh, great! You have her address?"

"No, I mean, she lives *on* the street. She's a bag lady, Marlene. Completely *meshuggeh*. Has been for years."

"She can't communicate at all?"

"Oh, yeah, she *communicates*, all right. You want to go through her *files*, as she calls them, and pretend that she's still a legal secretary, she'll talk your ear off. She carries pathetic piles of trash around in a couple of supermarket carts. Her *files*. Another casualty of what Jerry did."

"If he did it," said Marlene.

"Yeah, right, if he did it."

In a conference room in the organized crime division they showed Karp the tape of Guma talking to Gino Scarpi at Bellevue. The camera had been concealed in the TV set, and the audio treated with sophisticated electronics to remove the sound of the TV programs so that the targets' voices came through with clarity. After the viewing, after Eitenberg had turned up the lights, Karp asked Norton Peabody, "This is all you have?"

"Isn't it enough? It looks an awful lot like conspiracy to me. Your boy's in bed with the wise guys, and apparently has been for years."

Karp rubbed his eyes. He pointed them at Peabody, charged heavily with contempt. "Peabody, how old are you?"

The man hesitated, and then said, "Thirty-seven. Why?"

"Yeah, same as me. Ray Guma is fifty-eight, which means he was putting killers away before either of us got out of high school. He started with the Kings County D.A. in 1949. That was just after that office took apart Murder Incorporated. You have any idea what organized crime was like in New York in 1949, how powerful?"

Peabody affected a bored look. "Yes, I saw *The Godfather*, too. Where is this leading, Butch?"

Karp stared at Peabody until the other man dropped his eyes. "That's a movie, Norton. I'm talking about real life. Ray Guma started work in that environment, and three years later he got an offer from New York County and he went for it. He has over thirty years in the best homicide bureau in the country. He's probably put more actual Mafia killers in jail than anyone else in the United States. And you have the gall to call him dirty?"

Peabody shrugged. "So they threw him a fish

once in a while, just like a trained seal. He still looks like a trained seal to me."

Karp got up, and reflected yet again how nice it was to be big and tall. Peabody was, by contrast, well named. Karp loomed over the smaller man for a long moment, fists clenched, until Peabody discovered that it was urgent to turn off the VCR and retrieve his tape. He stayed by the machine, a comfortable three yards from Karp, who said, with conviction, "This is going to be an embarrassment for you guys if you try to construe that horseshit as serious evidence. And I know that Mr. Colombo really hates to be embarrassed in public. His long, scaly tail lashes around in fury and does all kinds of damage to the people close to him." He nodded politely to both men and left.

He trotted across Foley Square to the courthouse, went directly to Guma's office, knocked.

"I'm on the phone," said the occupant's voice. Karp barged in anyway and made urgent circular motions with his index finger.

Guma said into the phone, "Sol, I'll have to call you back, I got a crisis here."

He replaced the receiver and looked up at Karp, who said, "I just came from the Southern District. Your subpoena is because they got the prison ward thing on tape. You and Scarpi."

"Fuck! Ah, *shit*, I should've figured they had the place bugged."

Karp threw himself into an old-fashioned wooden swivel chair, making it rattle. "Well, according to them, said tape demonstrates that you're the Mob's mole in the D.A. They were pretty convincing.

Quote, I'm in the *famiglia*. Quote, you'll be the first to know. Quote, the fix is in. Unquote. Easy to misconstrue, no?"

"Misconstrue? Shit, Butch, you can *misconstrue* 'good morning' negative if you put your mind to it. What went on between Gino and me was just the usual horseshit I do with those guys. Nobody takes it seriously."

"Colombo does."

"Right, and he's a fuckhead, we know that. Next question."

Karp took a deep breath. "Okay, you're right. Jack will go a little ballistic, but who the fuck cares? Right is on our side, and that's what counts. It looks like shit, but I don't care about appearances, and you sure as shit don't either. I mean, Guma, *look* at you!"

Guma looked down at his chest and then at Karp. Then he laughed. Karp laughed, too, and said, "Meanwhile, I can't do anything about whatever passed between you and Gino, so you will respond to their fucking subpoena like a good citizen, and answer all questions asked, and explain what a jocular remark is, and fuck them if they can't take a joke."

Guma laughed briefly, then sobered. "It's a damn good thing grand juries are secret."

"Why?" asked Karp, and then it hit him. "Oh, you mean the boys might think you . . ."

"Guaranteed. This gets out, nobody in town with a vowel on the end of his name's gonna want to talk to me, and I'll be wearing Kevlar underwear for the rest of my life."

15

THEY WERE SITTING ON A WARM ROCK overlooking the 97th Street transverse in Central Park, eating pho out of styrofoam boxes and washing it down with black tea from cardboard cartons, when Tran gestured with his chopsticks at the humming traffic below and said, in Vietnamese, "Dear child, suppose you have two squads, say sixteen men. Where would you dispose them so as to block that road?"

Lucy sighed dramatically and rolled her eyes. "I would have them join hands and march down the middle of it, of course. Why do you ask?"

"She mocks her elders. I see you will have to be drowned after all, and here is a large body of water convenient to the task." He seized the back of her vest with his free hand and mock-pulled her in the direction of the reservoir. She giggled and shrugged away. "But truly, Uncle Tran, why at every street corner do you ask me, how would you attack that building, or defend it? When I was younger it was our game, but now it is peculiar. Ought I to worry about your mental powers?"

"Your concern for my failing mind is worthy and

I thank you. Nevertheless, the reason for my asking such questions is plain. 'Sea becomes mulberry fields and returns to sea.' As you have read. Things change in unpredictable ways. When I was your age, I knew without the slightest doubt that I was going to teach literature at the Lycée Chasseloupe Laubat in Saigon. My future was planned, arranged, and secure, just as you imagine yours is. In the event, however, it proved necessary for me to acquire skills I did not dream of then, no more than poor Kieu in her father's garden imagined she would serve in a brothel and live as a bandit queen. The potter's wheel spins, disasters come flying on the wind, as they say."

His eyes, as he said this, were both sad and fierce, and she felt a chill. "Very well, Uncle," she said, and between slurps of noodle and pointing with her chopsticks she designated the positions of the riflemen, the machine guns, the fixed charges, the rocket launchers, and the planned concentrations of mortar fire in the dead ground. Tran responded with more questions, and soon they had so effective a kill zone designed that, had it been put into effect, New Yorkers would have found it far harder to get across the park than was presently the case.

They finished their meal, and Lucy trotted over the rise to find a basket for the trash. Tran had been her constant companion during her outings to the Columbia lab these last days, which was nearly the only time she got out, except for church. She was stifling but resolved not to show it, least of all to Tran.

She returned to the rock shelf and sat. Tran was

still and silent, watching the road, as if he were preparing an actual ambush.

"Why are we waiting here, Uncle Tran?" she
asked after some minutes. "My bottom is sore from
this rock."

"Have you any pressing engagements?"

"Only with the remainder of my life, if you can
call it that," she sighed, switching to her native
tongue.

"In that case you can practice being still, a useful
attainment, as you know. Squat also, as I do, rather
than slouch like an empress on a divan. This will
relieve your . . . ah, you are saved. Here is what we
await."

A dark Ford van had pulled up on the shoulder of
the transverse, discharging an Asian man in a tan
suit and large sunglasses. He walked up the little
hill and stopped at the base of the rock ledge. Tran
formally introduced girl and gangster. They both
nodded politely, and then Freddie Phat said, "They
are back."

"Where were they, do you know?" asked Tran.

"Upstate, and in Connecticut, Hartford, pulling
home invasions. Kenny's telling everyone that the
first thing he's going to do is kill you."

Tran smiled unpleasantly. "Then I must flee for
certain. Tell me, is Leung with them?"

"No, still gone. What they say on the street is
he has traveled to Hong Kong, to report, and that he
will return with his own people."

Tran stood up, as did Lucy, who repressed the
desire to massage her aching knees. Tran said,
"That is interesting, and gives a certain urgency to

our task. At this moment a freight container with ten assassins in it might be unloading at some airport. Where are the Vo now?"

"Their apartment on Hester, off Lafayette. They keep girls there. What do you want to do?"

"Oh, by all means let us visit, and join the party. Perhaps Lucy will read us passages from *The Tale of Kieu*, and we can all have a good cry."

Tran and Lucy mounted the motorcycle, and they followed Phat in his van out of the park and downtown to Lafayette, parking both vehicles some distance from the junction of that broad avenue with Hester Street. Lucy sat in the back of the van and watched Phat talk to the man he had set to watch the house. There was some agitated conversation, and Phat showed considerable irritation. Lucy gathered that the two brothers had gone out a few minutes before. Tran and Phat and two of his boys went up into the house. The driver and the man Phat had used to watch the house sat in the front seats. The windows of the van were tinted to near opacity, and they kept the engine running and the A/C on, drowning out the sounds of the street. It was like being in a spaceship. The two men ignored her, nor did she wish very much to converse with them. (So, how do you like being a gangster . . . ?)

Instead she opened her *Kieu* and read about Kieu's romance with the bandit-rebel chieftain Tu Hai, fairly hot stuff, and this kept her occupied, reading and thinking that she was uncomfortably close to hanging out with bandit chieftains herself, until the van's door slid open and there was Tran, dragging by the arm a thin Vietnamese whom Lucy recognized from her kidnapping as Nguyen Van Minh, called Cowboy.

Tran threw the boy facedown into the space between the two rows of seats and kicked him flat, wrenched his arms around, and secured his wrists together with plastic cable tie.

"Do you recognize this garbage?" he asked Lucy.

"Yes, he's one of the kidnappers," she said, and added quickly, "but he didn't hurt me."

"Lucky for him."

"What will you do with him?" she asked.

"I believe *Ong* Phat will offer him hospitality," Tran replied, "and then perhaps his cousins, who seem to have stepped out for a while, will try to get him, and then we all sit down and have a talk about Mr. Leung and his various projects. You need not concern yourself."

He turned away to speak to Phat and Phat's minions. Lucy leaned over the Vietnamese youth.

"Cowboy, don't be afraid," she whispered in Vietnamese.

The youth twisted his head around. Lucy could see the side of his face and the livid bruise along his jaw, and a bit of swollen and bloody mouth, and one eye, white-rimmed and staring like a cow's.

"Don't worry, I won't let them hurt you."

He replied, "What can you do? You are only a girl."

"So was Kieu. Listen: Phat is the dog of Tran, and Tran loves me. Be calm and don't struggle or try to escape. I will see that you come out of this all right."

She left the van and went to Tran. Motioning him aside, she said, "I want you to promise me something, Uncle Tran."

"If I can," he said.

"See that no harm comes to that boy."

He frowned down at her, but she met his gaze. He said, "But, my dear girl, we require information from him. What if he does not wish to give it? These are dangerous people, and we must eliminate any danger that they pose to us. To you perhaps most of all."

"I will interrogate him myself."

Tran suppressed a smile. "Will you? I had not realized that was one of your talents. I look forward to learning much at your feet."

"You mock me, but I tell you he will speak to me. Now promise!"

The Vietnamese gangsters were staring at this colloquy, which to them had much of the effect of Fay Wray dressing down King Kong.

After a long, tense moment Tran grinned, nodded sharply, and said, "I promise. And I must say that this is a remarkable and romantic gesture. I had not expected such gestures from you, at least not for some time."

"Then you should not have given me that book," said Lucy.

Dinner that night at the Karps' was a subdued affair. Desultory conversation, and the click of utensils, a monastery repast almost, with each member of the family locked in private thoughts. Lucy excused herself early, kissing both her father (with an especially close embrace) and her mother (a more formal yet still tender one), something she had not done for a while. Marlene set the espresso pot on the flame and sat down to finish her wine. Karp, she noted, had poured himself a glass too: rarer that, even than Lucy's kisses.

"You look a little tattered," she said. "What's going on?"

"You look tattered yourself."

"No, *I* look *destroyed*. Ruined. *You* look tattered. What is it, the agony of command? Trouble being Queen for a Day?"

"Oh, not really. A little spat with the Southern District." He told her about Guma's subpoena and its sequelae.

"Jack will shit," she said with assurance.

"Uh-huh, but he'll be pissed at Tommy C., not Guma."

"Mmm. I take your point about not hauling Mr. Lie before your grand jury without some better idea of who the hell he is and what he's done, but is Jack going to sit with that, with all the political pressure he's under?"

"Roland thinks he'll roll on it. I mean, the upside is pretty clear and straightforward. He gets a grand jury witness who'll implicate Pigetti and maybe the Bollanos, and provide corroboration, give us the people who lifted Eddie, maybe physical evidence—"

"But you're concerned Lie'll also say, oh, and by

the way, I pulled the trigger on Eddie Cat and I also did some other little jobs for various people, and you won't be able to touch him on those."

"You got it, and also there's the real possibility that Pigetti didn't do it," said Karp, and took another drink of wine, toyed with a plastic soldier one of the boys had left at the table, and returned in his thoughts to the idea that had been niggling at him for weeks, the real reason he had not done the expedient thing and gone ahead and cleared Lie for the grand jury.

"Earth to Butch, hello?" said his wife.

"Excuse me?"

"I've been talking for five minutes, and you haven't heard anything I said. Where were you?"

"I'm sorry, Champ, what were you saying?"

"Never mind that, what were you thinking? Except, if it was an elaborate sexual fantasy not featuring me, I don't want to hear about it."

He said, "How can you drink a pint of espresso this late at night?"

"Don't change the subject. What's going on?"

"Nothing. It's just a feeling, a . . . an aura. I have the sense of some presence, some controlling force behind all this, the Catalano thing, the business Lucy's involved in, the Sing killings. Shit! And I can't figure out how the pieces fit. We have one low-ranking wetback Chinese gangster, who walks into the D.A.'s office, asking for me personally, with a half-wit lawyer, and says he's willing to act as a witness against Joe Pigetti, and this gangster seems to have a remarkably clear understanding of the immunity procedures available in New York

state. Why? Because he's scared that the Mob is going to get him, he says. Marlene, I looked this guy
in the face, and I have never seen anyone less scared
in my life. His *lawyer* was scared shitless, but *he*
wasn't. You ask me, the little bastard could eat the
whole Bollano mob à la marinara. And this guy has
no traces, none, no car, no bank account, no drugs,
but when we check him out with Hong Kong, we
find out he's really a guy named Nia who's got big-
time triad contacts over in the Far East. That's one
thing we do know for sure, from fingerprints: Lie
is definitely the man the Hong Kong cops know as
Nia. That's only mystery number one. Mystery
number two: the whole leadership of the Bollano organization is knocked out, except for the don himself: Catalano killed, Pigetti accused, Little Sally in
jail, charged with attempted murder, et cetera. Does
somebody have a big hard-on for the Bollanos? And
are they using us to get them?"

"But there's no connect between Little Sally and
the other two," Marlene objected. "He got in trouble
because his wife cut out on him."

"Yeah, right, it's a coincidence. Just like it's a
coincidence that two big triad guys got whacked
the same week as Eddie Cat, at which murder our
little girl might well have been a witness, and then
a Chinese gangster with triad connections comes
in and asks to see me personally, and shortly thereafter, another no-name Chinese gangster, Leung,
starts hiring people to threaten Lucy and find out
what she knows, among other things, to demonstrate to dear old dad how easily his daughter could
be snatched. That's mystery number three. Too

many mysteries in a limited area, Champ. I have this sense that somebody is sitting out there pulling the strings, some . . . some *intelligence*, moving around little plastic soldiers." Angrily he flicked the actual soldier with his index finger. It flew across the room, ricocheted off the refrigerator, and landed, clanging, in a steel mixing bowl awaiting rinsing on the drainboard of the sink.

"Two points," muttered Karp.

"Yes, and an example of the role of the random in our lives."

"What, you think all of that *is* just coincidence?"

"I don't know," she said. "The killings could be connected. Lie and Leung could be working for the same outfit. But I do know that the joker in your deck is Vivian. Why did she split just then after years of marriage to the scumbag? And in a way guaranteed to send Little Sal off the rails and get him into deep trouble?"

"I like that she was boffing Eddie Cat, and when he got it, she figured she was next and ran."

"No way," said Marlene. "Scarpi was right; it had been that, they would've used the knife, and made her watch. No, it was something from the deep past reached up and bit her on the ass. That's why this Jumping Jerry investigation is happening." And she told him what she had learned that day from Doherty and Abe Lapidus.

"That's interesting about Judge Paine being such a bad boy back in the old days," said Karp. "He's really cleaned up his act, if true. I've never heard a whisper about him being bent. The opposite, in fact. He's hell on the defendant, especially Mob defendants."

"People change," said Marlene. "Maybe. By the way, I went by Sophie's after I finished with Abe. I think I caught her and her enamorata in a compromising position. She was wearing a lavender wrapper with an actual feathered collar and silk mules."

"This is Jake?"

"Yeah. He stayed in the bedroom, probably in black silk pj's and a scarlet quilted monogrammed robe with tassels. Me and Sophie chatted briefly. I didn't want to take her away from a hot time, especially, God forbid, you can never tell if it might be her last one. And Abe was right, she didn't know any of the legal details, but she filled me in pretty good on the family and friends. A very fifties story. The king and the queen in paradise, with the perfect little girl, and of course they had the usual Jewish princess and rich daddy relationship, and also we got the best friend—"

"Kusher, the *gonif*."

"Yeah, but before he achieved *gonif*-hood. A swell guy, sort of the third wheel around Jerry and the lovely Ceil, his bride. Ceil's a little soft in the upper stories, according to Sophie, but very decorative, played a lot of guts canasta. Bernie's the jokester, the boys play practical jokes on each other, gag gifts, costumes, while they make a nice living defending the Mob."

"Was Bernie schtupping the wife, do you think?"

"God, I didn't think to ask! And I thought *I* was the one with the dirty mind."

"A possibility, anyway," said Karp. "It's always the best friend. A guy dies, suicide or foul play, you look at that the first day. And the man did vanish."

"Well, they were discreet as hell if so, because I haven't heard a whisper. Anyhow, into this paradise comes the serpent Panofsky. Jerry's being his usual amenable self, and Panofsky brought some family money into the firm, which never hurts, and the kid washes out as a trial guy and he becomes the fixer, et cetera, which we knew already, and also, get this, he conceives a passion for, guess who?"

"The lovely and talented Vivian?"

"Right, and naturally it's a joke," said Marlene. "She's a dewy sixteen, and a stunner, he's pushing thirty, and he looks like an armpit, as we know, a young armpit maybe, but still, and according to Sophie, he's hanging around her, weekends at the beach, it's embarrassing, he won't let up. Finally she tells him to take a hike in no uncertain terms. He still doesn't get the picture, so Jerry has a talk with him, nice but firm. Then he lets up. This is in August, say, and that fall, that's when the jury-tampering scandal breaks."

"You're saying Panofsky framed Jerry because . . . what, he was *spurned* by the beauteous Vivian?"

"Hey, far be it from me to cast aspersions at a distinguished jurist, but it does have a certain poetic resonance, a Jacobean flavor, *The White Devil* or *The Spanish Tragedy*. I can just see the ugly little fuck licking his lips and rubbing his hands together as he takes his revenge." Marlene rolled her eye horribly, licked her lips, and wrung her hands to demonstrate.

Karp shook his head and gave his wife a cock-eyed look. "And . . . after twenty-odd years, what? What happened to make her break out? And come to that, how do we go from spurning Panofsky to accepting a nasty psychopath, the young Bollano?"

"Oh, well, that was *after* Jerry's jump," said Marlene. "The girl is desperate, miserable, vulnerable, the mom is a dim bulb, and, you have to say, the mope at least is a handsome devil. Maybe he said, yeah, honey, some mobster aced your old man and by God we're going to find him and whack him out, and maybe he did, or he said he did. And then she finds out just recently he really didn't, he was blowing smoke to get her in the sack."

Karp laughed. "Makes a great movie, Champ, but . . ." He rubbed his thumb and index finger together. "Where's the beef?"

"Yeah, right," she agreed with a sigh. "But I still got people to talk to, Nobile the gofer and maybe I can dig up this bag lady, get her story. I called Paine's office for an appointment and got one for tomorrow."

"Oh, I'd love to be a fly on the wall for that," said Karp.

"Yeah, especially the part where I trade sexual favors for the straight poop. Euuugh!" She shuddered elaborately. "Meanwhile"—she consulted her watch—"want to watch some TV? That's all I have energy for right now."

"In a bit. Let me just go spend some time with Lucy."

He walked down the hall, feeling a bit of a sneak, because when she kissed him at the table, his daughter had whispered a request for him to do just that, later, in her room.

He knocked, got a "come in," and found his daughter in bed, reading *The Loom of Language*. She put the book down, and his heart sagged at how peaked she looked, like an abandoned nestling.

"What's up, kid?" he asked as he turned her desk chair around and sat.

"If I tell you stuff, like crime stuff, can I, like, stop telling you when I want, or do I have to tell the whole thing?"

"I assume this is not just hypothetical."

"No, it's real."

Karp waited a beat or two, nodded, and said, "Okay. Here's the deal. If you give me information about a crime or criminal activity, then I'm obliged to take official cognizance of it. I mean if you say, 'Dad, I saw Joe shoot Jim,' then I have to go after Joe and I have to name you as a witness. I got no choice here. The cops get called, they interrogate you, they interrogate Joe . . ."

He stopped because Lucy was shaking her head. "No, I mean, I just want to give you some information about a suspect. Like I saw a guy on a wanted poster and then I spotted him on the street. Do I have to say how I got it or if other stuff happened? I mean, I *want* to tell you, it's, like, the *right* thing, because it could stop a bad crime and people I know could get into trouble, but do you have to, like, *bug* me to tell you every little thingee about it, I mean, how I know and stuff?"

She was suffering, he could see it, and he wanted to enfold her in protective arms and make all this go away, and he thought about what Marlene had said in the hospital room that day, about who Lucy really *was*. A hug from daddy would not, in fact, make it all better.

"Lucy," he said, "let's keep it real simple. You just tell me what you want to tell me, and I won't bug you for any more. But I will take the actions I think are necessary, both as a member of the D.A.'s office and as a father, for your safety. Sorry, but that's the best I can do."

"We found the Vo brothers," said Lucy in a rush, as if the phrase were a bolus of poison she had to heave out or die.

"Where?"

"Two-oh-three Hester Street, off Lafayette, second floor in the front."

"Okay, good girl! You wait here, I'll be right back." Karp went to the hall phone and dialed a familiar number. Experienced in such instant mobilizations of force, Clay Fulton asked few questions as Karp filled him in.

"You want me to bring the Five in on this?" was one of them.

Karp thought of Phil Wu. He had been hard on Wu, and he figured it would be a decent gesture to let the guy in on a good collar. Clay Fulton was way past needing credit for big arrests. He said, "Yeah, Phil Wu's the man there. And make sure they have a Vietnamese interpreter along. I don't want these guys getting shot because of a mistake. Call me when you get it done, whenever. I'll be here."

After discussing a few more details, they hung up, and Karp went back to Lucy's room. This time he sat next to her on the bed and pulled her close. He noticed that she had washed her hair, a good sign, and, putting his face close to the herbal-scented dark curls, he said, "All right, that was the D.A. part. This is the Daddy part. Is there anything else you want to talk about?" No answer; he felt her head shake against his chest.

"I'm worried about you, Luce," he said. "We're a family. There shouldn't be any secrets in a family."

"Hah!"

"What, you think there *are* secrets?"

She pulled away and looked up at him, meeting his eyes, which he thought was a good sign. She said, "Are you kidding? You're running the D.A. and my mother is a part-time felon, so what do you think? And I'm probably a felon, too."

"You're not a felon, honey," said Karp, startled as this sentence left his mouth, for it was not one that he had ever imagined saying to a child of his.

"How would you know?" she snapped, and then sagged against him again, cuddling into his arms. In a weary voice, too weary, Karp thought, for the voice of a child, she said, "I don't want to be a *freak* anymore. And *don't* say 'you're not a freak,' because I am. It's a scientific fact. And I'm tired of all this . . . shooting and kidnapping and hospitals. I want things to be *regular*, like a regular family. And I love Tran, but he thinks he's still in the war, and we have to play soldiers all the time, and I used to like it, it was fun and exciting, but now . . . what's that called when soldiers go crazy from fighting too long?"

"You mean combat fatigue?"

"Yeah. I don't want this anymore. Sometimes, you know, like when you daydream? I dream that I have this room, with just my things in it, and attached to it is a big library with all the dictionaries and grammars in the world, and language tapes, and that's all, just a big white room, and it's on an island, with nobody else on it. And people could come by boat, or something, but they couldn't get on except if I wanted them to. And I could stay there and not be *bothered* by all this stuff. Crazy, huh?"

"Not really," said Karp. "Could we have cable? And bagels?"

She giggled. "Oh, right, we need one of those machines they have on *Star Trek*, a replicator, that gets you anything you need."

"Good idea, and we would need some hoops, full-court on parquet, like the Boston Garden . . ." He stopped because the girl's face had fallen. "What? No parquet? Okay, a half court, on planks. We're only going to play horse and one-on-one, anyway. Lucy, what is it?"

She shrugged. "I'm sleepy," she said. "I need to say my prayers now."

"Okay, Luce. But . . . I don't know how, but I'm going to fix this for you. This is wrong. You're a kid, you shouldn't be going through this now." He kissed her forehead.

She gave him a bleak, heartbreaking little smile, and he went out the door. Before he shut it, he looked back and saw her cross herself and kneel by the bed, her head down on her clenched hands, resting on the bed, her body stiff with concentration.

He could see the knobs of her spine through the thin cloth of her T-shirt, but he could not hear her murmurings, which, after the usual preliminaries, were, "Dear Lord, bless and keep my family and friends, and bless Tran, and take the violence and hate from his heart, he is really a good man, and help me to love my mother, and to be nice to her, and help her to love me, not just worry about me, which isn't the same, make her understand that, please, and don't let my father worry too much about me, it drives me crazy, and let Janice like me again the way she used to, and protect her and the Chens from the triad, and let them catch the guys who did it, and no more killing, please, and let them not hurt Cowboy, because I think he's really not a bad gangster, and give me spiritual strength, dear Jesus, and help me control my temper, and also, if it be Your will, please, please, could I have some breasts? Amen."

Always an uncomfortable moment for Karp, watching his child worship a God he didn't believe existed and in so alien a fashion. He sent into the agnostic void a hopeless quasi-prayer of his own that whatever she was praying for might be delivered, after which he gently closed the door and walked down the hall to the living room, where he found his wife sprawled on the red velvet couch, sipping coffee and watching television. She lifted her legs, he sat down, and she dropped her calves across his lap, having converted Karp over the years into a pretty good foot massager. But only a desultory rub did she get tonight.

Marlene muted the volume of the show, a sitcom

of no particular distinction except as an evening anodyne, and asked, "How is she?"

"Depressed. Exhausted. Marlene, we have to do something about this kid. I don't care what you say about her special qualities, she needs to be moved out from under this load she's carrying."

"What do you have in mind?"

"Get her out of town, for starters, until this thing blows over. Hey, it's the summer. She could visit John or Anna or Patsy, hang out with the cousins. We could send her to camp, or . . . I don't know, a summer program, anything to get her out of here, and get her mind off what went down in that goddamn stockroom."

Marlene considered this for some moments. "You're concerned she could be in danger?"

"Jesus, Marlene! Of *course* I'm concerned. Aren't you?"

"To an extent," she replied with unnatural calm. "So, what is it, you have visions of Chinese hit squads bursting in and spraying bullets at her?"

"Yeah, that's a possibility," he admitted, "and that's why—"

"And so you think the best place to put her is on my brother's or my sisters' suburban lawn with a gang of cousins? What, to absorb some of the bullets?"

"Don't be stupid, Marlene! I only meant that—"

"And you think that if someone wanted to get her, they wouldn't know how to find out where my relatives lived?"

"We could make arrangements to have her watched."

"By who? Rent-a-cops? Butch, I'm in the *business*! Please do me the courtesy of acknowledging that I know what I'm doing here."

"So what do we have now? The great and powerful Tran? That's it?"

She shook her head, irritated. "Butch, where do you think Tran is, right now, this minute?"

"I have no idea."

"Well, I'm not sure either, but"—here she lifted her eyes upward—"I would guess that he's slung in a hammock on our roof with a Kalashnikov across his chest. Anybody tried to come through that door, assuming they got through the cordon of tough little Viets he's had posted around this block since the kidnapping, he'd be down through that skylight in about three seconds and turn whoever it was into shreds. You think the Valley Stream P.D. out by my sister's would mount an operation like that for Lucy?"

Karp raised his own eyes to the ceiling. "He does this every night? When does he sleep?"

"I'm not sure that Tran does sleep. In any case, does that make you feel any better?" Karp stared blankly at the screen, letting the silent images bounce meaninglessly off his eyeballs. The sitcom was over, the commercials were selling bright goods.

"It's not just that, Marlene. This whole situation, the Chinatown stuff, the genius stuff, it's, I don't know, *eroding* her." He let out a bitter laugh. "Aside from getting pissed at you, I honestly don't know what the hell to do."

"Yeah, well, I realize the agenda here is if only

Marlene had been a normal mom, like both of our moms, if only we lived in a regular suburban house, and she went to a regular suburban school—we've been over this a million times, Butch. It's fruitless. If, if . . . if your grandmother had wheels, she could haul cement. There's no way out except *through* it, playing the cards as dealt. What you need to spend your energy on is lighting a fire under the cops to get these bastards."

"Good advice, Marlene. I'll tell you what, why don't you let me be in charge of legal affairs in this family? You seem to have your hands full with the illegal kind." Marlene huffed, but Karp had shifted the focus of his attention.

He grabbed for the remote, pushed the mute. A commercial for the news program scheduled for the next slot was on the screen.

". . . startling revelations suggesting Mafia infiltration at the highest levels of the New York district attorney's office," said the announcer, and on the screen was Ray Guma, winking slyly and saying, "The fix is in."

"All this and the latest weather and sports. Stay tuned," said the announcer.

Karp said, "Ah, shit! The stupid fuckers leaked the film."

They watched as the news came on and the screen showed the artfully edited tape, thirty seconds of Guma saying those unwise sentences to Gino Scarpi, ending with that wink and "the fix is in." After that there was an interview with Norton Peabody in the lobby of the Federal Building. Mr. P. was terribly upset that someone had leaked this piece of evidence, and an investigation was under way to find the culprit. Was there a federal investigation under way of the D.A.'s office? He was not at liberty to reveal whether or not there was. Would the federal grand jury take up the issue? The grand jury was authorized to explore all aspects of Mafia penetration of society, and the D.A.'s office was not excluded. Mr. Guma had received a subpoena and would be appearing before the grand jury in short order. The minute being up, the news switched to the doings in Lebanon, leaving Karp shrieking curses at the screen, and then the phone rang. Karp went out of the room to the kitchen and stood over the answering machine, glaring at it and snarling. It was a reporter. He left a message. Another ring. Another reporter.

Reporter. Reporter. TV reporter, could we schedule an interview for seven tomorrow? Another reporter. Then, "Butch! Jack Keegan. Pick up if you're there."

Karp picked up. "Are you having fun yet?"

"Goddamn it, I actually was until this goddamn tape got on the TV."

"Did they show it in West Virginia?"

"No, Mary just called and gave me the good news. Jesus, Butch, I'm here with every D.A. in the country, and it's out on network TV that I got a Mafia mole in my office. I'm gonna have to play golf tomorrow with a bag on my head. You saw it?"

"Yeah, Peabody showed it to me this afternoon. He's subpoenaed Guma based on the tape." He paused, while Keegan said nothing. "You know it's horseshit, don't you?"

"Oh, Christ, of course it's horseshit," said Keegan, "but that's not the point. It looks bad politically. I know you don't think that's important, but believe me it is. We could put the whole five families in jail and what people would remember is that fucking tape. Did he really wink and say 'the fix is in'?"

"I'm afraid so. What're you going to do?"

"Hell, I feel like leaving right now. Four hours by car to D.C. and I could be on the first shuttle tomorrow morning."

"Don't do that, Jack. It gives the fuckers more credibility than they deserve. Stay out of town and let me handle it. I'll do a press conference tomorrow morning and come out snarling. It should take the wind out of their sails a little, and if it doesn't work you can repudiate me, whatever."

He was glad to hear Keegan's laugh over the line. "Oh, I will, my lad, never fear. Meanwhile that sounds like a start. I'll work the phones tomorrow, I got some pals at Justice, and I'll call my tame reporters in the city. Counterattack is good. I thought you didn't do politics."

"I can do it," said Karp. "I just hate it."

He hung up shortly thereafter, and the phone immediately rang again. Karp cursed and listened, but it was not the press again. It was Fulton.

"We got one of them, Stretch," he said, "and we lost two." His voice was husky with exhaustion.

"What happened?"

"No problems going in, but two of the three weren't there. The guy we got is Vo Hoa Dung, they call him Needlenose. The big brother, Kenny Vo, was out. The other one, the cousin, disappeared this afternoon under circumstances yet to be determined. We found a bunch of weapons, too, including a couple of MAC–10 submachine guns. According to one of the girls, Kenny's packing one."

"Terrific. Was Phil Wu there?"

"Yeah, and I got to say the man has a pair of balls. He was the first one through after the ESU popped the door. He did the interrogation, too."

"Anything useful?"

A pause on the line. "Vo won't talk at all. The girls were saying that the Vo boys were yakking about how they were going to take out your Vietnamese buddy."

"Tran?"

"Him. And, Butch? Jesus, I hate to have to tell you this, but they said they were going after Lucy, too."

"Not if their asses are in jail. So out of the four original perps, one's in the prison ward at King's County, one's in custody, one's on the run, and one we don't know where he is. Is that right?"

"You got it. We're going to need Lucy down here tomorrow morning to ID Needlenose Vo in a lineup. You'll get her down to the Five?"

Karp said that he would. As he hung up, he reflected that, for at least part of the following day, his daughter would be in a police station and he could for a brief time stop worrying about her.

16

"NO MAKEUP," SAID KARP.

"It's only powder," said the television woman. She had approached him in the chaos behind the set of the *Morning Report* show. Karp had arranged to be on the show just after speaking with Keegan the previous evening, to answer questions about the Guma-Scarpi tape. By now the tape had been seen at least a hundred times on all the local stations and the networks, too (*The fix is in*: wink), and Dudley Bryson, the newsman who was about to interview Karp, had, at their initial meeting earlier that morning, practically to wipe the saliva from his chin, so eager was he to get Karp before his cameras. A dangerous man, according to Bill McHenry, the D.A.'s public affairs chief, who had lectured Karp on how to handle *Morning Report*, a detailed strategy that had gone in one ear and out the other.

The television woman said, "Everybody uses it. It takes away the shine." She smiled as for a recalcitrant child and leaned closer, paper bib and puff in hand. Karp gave her a knifing yellow look, of the type he ordinarily reserved for violent pedophiles.

"I. Said. *No*."

She paled and scuttled away, muttering.

A young man wearing a headset and carrying a clipboard approached and led Karp out to the set, a matte blue wall dressed with a coffee table and two tan padded chairs. Karp was seated in one and fitted with a tiny microphone that clipped to his tie. Asked for a sound level, Karp said, "I wish for this entire enterprise to be destroyed by fire from the heavens, destroyed utterly, leaving only ashes and horribly disfigured corpses," which apparently sufficed, and in short order the host came out, pancaked and hairsprayed to a mannikin perfection, and sat in the other seat, and had his mike attached, and attempted some small talk with Karp, not very successfully, and then the makeup person came out again and patted some powder on Bryson's thick orangey makeup, and he said something to her, indicating the guest with a gesture of his chin, and she shook her head and stalked off stage. Then the kid with the headset crouched in front of them and made three-two-one signs with his fingers and snapped his index finger pistol-like on the last count and the red light on the camera went on and Karp made a concentrated effort to relax the set of his jaw, which felt wired, and then Bryson was talking.

Karp tried to tell himself that this was just like a jury trial, that he was about to make a presentation to a jury of millions rather than just twelve, but he knew at some level that this was not so. Juries were grave affairs; whatever their origins, jurors were almost always ennobled by their function, which

was seeking truth, that tender thing, and while
Karp, if pressed, might agree that at its best journalism reached for something similar, what he was
doing now had little to do with journalism at even
its second best. What this jabbering little pimp next
to him was doing was entertaining slobs in hopes
that they would buy Miller rather than Bud, and
Pontiac rather than Ford.

The scant intros over, Bryson called for the tape,
and once again they all watched Ray Guma at work.
Bryson's false smile spoke: "Mr. Karp, many people
believe that what we've just seen suggests criminal
activity and the possible corruption of the district
attorney's office by organized crime. What's your
response to that?"

Karp said, "Oh, there's no doubt that it's evidence of a crime."

Bryson had expected wriggling here, and so he
was somewhat taken aback. "And what is the district attorney's office going to do about it?" he
asked.

Karp raised his eyebrows. "Nothing, with respect to prosecution. It's a federal crime."

The false smile grew confused; the face turned
to the camera to show it was not dismayed. "Excuse me?"

"Yes. It's illegal under federal statute and Department of Justice regulation to reveal the proceedings
of a grand jury, and that includes the evidence collected pursuant to those proceedings."

"But surely the First Amendment overrides some
regulation," said Bryson. "Think of the Pentagon
Papers—"

"Yes, but that's for a judge to decide. And I assure you that our office will protest most vigorously to Judge Oberst, the federal judge who empanelled the federal grand jury, regarding the release of this evidence. The issue of whether the U.S. attorney's office deliberately violated the seal of the grand jury in this case has nothing to do with your action as a member of the press to publish material you have in hand under supposed First Amendment privileges. The release itself is, in our opinion, frankly illegal."

Bryson was starting to feel uneasy. On a live show there was always the danger of an interview subject going ballistic, but the reporter had a vast faith in the power of television to produce awe and terror and bland agreeableness in the people upon whom its searchlight fell. People *wanted* to be loved by television reporters. He moved now to regain control. "But Mr. Colombo has denied any deliberate leak of the tape we just saw, and in any case, the issue here is whether Mr. Guma has—"

"I am not accusing Mr. Colombo directly," Karp interrupted. "It is entirely within the realm of possibility that an intrepid reporter penetrated the interior of the Southern District offices, got past dozens of armed federal law enforcement officers, located the tape in question from among hundreds and hundreds of evidence tapes, and purloined it. In that case Mr. Colombo would be merely incompetent and not culpable."

Bryson's face now arranged itself into an expression of pained forebearance, suitable to guests who claimed alien abduction. "Mr. Karp, as I said, the issue here is the *content* of the tape itself, and whether an assistant district attorney was in collusion with organized crime."

The camera focused in on Karp here, so as to watch him sweat out an answer to this one, but Karp was not looking at the camera. He was staring at Bryson. The show's director instinctively switched to a two-shot and got a good one of Karp's center punch of a finger pointing at the host. "I know you!" he cried. "I've seen you around my daughter's school. You were trying to trade heroin for sexual favors from little girls. Yeah! You're the guy!"

Bryson's face took on a rictus of surprise and horror, which the unforgiving camera recorded forever. The show stopped for two beats, and then Karp said, "Oh, gosh, I'm sorry. You're not the guy after all. It was someone else. Do you get it now, Mr. Bryson?"

"You're avoiding this issue, sir . . ."

"I beg to differ—this *is* the issue. Say I don't like you, Mr. Bryson. Say I hauled you into court on that preposterous charge, and brought up a cloud of witnesses who claimed to have seen you do awful things. I bet you have plenty of malicious enemies. Oh, you'd probably get off, and you might afterward sue for false arrest, but think of the cost! And then I might do it again. Why not? If we had a system where someone like me could make a baseless accusation against someone like you, even if the case proved false, your reputation would never survive. I don't even mention your bank account. That's why there are grand juries, and that's why they're secret. Before I can make you a defendant in a felony, before I can indict you, I have to convince a majority of twenty-three of your fellow citizens that there is enough evidence to hold you to answer for the crime at a public trial, and if there isn't, if the charge does not hold up, no one knows about it, *ever*. Absent that constraint, the authority of prosecutors to do damage is very nearly absolute. Absent that, I could tear you apart, Mr. Bryson. I could tear anyone apart."

"Yes, that's all very well, but you haven't answered—"

"Listen to me! We are your *dogs*, Mr. Bryson. Me and Mr. Colombo and all the others who are supposed to represent the people. You want us to keep you safe from the wolves in our society. But we have very, very sharp teeth and powerful jaws, and we need strong chains. The grand jury is one of those chains, and secrecy is its most important link. Weaken it, and even though greedy journalists think it's swell to get leaks from a grand jury, I guarantee you, you won't like what happens. Mr. Colombo's office has slipped that chain, and as a result a distinguished public servant, a man who has in thirty years of dedicated work done more to fight organized crime in this city than anyone I know, has had his reputation besmirched. You mentioned the Pentagon Papers? How can you compare the breaching of executive secrecy in a matter of transcendent national importance with a cheap political stunt by an out-of-control federal prosecutor?"

Bryson made a series of inarticulate noises as he tried to regain momentum. The director, who was one of the many who did not like Dudley Bryson, held the camera steady on this gabbling: "But, but, but, um, but, if that's the, I mean, if . . . then you . . . are not going to pursue any, disciplinary measures against Mr. Guma?"

The camera moved to Karp's face, on which there was a bemused expression that all New Yorkers could recognize as the one that appeared on their very own faces when trying to explain to a group of Korean tourists how to get to the Cloisters.

Cue commercial.

In the Karp home, all were glued to the little screen in the kitchen, watching the man of the house on *Morning Report*.

"Why is Daddy so shiny, Mom?" asked Lucy. "He looks weird."

"I believe that's the light of truth and justice issuing forth," said Marlene. "They usually don't let it on TV. It's like full-frontal nudity."

Zak was dancing around snapping a red plastic pistol and crying, "My daddy's on television!" repeatedly. Zik was not watching at all, which offended his brother, who urged him to lift up his eyes and gaze. "Watch Daddy, Zik! Daddy's on TV."

"Daddy's not on TV," replied Zik disdainfully. "Daddy's in *real life*!"

• • •

And back in real life, Karp got a round of applause and humorous cheers from those he passed as he went to his office, and within five minutes of arriving at his desk, he got a call from Jack Keegan.

"I haven't had so much fun since the pigs ate grandma," said Keegan without preamble.

"I'm glad you liked it," said Karp.

"Like is not the word. You added ten years to my life, boyo, and you set public relations back twenty-five. McHenry's been bending my ear for the last ten minutes. He's going to require sedation. He reminds me, and I now remind you, that the press never forgets. You made one of them look like a jackass, boyo. I hope you're prepared to live a life of absolute perfection from now on. You're a marked man."

Karp thought briefly not of himself but of Marlene and the extraordinary vulnerability and imperfection of *her* life and of what a couple of skilled investigative reporters could do to her with it, and then suppressed that unhappy line of thought. "Perfection? No problem," he replied lightly, and asked, "How are your peers responding?"

"Mixed. I like to imagine all the honest ones are on our side. The guys I watched the show with were cheering, at any rate. How's Ray holding up?"

"I sent him home with one of the guys from the squad for company."

"You don't think he's in any serious danger?"

"I got the word out he didn't know about the bug, but whether that will satisfy Scarpi and his brothers is another question. But fuck them, they're the bad guys. I'm more worried about the good guys."

"Meaning?"

"Well, Jack, not to put too fine a point on it, Ray Guma, in addition to being, as I said to millions, a helluva crime fighter, is also, as you well know, excessively fond of dipping his wick, and he has dipped it on occasion in places where maybe he shouldn't have, being an officer of the court. Lovely witnesses, for example. Lovely former defendants, for example. High-class ladies of the evening with strong ties to some prominent Italian-American gentlemen, for example. Colombo puts the full-court press on this, he's going to come up with a lot of dirt, and the media will eat it up. D.A.'s man in Mafia sex ring. Keegan's Italian stallion in bed with Mob . . ."

Keegan cursed briefly, and then there was an ominous silence on the line, leaving Karp to imagine that Keegan was thinking nasty thoughts about how to cut Guma loose, and about what he, the district attorney, could plausibly have known and when about the fellow's deplorable lusts. Karp decided to save Keegan embarrassment by changing tack.

"Which means we have only a limited time to derail this entire operation and make Tommy look like a horse's ass not only on the Guma thing but on the Catalano thing as well, so much so that the jackals will forget Ray. So I need some scope, and I need some cover."

"What do you have in mind?" growled the D.A.

"Not a goddamn thing right now," said Karp. "But I'll think of something."

• • •

Tran came to convey Lucy to the cops for her lineup, and Marlene and Posie, the kids and the mastiff, piled into the Volvo. All but Marlene exited at Central Park South for a healthy romp, and Marlene headed north and east. James Nobile was in the phone book, which meant that Marlene needed no detection skill greater than the ability to find a large tan apartment building at 70th and Third.

There was no doorman, and Marlene entered with the standard ruse: being well dressed, with nice legs, and fumbling with keys while a legit male tenant was entering.

As usual, Sym had called to determine if the man was home, and he opened the door at Marlene's ring. She looked down, trying to hide her surprise. Abe had not mentioned anything about Nobile's physical appearance, so she was unprepared for a man less than five feet high. Paint him red and screw a big hex nut into his skull, and he would have passed for a fire hydrant on a dim night. He must have been near seventy, and he had retained, or returned to, the face of an irascible infant.

"Yeah?" he snapped. "What is it now? And how did you get into the building? If this is another goddamn charity collection, you can forget it."

"Mr. James Nobile?" Marlene inquired.

"Yeah?"

"Did you work at the law firm of Fein, Kusher and Panofsky in the fifties and sixties?"

"What if I did? Who are you, lady?"

Straight is not going to work with this guy, Marlene thought. Doherty might have been a bent cop, but as a human being he was relatively decent; this little fellow was warped to the core. She smiled and said, "My name is Ariadne Stupenagel, I'm a freelance writer, and I'm doing a story on famous suicides in the New York area. Can I come in?" So saying, she used her hip and entered the apartment, closing the door behind her.

"Hey," said Nobile, "I didn't say you could come in here."

"I won't take up much of your time, Mr. Nobile," said Marlene, looking around. Musty, the smell of whiskey in the close air. Expensive, flashy furniture from twenty-five years ago, the low point in American design, crowded the living room, lots of crushed velvet, a Barcalounger, a twenty-one-inch television in an immense mahogany console, a nude on velvet on the wall; no sad clowns, but he might have saved that for the bedroom.

She chivvied him into letting her sit on his sofa; he sat in a fading brocade armchair facing her from halfway across the room, as if she were carrying a communicable disease.

"Now, what I wanted to ask you about was the suicide of Gerald Fein, one of the partners in the law firm you worked at. Do you recall that tragedy, Mr. Nobile?"

"Sure, yeah, but I don't know anything about it. I mean, all I know is from the papers and whatnot."

A lie, thought Marlene. A whopper. She was always surprised at how badly ordinary people lied. Being careful to stare into the interrogator's eye more than was common, that was one sign. Nobile's eyes were like some curdled dessert, a dab of grainy chocolate in stale, yellowing crème.

"But you worked for the firm at the time. You must have seen Mr. Fein every day, just about. Did you get the impression that he was troubled?"

"Hey, I just did my job. I didn't poke into anybody's business."

"Mr. Panofsky thought that Fein was troubled, though, didn't he?" Shrug.

"Did he ever mention it to you?"

"Hell, lady, it was twenty-five years ago," Nobile said irritably. "You think I keep crap like that in my head? He must've been crazy or he wouldn't have jumped off of the Empire State."

"Uh-huh. Well, you're right, it was a long time ago. I guess you're retired now yourself." She looked around admiringly. "You must have a nice pension to afford this place. Upper East Side, wow! I'm jealous."

"Not a pension. Those days only the big guys gave pensions. Nah, I got Social Security and I got investments."

"Lucky you! So, tell me, how did you come to work for Fein's law firm?"

"I answered an ad in the *Journal-American*. I was with them seventeen years."

"Uh-huh. And before that?"

"I was in building management." His look grew narrower. "What do you want to know this stuff for?"

"Just background, Mr. Nobile. So, was carrying important packages part of your work? Confidential information and so on?"

"Yeah, I did that, I did a little of everything. What does that have to do with the suicide?"

"I'm getting to that. The packages were mostly from Mr. Panofsky, weren't they? Thick envelopes. You took them to politicians all over town, didn't you?"

"You're not a reporter," said Nobile, and shot to his feet.

"But you took them from Panofsky, not Fein, didn't you? Fein wasn't in the thick-envelope business. Except once."

"Get out of here!" Nobile's clay-colored face was going red around the edges.

Marlene got up and stalked slowly toward him. "Except once, and that envelope was the one that got him disbarred. I bet you could tell me a lot about that deal, couldn't you? Is that how you got your *investments*?"

Sometimes they talked when they were scared, and sometimes they fought, and if they were decent folks, they called the police. Nobile was terrified, she could see that, but not necessarily of her. He turned and ran into the kitchen. Marlene heard a drawer violently open and metallic rummaging sounds. Gun, or knife, or hammer? She recalled that she was unarmed and dogless, and beat a retreat.

Tran and Lucy were about to leave the loft when the phone rang. Lucy picked it up. "Lucy Karp, please," said an unfamiliar voice.

"Speaking."

"Good. Listen, this is Detective Wu from the Fifth Precinct. You're supposed to come down here and look at a lineup."

"We were just leaving," she said.

"Your mom's there?"

"No, I'm coming with a friend."

"Well, your dad said I was to go pick you up. I'll be by in ten minutes. Why don't you be outside your building, okay?"

"Wait a second, how come I can't—"

"Just be outside, okay?" He hung up.

When she told Tran about the change in plans, he frowned. Tran did not like changes in plans at the last minute.

He said, in French, their best mutual language, "Let us go look at this policeman before he drives away with you. Anyone can say he is of the police."

They went down in the elevator, and Tran led her a few buildings away and across Crosby Street, where they waited in a deeply shadowed doorway. A brown sedan approached from Howard and stopped in front of the Karps' building. After a few minutes, a neatly dressed Asian man emerged and pressed the Karps' buzzer.

"That must be him," said Lucy. "The detective." She began to wave and walk forward, but Tran swept her up, pulled her deeper into the doorway, and clapped a hand over her mouth.

"Be still," he whispered. She could feel the warmth of his breath and smell his scent: *nuoc mam* and lilacs. "I have seen that man before, accepting something from our Mr. Leung. You mustn't go with him." He took his hand away from her mouth.

She stared at the man, who was now gazing up at the windows of the family loft.

"Are you sure? I thought he was a cop."

"Whether he is or not, which I will determine later, I do not care to have you go off alone with anyone who takes thick envelopes from a triad agent. Ah, good! He is going into your building. Now we will make our *getaway*."

"Where will we go?" asked Lucy, trotting along beside him.

"Well, as to that, here is the problem. We believe Leung has corrupted one policeman, but perhaps there are others who are *on the take*. A policeman comes up to you on the street, shows his badge, orders you into his car, and you go, and poof! No more Lucy. He *takes you for a ride*, yes? So properly, we should *blow town*."

They reached the alley where Tran kept his elderly Jawa. Lucy said, "Uncle Tran, I don't think people say *blow town* anymore."

"Do they not? You astound me. In any case, I believe we will not do that thing at all, but instead travel to the Queens, where we will be quite safe. Climb on! I want you out of sight before he realizes you are not going to place yourself in his hands."

If it was a tail, Marlene thought, it was a stupid one, or maybe they figured she would think that. Nobody sane would use a dirty red Dodge pickup with a pale green front fender to tail a car in the city. The vehicle had impinged mildly on her consciousness when parking near Nobile's apartment building, and then moved up on the awareness scale when it appeared in her side mirror as she drove south on Second Avenue. She cocked her head to center the rearview in her good eye. There it was, two cars back. A man driving, wearing sunglasses and a dark ball cap—could be anyone. When paranoia strikes, Marlene believed, respond as if the danger were real, because all in all a little social embarrassment, even including a brief stay in a nice clinic enriched with soothing medication, is better than being dead. Consequently she signaled, hung a right at 54th Street, and was not really that surprised to see the Dodge make the same turn, nor to see it again after her left onto Third. Marlene now demonstrated why you need at least three cars in radio communication to set and keep a proper tail in a city. By 48th Street she had maneuvered herself so that when the light at that corner turned red, she was right at the crosswalk, and then, just before the cross-street traffic entered the intersection, she leaned on her horn and shot through, scattering pedestrians and summoning forth the usual cacophony of honking horns and screamed curses in several languages. The tail was pinned, and Marlene cut west at 45th, parked in a loading zone for fifteen minutes, and then continued south.

She left the car in a garage of a hotel on Madison off 34th and set out on foot. At a bank she changed a hundred dollars into a stack of crisp ones and fives and went looking for the homeless. After a couple of hours she was thirty-five dollars lighter and not much wiser. The homeless are not your best informants, especially when trying to locate one of their number, most especially when you don't have a good recent description of your quarry. Shirley Waldorf could have been the Tinfoil Lady, or the Dog Lady, or the Leopardskin Lady, or Crazy Annie. She could have been the Demon Queen that haunted one particular person who, dressed in a toga and a paper hat bearing mystic signs designed to fend off just such evils, assured Marlene that the woman she sought was just across the street, but currently invisible.

"I know who you mean," said a voice behind her.

A Latino man in kitchen whites was puffing on a cigarette under a ventilator blowing grease and coffee smells out onto 33rd Street. Marlene slapped a buck into the filthy palm of Toga Man and turned to her new informant, who had clearly overheard her recent conversation with the nut.

"You know Shirley Waldorf?"

"Oh, yeah, I know Shirley. She come by in the mornings, and I give her a cup of coffee and a bagel. A old bagel, you know? She give me fifteen cents." He laughed. "Old lady think a cup of coffee and a bagel still cost fifteen cents. Crazy but never give me no trouble. But I ain't seen her, three, four days now." He raised his eyes to the vast gray cliff of the building across the street. "She was always going on about that Empire State. She used to work there or something, I don't know. Anyway, maybe something happen to her. You check with the cops or the hospitals, I think that would be the thing to do."

Marlene asked a few questions, but the man knew little more than he had already offered. He accepted a five-dollar bill and a card with her number on it, and promised to call if Shirley Waldorf ever came by again for a bagel and coffee.

Back in the Volvo, Marlene drove downtown to her appointment at the courthouse. The red pickup did not show, which meant little. There could be other cars. How about that tan Mercury with the two guys in the front? Control the paranoia, Marlene. Of course, she did have more than the usual number of enemies; still she was having trouble assuring herself that she was operating at her best. It seemed to take more effort just to keep focused, and she wondered about neuron loss.

She was an hour early, on purpose. She wanted to see Judge Paine in action, and so she slipped into Part 52, where the current show was *People* v. *Macaluso*. Jilly Macaluso ran a crew for Salvatore Bollano, and his prosecution for extortion and other felonies was a part of Frank Anselmo's crusade against that crime family. Jilly had been nailed in the hope that he would turn and implicate higher-ups, but Jilly was a stand-up guy and here they all were.

Marlene sat on the hard and shiny seat and reflected upon how dull trials were, if you were not a principal player. It was always a wonder to her why the media had seized on this slow-motion institution as the symbol of dramatic tension—the wizardry of cutting, perhaps, otherwise "legal thriller" would be another oxymoron. Batting for the People was a guy named Motile, a senior rackets ADA, and on D. was, of course, Marvin P. Kronsky. Kronsky was having a bad day, but the smile on his broad, perfectly shaved face was intact, and his voice as he objected had the even resonance of an oboe in low register. The source of the bad day was up there on top of the presidium, a lumpy, chinless, Brillo-fringed head bobbing above the expanse of black serge like the noggin of a hand puppet. Paine was batting down Kronsky's objections to the line of questioning, which, as far as Marlene could see, were perfectly legit. The testimony was hearsay, and did not fall into any of the numerous exceptions to the hearsay rule. Of course, she had not been in a courtroom for several years. Maybe the law had changed, and the exception had broadened. In any case, the witness was more or less allowed to spin out his inculpatory tale. On cross, Kronsky brought out that the witness was as much a slime-ball as his client, and then they broke for lunch.

Marlene walked down the hallway to Judge Paine's office, identified herself to the secretary there, and shortly Judge Paine himself appeared, still robed, to greet her. He gave her a big smile and, after a glance at her face, addressed his remarks to her nipples.

How nice to see you again, we don't get many attorneys as gorgeous as you (taking her arm, the backs of the fingers pressing against tit), sit down in that chair and I'll sit here (unspoken: so I can look up your skirt), did you hear the one about . . . (a mildly dirty joke), and the rest of the usual pre-lims with this kind of asshole. Marlene was used to it, knew the routine, smiled and giggled at the right times. Jesus, she thought, it was like working with a hot wire and a pithed frog, and after a good deal of this they got down to the reason she had come.

Gerald Fein? Oh, of course he remembered Gerald Fein. Marlene watched him closely as he spun what must have been a familiar tale. He really was an ugly little fuck, she thought, and this must have colored his life. People trust the handsome more than they do the ugly, she recalled, and it must have been . . . what? Excruciating? To be working with a couple of slick, good-looking men like Jerry and Bernie. He told the story well, and Marlene entertained the thought that he'd been tipped to expect her.

"Judge, tell me one thing," she interjected at a pause. "I have not been able to find anyone else besides you who recalls Jerry Fein being despondent in the days before the event. How do you explain that?"

The genial smile lost some of its temperature. "I don't have to *explain* it, Marlene. This isn't an interrogation. I'm telling you what happened as a courtesy, so that you won't go down any wrong paths. Jerry was severely depressed about the loss of the appeal. He didn't want to go on. I tried to cheer him up, but it was, obviously, not enough. I've always felt guilty about that. Maybe if I'd said something else—"

"Well, it really wouldn't have mattered what you said, if he was killed. If the suicide was phony."

"There's absolutely no evidence for that," Paine said sharply. The smile was but a ghost of its former self.

"Actually, there is, and I have some of it, and I hope to gather more," said Marlene, lying for effect.

The smile was dead and buried, replaced by a look honed to be terrifying if one was a prisoner awaiting sentencing. "You know, Marlene, if you poke a stick into a hornet's nest, you're liable to get stung."

"Oh, God, that's good!" said Marlene brightly, flipping up a fresh page in her steno pad. "I have to write that down. To whom shall I attribute it? The Honorable H. I. Paine, distinguished jurist, or Heshy Panofsky, the payoff man for the Mob?"

Paine went white around the eyes and lips, the lips pressing into an almost invisible line. He pressed a button on his desk. Five seconds later, a side door opened and a uniformed guard appeared.

"Out," said Judge Paine, "and remember, there are laws against spreading slander."

The house was in Elmhurst on one of the short, anonymous streets that lie between Queens Boulevard and Corona Avenue, a two-story wooden structure painted light green, with an unkempt, slanting yard out front surrounded by a low chain-link fence. The houses on this street had been built in the twenties for big Catholic families escaping from the tenements of Manhattan, and they all had more or less the same plan: big front parlor, seldom used, big kitchen in the back, narrow hallways, lots of small bedrooms, one bath on the second floor, a toilet near the kitchen. Now the block was full of big Asian families, although a few of the houses contained truly remarkable numbers of people whose only relationship was that they all hailed from Quang Ngai province or were all semi-serfs of the same sweat-shop, or had no connection at all except that they were all single men trying to make it in *Meiguo*, the Beautiful Country.

This was the case in the house Lucy and Tran now entered (the heavy glass-paned door opened to Tran's knock by a surprised young Vietnamese) and moved through from warm sunlight into shadows scented with the cuisine of Southeast Asia: mint, fermented fish, chilies, coriander, the wet, heavy odor of boiling noodles.

Four men were in the front room, playing cards around a folding table, while a large television showed a silent soap opera. They looked up when they saw the two newcomers, and one of them stood to greet them. Lucy recognized him from the raid on the Vo brothers in Manhattan: Sonny Thu, the *dai lo* of this crew, and one of Freddie Phat's main men. He was large for a Vietnamese and wore his hair in a rooster crest in the front and long in the back; two thin wisps of hair grew from either side of his wide mouth, lending an animal look to his hard face. They all had hard faces, thought Lucy, although none of them could have been over twenty-five. They were all people whose childhoods had been shattered by the American war, and Lucy found it hard to imagine them as cherished moon-faced little Asian babies. Being an Asian from this class is a rough lot, but Chinese and Vietnamese babies, especially male babies, live in the closest thing to paradise this earth affords. Contemplating the sort of lives that had converted those semi-divine infants into these terrible-looking men made her inexpressibly sad.

Tran was speaking to Thu in low tones over to one side of the room. Discussing what to do with me, she thought, and she found herself irritated. Once again, nothing normal for Lucy. In a loud voice she said, in Vietnamese, "I have to use the toilet. Where is it?"

One of the card players giggled humorlessly. Thu told her where it was, and she walked out of the room.

"I thought I would find you here," she said.

Cowboy looked up from the cluttered sink, where he was scrubbing out a pan. He turned and wiped his hands on a towel. "What are you doing here?" he asked. He seemed startled to see her, and nervous.

"I am hiding from the villains, like you."

"I'm not hiding, I'm a prisoner," he said with dignity.

"Excuse me. Are you well treated?"

He shrugged and said, "I wash pots and sweep and scrub toilets. They don't beat me." His eyes slid away from her. He mumbled to the laden sink.

"What did you say?"

In a louder, defiant voice he snarled, "What do you care?"

He was agitated and upset, and seeing him thus gave Lucy an odd feeling of power. It was rather like it was with Warren Wang, and very unlike how she behaved with the teenage boys who hung out with her male cousins, or most of the boys in middle school, and she wondered why. Was it that they were Asian? No, she decided; it was her, *she* was different, she *felt* different and behaved differently, and it was because of . . . the situation, yeah, that, she thought, but really it was that with both boys the situation—mystery with a lurking danger—allowed her to slide out of freak hideous Lucy into being someone else, into one of those personas her reading had supplied, like crisp dresses just back from the cleaners, hanging in plastic in a closet, ready to wear. Or more than one, as now, as she added to the mix of Kim and Claudine the exquisitely sensitive and long-suffering Kieu.

"'That we have met means fate binds us,'" Lucy quoted. "'The will of man has often beaten back the whim of blue Heaven, but should the knot that ties us fail, I'll keep to what is etched on bronze and cut in stone, and die.'" He gaped. Lucy placed her hand on her cocked hip, smiled, and batted her eyelashes rapidly. After a stunned moment he burst into laughter. Which she joined.

And after they stopped laughing she said, "I wasn't really joking, Minh. I *will* be your friend. You're not like the others out there, or the Vo."

But he hung his head and looked away. "I have to get working. They want me to cook the *pho* for lunch, and I haven't finished cleaning."

"Go ahead, I'll make the *pho*. Where do you keep all the stuff?"

"You can make *pho*?"

"Don't be ridiculous, I was making *pho* before you were born." Again, startled, he laughed, and his face was again transformed into that of a real kid, the dull mask of the hard man cast aside for an instant. She seized the moment to say, "Only trust me, Minh, you'll see. Listen, those others, they can't help what they are, and I don't blame them, no, and I don't hate them. I love Uncle Tran more than anyone besides my family, and he is a very bad man. He could eat them all. But you're still young . . ."

He looked at her now out of his real self. "You don't know. You don't know what I've done."

"You've killed people, right?"

"Yes. And robberies. And worse, torture to make them tell . . ."

"But you're not going to do that anymore, are you?" God will forgive you, she thought, and almost said it, but her native good taste intervened.

He held the look for a moment longer, and then it fell away. He went back to the sink. "All the food is in the refrigerator," he said. "We have rats."

Marlene called Osborne on the car phone as she drove south on Second Avenue and got a woman named Meg Morrison in the research unit and asked her to generate a full history on James C. Nobile. She could've asked Sym, but Osborne would be quicker, and Marlene had a feeling that time was beginning to press in this case, after twenty-some years, and she had other things for Sym to do. She definitely did not like that Shirley Waldorf was missing from her accustomed streets.

"Credit and criminal only?" asked Morrison.

"And employment history, as far back as it goes."

"By close of business all right?"

"That'll be fine," said Marlene. She hung up and turned east on Canal. The phone buzzed, and it was Tran. She had a short, unpleasant, and unsatisfactory conversation with him. She did not want to hear, or believe, that the NYPD was dirty with triad money. That was too much. She said so. Tran was silent, waiting. Marlene found herself thinking about how she was going to explain this to her husband. An unusual thought: Marlene in general did not much concern herself with explaining her actions, but this affair had moved beyond even her generous boundaries of what was acceptable in family life. She inquired after her daughter's health, was told it was satisfactory, that the child had made a lunch for the gangsters. Perfect. Karp would be *so* pleased. She told Tran to sit tight and she'd be in touch.

The cherry on top of this marvelous morning was that when she pulled into the little parking lot near her office, there was the red pickup truck with the green fender parked across the street, empty. Cursing, she got out and walked over to it. It was locked. The gun rack behind the cab was empty, but peering through the dirty window, Marlene could just make out a box of Remington double-ought twelve-gauge shells. Charming. She wrote down the number of the Jersey plates and tried to think who she had offended in that state recently, and came up blank.

In the office she lunched on cottage cheese, a chunk of pepperoni, black coffee, and a cigarette, and got Sym involved in calling the city's homeless shelters and hospitals to inquire whether they had a Shirley Waldorf. Marlene called Jim Raney and asked him to run the plate number of the pickup. He called back twenty minutes later with the news that the registered owner of that truck was a firm called Buttzville Landscaping, of that town, and they had not reported their license stolen either. Marlene laughed, only semihysterically, and Raney said, "You've been sneaking off to Buttzville again, Marlene, and doing it with the sod crews and now it's coming back to haunt you."

"What can I say, Raney, the smell of cut grass gets me off. Or maybe I forgot to pay for a load of mulch."

"Yeah, I always forget the mulch bill, too. You want me to drop around, have a talk with the guy when he comes back?"

"Thanks, Jim, but no. I got too many factors going on in my life, and I'm just going to forget this guy right now. Tell the truth, it could just be my imagination, or coincidence. And if not . . . well, if I can't handle a shotgun-wielding hick gardener from Jersey, it's time to hang it up."

The calls drew a blank on Waldorf, and at three Marlene left and went to pick up the kids and Posie at the park. The pickup truck was gone when she looked. Maybe it *was* my imagination, she thought, or maybe it was the Mercury, and when she reached the park twenty minutes later, and Green Fender had not appeared behind her, she had nearly bought the story.

Posie and the boys were waiting at the appointed spot on Central Park South as Marlene pulled up.

"We got kidnapped, Mommy!" Zak screamed gleefully as the twins, Posie, and the dog piled in.

"I want to tell it, Zak," Zik complained. "It's my tell, because, I got kidnapped, not you."

Marlene looked at Posie, who rolled her eyes. "It was nothing, some creep . . ."

"My tell! My tell!" screamed Zik.

"Okay, darling, you tell Mommy," said Marlene, heart in throat.

Zik said, "Once upon a time, Zik was playing in the sandbox in the park . . ."

Zak said, "And Zak was playing in the sandbox, too."

Zik shrieked out the rage of the thwarted artist and had to be calmed and Zak had to be made to promise to let Zik tell the whole thing in his way, and then Zik began with the same trope and then, ". . . and I was making a duck with my red duck mold, I was making a whole long line of ducks in the sand, and this man came over and he said, hello, Zik, and he said, I know where there is some real-life ducks you can play with and you should come with me and I said could Zak and Posie come too and he said no, just you, Zik, and he came over me and held my hand and then Posie yelled and Sweety scared him away. The end."

"Could I tell my story now, Mommy?" Zak shouted.

Marlene felt the hot, penetrating band between her eyes that signaled the start of a major, soul-threatening headache. She gripped the wheel until her knuckles glowed and said, with preternatural calm, "In a little bit, honey, but now it's *Posie's* turn to tell all about the man in the park. Posie?"

"Marlene, honest, it was no big deal. I saw this guy leaning over Zik and I watched him, and when he grabbed Zik's hand, I yelled and he started to pull him up and I yelled again and grabbed Sweety's lead and ran over there and Sweety was real upset and doing his Turner and Hooch thing, growling and slobbering and the guy saw it and booked. That's it. Oh, yeah, and I caught a cop passing by and gave her a description of the guy."

"Uh-huh. Good. Uh, Posie, this was an Asian guy, right?"

"Asian? No, he wasn't Asian. He was, like, a regular American guy. But big, like a football player. He had wraparound shades and a suit and a shirt but not a tie kind of shirt, more of a . . . what do they call those guys who hang around in Vegas? In the casinos?"

"You mean gangsters?" Marlene inquired in a weak voice.

"No, there's another word . . . oh, yeah, like a bouncer. He looked like a bouncer. He had a bunch of gold chains, I saw that, and black shoes. Marlene, are you okay? You look green."

17

MARLENE WAS LYING IN THE DARK-
ened bedroom with a cold compress across her eyes
and two Tylenol plus codeine caps dissolving not
quickly enough in her stomach, when her husband
walked in. He said, "What's all this about somebody trying to grab Zik in the park?"

"Later," she whispered.

Later, about ten that night, she emerged, wearing her flamingo kimono, and plopped down next
to him on the couch. She picked up the remote and
switched off the television. Karp immediately forgot what he had been watching and watched his
wife, who slumped against his shoulder like a sand-
bag. "Take care of me," she said.

"Excuse me?"

"Take care of me. I can't think anymore. My
brain doesn't work right. They're going to kill my
kids, and I can't think of how to get out of it."

A thrill of fear. Karp shifted himself to face her.
He gripped Marlene's shoulders and stared into her
face. Her head flopped, as if she were drunk, but
she was not. She was crying, slowly, fat tears like
glycerine flowing down her flawless cheek from the

one duct that still worked, the other eye gleaming brightly, falsely, undisguised by the usual veil of hair.

"Marlene, are you okay? I mean, should I call the doc?"

"Does he pack a gun? Call the Army, call out the Marines. Call out the Monsignor Ryan High School marching band. *I can't do it anymore.*" This last came out as a high-pitched whispery noise that would have been a shriek had it any energy behind it.

Karp took a couple of deep ones against the rising panic, and when he thought he had his voice under control, he said, "Marlene, okay, I'll take care of it, but you have to tell me what 'it' is. What happened in the park today? I got the story from Posie, but there's more, isn't there?"

"Yeah. A guy's been following me in a red Dodge pickup with a green fender. All day. And he must have gone after Zik, but the dog scared him off. A wise guy. Not from Buttzville. They killed Jumping Jerry. They probably got Shirley, too. I checked out Nobile. Building maintenance. Osborne called. You know what building? Guess!"

"Marlene, I don't know what you're talking about. Look, I'm going to call the doctor—"

She grasped his wrist hard, her nails digging painfully into the soft flesh of the underside. "No! Listen to me!" In a crazy voice she said, "I'm *not* crazy."

Karp removed her hand and held it tenderly. "Okay, you're not crazy, but you're not making much sense either. Slow down, take a deep breath, and tell me the whole thing, from the start."

There must have been few people in town more suited to elicit a complex story from a distraught witness than Karp, and he fell back on his professional skill to extract the entire tale of the Fein investigation up to and including the intelligence that before being hired at Fein's law firm, Nobile had been a superintendent at the Empire State Building.

"That's where they got the key," Marlene concluded. "Panofsky must have set things up for his Mob friends. The fixer. He took care of Nobile, and Nobile got the key to the outside deck, and kept his mouth shut after, and Panofsky gave the key to whoever, and they lured Fein up there to the observation deck and then they hustled him through the door and put the key on him and tossed him over."

"Whoever," said Karp. "You think it's connected, what happened in the park today?"

"Why else? A guy looks like a Vegas mobster tries to take Zik. It's a subtle message. We don't like what you're doing."

"Yeah, but, Marlene, the Mob doesn't usually go after family. You know that. And they usually drive around in Town Cars and Crown Vics, not old pickups from Buttzville." And saying the word "family" triggered an uncomfortable thought in Karp's mind. "Where's Lucy?" he asked.

Marlene uttered a series of whooping sounds that could have been laughter or weeping. "Oh, yeah, Lucy. How could I forget? Lucy is with Tran. A cop came to pick up Lucy this morning, and Tran spotted him as someone in deep with our old pal

Mr. Leung; hence he decided not to let her go with him, and also decided that if one cop was bent, another might be, too, so she is in protective custody among a bunch of Vietnamese gangsters he hangs out with." And some noises indicating incipient hysteria. The mastiff clumped in from the kitchen, drawn by dog emotional radar signals, and placed his great head on her knee. She crumpled one of his hot velvet ears and began cooing doggy talk.

Karp snapped, "Stop it! Goddamn, Marlene, what the hell is this! What cop?"

"Detective Wu. Who else?"

"Jesus! Wu's dirty?"

"Yeah, Tran checked it out after. I guess that explains why they haven't been making stellar progress on the Asia Mall killings and why the Chens are so freaked out. Everybody in Chinatown must know Wu is bent except all of us *lo faan* round-eye assholes."

"You knew about it this morning, obviously," said Karp a little testily. "Didn't you think to call me up? I could've had Tran downtown talking to IAD. Christ, we'll tear that whole precinct apart—"

"Not with Tran you won't, and that's all you have right now."

"What, you're saying Tran won't talk? Why the hell not?"

Marlene sighed. She thought briefly of trying a couple of fancy lies, but no longer possessed the energy necessary for fabrication at a level that would pass; nor did she feel any longer like the Marlene who thought that sort of thing was cool.

"Because he's not Tran. Because he's a Viet Cong. Because he's some kind of war criminal besides. Because he was also a hit man for the triads in the Philippines. He won't cooperate with the police; he can't. That's why."

There was a longish silence as Karp came to a boil. She stroked the dog's head.

"You *knew* this?" he cried. "You let our daughter hang out with someone like that?"

She started crying again. "Oh, Butch, he's just a big, fierce dog. He won't hurt her any more than Sweety would. Don't beat on me, Butch. Not now. Just fix it. He's on a beeper; his number's in my Rolodex."

"Marlene . . ."

"Honestly, Butch, I'm so tired," she said, and drew her legs up and cradled her head in her hands. The dog caught the tone of the argument and gave Karp a baleful look, growled briefly, and sank to the floor below her, breathing noisily, on guard.

Karp, not having had brain surgery a few scant weeks ago, was better able than his wife to deal with a number of complex issues at once. He was angry and satisfied at the same time; his Pleistocene male instincts did not get much feeding around Marlene, and now there was warm defense-of-wife-and-family red meat. He pounded out the beeper number he found, made a couple of brief calls while he waited, and then the phone rang.

Karp heard something in French, which he didn't get, and he said, "Do you speak enough English to understand what I'm saying?"

"Yes. I understand."

"Good. Here's what I want you to do. I want you to bring my daughter home. Now."

A pause, then, "If you wish."

"I wish," Karp said, and hung up.

He made another call and then came back to the living room. Marlene had not moved, nor did she budge as he sat next to her.

"Okay, I fixed it," he said.

She shifted to bring her real eye around to look at him. A pang of sympathy plucked at his heart, and he tried to keep it from his face. She had the bristling, fierce, helpless, desperate look of an un-fledged eaglet. Her glassie had rolled out of position and now seemed to be looking at the dark TV; the staples holding her scalp together glinted hor-ribly against the black fuzz on her scalp.

"Do you want to hear this now?" he asked gently.

"Sure."

"Okay. Tomorrow, you, me, Posie, and the kids are going out to Long Beach to stay with Sophie at the house. I've arranged for Ed Morris and Debbie Bryan to come along."

"Who's Debbie Bryan?"

"A PW on the squad. She's good, you'll like her."

"Uh-huh. What about Tran?"

"No Tran. No Vietnamese shooters, Marlene. No more. This is straight up, by the book. We'll stay out there until this goddamn mess is resolved."

Marlene mumbled assent.

"I called Harry. I told him you're off the Fein thing until further notice. I got Clay Fulton work-ing on the Wu business. They'll put a team on him and see if he makes contact with Leung again."

"Uh-huh. What about your work?"

"Fuck it! Crime will be rampant for a week while I'm out of town. Jack will be back tomorrow, and I've got about a thousand hours of leave. He doesn't like it, he can lump it. You need to rest, and I'm going to make sure you do if I have to sit on your head."

The phone rang. Marlene visibly cringed. "Don't answer it!"

It rang three times, and the machine cut in. A crackle of static, then, "Marlene, pick up! Marlene, this is an emergency! Marlene? *Chingada madre!* Look, Marlene, Brenda Nero just went crazy. Chester dumped her and left town and she thinks you got him to do it and she was screaming about how you ruined her life and she started a fire here and while we were running around like cockroaches she got into my office and stole my Colt. I think she may come looking for you. Marlene? Christ! Just call me, okay?" Click.

Marlene uttered a loud groan, almost a howl. The dog sat up, startled. Marlene burrowed into the sofa and dragged a pillow over her head. Karp stroked her back and made soothing noises, as did the mastiff, in his way. This went on for some time. They heard the elevator rumble into life, and shortly Lucy came stomping in, as if returning from the junior prom.

"Hey, what's going on?" she asked brightly. "What's wrong with Mom?"

"Your mom's a little out of it right now, Lucy. What's going on is that we're going out to the beach tomorrow, Aunt Sophie's."

"All of us? What about my lab?"

"Take a break. You'll still be a genius when we get back."

"Can I bring Mary Ma?"

"No."

"I'll go call her," she said, not hearing, and started for the phone.

"Lucy! I said—"

Marlene said, "Let her. One more won't make a difference to Sophie, and if she doesn't have someone to hang out with, she'll get bored and bitchy and she'll pick at me and the boys and she'll drive me crazy. Crazier than I am. Please."

So the next morning early the Volvo was packed, after the usual alarms and shrieks about forgotten things, several trips up and down the elevator, Karp admirably keeping his temper, acting as major domo, Marlene listlessly observing, and they set out. Karp drove the car, something he ordinarily did as little as possible, blessing its automatic transmission, and Marlene sat next to him, wearing huge wraparound sunglasses, a head scarf, a straw hat, a short-sleeve shirt, and blue linen shorts (looking wan and exhausted like Judy Garland in her final year), and in the rear seat sat Lucy and Mary Ma (who knew what oriental stratagems she had used to convince her parents to let her go?) and Posie, wearing a tank top (braless, as Marlene had—uncharacteristically—not even noticed until it was too late) and a pair of jean cutoffs heavily embroidered and more holes than not, and the two boys shoved down among them like chickens on a third-class Honduran bus, squealing with excitement, and the dog wheezing in the luggage compartment, squashing the bags and drooling from time to time on the bare necks of the girls.

As they pulled onto Canal Street, a dark Plymouth slipped into line behind them, this carrying Ed Morris and Debbie Bryan. Bryan was a chocolate-colored woman with a cropped afro and a long neck, her upper body stuffed fetchingly into a red tube and the lower encased in loud print culottes. Morris was wearing a pink shirt and bermudas. Neither of them was complaining about this particular duty. Cop work was rarely a day at the beach, but now it actually was.

The small caravan went through the Battery Tunnel and onto the Belt Parkway, heading south around the pregnant bulge of Brooklyn. Karp knew the way by heart, having traveled it virtually every summer day of his childhood to his family's beach club on Atlantic Beach. He and his two brothers would nearly come to blows during the ride over who would get to pay the toll on the Marine Parkway bridge (the loser getting to pay the toll on the Atlantic Beach bridge, but since there were three of them there was always one absolute loser and since Karp was the youngest, it was usually him). They had not been particularly pleasant trips, he recalled, having been full of the civil sadism of unhappy families. This one was much better, he thought, so whatever happened he was that much to the good. Posie (the sort of person who never would have been admitted to the precincts of the elder Karp family) had devoted virtually all of her brain cells that had not been fried by drugs or required for basic body maintenance to the memorization of rock 'n' roll lyrics, from the fifties unto the present day, and she was not shy about sharing them. Aside from Karp and the dog, everyone sang. Even Marlene, Karp was happy to observe, kicked in on "Big Girls Don't Cry," and Mary became reasonably competent at providing doo-wah backgrounds after Lucy explained, amid general hilarity, that doo-wah did not in this case mean "inverted Chinese" as it does in the language of Guangdong. It was all in all very nearly like a happy family outing rather than a flight from killers.

Sophie Leontoff's house was large and white, with a long screen porch across its front supported by squat pillars. It sat behind a large lawn on a side street in the town of Long Beach, alongside similar houses, most of them the property of New York's old middle-elite, the money from *schmatehs* and other material substances rather than from advertising and media and show business, as in the Hamptons. Comfortable and unhip was Long Beach and this house.

Karp had debated whether to let Sophie in on the full situation and had decided to do so, first because he disliked prevarication (and a fake story that would explain two cops would have to be a doozy) and because he thought a lady who had spent three years in Paris running from the Gestapo and later survived Ravensbrück could probably handle a mere squadron or two of hit men. He was correct in this; nor was Aunt Sophie at all put out by the extra people arriving at a house with only three bedrooms. The children were shipped up to the attic, reached by a drop ladder, to the delight of the twins, and also of Mary Ma and Lucy, who got to share an ancient, lumpy four-poster in an alcove, a prime staying up to all hours giggling locus, which left one bedroom for the Karps, one for Sophie and her paramour, Jake (who sat chewing a cigar, observing the invasion with wry good humor), and the small one in the front of the house for Posie and Bryan. Ed Morris got the sofa bed on the sun porch in back. Karp noted that this arrangement meant one cop was stationed by the rear door and one overlooking the front lawn, and wondered if Aunt Sophie had figured that out by herself.

Settled, unpacked, fed (an immense tray of sandwiches from the Long Beach deli, pickles, cole slaw, beer, wine, and sodas, gorged upon), warned not to swim before digesting, the party set out for the short walk to the beach club. The twins insisted on going to the men's locker room, so Karp had the duty of getting his kids changed into their tiny swimsuits, in a replica of the damp-smelling closet in which he and his brothers had changed a million years ago, or maybe it was exactly the same one, for this was the very beach club to which his own family had come in the forties and fifties.

"The Feins came here, too," said Marlene when Karp happened to mention this later.

"Yeah, I guess they did," said Karp. "A long time ago."

"*Où est les sables d'antan*?" said Marlene. "Still clinging to our belly buttons. It probably doesn't seem like long ago to Vivian Fein Bollano."

Karp looked over at his wife. They were lying in awning-striped sling beach chairs on the sand. Marlene was wearing her faded red Speedo suit, and he observed that her hip bones were pushing up the thin fabric and her collarbones were staring through skin that looked as thin as the nylon of the suit. Some people eat under stress; Marlene starved. She had her hat on, and the huge sunglasses, so he could not see her face very well. A magazine, an old *New Yorker*, stained with suntan oil, sat on her lap unread, its pages riffling in the soft breeze.

"Are you still thinking about her, about the case?" he asked cautiously.

"Not really. I seem to have lost the ability for coherent thought. About anything."

He saw her stiffen and raise her sunglasses, and followed her gaze toward the shore, where Zak had dashed into the surf to scoop up a bucket of water. The boy returned to his sand castle, however, and was not swept out to sea. Marlene relaxed a notch. Close by, but separated by a decent interval, his brother made mold after mold, fish, duck, star, in elaborate patterns on a carefully smoothed plateau of sand, delineated by seashells. In a short time its perfection would become unbearable to Zak, who would accidentally on purpose trample one of the shapes, and there would be a screaming fight and Zak would spitefully attempt to destroy the rest of the pattern, and Posie would scramble up from where she was sunning herself facedown on a blanket in a barely visible bikini and snatch both of them up for a splash in the mild surf, perhaps even forgetting to tie up her suit top.

Marlene waited, as she had since the previous evening, almost comfortable now with the waiting, with being passive. Something would happen and then she would respond, if she could. She concentrated on her breathing, on feeling the sun on her winter-pale skin, on listening to the seashell hiss of the surf. Zik screamed. He threw sand at his brother, who burst into tears and retaliated with a plastic shovel. Posie leaped into action, and did forget. Breasts jiggled. A yacht cruising offshore blew its air horn in appreciation. Marlene didn't budge. She was being cared for.

Behind the Karps was a sort of pavilion or shelter, six rustic posts holding up a shingled roof over a concrete base, on which rested a brick barbecue grill and a round concrete table, around which, on deck chairs, sat Sophie, Jake, Mary Ma, and Ed Morris, playing pinochle for a penny a point. Mary Ma, who had never played pinochle before this and who had spent about four minutes learning the rules, was murdering them, much to the delight of Lucy, who had tipped her pal that a kid with an eidetic memory for numbers and a total command of the laws of probability could clean up. Lucy sat behind her friend kibitzing and giving advice in Cantonese, and on the side talking with the cop, Bryan, about the cop life ("Believe you me, sugar, it is rarely like this; this is unreal") and about religion, Bryan being in the same class of devout as Lucy herself, although a Baptist.

Thus they disported themselves, as the sun moved its slow circle toward Jersey, and the sea breeze sprang up, and when the shadows lengthened they all gathered their impedimenta and the resisting children and went back toward the house, where there was another feast, the usual chicken and hot-dogs grilled, with gallons of wine. Posie, of course, having no mommy to look after her, picked up a nasty sunburn, and got slightly drunk and retired early, which Marlene did not at all mind. She immersed herself in the domestic, the mindless chopping, serving, washing, cleaning, grateful for it, even, working calmly and with some delight, helped by Mary Ma and her daughter in near-Confucian harmony. Sophie, as she announced, never touched a pot (I sew, dolling, I don't cook), so there was no tension in the kitchen. In truth, as Karp observed with relief, there was no tension anywhere. By some benign influence, the crowded house was a model of concord, as if all had agreed to savor the delight of the moment, and forget what was really going on.

After dinner, more cards, a game of penny poker, at which Jake was the master, so that Mary Ma learned that poker was not entirely a matter of statistical analysis, and after that, with the twins put down, music from an elderly machine Sophie called the Victrola, from a vast collection of brittle, scratched 78s, songs from the thirties and forties and the early fifties. "Bessame Mucho." "Begin the Beguine." "Embraceable You." "Miami Beach Rhumba." "Cherry Pink and Apple Blossom White." They danced, Karp and Marlene, Sophie and Jake, and the cops, and the girls learned to dance, taught by Sophie and Marlene, fox-trot, rhumba, cha-cha, mambo.

"We haven't done this in a while," said Karp. It was later, the house was silent but for refrigerator noises, surf and wind and insect tappings, and the rush of the big-headed shower under which he stood, clasping his wife, enjoying that prince of showers, the après-beach.

"No, we haven't," she said, and pressed herself against him and drew his head down for a kiss steamier than the water pouring down.

After that he said, "Wow. This is like when we first met in my old place, in the shower, remember?" And she said, "Yeah, but I don't want to talk now."

Nor did they; no, Marlene leaped up and wrapped her legs around him (Karp barely managing to turn off the shower), and they staggered out of the bathroom uncaring of anyone venturing forth for a late pee, and through their bedroom door (artfully kicked shut by Marlene), where they crashed onto the bed dripping, like a pair of freshcaught smelt. Marlene rolled on top and proceeded to pound away like a punch press making grommets, nor did she spare the sound effects. At some level (the one below the one occupied by holy shit she's gonna wake up the whole house) Karp understood that Marlene was seeking oblivion, but he thought also that this was, at least, something he could give her, and after she collapsed on his chest, he rolled her over and pounded them both into black zero.

Until she awoke with a start, wide-eyed, at 3:10, out of an obscure dream about losing the Volvo on a complicated bridge in Tokyo. Karp was, as usual, sleeping the sleep of the just, to which she thought him perfectly entitled, and so she slid off the old-fashioned high bed, into a tatty, soft chenille robe she found on a closet hook, and her flip-flops, grabbed a pack of Marlboro Lights from the dresser, and went through the door. The mastiff, sleeping across the threshold, stirred, shook himself, stretched, and followed his mistress without a word of command. The two of them went out the front door and into the cool, sea-heavy air of the night.

The street lay dark and quiet under the leaf-filtered glow of a low quarter moon and the yellower glare of the old-fashioned street lamp in its crinkled tin shade down at the intersection. She put a cigarette in her mouth and looked both ways, and saw, as she had expected, a tiny orange spark in the deep shadow cast by a large hydrangea in full leaf. The dog huffed and walked in that direction, and she followed, as if on a leash.

"A pleasant evening, Marie-Hélène," said Tran.

"How long have you been here?"

"Not long. Would you like a light for that cigarette?"

She nodded. In the match flare he studied her face. He said, "You are tired, my dear friend."

"I am ruined. I feel like a piece of trash in the gutter."

"Yes, I know the feeling. Is there anything I can do?"

You could testify against Wu, she thought. You could expose yourself and be deported and end up in a cage in Vietnam, or here. She said, "I don't think so. What's going on in town?"

"I'm afraid your business is somewhat in suspension. Mademoiselle McCabe is refusing new clients, but on the other hand, she has been able to mobilize your freelance people to carry out necessary tasks. Madame Duran is distraught and calls many times. She demands to know where you are, which knowledge I have naturally refused her, and the same with La McCabe. M. Leung remains missing. Kenny Vo was spotted with a group of White Dragons, in the Queens. By this I surmise that M. Leung is still in play and plans some stroke. I assume you and the family have adequate protection?"

"Adequate, yes."

More hesitantly he asked, "And the girl is well?"

"Well. Thriving. She is in the midst of people who love her, she has a good friend. As the days pass, I hope we will become closer again." She paused, took a deep drag. "I notice that you do not mention what follows from the connection between the Vo and the White Dragons."

"It will be a sad thing for her," Tran agreed. "Unless the Chens wish to act against the interests of their own tong, we must regard them, and their girl with them, as . . . perhaps *enemy* is too strong, but hostile neutrals."

"Yes," she said, and abruptly stood up, flicking the cigarette into the road. The pinched feeling behind her eyes was coming back. She wanted it to depart and took several deep breaths of the salty air. Tran stood, too. She shook his hand and kissed him lightly on both cheeks. "Thank you for this, Tran. But . . . how can I say this, you have done so much for her . . ."

"I quite understand, Marie-Hélène. I will keep my distance. Believe me, I am under no illusion as to what I am and what she is. I wish you good luck on your recovery. I wish you a peaceful vacation."

"If it lasts," she muttered and walked away.

Karp had over the three idyllic days that followed kept his vow not to call the office, and his office, exhibiting more decency than he had expected, refrained from calling him. The sole TV in the house was a small black-and-white with a rabbit-ear antenna that sucked in mainly snow, and no newspapers were delivered. Every morning Sophie and Jake drove to the small commercial strip to buy a *Times* so that she could check her investments (and, Karp suspected, grab some time alone with her man), but she did not bring it back to the house. They all might have been on Mustique.

Nevertheless, Karp's thoughts returned at odd moments to the problem of Willie Lie and his promise to Keegan to think of something to take the heat off Ray Guma. At one of these moments he was sitting in the beach shelter playing pinochle with Jake and Sophie and Mary Ma. Lucy had just gone off to the club to collect some drinks. They had just finished a game and Sophie was totting up the score when Karp's attention was distracted by a shrill cry. Twenty yards away, two seagulls were fighting over a long bit of carrion. Neither would let go as they leaped, flapping into the air. The birds had attracted the attention of the twins, and Zak had decided that it would be fun to catch a seagull. Naturally, and fortunately, the piece of garbage broke off, and the two birds flew their separate ways, but watching the brief vignette cast Karp's mind back to the saying Willie Lie had written on the legal pad in Karp's office. He grinned and turned to Mary, who had also watched the same thing and remarked, "When snipe and clam grapple, the fisherman benefits." Her face lit up. "That's a Chinese saying," she said, and he said, "Yes, I know," and at that moment Sophie asked him to reach down for a towel that had been slung over a roof beam, and a little light turned on in Karp's mind.

"Say, Mary, how do you say 'roof beam' in Chinese?"

"Roof beam? In Mandarin it's *liang*. In Cantonese, *leung*."

"And, ah, Leung: that's a name, too. I mean, the same character is both, right?"

"Yes. Leung is a very common name, and it's the same character, but you say it differently in different parts of China, like Leong, Long, Nia, Liao, Liow . . ."

"What!" he cried.

They all looked at him. Very carefully he said, "Mary, what you're saying, Nia and Leung are the same name?"

"Yes. Sometimes names are very different in Chinese, and when two strangers meet, sometimes they draw the characters of their names on the palms of their hands, so maybe they are relatives?"

"What about Lie? Is that the same, too?"

"Oh, no, Lie is different, Lie and Lee and Louey, those are not the same at all. Lie means plum."

Jake said, "Something wrong, Butch?"

"No. Yeah, actually, I just found out something I need to tell someone about. In fact, I think I'm going to have to go back to the city."

"But you'll be back?" asked Sophie, worried.

"Yeah, soon as I can."

He went to where Marlene was lying in the sun. He told her his recent surmise and what he intended to do.

"Okay," she said, "see you later," as if he had told her he was going to run out for a carton of milk.

He looked at her. "Are you all right, Champ?"

"I'm fine. Just a little sleepy."

"You seem to be getting along better with Lucy," he said tentatively.

"We're not fighting, if that's what you mean. She has a lot of distractions and less pressure on her. It helps."

"Do you think you can talk to her? I mean about what she saw. It's the key to this whole damn mess. If she can actually *put* Leung at the murder scene . . ."

She took off her sunglasses and looked at him, and the exhaustion in her face and in her eye was so profound that he felt a pulse of shame. He grasped her hand, patted it, said, "Okay, forget it, I'll take care of it some way. Just rest and don't worry."

She put her sunglasses on again and continued her observation of the twins.

After a moment he said, "I'm going to drive in with Ed. Debbie will stay here with you and the kids. I'll be back as soon as I can." She nodded. He kissed her on the cheek and departed.

Somewhat over an hour later, after a stop at the loft to change clothes, he was back at Centre Street, but in Clay Fulton's tiny office. Karp was not officially back from leave. It was ten degrees hotter in the city, and the air had acquired the acrid fug of summer.

"Explain this to me again, Stretch," said Clay Fulton. "Lie is Leung?"

"Lie is Leung and they're both Nia, the triadnik. I figured they were connected, maybe working together for someone else, but they're the *same* guy. He engineered the setup that killed those two Hong Kong triad guys in Chinatown, he set up the Catalano killing, he kidnapped my kid, he bent Detective Wu, same guy. He came to me to act as a witness to frame Joe Pigetti, and he bolted when I wouldn't give him a free ride and went to the feds. He's been sitting in one of their hotel rooms someplace, being *protected* by the federal government, laughing his head off."

"Okay, okay, say you're right about that—what does it buy us?"

"Well, for one thing, it explains why we can't figure out a Mob angle for the Catalano killing. There *is* no Mob angle. Leung did that freelance and he's fingering Pigetti for it. That fancy work about the clock in the car wasn't an alibi for Pigetti, it was an alibi for Lie, but with Lie's testimony it becomes an *incrimination* against Pigetti. Brilliant, when you think about it. And I would be willing to bet that he had a lot to do with getting Little Sal in the shit he's in, maybe slipped some new information to the wife, maybe told Sal where she was hanging out. And the result, the Bollanos are stripped of leadership, ripe for the plucking."

"Jesus, Butch, by who? We got absolutely no evidence that the other Mob families are moving in on—"

"Not the Mob, Clay. The triads. Or *some* triad."

But Fulton was shaking his head. "Butch, they don't ever do that. They may ship in China white, sure, but they sell it to the locals. That's the deal."

"It *was* the deal," said Karp grimly. "Take a look at the streets, Clay, the faces. The city's changing. It's not the place we grew up in. I remember when cabbies were Jews and Italians. They had Brooklyn accents: T'irty-t'oid and T'oid."

"And they got turbans now. What's your point?"

"Different times, different wise guys. The old Italian Mob is dying. You compare someone like Little Sally to guys like Lansky, Luciano, Joe Adonis—it's a joke. And fucking Colombo is a joke, too, going after those mopes like he was saving the city."

"So . . . you're saying it's the yellow peril now?"

"Come on, Clay, it has nothing to do with race, it's culture and it's numbers. There are ten million Sicilians and a billion Chinese. They got a criminal culture that goes back I don't know how long, but older than the Mafia for sure. We got next to no intelligence on them, we got lousy contacts in the community, and this city is the richest target in the world. You figure it out."

Fulton held up a hand in surrender. "Okay, okay, a triad's trying to take over a New York crime family. Why kill the two triad guys, then?"

"Not from his triad."

"So?"

"Want my guess? Leung invites a couple of Hong Kong big boys from a *different* triad over for a meet with the goombahs, or so he says. Then they get hit and Leung goes, oh, those evil Italians, look what they did! In one shot he knocks out a couple of rivals, maybe to get him in good with his own guys, spreads the word the Mob isn't to be trusted, and he clears the way to do something maybe the Chinese community, the tong structure, the local gangs, might not otherwise be willing to support."

Fulton said skeptically, "That's a big pot of soup you made out of one bitty little ham bone. What've you got besides the names? Because if you take this to a judge, he's gonna laugh in your face."

"Good point! Faces. Set up a photo lineup, including that Vo we pulled out of Hester Street, and get someone to run it out to Long Beach and show it to Lucy. She'll pick the guy out, and then we'll have something to beat him over the head with. He'll give us Leung as the guy who set up the kidnap."

"You're pretty confident."

"Oh, hell, this guy's not going to stand up to an A–1 felony charge. He's looking at fifteen to twenty-five for the kidnapping one, plus something on the assault, and after he gets out, he goes right back to the People's Republic of Vietnam. Not a thrill, and I'll work with him and his brother on it if he gives me Leung. He'll roll, you'll see."

Karp clapped his hands. "Okay, let's hustle on

this. The pictures . . . oh, and slip one of Leung in there, see if Lucy or Mary Ma will pick him out—maybe they saw him somewhere. And the Chens. I want them pulled in, the whole family, kids and all. And Mr. Yee. Get a Cantonese translator. What about Wu?"

"Oh, he's finished, the fucker. We checked his bank account. Nothing unusual there, but it turns out that over the past four months Wu's bought teller's checks for amounts ranging from four grand to nine grand, a total of fifty-eight K. Lucky at the track? I don't think so. We're still looking for other accounts. We got a phone tap, too. He called a number in the Bronx twice, the Marston Motel, which turns out to be where they're keeping Lie. Pretty sloppy for a conspirator, I mean, Jesus, kids in diapers know to use a pay phone you're gonna talk dirty."

"Uh-uh, Clay," said Karp, shaking his head, "why should these guys be careful? They're invisible. They're like the Mob was before Appalachin. Triad? What's a triad, mommy? That's why that little shit left that paper right there on my pad. It never occurred to him that anyone would care, or understand if they did care. Okay, let's get IAD to snap Wu up and sweat him on that phone call and the money. We got to move like lightning on all this, Clay, or all these jokers are going to get together and concoct a story." He stood and so did Fulton. He grasped the detective on the shoulder. "Go," he said. "Make it happen."

Karp sat down at Fulton's desk and waited, resisting the urge to use the phone to check on his minions. Having delegated all his routine tasks for a week, he had nothing to do. He doodled. He crumpled up the doodled pages and tossed them across the room into a wastebasket propped up on a bookcase. Swish. Swish. Bored, irritated with himself for being bored, he stalked out, descended the staircase, bought a coffee and a greasy cruller from the snack bar on the first floor, walked out to the park to eat it. The homeless cruised by, and he distributed modest alms. He saw the woman coming toward him across the grass, waving a sheaf of soiled papers, and he pretended not to see her, and escaped back into the building.

The call from Fulton came in ten minutes later. Lucy had made the ID of Vo Hoa Dung, aka Needlenose. Neither she nor Mary Ma had identified Lie-Leung. Needlenose had been braced in the Tombs and, as expected, had given up Lie-Leung as the author of the kidnap. Good.

"You want me to pick him up now?" Fulton asked.

"No, wait on that. I need to get Jack up to speed. But get a team ready to move on my call."

Karp went next door and found Keegan's office full of Fraud people, including V. T. Newbury. He smiled and waved Karp over.

"Isn't this great? Today's the day the green eyeshades have their picnic. Some of these guys haven't been out in the sunlight since 1956."

"What's the occasion?"

"Difficult to explain to a layperson such as yourself, Butch, but it involves naked puts and several bent officials of the New York Stock Exchange, plus one of our fine congresspersons. It's political as hell, and we're going in there to brief Jack."

"Mazeltov. Can I sneak in there for five before you get going?"

"We've been waiting eighteen months," said V.T. "Be my guest."

"Thanks," said Karp, and paused. "Oh, by the way, any progress on the Chinese puzzle?"

"Not really, I'm sad to say. But I did have one thought. The Chinese approach to banking, as to fire drills and handball, is sometimes strange. It's similar to what European banking was like in the fourteenth century. For example, suppose the Medici bank wished to tranfer ten thousand gold florins to Frankfurt—"

"V.T., could we bring it right up to present? I'm on a tight schedule."

V.T. pouted but complied. "The *Sesame Street* version, okay: it seems Chinese merchants often have a sideline in money holding and transfer. You give them cash, they give you a ticket. Show that ticket in Hong Kong or Canton, say the magic words, and you get your money back, without any pesky questions from governments about currency transfer."

"So that could be how our boy Leung got operating funds into New York?"

"I'd say it was the only way, unless he portered in cash."

"Thanks, V.T., we'll check it out."

"Wait a minute, who's Leung? I was talking about Lie, alias Nia."

"They're all the same guy," said Karp, and went through the door.

Keegan was riffling papers when Karp entered. He looked up and said, "You got some color in your face. I thought you were taking a week."

"I am, but this couldn't wait," he said, and gave Keegan the *Sesame Street* version of the truth about Willie Lie.

"Interesting," said Keegan, and twirled his Bering. "What're you going to do?"

"Mimi Vasquez is getting a warrant signed for Lie's, or Leung's, arrest as we speak. But before we grab him, I'm going across the street and give Colombo a heads-up on it. Give him a shot at doing the right thing and save him some embarrassment."

"You're hoping he'll be so grateful he'll lay off Guma?"

"That too, but the main thing is to reestablish some fucking civility between us and the feds. If we don't get our acts together on this Chinese mob business, this city's going to look like Macao in a couple of years. I think clear evidence that a triad is moving in on a Mafia family should catch Tommy's eye, don't you?"

"Maybe. But I think you should remember that when the words 'gratitude' and 'civility' are spoken, Tommy has to look them up in a dictionary. What's your plan if he laughs in your face?"

"Oh, in that case I intend to drive the little fuck into the ground like a tent peg. He'll have to wear a Reagan mask on his face for a year."

Keegan laughed, a big, slow, hearty sound. "Ah, Butch, you're the last true gentleman in the business, you know that? It's your glory and your shame.

Now, go and conquer, and send those damned pencil necks in here."

The first thing the U.S. attorney said when Karp entered his office ten minutes later, even before asking him to take a chair, was "I hope to hell you're here to apologize."

"No," said Karp, "actually, I—"

"Goddamn it! Do you think I'm going to let you get away with that kind of irresponsible calumny on a national news show?" Colombo went on like this for some minutes, his face red with a mist of forceful saliva forming in front of it as he ranted. Karp imagined it must have been an alarming display were you one of the man's subordinates. Karp waited calmly for Colombo to pause for breath, and interjected, "I'm here to save you from making a serious mistake. If you don't want to hear it . . ."

"What mistake?"

Again Karp told the Lie-Leung-Nia story, with the theory about a triad taking over the Bollanos. At the end, Colombo did actually laugh in his face. It was a whinnying, unpleasant sound, quite unlike Keegan's.

"You have to be joking. You expect me to abandon my key witness against the Bollanos because of this . . . *farrago* of supposition and bartered testimony?"

"He's not a witness, Tom, he's a participant. No, he's the *mastermind* behind the whole thing. He did Catalano on his own, and he's trying to frame Pigetti for it. He did the Sings, too, which is why he tried to kidnap my daughter. He's playing us. I was hoping you'd want to cooperate, but in any case, I'm having an arrest warrant prepared and I intend to charge him at least with the kidnap and assault. I have no doubt that once we're focused on this, we'll be able to generate a good case for the three murders as well."

Colombo laughed again. "Oh, great, the evil oriental genius strikes. Hey, I appreciate you're worrying about your daughter, maybe you ought to talk to her about who she's hanging out with, but this is a pile of horseshit. A Chinese gangster uses a couple of aliases and then a little girl picks out a picture, and some lowlife Viet picks out a picture, and that's your case? What I should do here is start asking some serious questions about why the D.A.'s office is so concerned about shying away from pounding the Bollanos that you'd concoct this fairy tale."

Karp waited until his temper subsided and then asked, "Are you being deliberately obtuse, or do you really not grasp this? I'll say it again: a Chinese triad is taking over a New York crime family, and you're helping them do it."

Colombo's smile vanished into his face like a bit of toilet paper sucked down a drain.

"If that's it, Butch, I got a meeting," he said.

"Go ahead, get him," said Karp into the phone. More waiting after that, a half hour, an hour. The phone rang, the private direct line. Karp snatched it up.

"Well?"

"Sorry, Stretch, we came up empty," said Fulton.

"Oh, *shit*! Colombo, that son of a bitch, *moved* him? Jesus, I'll fucking arrest him for obstruction of—"

"Hold on there, son. The marshals watching him were as surprised as we were. He wasn't moved. He took off, out a bathroom window. He got a call, maybe a half hour before. They listened in, of course, but it was in Chinese, and real brief. Then he goes in to the can, and that's the last they saw him."

"I can't believe this!"

"Believe it, son. Wily Willie has flown the coop. Not hard, when you think about it. He's supposed to be *scared* of what's out there. They're protecting him, not particularly guarding him from escaping."

"You got him out on the air, right?"

"Yeah," said Fulton, "and I got cars cruising the district and people covering the subways. Nothing yet. The little bastard's gonna be a tough one to nail if he gets into Chinatown."

18

LEUNG SAT IN THE REAR OF THE VAN, surrounded by the silent White Dragons. In front of him Kenny Vo mumbled to himself and snapped the slide on his MAC–10 machine pistol. He had been acting strangely from the moment he had made the prearranged pickup up near the motel at which the Chinese had been a guest of the federal government, and Leung bitterly regretted ever having made use of him. If he'd had a team of Hong Kong boys, none of this disaster would have happened, but that, of course, was precisely the catch. He was not here as an agent of the Da Qan Zai, but on his own, hence without real triad support. It had been a gigantic, a colossal bluff, and it had nearly come off. For if he had gained control of a Mafia family, their connections, their net of influence, their sources of income, then his triad would have welcomed him warmly, and his superiors would have basked gladly in the credit. He realized that he had badly miscalculated when his ma jai had been so neatly lifted off the street. He had thought it was the Italians, grown suspicious, sending a message. But the Italians were asleep and stupid. No, it had been that girl, and some strange Vietnamese who unaccountably held her in some value.

He cast a sour glance at the boys sitting next to him. If the tong knew his true position, any authority he still had over these dog farts would immediately vanish, and shortly thereafter so would he. Meanwhile the terror of the triad still held sway, and perhaps something could be done to save things even now. The girl, first of all. It was by now perfectly apparent that she had seen him and had at last told the prosecutor. How they penetrated his persona as Lie was still obscure, but this was not of any importance absent the testimony of the Karp girl connecting him with the Sing killings. The Chen girl and the daughter of the illegals, Ma, would remain quite silent for the moment, and could be disposed of in the future.

If there was one. He must make prompt inquiry as to where the Karp family could be found. Apparently, like many Chinese officials, they had decamped to the villages, where, without doubt, they were lording it over their rural relations. The particular village would have to be located, although he had no idea how to do this. Meanwhile they were embarked on this absurd vendetta of Vo's. Leung had agreed to it in order to secure the cooperation of Vo, which he still needed. Another item for future disposal.

His thoughts kept moving back to the girl Loùh-sì. A non-Chinese Chinese, a monster that could never have existed in civilized lands. Chinese saw but were silent; the *lo faan* were not silent but were blind. That was the way things were. And for her to have such a father, another piece of rotten luck. Perhaps it had been a mistake to go to the father, but no, it had been important to find out his character. Would his own greed fool him? Could he be influenced by threatening the daughter? Clearly neither was the case. Well, he had found another greedy fool in Colombo, and all that was necessary now was to eliminate the daughter. Not an impossible task, surely. She was, however talented, only a girl. The van was slowing, turning. It had left a heavily trafficked road and was now on some residential street. Vo turned in his seat and spoke to the White Dragons. He spoke a crude and badly accented Cantonese. "In and out. No problems. Get the boy. Anybody try to stop you, shoot them." The van stopped.

This is like being pregnant, thought Marlene, like waiting for delivery (and why do they call it "delivery" since nothing less like receiving a package from a postal employee could be imagined?), but in this case it would not be new life in the offing but the end of something. Maybe of her, but not, if she could help it, of her children. She lay torpid as a gecko on her sling chair, under her hat, behind her sunglasses, her vision and her interest restricted to the three bright bands before her, beach, sea, sky, like the flag of some extremely laid-back tropical nation, and on it, the boys playing, Posie toasting foolishly on a blanket, the breeze bringing to Marlene's nostrils the scent of her Noxema. The older girls had gone walking down the beach, with the dog and the policewoman. She could barely make them out as shimmering stick figures, identifiable among the other bathers only by the dog leaping into the surf after a tossed Frisbee.

Also in her field of vision, a distant rusty freighter, a large sailboat with all sails set, and closer in, a large white motor yacht. From behind her she could occasionally hear, borne on some favorable breeze, the sounds of Sophie and Jake and a couple of beach club friends playing rummy. Marlene tried to read, but the usual concerns of *The New Yorker* are not enticing when your kids are in danger. She called out to Zak not to venture so far into the surf. Out on the motor yacht they had launched a black Zodiac boat. The whine of the motor came intermittently to her as the two men in it gunned the outboard and raced around the mother ship, bouncing high off the choppy waves. She thought that looked like fun, although requiring more energy than she currently had to bestow. She wondered what had happened to her, to the recently competent, active, heavily armed Marlene, whether it was what the Jungians called regression in service of the ego (from which a more mature, self-realized woman might shortly emerge), or an old-fashioned nervous breakdown, or a leaky blood vessel that the docs had overlooked, which was on its way to reducing her to a persistent vegetative state. Generalissimo Franco, she recalled, used to keep two boxes on his desk, one labeled "problems that time will resolve," the other, "problems that time has resolved," and his administration consisted in moving, every six months or so, the entire stack of documents from the former to the latter box. Marlene typically had little in common with the late fascist, but with respect to her current state they were in perfect agreement: only time would resolve it. Out at sea, the Zodiac had stopped its circling. Now it was heading for the beach.

"Marie Hélène? I am hoping you will call in and get this message. Phat has just called. There has been a raid on the house in the Queens where Lucy was staying, and the boy they call Cowboy has been taken away by his cousin, Kenny Vo. One of Phat's people was shot. Marie Hélène? I do not wish to worry you unduly, but a man who must be our old friend Mr. Leung was with them. I cannot imagine that Leung will have any more pressing interest than to get his hands on Lucy and her friend. I suppose they do not know exactly where you are, which is a benefit. Please, I urge you, do not attempt to return home until these people are captured. Meanwhile, I have taken the liberty of assembling a small group and will be leaving shortly for Long Beach. Call me as soon as you can. Until later." Tran listened to the hiss on the line for a moment and then hung up the pay phone. He climbed into the back of Phat's van and urged the utmost speed.

"How're we doing, Clay?" Karp asked the telephone.

"Well, Stretch," replied Fulton in an overly patient voice, "we're doing about the same as we were doing fifteen minutes ago, when you called me the last time. No, Leung has not turned up. Yes, we have Chinatown in Manhattan crawling with cops. Every cop in the city will have the guy's picture when the shift changes. We have ESU standing by in Chinatown and Elmhurst and Flushing. Bridges, tunnels, and airports, check. You want to hear the whole thing again?"

"What about that gunshot wound in Elmhurst Hospital?"

"Nothing there yet. The guy was Vietnamese, not Chinese. They're on the case, waiting for a translator. Butch, I swear to God, anything changes I'm on the line to you next second."

"What about my family?"

"Butch, aside from me and you and Ed, nobody knows where they are. They're quote, at the beach. What beach? Can you imagine a Chinese guy walking from Coney Island out to Montauk on a hot holiday weekend looking for Marlene and the kids? We got a unit stationed at your loft."

"We should send some people out to Long Beach, too."

Karp heard an irritated sigh on the line. "Butch, that's not a good idea. We'd have to work through the Long Beach P.D. and the Nassau sheriff and the staties, and you'd have more of a security risk than what you got now. We know this guy has bent cops . . . we still don't know who or how many. Look, you're eating yourself up here, Butch. Leave this to us and go home. Have a shower, pour yourself a cold one, watch the Yankees game—"

"No, I'm going to drive back out to Long Beach with Ed. I want to be with them."

"Suit yourself," said Fulton.

"You got the number out there?"

"Tattooed on my hand, for crying out loud. Would you just relax!"

Mary Ma had been to the beach only once before this. She did not remember it well, for she had been only a baby, the sun had long descended behind Hong Kong Island, and the Ma family had spent as little time as they could on the sands, as they did not wish to encounter the immigration police. So she was happy, as always when discovering some new aspect of America, and she had, in addition, Lucy all to herself. They were, as the Chinese say, breathing through the same nostrils. The only thing that marred the perfection is that Mary wanted very much to have a bathing suit. She did not own one, no one in her family had ever owned one, she had the money to buy a cheap one, but out of sensitivity to her friend, she did not press the issue. Lucy was wearing a baggy shorts and T-shirt combo that obscured her despised body, and Mary wore a similar one, although in her case the round little body showed forth at the correct places. She was no Janice Chen, of course (ah, yes, another reason for delight in Janice's absence), but was clearly distinguishable from a boy. Thus, Mary was not enthusiastic when Lucy said, without preamble, "I want to call Janice."

"Why?" Mary blurted, without thinking.

Lucy gave her a startled look. "Because she's our friend. *Wen jing zhi jiao*, remember? I miss her." She pointed to where a blue pay phone sign rose above the boardwalk. "Give me a couple of quarters." Which Mary did, and they yelled to Debbie Bryan, who stopped, watching, and then they trudged up through the hot sands.

Lucy called the Asia Mall, and was told that Janice was at home, which she found very strange, and then they had to find someone to change a dollar and then Lucy called the Chen home and found Janice there. Lucy greeted her and began an excited recitation of their recent doings, but soon noticed a curious flatness in Janice's responses.

"Jan, what's wrong? You sound weird."

"No, I'm okay. A little tired is all."

"What've you been doing?"

"Nothing much. I went to see *E.T.* with Susan Lu and Amanda."

"Amanda Shaw? Janice, we *hate* Amanda Shaw. She's a complete dweeb."

"Oh, and Mary Ma isn't? At least Amanda speaks English."

Lucy sensed this was not a profitable line of discussion and asked about the movie instead, and she got a synopsis, and things seemed to be settling down when Janice put her hand over the receiver. She seemed to be talking to someone else. When she came back on, she said, "Um, Lucy? Maybe I could get my brother to drive me out there for a day."

"Oh, that'd be super cool! Like tomorrow?"

"Yeah, um, what's the address you're staying at?"

"It's in Long Beach, 210 East Penn. When will you get here?"

"I don't know yet. I'll have to call you back. Look, I got to go now. I'll call you later."

"Okay, the phone number's area code—"

Mary Ma said, "What's wrong?"

Lucy looked at the telephone and jiggled the switch on the box. "I don't know," she said. "I think she hung up before I could give her the number."

"On purpose?"

Lucy shrugged, burying her doubts. "Oh, you know Janice. She's weird sometimes."

The black rubber boat cut its motor and coasted in through the low surf, hissing to a stop a few yards from where the twins were playing. Marlene sat up, rigid. "Boys!" she called. It came out a quaver, plucked away by the sea wind. She shouted again. One of the men left the boat, knelt and said something to the boys, and they both dashed up the beach to her, the man following. He did indeed look like a casino bouncer, six-two, maybe two-thirty. He was wearing a thin red nylon Windbreaker, a pair of yellow swim trunks, and a maroon net shirt. Several strands of massy gold adorned his thick neck. His skin was tanned bronze, and as he approached more closely, she could see that he was pelted heavily in black.

Zik put his face against hers and whispered in her ear, "That's the kidnapper man, Mommy."

On her other side Zak said, "That man said we could have a boat ride, Mommy. Can we?"

The man squatted by the side of her chair and pushed his sunglasses up on his head, so she could see his psychopath eyes. "Marlene Ciampi, am I right?" He was grinning. He had even, capped teeth, very white against the tan.

"Yes. What do you want?"

"These are your kids, huh? Jeez, they're really twins. How do you tell them apart?"

"I'm Zak!" said Zak. "I'm the oldest." Which was his usual response to this familiar conversational gambit.

"Yeah, you are," the man said, and tousled Zak's hair. Marlene shuddered.

"I'm Vincent Frasciotti," the man said. "They call me Vinnie Fresh. You ever heard of me?"

"No."

"Yeah, well, I don't advertise. And I'm not from here. I'm from L.A. I usually work for John Tona. You heard of *him*, right?"

"Yes."

"I figured. Yeah, well, I'm what they call a mechanic: something ain't right, they call me in, I fix it. No muss, no fuss. So, Mr. Bollano . . . you heard of *him*, I guess?"

"Yes."

"Yeah, Mr. Bollano got this little problem, and he asked me to fix it for him. Mr. Bollano thinks it's a shame that a nice mommy like yourself is spending all her time poking into stuff happened a long time ago, coming between a husband and his wife, shooting people, and so forth, and not watching her kids like she's supposed to. Mr. B. is a big believer in the family. He's concerned, you could say, something could happen to these nice kids while you were out doing stuff you shouldn't be doing in the first place, if you catch my drift."

"Yes," said Marlene. "Okay, I'll stop."

Vinnie's smile faded a tiny bit. He was disappointed, Marlene thought. This was too easy, and he hasn't got all his menacing jollies yet. "You'll stop," he said, flat-toned.

"Yes. I won't work for Vivian Bollano anymore, I'll stop the investigation."

"Yeah, well, that's very reasonable of you, Marlene. I heard you were a hard case, but I guess you're not so hard, huh?"

"No. I'm a soft case. I don't want anything to hurt my kids, okay? You made your point. I'm out of it."

"Yeah, good, but"—now he leaned closer, close enough for Marlene to smell the coconut scent of his suntan oil, and ran his index finger under the leg band of her Speedo suit, near the crotch, drawing the fabric up, exposing a small patch of pubic hair— ". . . but maybe we should go out to the boat there, the four of us, and discuss the details, you know, in a relaxed setting, make sure we understand each other."

Marlene was watching his face, watching him enjoying it. She had kept her own face blank, but now she saw that this had been an error; he would not relent until he had seen her break. And if he got her off this beach, with the boys, she would break, she was under no illusions about that. Vinnie Fresh would smash her in a way that precluded any recovery. That was what he did, and he was good at it, she could see that in his face.

Then his face changed. He frowned. He was looking at something behind Marlene. Sophie's voice called out cheerfully, "Boys, boys, who wants ice cream sodas? Come with Aunt Sophie!"

The twins shrieked and darted off like young rabbits. Sophie had them each by the hand and was moving with surprising speed toward the beach club.

"Hey . . ." said Vinnie.

Then Jake Gurvitz stepped into Marlene's field of view. He had a white terry-cloth robe on over his swim suit, and his thin white hair was blowing around his head like banners.

"Take a hike, sonny," he said to Vinnie, his voice grinding.

"This is a private conversation, grandpa. Get lost, and tell that old bat to bring those kids back."

Jake pulled a pistol out of the pocket of his robe and showed it to Vinnie. He showed it, and then let it fall down by his side, so that it hung by Marlene's face. She saw that it was a serious gun, a Smith .38 Model 10 with the four-inch barrel, the bluing worn, the handle wrapped with old-fashioned black friction tape, the classic gat of thirties gangster movies.

Vinnie shot to his feet. "What're you nuts? You pulling a gun on *me*? You know who I am, you old fuck? Get the fuck out of here before I shove that piece of shit up your ass!"

Jake said, "Shit for brains: shut up and listen to

me! You go back and tell Salvatore that Jake Gurvitz says he should lay off these people, this family. Tell him it's my family. Tell him Jake saved some paper from the old days. He doesn't want to see it on the television, he'll lay off. You got that, or do I have to repeat it?"

"What the *fuck*! Who the fuck are you, some maniac?"

"No," said Jake. "Like I said, Jake Gurvitz. Now, go ahead, get out of here."

They were separated by about six feet, Marlene estimated, Vinnie on the right side of her chair and Jake on the other. Vinnie now started to move around the foot of the chair.

"Give me that goddamn gun, asshole . . ." he started to say and then stopped, because Jake had raised the weapon and was holding in an old-style but undeniably expert two-handed grip, his left elbow dug into his broad belly, his left hand making a platform for the Smith, which Marlene could observe was trembling about as much as the boardwalk.

"Don't move your head," Jake said in a conversational tone. "I'm going to shoot your ear off." He cocked the hammer and leaned his head slightly into his grip, squinting at the front sight.

Vinnie had gone noticeably paler. He said, "You pull that fuckin' trigger, you're dead, man. And your fuckin' wife, and your fuckin' kids, and your fuckin'—"

The pistol fired, its report flattened and carried away instantly by the wind. A flock of seagulls bounced into the air, yelling and wheeling out over the sea. When Marlene finished her blink, she saw that Vinnie was sitting on the sand, his mouth an O of shock, his left hand held to the side of his face, blood pouring from between his fingers. A long piece of flesh, dripping red, hung down like a dreadful earring below the line of his jaw. His sunglasses had gone flying, and Marlene could see his eyes. They were full of disbelief, and horror, and the knowledge that a man who could shoot your ear off at six feet could remove any other part of your body he chose to, and you couldn't do anything about it. The other man ran up from the Zodiac and helped Vinnie to his feet, and together they went back to the craft. He manhandled the boat out into waist-high surf, helped Vinnie into it, paddled twenty yards farther out, cranked the outboard, and departed.

"You okay?" said Jake.

"Yeah. Yeah, Jake, I'm fine. Thank you."

"No problem," he said. With a movement of his head, he indicated the yacht and the Zodiac approaching it. "You might want to get off the beach," he added. "They could have a rifle."

He turned and walked back up the beach, past the wondering stares of the two other rummy players, and into the beach club.

It was not a good day, Karp found, to travel from Manhattan to the Long Island shore.

"You didn't realize it was July Fourth weekend?" asked Ed Morris incredulously.

"No, because the Fourth falls on a Tuesday this

year, and I had other stuff on my mind," said Karp. "Christ, the summer just started. We just had Memorial Day."

"Yeah, I hear you. The summer used to last a million years. Now . . ." He snapped his fingers. "Speaking of a million years, that's about what it's going to take us to get through this tunnel. I assume you want to avoid the Belt?"

"Hell, yeah! Take Flatbush. Use the goddamn siren, too."

Which they did, and made good time from the egress of the Battery Tunnel to the approaches to the Marine Parkway Bridge. There they found another fuming parking lot. Morris used the police radio to find out what was going on.

"A truck fire on the bridge," he said. "We're fucked, unless you want to call for a chopper."

Karp cursed briefly. "No, just patch into a land line, get in touch with Bryan, and tell her about Leung being on the loose. Tell her to keep them all close, in the house. And tell her to make sure that nobody tells anyone that Marlene and the kids are there. Tell her that we should be in Long Beach in, what . . . ?"

"Figure three hours," said Morris glumly, wiping off sweat.

"Shit!" After a few sweaty minutes, Karp leaned over and pulled his tattered cardboard portfolio onto his lap. He pulled from it a stack of case files and a Sony microcassette recorder.

"I might as well get some work done," he said.

"There's no one home," said Morris after a few minutes. "They must all be at the beach."

• • •

Nobody at the house spoke of what had happened at the beach. Marlene tried to thank Sophie, but came up against that lady's remarkably well-developed ability to place unhappy or violent events outside her consciousness. Jake was a sphinx in general, and when the girls and Bryan returned, Marlene was aware of her reluctance to involve the policewoman. The center of attention that afternoon was, in fact, Posie, and Posie's sunburn. When she emerged from her room, mottled, blistered, stinking of Noxema, Zik burst into tears, and Sophie, after a brief inspection in the bathroom, decided that she had to be taken over to the emergency room at Long Beach Memorial. Jake volunteered to run the two of them over in his Lincoln.

When they were gone, Marlene slipped into Sophie's bedroom and used the phone, charging the call to her office number.

"Guma? This is Marlene. *Comu stati?*"

"Champ? Jeez, you're the first call I had in three days. I'm some kind of non-person now, like in Russia."

"You're holding up, though."

"Yeah, yeah. The fucking press is camped outside, so I can't go out. I'm watching my Jane Goodall tape. Christ, that woman turns me on, those long legs in those little shorts—be honest, Marlene, do you think I got a shot at Jane Goodall?"

"To be honest? I think you don't look quite *enough* like a chimpanzee."

Guma laughed. "God, Marlene, I think that's the

nicest thing you ever said about me. How's by you? Got sand in all your orifices?"

"So far, so good. Look, Goom, I need to pick your brain. Ever hear of a Jake Gurvitz?"

"Hm, Jake Gurvitz, Jake Gurvitz . . . oh, yeah, late thirties, forties, into the fifties, a labor goon, a head breaker, a Brooklyn guy, he came up with all those Murder Incorporated Jewish fellas, Pittsburgh Phil, Kid Twist Reles, and all of them. Worked for, let's see, he worked for Albert Anastasia, and after Albert got clipped in fifty-two, he worked for the Bollano outfit. As a contractor."

"He did murders?"

"Not that we could ever prove. A slick guy. They called him Jake the Baker, or Bakin' Jake. The feds finally got him for some dicky little thing like the feds do, tax evasion or perjury, I forget. He did a jolt in Marion, early sixties or so, and I guess he must've kicked off, because he sure hasn't shown up recently. What's your interest?"

"Oh, just following up on something. Why did they call him Jake the Baker? Because of the baker's union connection?"

"That, and he used to put guys in bake ovens and turn on the flames. You piss him off, he turns you into a bagel. A real sweetheart, from what I heard."

Marlene had scarcely hung up the phone and had not even begun to digest Guma's story when Lucy popped in.

"Can we go shopping in Long Beach? We need some things."

"Things? What things?"

"Oh, you know, items. Mary wants to get a

bathing suit. I need new sunglasses, and a hat. Could we?"

"I'll talk to Detective Bryan. And anyway, we have to wait until the twins wake up."

"Why do we have to take them? Why don't we just go now, the three of us? It won't take more than an hour at the most."

Marlene sighed. She didn't need this just now, and she was thinking that it would be a good idea to go up to her bedroom and turn on the fan and, after a slow shower, lie naked on the white bedspread and drift off herself. She said, "Lucy, you're forgetting the situation. We have to stay with Detective Bryan."

"We could walk over to Beach Bazaar, it's not that far. Come on, Mom, nothing's going to happen."

"Lucy! Are you completely nuts? I *said* . . ." A glare with this hot enough to fry eggs.

"Okay, okay, you don't have to yell." Lucy flounced off, muttering, leaving Marlene to reflect that her daughter, despite her gifts and the remarkable resourcefulness and sophistication she often displayed, was not immune to the fits of brainlessness that afflict adolescents. She did not know whether to be annoyed or happy at this. She lay back on Sophie's bed, still in her bathing suit, and conked out, to be awakened after what seemed like four minutes by the twins, who were cranky and demanding of different and incompatible things, and had to be cozened by the promise of a commercial expedition.

The children ran happily into the Volvo, Marlene

drove, Bryan rode shotgun, and everyone else piled into the backseat. Marlene locked the door, and they set out. In the house behind them, the phone rang.

"Where could they be?" Karp asked.

"Gosh, Butch, for crying out loud, I said they're at the *beach*," replied Morris. "I mean, that's what you do, you're at a beach house, you go to the beach."

"Well, we're out of that traffic anyway."

"Yeah, relax, we'll be there in twenty minutes."

What I should really do now, thought Leung, is open the door of this van, get out, and simply walk away. I should walk to the nearest public transport, go back to Manhattan, get the money, and leave. Their route from Queens to Long Beach had taken them on the Cross Bay Boulevard, where the airliners roared overhead on their way to and from JFK Airport. He wanted to be on one of those planes, headed east, instead of in this van, heading to an unplanned operation, with four frightened local *ma jai*, and the crazy Vietnamese gangster and the resentful boy they'd just snatched. But he had no money, not for a ticket, or to buy a fake passport, or even to bribe his way into a freight container. All his money was in Chinatown, and all the money in the world would do him no good as long as the girl was free and able to talk. If the girl could be taken, without notice, then he could recoup, slip back into federal protection, testify against the Italians, then vanish and change into someone else, after which the rest of the plan would be simple to accomplish.

He leaned back and lit another cigarette, although the air in the van held so much smoke that it was hardly necessary. He looked out the window. The van had turned left after leaving the Cross Bay Bridge and was now heading down a wide road, moving slowly in the heavy traffic. It was some sort of holiday, it seemed, which might be helpful in the event an escape became necessary. Another bridge and a smaller road, this one leading through a beach community, low houses and one-story shops. Park Street, Leung read on a sign. Vo had a map spread out, and he was barking directions in bad Cantonese at the boy driving, a White Dragon named Lau, the sole American-born Chinese in the group. Presently, after several wrong turns, they came to a large white house with a pillared porch. Vo was about to jump from the van as soon as it stopped, but Leung placed a restraining hand on his shoulder from behind.

"Wait. We don't know who is at home. There are no cars in the driveway. Perhaps they have already left." Leung felt a faint surge of relief. If they had gone back to their residence, if they had picked up their normal routine again, taking the child would be vastly simpler. They waited. In the house nothing stirred, no sounds of occupation came through the open windows.

"They've left," said Leung. "Let's go."

Lau said, "That doesn't make sense. Why would they leave? It's the Fourth of July weekend. They're probably just down at the beach."

"That's right," said Vo. "We should wait."

"But not here, in front of the house," said Leung. "Drive on, and turn left at the corner."

As they turned past that junction, another Dodge van approached from the direction of Park Street. It could have been the twin of theirs, except that it had tinted windows and was black, where theirs was gray. The vans passed each other slowly, their speed suited to the narrow, sand-dusted residential street.

Freddie Phat, at the wheel of the black van, made a startled movement and craned his neck to look at the other vehicle as it passed.

"What's wrong?" asked Tran, who sat beside him in the front seat.

"Strange. It looked like Kenny Vo sitting in the passenger seat of that van."

"Stop!" cried Tran. "Turn around and follow it!"

Phat hit the gas pedal, shot forward to the next intersection, and spun the van skidding around. The three hard faces in the back rocked, and their automatic rifles clattered on the floor.

"That's their car," Leung shouted.

"Where? Where?" Lau saw nothing ahead but empty roadway.

"An orange Volvo," said Leung excitedly. "It just passed the next intersection, going to the left."

Lau accelerated, turned, and soon they had the square orange car in view. "Stay back," Leung ordered. "I don't want them to see us. That's good, let a car get between us. They are heading for the shops. Good, they're slowing, they're turning into that parking lot. Follow them! No, no, not right next to their car! Idiot! Park over there, right next to the exit. Good."

They parked. The lot was crowded with shoppers and their cars, as were the narrow sidewalks of the shopping strip, which was anchored by the Beach Bazaar and a large Grand Union supermarket. Those in the back crowded forward so they could see out the windshield, from which they had an excellent view of the Volvo. As they watched, its passengers left, the two girls running into the Beach Bazaar, a substantial emporium whose striped steel awnings dripped with beach chairs, inflated animal-shaped swimming toys, large beach balls, air mattresses.

"Who is that black woman?" Vo asked.

"A nursemaid, no doubt," said Leung. "She is not significant. Our luck has changed, it appears. I am going to examine the situation in the store. All of you, wait here and do nothing!"

He was gone ten minutes. When he returned, he was carrying two yellow smock shirts, embroidered with the logo of the Beach Bazaar and the names of two employees. Back in his seat, he said, "It is perfect. They are scattered throughout the store, and the girls are isolated in the swimming costume area. This is what we will do. Lau and Eng will stay with the car. I and Vo and Cowboy will enter the store. Cowboy and I will wear these shirts. Cai and Yang will take up a position outside the store. The girl knows Cowboy; that will put her off her guard. He will lead her to the back of the store. I will join him there, and together we will take her through the stockroom, to the rear exit. There is an alley there, and a loading dock. When Vo has seen us enter, he will signal to Lau, and he will take the car around to the alley, get us and the girl, and then come around and pick up the three others."

"What about the other girl?" asked Vo.

"If she sees anything, we will take her, too," said Leung. "Does everyone understand what he is to do? Cowboy?"

The youth nodded sullenly. Leung asked each of the others and, where there was doubt or confusion, gave crisp instruction. They were nothing like a Hong Kong triad team, he thought, but far better than Red Guards, and it should be a simple operation. In and out.

There was an odd smell in the store, an old-fashioned place with circulating ceiling fans, wooden floor, a high, stamped tin ceiling, long counters, and bins. Cowboy thought it must be some sort of confection; it was sweet and heavy, and to him as exotic as five-spice powder would have been to nearly all of the store's clientele. It was crowded with these, and getting more crowded as people came in to pick up the various necessities they had forgotten to pack in their rush to leave the heat of the city for the big weekend.

Cowboy walked quickly to the place Leung had indicated, where swimsuits hung on chromed racks and headless, armless models showed them off. He could not see Lucy, and felt a sudden and surprising sense of relief. Perhaps they had suspected something and fled. But no, he now saw a short Asian girl selecting suits with intense concentration, reading the price tags and the labels as if they were oracles. She did not notice Cowboy.

Then the curtain that led to the changing room was thrust briskly aside, and there she was right in front of him, swimsuits draped over her arm. She saw him.

"Cowboy? What are you doing here?" she asked in Vietnamese, looking curiously at his shirt, which bore the name IRIS embroidered in red thread.

"I have to see, I mean, to talk to you. It's very important."

Lucy looked over at Mary, who was utterly absorbed in the mathematics of assessing clothing value, and nodded to Cowboy. She tossed her suits over the top of a rack and followed Cowboy toward the back of the store.

"In here," said Cowboy, pushing open the swinging door to the stockroom. Lucy went through, and Leung grabbed her, clapping his hand over her mouth and pressing a pistol muzzle into her back. He pulled her into a dark alcove formed by large cardbord crates containing plastic swimming pools. In Cantonese he said, "Is it true that you can speak Cantonese?"

She nodded. He said, "Are you going to scream or do anything foolish?"

She shook her head, and he removed his hand from her mouth. She looked at Cowboy and said, in Vietnamese, "With Heaven rest all matters here below: harm people and they'll harm you in their turn. Perfidious humans who do fiendish deeds shall suffer, and cry mercy in vain." Cowboy reacted as if slapped. He looked away from her, his jaw quivering. Every Vietnamese knows the scene where Kieu and her lover, Tu, the rebel chieftain, take revenge on all who have abused her.

"What did she say?" Leung demanded.

"Nothing," Cowboy mumbled. "Just some poetry."

Leung snapped, "Go out to the loading dock and see if they are there." Cowboy trotted off.

Leung turned Lucy around and gave her an appraising look. He shook his head. "Incredible! So you speak Vietnamese, too, even poetry. You know the saying, *cai tai, cai tai,* and so on?"

"Yes, because of the rhyme. Talent and disaster are twins."

"Particularly true, it seems, in your case. You have caused me an enormous amount of trouble, little girl."

"Are you going to kill me?"

"I suppose I will have to, although it seems a shame. There is a white-girl brothel in Macao that would pay nearly anything for someone like you. Perhaps I will pump you full of heroin and pack you in an air-freight container. How would you like that?"

"I think it would be wisest to kill me. If you did that other thing, I would escape and find you, wherever you were, and eat your heart."

To Lucy's vast surprise, Leung replied in English with a decided New York accent, "Oh, don't be a schmuck!" He looked at his watch and said, in the same voice, "Where the fuck is that goddamn kid? What is he, jerking off out there?"

Lucy's linguistic curiosity overwhelmed her fear and burst forth. In English, she asked, "Where did you learn to talk like that?"

Leung switched back to Cantonese. "You are impressed. To confess the truth, I have only a few phrases like that. I learned my English from an American, a native of this city, in Macao. I was escaping from the Cultural Revolution, and I had a septic wound in my leg. It was from being beaten with chains and thrown into a vat of pig manure. He took me in and taught me a great deal about your wonderful country before—"

Cowboy came running then, a worried look on his face.

"They are not there," he blurted.

Kenny Vo was pacing to and fro in the front aisle of the Beach Bazaar, where they kept the shopping carts and the soda machines. He kept looking out of the window, expecting the gray van to pull up with Leung and Cowboy and the girl. But the van did not come. The parking lot was growing more crowded.

It was not hard for Tran and his associates to overpower Lau and Eng. They simply worked their way crouching through the parked cars, appeared at the unlocked side door of the gray van, jumped in, and stuck pistols in the faces of the amazed White Dragons. Nor was it difficult to get the details of Leung's plan from Eng, who was, in fact, one of the two *ma jai* Tran had snatched earlier, and he required no additional demonstration of what lengths Tran would go to in order to extract information.

Tran snapped out directions for the counter-attack and left Freddie Phat and one of his men in the van, while he walked out into the parking lot with the two others. They spread out, winding through the cars, stepping lightly around the clusters of harried parents and their children, the clumps of teens in bright beach wear, the occasional slow-moving elderly couple. Each of the Vietnamese carried a long beach bag tucked under his right arm.

Vo looked through the plate glass and saw them coming. He let out a curious high-pitched cry. The checkout ladies and their customers looked up. They saw a stocky Asian man in a sports jacket, dark trousers, and black loafers—not dressed for the beach. The man let out another sound, this one a combination groan and hiss, as if from a pressure vessel about to pop its safety valve. The nearest checkout lady raised her hand to attract the attention of a manager.

Vo saw the man who had ruined his life walking toward him; the rage burned away the last of his modest store of rationality. He yanked the machine pistol from his waistband and directed a stream of automatic fire at his enemy. He fired one-handed in his zeal and the weapon flew upward, blowing out the plate-glass window in a hail of shards before directing bullets at the parking lot and the sky. He heard something snap-snap-snap past his head. He dropped to the floor. Someone was shooting a Kalashnikov at him, disciplined fire in three-round bursts, the habit of the thrifty little army he knew so well. On his knees, sheltered by the bulk of a Pepsi machine, he fired the rest of the magazine blindly out the vacant window, and fumbled to replace it with a fresh one.

Sounds of firing came from outside as the two White Dragons blasted away; then that firing ceased. More bullets came flying into the store, in the same precise rhythm. An overhead fixture shattered, raining glass onto customers and staff cowering in the aisles. People were screaming, shouting. Vo couldn't think in all the noise. He wanted to shoot the screaming people. When the new magazine finally clicked in, he cautiously peeked around the Pepsi machine to find a target.

"Drop the gun! Now!" It was a woman's voice, and American, behind him. *Behind him?* Vo spun on his knees. It was the nursemaid, crouching low, pointing a gun at him. *The nursemaid?* He raised his weapon, and Detective Bryan shot him through the chest four times with her service revolver.

Around this scene, chaos. A hundred or so screaming people were attempting to leave by the two exit doors, parents were crying for their children, children were howling their heads off, several brave souls leaped through the broken window, a couple of men knocked Detective Bryan down as they rushed by. One person, however, brooked the human tide and walked calmly through the one-way entrance door.

• • •

Leung heard the automatic fire from the front of the store and realized that something had gone badly wrong. The plan was therefore finished. A shame, but he had already accomplished much. He would have to escape and attempt, somehow, to recoup. But first.

Cowboy saw the Chinese point his pistol at Lucy's head. Without a thought his arm shot out and struck Leung's elbow. The gun exploded. Lucy reeled backward, tripped on a low carton, and fell sprawling to the floor. Leung stared for a moment at Cowboy, unbelievingly, and then shot the boy twice in the chest. The youth fell, grasping at Leung, hooking his hand on Leung's trouser pocket, ripping the fabric and tearing the pocket out as he collapsed. Coins jingled and scraps of paper flew to the floor. Leung cursed, ignored the coins, scrabbled for the small papers.

Leung heard a voice shout in a language he did not understand. It sounded a little like the Portuguese he had picked up in Macao, and he recognized the name, Lucy. He had to kill the girl quickly and get away. But where was the girl? He saw the gap in the pile of cartons. She had wriggled into some crevice. The shout again. Steps, coming closer. Leung fired some shots blindly at the cartons and took off, dodging down the narrow aisles. He saw the daylight of the loading dock and ran toward it. There were pursuing steps. He ignored them and raced on, out onto the loading dock and down into the service alley.

• • •

"Fireworks must be starting early," observed Karp as they rolled down Park Street in Long Beach.

Ed Morris frowned. "That's not fireworks, Butch. Somebody's shooting auto."

Then they heard the sirens. "What should we do?" Morris asked.

It did not take Karp long to decide. The possibility that someone was firing an automatic weapon in a beachside community in which his wife was resident and that the discharge did not in some manner involve his wife was too remote to be credible.

"Follow the sirens," he said, his heart bouncing yet again into his throat.

"Lucy, are you there? He is gone. You may emerge now."

Hearing Tran's voice, Lucy crawled on hands and knees from her hiding place. She crawled backward, for the space in which she had wedged herself was barely eighteen inches wide. She felt wetness on her bare knees, and then on her hands. When she was free of the tunnel, she turned and saw Tran and saw that the wetness was Cowboy's blood, spreading out from his body, looking black in the dim fluorescent light, like the blood in the Asia Mall stockroom, from the men Leung and . . .

"Is he going to die?" she asked. There was a piece of white paper stuck to her knee in blood. She pulled it off and crumpled it in her fist.

"I think so," said Tran. "He is shot through the lung and blowing bright blood."

"Did you kill Leung?"

"No, I didn't see him. I heard someone running away, but I first wanted to see that you were safe." He paused. "I must go now. Some of the Chinese have been shot, and I do not wish for my friends and I to be imprisoned." He shook his beach bag, which made a Kalashnikovish noise against the floor.

"I'll see you," said Lucy.

"See you later, crocodile," said Tran in English, and left.

Lucy crouched over the Vietmanese and took his hand. He opened his eyes. "I'm sorry," he said. "I am ashamed, but they made . . . I'm so sorry."

"Don't be sorry," she said. "All this is my fault."

Then, as if magically, as if in a dream, the alcove was full of people. Her mother, her father (her *father?*), Detective Bryan, Mary Ma, two paramedics, several policemen.

"Lucy, come away, honey," her father said. "Let these guys get to him." He knelt down and placed his arm around her.

Cowboy said, "No!" with such vehemence that he coughed up a froth of blood. He gripped Lucy's wrist so hard her tanned skin turned white around his bloody fingers. He began to speak rapidly in Vietnamese, interrupted by spells of coughing. Lucy answered softly in the same fluting language. Tears were pouring from her eyes. Karp held his daughter tightly, and in his other hand a Sony soundlessly rotated, recording the best possible exception to the hearsay rule, a dying declaration.

19

"YOU DON'T HAVE TO DO THIS NOW," Karp said. "You don't have to do it at all. I can get a Vietnamese translator tomorrow—"

"No," said Lucy firmly. "You said the faster we can get this done, the faster the cops can start looking for Leung. And I want to do it. He was my friend. It's my fault he's dead."

"Lucy, now stop it! It's not your fault." She shriveled and started to weep again, a slow snuffling drip, almost soundless, that had been going on almost without break from the time the dying boy had grasped her hand. They were in the Karps' bedroom at Aunt Sophie's house, where they had returned late, after endless exhausting interviews with the local cops and then the homicide cops from county and state police, and a couple of well-dressed gents from the FBI. In fairness, it was a complex story and the telling took some time, how a Chinatown double murder and a Mafia assassination had led to a machine-gun shoot-out in a beachside shopping center, and how Lucy Karp fit into all of it. Karp had been by his daughter's side throughout, and thought she had handled herself well.

Leung was the man she and Mary and Janet had seen at the murder—there was no point in hiding that any longer, and Mary confirmed it. But the locals and the staties were interested in the four corpses on their patch. Miraculously, no one else had been killed, although there were numerous injuries among the bystanders, some grave. Of the dead, two were simply explained: Leung had killed Nguyen Van Minh, aka Cowboy, and an NYPD police officer had killed Vo Van Hai, aka Kenny Vo. There were two other Asian corpses outside the Beach Bazaar, Cai Wenshi and Yang Wo-ming from their ID, and no one knew who had shot them, or whom Kenny Vo had been shooting at, or why.

Lucy professed ignorance of these details. Karp was not so sure. The list of people who could both mount a disciplined assault with automatic weapons and who were pals with his daughter was a very short one; perhaps it had only one member. Despite this, he did not press her on it. The other great mystery of the day was what had become of Mr. Leung. By four that afternoon several hundred officers from a half dozen police agencies had searched the area of the shopping strip and beyond, stopping cars, peering into crannies under the boardwalk, and questioning people, but with no success. Leung had vanished, and Karp believed that Cowboy's last words might hold a clue to his plans. He prepared pad and pencil and pushed the recorder switch. The sound of coughing and then the boy's voice.

Lucy said, "He says, 'I am sorry. He is a bad person, my cousin, he . . . does not know how to live as a human being. I am bad, too, although I did not want it to . . . listen, it was Leung's plan, all of it. First, we captured the Italian man, Catalano . . .'"

Karp heard his own voice saying, "Did you kill Catalano?" and then Lucy's translation and Cowboy, again. Lucy translated: "No, I drove one of the cars. Kenny killed Catalano. Leung was there. He looked at the clock and said when to fire. They fired through the man's head. I was sick. Kenny laughed and he said, 'Next time, you will do it yourself, it's about time,' and other things. They all laughed at me. I wanted them to stop laughing, so I did it. I came in through the back door and I shot them both, as Leung had ordered, in the body and in the head. I went on home invasions, too. In one place we raped a woman, and I pretended to also, but I was too ashamed. I did not want this kind of life in America. He knew you were the one, that day, you saw everything. He found out from the Chen. You called, they got the address where you were. She asked you. I should have shouted out or warned, but I was afraid. We came out here. I didn't want to, but . . . Lucy, do you think . . . Lucy, do you think . . . Lucy . . ." And the sound of crying. Karp flicked off the machine.

She was sobbing now, and she brought forth from the pocket of her cutoffs a wad of tissues the size of a softball, bits flying everywhere, and dabbed her eyes with it and blew her nose. Karp tossed his pad away and hugged Lucy to him, making comforting sounds without meaning, until the whooping sobs stopped and she relaxed against him, snuffling and exhausted.

"You should get some rest," he said.

"Everybody thinks it's my fault, don't they?"

"Nobody thinks that, Lucy."

She pulled away and faced him. "No, don't be a *daddy*, tell me the truth! None of this would've happened if I just came to you and told what I saw in the Asia Mall."

"You want the truth? Okay, yeah, it would've been better if you came forward with it—for you. For *you*, Lucy, not necessarily for the other people."

"I thought I was doing the right thing. For Mary, I mean, and Janice. Dad, how *could* she have? I don't understand. I thought she was, they are—were, like my family. I *loved* her. *Wen jing zhi jiao.*"

"What's that?"

"Friends who would die for each other. I thought . . . oh, God, what a mess." She stood and gave her face another wipe. "I want to go see Mary now, all right?"

"Sure, baby, go ahead. I'll see you later."

He checked over his transcription and put it away, and bent to pick up the scraps Lucy had scattered on the floor, placing them in a large tin ashtray on the bedside table. He did a good job, glad, actually, of one mess that was easy to clean up.

Marlene made a big batch of Spanish omelettes and buttered toast for the house, but the table was far from the merry assembly it had been on previous nights. Two people were missing: Posie had been kept by the hospital for a day of observation, and Detective Bryan, placed on routine administrative leave after the shooting, had gone back to the city.

The rest ate with poor appetite, in relative silence. Even the twins were subdued. The girls left for their attic as soon as they could, and Sophie left early, too, complaining of pains in her hip. Karp took the boys for a walk on the beach before bedtime, accompanied by Ed Morris, while Marlene washed up. As she stood at the sink, Jake Gurvitz came in, picked up a dish towel and started to dry.

"Don't bother, thanks," she said. "They'll drip on the rack."

Jake smiled. "That's what Sophie says." He took a seat at the kitchen table. Outside, it was drifting into deep blue, and moths were beginning their *totentanz* against the back-door lightbulb.

"How is she?"

"Not bad for an old lady who just had a goddamn thing the size of a pipe wrench stuck in her body. Amazing what they can do nowadays."

"Yeah, amazing." She turned off the hot water, racked the egg pan, and faced him, leaning against the sink. "Was she upset about this afternoon?"

"Upset? Sophie's hard to upset. Something don't go right, she puts it out of her mind. You think of what she's been through, it's probably the best thing."

Marlene pulled out her pack and stuck a sandy, crumpled filter tip in her mouth. Jake lit it and lit a panatela for himself. "Yeah, no point in carrying all that stuff around with you, except if you plan on doing something with it. And, speaking of the past, does she know about you?"

"She knows I wasn't teaching in a girls' school," he said after a brief pause. He was watching her closely.

"But not that you were Jake the Baker."

"Huh. You're some detective. Where'd you hear that?"

"Around. Does she?"

"That? No. Why, you going to tell her?"

"No, of course not. You did a good thing for me and my kids today. I owe you. But as a matter of curiosity, and because I got a stake in it, what kind of paper would it be that Salvatore Bollano wouldn't like to see on the TV?"

Jake released a long stream of cigar smoke and studied a large gray moth battering against the kitchen window. He took a deep breath and let it out. "You know I worked for Sally back then?"

"Uh-huh. What as, exactly?"

"I kept the union in line, made sure Sally got his cut of the dues, took care of the pension funds for him. Moved money from here to there and back. Like that."

"And put guys in ovens?"

Jake chuckled. "You don't want to believe everything you hear, Marlene. Anyway, a lot of cash moved around, and there were markers, little pieces of paper that said who got paid what—like receipts, you know? The guy's initials, the amount, and who cleared the payoff. That was usually Sally himself, but me, too. We called them tags. Like a guy would say, 'Tag so-and-so for fifty G.'"

"A guy like Heshy Panofsky?"

Jake raised his eyebrow and smiled. "Oh-ho! Now I see why Sally sent that kid around to see you. No, as a matter of fact, Panofsky was at the other end. He was a cutout, if you know what that means. The politicians didn't want to know from where the dough really came. But they get it from Panofsky, they could tell themselves it was clean."

"So Panofsky collected money from the Mob and paid it out. I figured that out already."

"Uh-huh. He would keep track of it in a book he kept locked up in his office. The tag book, they called it, like a ledger. Initials, dates, amounts, the whole *megillah*."

"That'd be an interesting book to read."

"Interesting, yeah, but not healthy," said Jake, and Marlene asked the inevitable next question: "This has something to do with why Jerry Fein got killed, doesn't it?"

Jake's face darkened, and he looked again at the window. The moth was stationary now, exhausted, longing for the light. "That's a whole different story. You don't need to know about that."

"Oh, Christ! Jake, tell me you didn't do him!"

Jake looked at her, meeting her eyes. She thought, What is it about me that attracts the bad boys of the world? What do they want from me? Why do I like them? Thinking thus, it seemed like a long while before he answered.

"No, I didn't do him. Little Sal and Charlie Tuna did him. I knew about it, though. I found that scumbag Nobile for them."

"For the key."

"Yeah. The key."

"Was Panofsky involved?"

"Nah. They wouldn't involve Heshy, a thing like that. He was their gate into legit stuff. They wouldn't want him to get his hands dirty. Did he know about it? Hell, yeah, he knew about it. Had to."

"So, why, Jake? Why did they kill their own lawyer?"

"Why? Because he found out who framed him on the jury tamper. Thing about Jerry, see, he played it straight up. He gave you his best shot, and he was good. But Sally, on that Gravalotti thing, his own ass on the line, he wasn't gonna take no chances. So he tells Heshy, put the fix in, Heshy, get to a juror, a couple of jurors. So Heshy does it. But he works it so that when it comes out, Jerry looks like the one done it. And he, I mean Heshy, makes sure it comes out."

"Why would he do that?" asked Marlene.

"Hey, what do I know? But Panofsky had this hard-on for Jerry Fein. It was a known thing. Everybody but Jerry knew it, but Jerry, he couldn't take it in. He brought the guy into the firm, covered his ass, he's making a good living . . . what's that thing about punishment, something about a good deed?"

"No good deed goes unpunished."

"Yeah! That was them."

Marlene thought for a moment about what she'd learned from Abe Lapidus. Heshy'd done the frame, Fein had taken the fall to protect Bernie Kusher, but then found out that Heshy had screwed him. He'd be mad as hell, but . . . She turned a puzzled face to Jake. "But . . . okay, say Jerry found out about the frame. He threatens to expose Panofsky. What's that got to do with the killing? Bollano killed Jerry as a *favor* to Panofsky?"

"Nah. No way. No, that's something I could never figure out. Sally was really mad at Jerry, *really* mad, and Sally, you know he was usually a bucket of ice about business. No, this was something else, something personal. Because it looks bad, guys in that business don't usually knock off their lawyers. Lawyer's no danger to them, because of that rule— they can't rat them out."

"Right, client privilege. So, tell me, what was the paper you're going to scare Big Sally with?"

Jake shrugged, raised his eyebrows. "Oh, that. Hell, that was mostly bluff. I handled a lot of paper for Sally, he don't know what stuck to my fingers. Tags and stuff. I got some stuff with my lawyers, anything happens to me . . . you know. But the tags ain't worth much without the tag book."

"And I presume that's gone by now."

"Hell, yeah! I mean, they're not stupid. After Jerry went, Panofsky cleaned out the office, dumped Jerry's secretary, got rid of Bernie Kusher—"

"I thought Kusher embezzled some money and took off."

"The way I heard it, Heshy was about to rat him out, but Bernie beat him to the punch. He cleaned out the safe, all of Sally's payoffs for the month, had to be seven, eight hundred large. Heshy had to loot the trusts to pay it back, which he stuck on Bernie. Neat trick, when you think about it. Always a joker, Bernie."

Not a million, though, thought Marlene. Some of the trust money had stuck to Heshy's fingers. She said, "Yeah. Speaking of funny, aren't you worried about Vinnie Fresh? He doesn't strike me as the kind of guy who you blow his ear off he's going to laugh and forget about it."

Jake ground out his cigar and laced his hands behind his head. "Well, I tell you, Marlene: one, I'm seventy-two. If not this, it'll be the prostate or some other damn thing. I never figured to last this long in the first place. Practically everybody I came up with is dead. All this with Sophie—it's a bonus I never expected. And two—these guys they got to-day, they ain't the same as guys like me. They ain't tough the same way. I'd've pulled a stunt like that on the beach, in the old days, I wouldn't be here talking to you now. I'd be feeding the crabs. We used to get any shit, boom! Come right back at you, none of this fucking around. So, I ain't worried. I can take care of myself. Believe me, Salvatore knows that better'n anybody alive."

There was a commotion at the door, and Karp came in with the two boys. They came rushing up to their mother, and each dumped a large, stinking marine rock on the clean table.

"We collected rocks, Mommy," cried Zik. "Look, mine has seaweeds and a little crab. But he's hiding now, and a clam stuck on it."

"A barnacle. It's beautiful, darling!"

"My rock is bigger," said Zak. "Mine has red worms on it."

The rocks were admired, placed in plastic bags, were banned from the bathwater, despite strenuous objections, and the Karps soon afterward put their boys to bed. The two girls had meanwhile taken over the front bedroom vacated by the departure of Bryan and Posie. In their own bedroom, the Karps flung themselves full-length on their high bed, hooting and giggling with exhaustion.

"Good thing this is a vacation, or I'd be tired," said Karp.

"Yeah, any more relaxation and we'd start to get stale."

"Right. Say, Zak kept going on about going on a boat ride, and Zik said something about the kidnap man coming in a boat. What was that all about, or were they making stuff up?"

"No, just some asshole in a rubber boat trying to mess with my head. They see a woman alone on the beach, it goes right to their gonads. It was nothing."

"Really?"

Marlene ignored this, for she did not have the energy to deal with Karp's worry. They had, she thought, enough to worry about. She moved closer to him and nestled her head into the hollow of his shoulder. "You're so good," she said. "You uphold the law. You don't kill people. You don't even *want* to kill people."

"Well, George Steinbrenner . . . if I could get close enough . . ."

"No, *seriously*, Butch. I keep feeling it's all my fault, the violence, that there's some, I don't know, *lust*, I have for it. I was just thinking, just now, who are my friends, who do I attract, who am I attracted to: Mattie Duran, a killer; Tran, a stone killer; my best friend on the cops? Jim Raney, who's killed more people in line of duty than any other serving officer. Jake Gurvitz—"

"Our Jake?"

She told him who Jake was. He said, "Jesus!"

"Jesus, indeed. So I'm in this life, I chose it, for

whatever reason, and I have to say, Lucy's in it, too. Bad genes. I don't worry about Lucy; I mean, I worry about her hating me, and not being happy, but I don't worry about her safety the way you do. Irrational? Maybe, but that's how I feel. But, Butch, when that guy went after Zik, I fell apart. Complete paralyzed jelly. They're not like Lucy, they're just little tiny boys. And I can't protect them, not twenty-four hours a day, not and do anything else. Does this make sense?"

"Honestly? No, but I know that's the way you feel. The question is, what are you going to do about it?"

"Well, first I'm going to have a ciggie." She got her pack out, opened the window wide to the sea breeze, went over to the nightstand, and picked up the ashtray. She looked at it in distaste.

"What is all this crap?"

"Lucy's crying debris. Kleenex from her pocket."

"Butch, this is *blood*."

"Where?" Together, they examined the crumpled, brown-stained piece of paper together.

Karp said, "This must have come from the murder scene. It's got Chinese writing on it. It looks like a betting slip. See, the number 4,500 and the characters around it."

"Could it be evidence?"

"Sure, but I don't know of what or what it's worth. In any case, we have more than enough to nail Leung."

"If you can catch him," Marlene observed. She placed the slip in the drawer of the nightstand. "There's no point in bothering her any more today.

Show it to her in the morning, and we'll see if it's worth keeping."

"It's a deposit slip from a Chinese named Kuen," said Lucy the next morning as they all gathered for breakfast. "He's kind of a banker. You give him money and he gives you these slips, with your name and his name and the amount, or you give him a slip and he gives you money. It could be his own slip or a slip from someone he knows, in China or Hong Kong or wherever."

Karp recalled his brief conversation with V.T. Clearly this was how Leung had moved money in and out of the country. He experienced another brief moment of irritation as he thought of the man-hours wasted searching for Leung's financial trail, when all the time his darling daughter . . . but there was no point in getting into that now. He said, "Interesting. And this slip—Leung dropped it?"

"No. When Nguyen fell he grabbed and ripped Leung's pocket out. He had a bunch of them."

"Okay, I'll call it in. Maybe he'll show up at this Kuen's place, providing we can find it."

"It's on Doyers Street," said Lucy. "It's where I bank."

"Where *you* bank?" asked Marlene, who was cracking eggs at the kitchen counter. Karp was beyond being stunned.

Lucy calmly sliced another bagel, holding the circle against her chest and plunging the knife in the direction of her heart as she cut. "The lab pays me. I went to Kuen because I'm underage to get an account at a regular bank and I didn't want you guys to know about the money."

"Lucy!" Marlene exclaimed. "But why not?"

The girl shrugged. "I don't know. It seemed important at the time. Everything's changed now." She sniffled, seemed close to tears, swallowed hard and gained control of herself. "I hope you get him," she said.

"We'll get him, if we have to put a cop on every corner in Chinatown," said Karp grimly. "One thing in our favor—the guy has to stay in the community. An illegal from Hong Kong, on his own. He wouldn't know where to start on the outside."

"You know, Dad, that might not be true. He can talk English with a New York accent when he wants to. He might be a lot slicker than we think. And he's from Macao, not Hong Kong. He knew an American there who taught him all kinds of stuff. He said." She resumed her slicing. Karp and Marlene exchanged an eye-rolling look, and then Karp went to the phone to call in these revelations to Clay Fulton in the city.

After breakfast Marlene set the girls to washing up and dialed her number at Osborne. She punched in her voice-mail code and listened to the messages from Tran, then pushed the numbers to erase it. Tran's involvement in the Beach Bazaar affair vanished into electronic chaos. The next three message were from Mattie Duran. She ignored these. Maybe she was out of the business, maybe not, but the ladies would have to get along without her for a while. The next message was from Tran.

"Marie-Hélène, I am in Bridgeport, in Connecticut state. I thought it wise to continue east, rather than heading west to the city, in case there should be inquisitive policemen along the way back. We took the ferry from Port Jefferson. Do you know, there is a considerable Vietnamese community in Bridgeport? Perhaps I shall stay here awhile. I am *splitting the town*, as you say. Perhaps I shall once again enter the noodle business. Accept my tender regards, dear friend, and offer them as well to your daughter. Tell her she can keep the book for the time being. Until next time."

Marlene punched the buttons and erased this message, too.

Leung spent nearly ten hours at the bottom of a Dumpster outside the Grand Union less than a hundred yards from the Beach Bazaar, covered by layers of rotting vegetables, meat, and fish, surrounded by dozens of searching cops. The dumpster was opened several times, and sticks were pushed down into it, but he was not discovered. Leung thought that American policemen would not wish to burrow through rotting garbage on a scorching day, or even imagine that anyone would be able to stand being buried in such a place, and he was correct. It was far from pleasant, but he had been in worse places. He kept a carton wrapped around his head, and enough air filtered down through the stinking mass to keep him alive. In the early morning hours of the next day, when the search had moved far away, he dug himself out, walked down to the empty beach, and bathed in the sea. He threw his clothes in a trash basket, except for his undershirt and trousers, which he cut down into shorts with a pocketknife. Barefoot, he walked west on the beach under the shadow of the boardwalk. When he judged he had gone far enough, he crossed the boardwalk and entered the town. This would be the most difficult part. There was always a chance that a police car would blunder down the street he was on, but he counted on a beach town patrol not looking twice at what looked like a man in swim shorts and T-shirt without shoes—a citizen walking back from a party, perhaps. It was unlikely that they would come close enough to find that he was an Asian. He crossed the narrow sand spit on which Long Beach lay, following the signs he had noted earlier to the New York Avenue marina. Up to the age of twelve, Leung had lived on the estuary of the Pearl River, outside Guangdong, and later, in Macao he had worked as a smuggler. There was little about boats he did not understand, and so found it easy to steal a twenty-four-foot Bayliner from the marina. The boat was well supplied with charts. He moved at low speed out of the marina into Reynolds Channel and East Rockaway Inlet.

Navigation was easy, with the surf beating at Rockaway on his right and the lights of the great city behind it. He ate a box of Oreos and drank some warm beer he found in a cooler. He entertained the idea of sailing back to China, and it made him laugh. By dawn he was rounding Breezy Point, and then it was just a few more hours to cross Rockaway Inlet and reach Sheepshead Bay. He tied the boat up at a vacant slip where the charter boats docked, and walked east on Shore Boulevard. When he found an open store, he bought a pair of zoris, a pair of khaki pants, a white shirt, sunglasses, and a white terry-cloth hat. Shore Boulevard merged into Neptune Avenue. He was in Coney Island. He had heard a great deal about Coney Island; the American had painted it as a boy's paradise. It did not look like much in the light of day and without the scrim of happy memory. But there was a subway here, Leung recalled, and he found it without difficulty. He took the F train to Grand Street. By noon he was in Chinatown.

The Karps spent another day at the beach, but by Sunday they (or at least the adults) had had enough, and they decided to drive back to the city and deal with the unfinished pieces occasioned by the recent drama. Karp wanted badly to be in on the kill when they finally got Leung, and to ensure that the legalities were strictly observed. He also wanted to be the one to inform Tommy Colombo of what had been discovered. Karp was not much of a gloater, but he felt that a situation so flamboyantly gloatable should not be allowed to pass unobserved.

In the afternoon Posie returned, a walking advertisement for why you should not, if you have lard white Appalachian-person skin, spend eight hours in the sun of a New York scorcher wearing only a string bikini. They'd given her a lot of codeine at the hospital, and Marlene thought that Posie considered this access to legal downers a fair exchange for having most of her skin fried off. For her own part, things were starting to work again in her brain, slowly, like the first groaning movements of a locomotive setting out from the station, but in a direction she could now see clearly. She knew pretty much why everything that had happened since early June had happened. Two people had the remainder of the answer, of whom only one was available, but Marlene was determined to see her, brace her, and extract the truth.

The ride home was uneventful, punctuated only by an occasional scream from Posie as the dog licked her lobster-colored neck with his rough tongue. The twins slept, the girls talked earnestly in whispers, the radio stayed silent, as did Karp and Marlene. Traffic rather than ethnic gangs barred their way on the Belt Parkway. They dropped Mary off and pulled up in front of the loft just after six. Ed Morris got out of the follow car.

"You want me to stick around, Butch?"

"I don't think so. Just go up with Lucy and check out the loft. I think we can survive the night."

Morris, Lucy, and Posie rode up on the elevator, with the dog and the first load of bags. Karp leaned deeply into the Volvo's backseat to unbuckle the sleeping boys from their car seats. Zik, he saw, had taken his beach rock out of its bag.

Marlene had the rear hatch of the Volvo up. She

was gathering all the bits of travel debris into a sailcloth beach bag when she heard the sound of a car stopping suddenly and looked up. A black Trans-Am had parked in the middle of the street. The driver's-side door was flung open, and out stepped Brenda Nero, dressed in pink bermudas, a sleeveless top, and Mattie Duran's Colt Peacemaker .44. She walked around the front of her car, staggering slightly. Marlene saw that she was drunk, or high.

"I'm gonna kill you, bitch!" she shouted, and raised the pistol.

Marlene put down her beach bag. "Brenda, give me that damn gun before you hurt yourself!" she said.

Karp had been leaning into the car, fumbling with Zik's car seat strap, but when he heard the woman yell, he came out and stood up and stared at the scene on the street. The woman was pointing a huge shiny gun at his wife's head. At the same time he saw an old red pickup truck with a green fender draw up and stop behind the black Trans Am. Its driver, a burly man wearing a baseball hat, reached behind him and took a shotgun down from the gun rack and came out of the car. He jacked a shell into it and started walking toward Marlene.

Brenda Nero pointed the Colt at Marlene's head and pulled the trigger. A confused look came over her pretty, stupid face. She squeezed harder.

Marlene took two steps forward, grabbed the barrel of the pistol, yanked it out of Brenda's grasp, and socked her in the jaw. Brenda staggered back, tripped on the curb, and fell down. She started to cry.

"It wasn't loaded!" she wailed.

"It is loaded, Brenda," Marlene said. "It's a single-action gun. You have to cock it first." She demonstrated the cocking action.

"Marlene!" shouted Karp. Marlene looked up and into the muzzle of a twelve-gauge shotgun. She had no idea who the man pointing it was.

Karp's arm whipped around almost without volition, and Zik's smooth round stone, with its tiny passengers aboard, flew through the intervening space and struck the man on his right forearm. The shotgun roared, sending nine 00 pellets winging over Marlene's head and into the side of the building.

Marlene pointed the big pistol and shot the man from the red pickup, the bullet entering about three inches above the left nipple. The man dropped the shotgun and sat down in the street. In a Western movie, guys shot with a Colt .44 often ride long distances on horseback, punch out the bad guy, and save the girl from the burning ranch house, but in real life they usually want to lie very still in a quiet place, and this man was no exception. Marlene walked over to him and kicked the shotgun away.

"Sir," she said, "would you mind telling me who the fuck you are?"

"Reginald P. Burford," the man said.

"Reginald P. Burford, the right-to-life vigilante?"

"Yes, ma'am. Could you please call me an ambulance?"

"I'd be happy to," said Marlene. "Why were you trying to kill me?"

"It's the Lord, ma'am. Because of the baby killing. I saw you on the TV protecting those baby killers, and I opened the Bible to see what I should do and it opened up to Jeremiah 16:4. 'They shall die of grievous deaths; they shall not be lamented; neither shall they be buried' . . . And, you know, I fought it back, but the Lord, He kept after me, like unto Jonah, and made me stretch out my hand against. It ain't nothing personal, ma'am."

"Oh, I'm sure, I'm sure," she said. "It never is." Then she stood in the middle of the street and howled to the sky, "Anybody else? Let's go, people! Step right up! Take your shot! Here I am, Marlene the walking fucking death wish! Come on, you fucking crazy bastards! Come on!"

Karp ran to her and wrapped his arms around her. She collapsed against him, sobbing. "It's over, Marlene," he said. "It's all right."

"It's not over," she sobbed. "It's not all right."

Later, after Morris had organized the police necessities and Karp the domestic ones, Marlene paced her kitchen floor, smoking as she had not for many years, one after another. Karp sat on a kitchen chair and watched her with growing apprehension, glad that there was for once no gun in the house. There was on her face a look he had not

seen for some time, her Medea look, made even
more horrible by the absence of a softening coif-
fure. This was not the same woman who had lately
built sand castles with her little boys and sung them
gently to sleep.

At last he said, "Marlene, for crying out loud, sit
down! Relax!"

She stopped short and stared at him, her eye
glittering. "Relax. Good idea, but not quite yet, no.
What just happened, Butch, out on the street? A
woman I tried to help just tried to kill me. No good
deed goes unpunished. And a guy gets a message
from God, and what does it say? The envelope,
please. Shoot Marlene Ciampi. *I* don't get messages
from God. God only talks to assholes from Buttzville, New Jersey. Tell me, is this my *fate*?"

"What can I say, Marlene? You know how I feel
about what you do."

"Yes. Yes, I do know. And you know what? *I feel
the same way.*

> I know that I shall meet my fate,
> Somewhere among the clouds above.
> Those I fight I do not hate,
> Those I guard I do not love.

"Yeats. I have to go out."

"Marlene, don't be crazy."

She came up to him and touched his cheek and
kissed him. "You poor man. I'll be fine. I'll walk between the bullets."

Before he could say another word, she ran into
the bedroom and came out carrying her purse. She

stalked up to him, grabbed his head, and kissed him again, this time solidly on the mouth.

"I'll be right back," she said. "Don't worry."

Then she was out the door. He heard her running down the stairs, and began to worry.

20

THEY HAD REPAIRED THE DOOR AT THE East Village Women's Shelter. It was now a steel-sheathed monster with a small glass porthole in it, suitable for a nuclear submarine. Marlene pressed her face against it, and Vonda buzzed her in.

"Nice door, Vonda," said Marlene.

"About time you showed," said the guard, with her usual glower. "She's in the kitchen."

Marlene sought the woman out and found her on her back, surrounded by tools, replacing a fitting behind the shelter's ancient gas stove. She lifted her head an inch when Marlene came and stood at her feet. The work light shining on her grease-smeared face gave it a theatrical Phantom of the Opera look. She frowned when she saw who it was.

"Where the *hell* have you been, girl? I've been trying to get in touch with you for a week. Have you heard from Brenda?"

"In a manner of speaking. She tried to kill me with your gun."

"*Chingada!* What happened?"

Marlene told her. Mattie was not pleased. "You

had her arrested? Jesus, who the fuck's side are you on? What about the goddamn boyfriend? He's the one should be in jail."

At that, Marlene felt she had two possible options: smash the woman's skull with the fourteen-inch pipe wrench that lay conveniently to hand, or laugh. She laughed, ever the correct response to fanatics, and walked away.

"Hey, when am I gonna get my gun back?" Mattie called after her.

Up in room 37, Marlene found that Vivian F. Bollano had settled in for a long stay. The small room now held a color TV, with VCR, both set up on a new chest of drawers, a larger bed with a thicker mattress, a thick rust-colored area rug, and a teak and leather sling chair. A tape of *The Sound of Music* was playing on the VCR. Vivian switched it off after letting Marlene in, and sat on the bed. Marlene sat opposite in the sling chair and examined her client. Vivian had had her hair done, by whom Marlene could not imagine, and looked rather more doll-like than she had before. But there was a fuzziness about her expression that indicated the presence of dope, probably prescription downers, since Mattie had a ferocious rule about the nonprescription sort. Aside from that, Marlene imagined, Mattie was perfectly happy to indulge this resident in every legal way. There was a sliding scale of payment at the EVWS: most women owned only the clothes they fled in and paid nothing, but Vivian was clearly at the top of the scale. She could probably have had a suite in the Plaza for what she was paying here, for the day or so before the Bollanos found her and dragged her through the gilded lobby by her hair.

"Well, Vivian, since our last interview, I'm happy to report I've made some progress."

"Oh, yeah?" Mild interest only: she *was* tranqued out.

"Yeah. Your father did not commit suicide, as you suspected. He was murdered."

"Uh-huh. Do you know who killed him?" No excitement, no shock, Marlene noted, and put that down to the meds.

"Yes, your husband did it, assisted by a man named Carlo Tonnati. I'm reasonably sure of my informant, and there are some other suggestive pieces of evidence. But I don't know why it was done, and I don't have enough at present to go to the cops with."

Vivian nodded, and her face seemed to deflate a fraction.

"You don't seem all that surprised," said Marlene.

The woman shook her head and turned her face away. "I guess that's it," she said in a ghost's voice. "Thank you for your help."

"Well, actually, Vivian, it's not quite *it* yet. Because when you enter into a contract like we did, there are mutual obligations. My obligation is to give you honest service and keep your secrets. Your obligation is to tell me everything relevant to the case. You fail to do that and I could poke into a hole that I think's got no bear in it, and the bear is waiting and I get my head bitten off."

"I don't know what you're talking about," said Vivian to the blank television. "I just had some suspicions and—"

"No, Vivian, you had much more than suspicions, and ordinarily I would let it slide because it comes with the territory—clients lie, or they conceal. What else is new? But this time I got blindsided, because when you mess with the Mob, you might put yourself at risk, but not your family, because by and large, the Mob doesn't go after family. It's not like Sicily here. But because you didn't tell me what was really going on, my children were put at risk. Your father-in-law sent a thug after my babies. And I thought to myself, What would make a don send a thug after my babies? It would have to be something *outside* the normal run of Mob business, wouldn't it? What was it, Vivian? What's got Big Sally so scared?"

Her mouth was slightly open, like a hungry little bird unsure of whether that large shadow was really its mother. She shook her head again, reached for a beaded purse on the nightstand, took from it an amber plastic vial. Marlene jumped from her chair, snatched it away, and moved back to the chair. She tossed the pills into her own purse.

"Excuse me, I have to take my medication. What do you think—"

"No, Vivian, no pills. We'll save them for after, okay? Don't want to talk, huh? Vivian, I will have the truth out of you, if it takes all day and all night." Dumb silence. The woman now had the glazed and stupid look of a shot antelope. "Okay, Vivian, let's see if we can prime the pump. We start with the peculiar case of the Chinese gentleman Mr. Leung. Or Mr. Lie. This person has some interesting characteristics. He is a gangster, a triad member, in fact. He is in business with your husband's organization. He seems to have an uncanny understanding of American law. He went through a lot of trouble to kill one of your father-in-law's two chief subordinates and hang the murder on the other one. It seems that Mr. Leung doesn't like the Bollano family at all. No reaction? Well, you might say he's a gangster trying to take over the Bollano family. True enough, but that's not all that's true. This particular Chinese had a relationship with an American in Macao. My daughter found this out, by the way. Mr. Leung can speak English with a New York accent. So, now remember, Vivian, Mr. Leung knows something about New York law, can speak phrases with a New York accent, has it in for the Bollanos, and was in close contact with an American in Macao. Can you make a guess as to whom that American might be? Excuse me, I didn't hear you."

"Bernie Kusher," said Vivian, just above the limits of audibility.

"Yes, it would explain a lot that is otherwise very strange indeed. It would explain one of the two big questions I've been wanting to ask you ever since I started on this, and which I would've asked you if your husband hadn't kicked me in the head that night. Why you suddenly, after twenty years, bailed out on Little Sally. Bernie's dead now, apparently, but he was obviously working on this a long, long time. He didn't want to contact you until he had his little guided missile in place and ready to fire. Leung saw you, didn't he?" Nod. "And he brought word from Bernie about who really killed your father, didn't he?" Nod.

Marlene made an exasperated sound and crossed over to sit on the bed beside Vivian. She put her arm around her, and found that she was trembling like a caught mouse.

"Look, Vivian. This has to come out. It has to *all* come out, right now, so your life can start up again and the people who murdered your father can get what they deserve. It's like vomiting, Vivian: if you try to hold it back it gets worse and worse. Just heave it up, and brush your teeth and it's over."

"Please, could I have a . . ." Her hand twitched toward Marlene's purse.

"No. First talk. Leung came to see you, didn't he?"

The woman uttered a small sigh, and Marlene knew that it was the sound of the cork going on a magnum of poisoned mental champagne; it would all come out now. "He called first. He said, 'Hiya, princess,' which is what my dad used to say, and then Bernie picked it up, too. I almost fainted, because the accent was so right on. He said he came from Bernie, that Bernie had died in Macao and had told this guy to come see me. He wanted to know could we meet, and I said, yes. I would've crawled over broken glass. So we met the next day in some hole-in-the-wall place in Chinatown. He said Bernie had saved his life after some war they had there, I didn't follow that part. He said Bernie had landed in Macao, which is kind of a wide-open town. If you have money, they don't care what you did anyplace else. And Bernie had plenty of money. He bought some real estate, had some businesses. He got into opium, too. And when he was high, he would talk, about what happened to my father, about what Panofsky had done, to my dad and him. He couldn't go to the cops with what he knew, or guessed, because the cops were all bought by the Bollanos. So he just stayed in Macao, talking to this kid. The kid got into the triads—they practically run Macao anyway, and Bernie was connected with them too. And they figured out this plan. The first step was to come to me and tell me that Sal had killed my father."

"You never suspected this? Before, I mean."

Vivian seemed surprised at the question. "No. Why should I? Big Sally came to me right after it happened. He told me . . . oh, God, it's so screwed up. I can't remember which lie came first. Look, I'm sixteen. My father's dead. My mother . . . well, she's not much help. She's a little vague, Mom. There were two people I could count on. One was Bernie, and the other was my dad's secretary, Shirley Waldorf. Both of them thought he'd been murdered, and they were going to try to prove it. Then, all of a sudden, Bernie runs away and Shirley gets fired instead of Panofsky."

"Panofsky was going to get fired?"

"Yeah. He was . . . he was always hanging around me, coming on to me. Christ, I was sixteen! My dad saw him grab me once, and he blew his top. He said if he ever did anything like that again, he was finished. But he wouldn't stop. No. Then, after Shirley disappeared with the ledger, Big Sal came to our house one night and . . ."

"Wait a second, Vivian, what ledger?"

"Oh, that was part of Shirley's craziness. She

started acting weird after Bernie went away, after the scandal. She just couldn't handle the changes. Hah! Like *I* could, right? She kept every birthday card my dad ever gave her, and she came over here one night, with all of them and a whole bunch of office papers and laid them out on the coffee table . . ."

"You don't mean *here*, Vivian, you mean your home, in Brooklyn."

"Oh, yeah. Anyway, she had the cards, and some diaries of my dad's, and she gave us this, I don't know, some kind of *lecture* about how my dad couldn't have killed himself, and there were papers all around our living room, and my mom, who's not too tightly wrapped to begin with and the doctor had been giving her prescriptions, she fell asleep in the middle of it and there I was, sixteen, trying to follow this crazy woman. She was paranoid, too, she thought people were following her, they were going to kill her if anybody ever found out she had these papers, and that I wasn't supposed to tell anyone. And I didn't. She got fired after that. I guess she must be dead, because I never heard from her again."

"Okay, go back to when Big Sally came over."

"Uh-huh. That was a couple of days after Shirley was by. He was really serious and calm, and it was a relief after Shirley, you know, to think someone was in charge. I didn't know who he was or what he did. He was just a businessman, a client of my father's, and he was with Panofsky, so he was all right. And Sal was there, too. My future husband. And they told me that my father *had* been murdered, and they were going to find out who did it and get him. And a few weeks after that they sent a car to get me, after dinner, Little Sal and some of his men. We got the guy, is what they said. And we drove out to south Brooklyn, by the bay. You could smell the ocean, and you could smell the garbage dump, I remember, a sweet, horrible smell, and we went to a big building where they made cement, you could see lines of cement trucks parked outside, and inside the building it was dark except for the one bright light they had on and Big Sal was there and Charlie Tonnati, and they had this guy tied to a chair. They must have burned him. You could smell that burned-feather smell, and gasoline. This was the guy, they said. And Big Sal said, tell her, and the guy started talking, in this soft, tired voice, like he'd just walked a thousand miles, and he said he was from another gang and they wanted to kill Big Sal, and they were trying to get my father to sell him out, because they knew Big Sal trusted my father more than anyone, but my father wouldn't do it. This was up on the deck of the Empire State, where they met, where my dad had his office, and when he wouldn't they dragged him outside and held him over, to frighten him, but he still wouldn't and then they dropped him off."

She fell silent. Marlene asked, "What was the guy's name?"

"Frank Crespi."

"Who was he working for?"

"I never found out; they never told me and I didn't ask."

"And what happened after that?"

"Nothing. They took me home. Nobody ever mentioned Frank Crespi to me again. I guess they killed him. I was glad. Then I had my life, and then this Chinese guy walks in and tells me it was all a lie, that Sal killed my father. I guess the joke's on me. Ha-ha."

"Did he give you any proof, Vivian?"

She shook her head. "No, but I knew that it was true, and . . . that scared me. I thought I was going crazy, maybe. Maybe I invented this weird Chinese guy. I don't have a happy life, Marlene. Sal found out I'd been out to see somebody, and he asked me who it was and I wouldn't tell him, so he whipped me and put out a cigar on my . . . skin, and . . . did other stuff to me, but I still wouldn't tell him, so he locked me up and took away all my clothes. But I got out a window and called a cab, and came here. Naked came I. Heh. Not a *happy* life. That's why I take a couple of pills once in a while, when I'm a little down. That's why I hired you, to see if there was anything in it. And there is, so . . . now I know. Okay, I told you everything, could I please have my pills back?"

Marlene ignored her. "Actually, Vivian, you've only answered one of the two questions. The other one is, why did you marry a nasty little psychopath like Sal Bollano Jr."

"I don't see why that's any of your business," said Vivian stiffly.

"Humor me."

Vivian looked longingly at the television screen, as if it had the answer to the question asked. Her breathing was rapid and there was a glint of sweat on her upper lip. "He was around. It's not like I had a lot of dates. Sal tended to discourage interest in me by other guys. I had to take care of my mother, and the Bollanos were very generous to us. Now, could you *kindly* return my *medication*?"

"So, you're saying Little Sal commits several major felonies breaking in here, and the don hires a high-priced mechanic to scare the shit out of me, because . . . why? Because he thinks you might have learned about who killed your father? Bernie and Leung brought you speculation, stories. That's pretty much all I brought you. It's like who killed Kennedy; there's no danger to the Bollanos in it, because only they and Charlie Tuna know the real story and they're not talking. So, Vivian, tell me, why is Big Sally nervous? Why is the coolest, most cautious don in the city taking these chances?"

Marlene took the pill vial out of her bag and shook it like a maraca. Thirty seconds went by, with the only sound in the room the hiss of traffic outside, and the communal noises of the shelter, and the rush of Vivian's rapid breathing.

Then she sprang across the bed at Marlene, snarling and whining, inarticulated phrases of desire spurting from her mouth, grasping for her pills. Marlene flung the vial against the far wall of the room, where it cracked open, spilling its contents. Vivian squealed and tried to escape, but Marlene backhanded her across the throat with her left forearm, throwing her body behind it. She pinned Vivian prone across her bed, with her head against the corner of the wall, and lay atop her, her fingers

gripping the woman's hair. Vivian's eyes were bulging in their sockets. Marlene relaxed the pressure of
her forearm and hissed into Vivian's ear. "What was
it? Tell me! Goddamn you, he threatened my *children*! Tell me!"

"He . . . he . . . he made me . . . he made me have
sex with him. After . . . after . . . Crespi. In the car,
after Crespi."

Marlene was dumbfounded. "What? Jesus, Vivian, you were sixteen, that's not even statutory rape.
Little Sal wouldn't even think twice about something like that. And he married you later. It doesn't
make any—"

"*No!* Not *Little* Sal. *Big* Sal."

"Oh," said Marlene. "And his son *knew* about
this?"

Vivian Bollano's face changed now into something that needed snakes on top of it instead of a
rinse and set, and from deep in her throat issued a
burbling sound that rose through the register and
increased in volume until Marlene's ears rang with
it, the hopeless cry of a ruined soul. It would have
been unbearable were it mere noise, but there were
words in it, which made it worse.

"*Know* about it? Did he *know* about it? Oh, yeah,
he *knew* about it. They took *turns*, except where it
was both at once. And each other. And they brought
girls in, too. And boys." Once started, Vivian did
not seem capable of stopping. There followed in a
rush a litany of details that might have fit, without
editing, into *Justine*, by the Marquis de Sade. After
a good half hour of this, Marlene asked, "Vivian,
how long did this go on?"

"How long? Until three days before I left. Now, for the love of God, please, please, please, please . . ."

For twenty years? Twenty *years*? Speechless, Marlene rolled away from her, and watched as Vivian Fein Bollano scrambled across the floor on her hands and knees, snatching up the scattered yellow pills and popping them into her mouth.

Twenty minutes later, Marlene was back at the loft, having stopped for a quick vomit on the corner of First and St. Marks, attracting little notice, it being quite the custom in that quarter. She went immediately to the bathroom and brushed her teeth and washed her face. Karp was not in bed, or (when she looked) in the living room. She heard a noise from the kitchen and went there. Lucy, dressed in one of the gigantic T-shirts that were her favored sleep apparel, was sitting at the kitchen table with a book, a glass of milk, and a pile of chocolate chip cookies.

"Hi. Where's Dad?"

"He had to go out. They caught Leung."

"Oh, thank God! Where?"

"At Mr. Kuen's place. They tapped his phone, and Leung called up and said he was going to come by that night and for Mr. Kuen to have a lot of cash ready. They had the place staked out and they caught him."

"Anybody hurt?" asked Marlene, and sat opposite her daughter.

"Dad didn't say. I don't think so. Do you want a cookie?"

"No, thanks, dear. How are you feeling? You still look tired."

"I'm okay, I guess. Sad, is all. Hollow. I keep wanting to call Janice, or thinking about going by their apartment or the Mall. It's like somebody died. Mom, why did she do it? I mean, it's one thing to like have a fight, or an argument, like kids do, but she must've known Leung wanted to kill me, and she got Aunt Sophie's address out of me and gave it to him. I can't understand it."

"Probably she was scared. People do a lot of nasty, irrational things when they're frightened. And, you know, her parents were involved. Janice . . . well, she does what her parents tell her to do. Plus, maybe there was some jealousy involved."

A cookie halted halfway to her mouth, Lucy goggled at this. "Jealous? Janice is gorgeous. How could she be jealous of *me*?"

"There's more to a person than tits and ass, darling, though it may not seem so," said Marlene, and was rewarded with the sight of a blush springing to her daughter's cheeks.

"Easy for *you* to say," snarled Lucy.

Marlene rose. "Wait here," she said, and left, and was back in three minutes holding a fat brown envelope. She sat again and dumped a stack of photographs out on the table, old-fashioned snapshots, with pinked edges. After riffling through them she selected two and handed one to her daughter. Lucy examined it. Four girls she didn't recognize, in one-piece bathing suits, squinting into a summertime glare with the sea behind them.

"That's me, second from the right," said Marlene.

"This is *you*?"

"Yep, age thirteen. I was a pool table that summer, dead flat. This," handing over the other snap, "is the next summer."

Here was a recognizable Marlene, grinning glorious in a nicely filled two-piece bathing suit, supported on the shoulders of a pair of adoring lifeguards.

"You never showed me this stuff before," said Lucy sulkily.

"I would have, but we haven't had a civilized interaction in at least a year."

"You were too busy."

"And you were too ratty. Why don't we call it even?"

"Snarl," said Lucy around a tentative smile.

"Snarl yourself. How much money have you got in the bank of Kuen?"

"About a thousand fifty."

Marlene whistled. "What are you going to spend it on?"

"Oh, you know, drugs, maybe a tattoo. Condoms. How much does Sacred Heart cost?"

"Why? You said suicide was preferable. Change your mind?"

"Sort of. I guess . . . I guess I need a break from"—she waved her hand around—"Asia. I don't mean . . . the Chens and Tran and all, the street, Chinatown, it's in my heart, it's always going to be part of me, but . . . it's not *all* of me. I'm not Kieu. I don't have to haul that weight, do I?"

"No, you don't," said Marlene, thinking of Vivian Fein, of what she must have been like before her father died and what she was now. Tears ate at her eyelids, but she turned them back.

"Also, if I go to Sacred Heart, Mary will be there . . ."

"What? Mary's going to Sacred Heart?"

"Yeah, it's all arranged, I sold her on it. I told her parents it was like a cadre school, and I was going there and they think we're like the lords of creation. She'll apply for a scholarship and get it—I mean, they'd have to be crazy not to—and she likes the idea, and if I'm uptown, I can run across to P and S, and keep up at the lab. Dr. Shadkin's got a lot of new stuff he wants to try out on me when the regular term starts."

"Um, Lucy, Sacred Heart is a lot rougher than anything you've done in public school. Do you think you'll have the time?"

Lucy frowned. "It's *my* life, Mom."

"Oh? Actually, it isn't. It's *my* life. When *you* have a daughter, *then* it'll be your life. Meanwhile, you'll fill the emptiness caused by me trampling on your spirit by an orgy of neurotic consumption, thus spinning the wheels of capitalism ever faster. It's the American way, kid. Better get used to it."

When Karp came in a few minutes later, they were still at the table, still laughing and poking one another and cracking jokes. Karp thought, this makes a nice change.

"Did he spill his guts, Daddy? Did you hit him with a phone book, please please?"

"Ooh, I *knew* I forgot the phone book. That's probably why he stood on his constitutional right to remain silent and requested an attorney. Not that it'll do him any good, the evil little bas—bad person." Karp poured himself a glass of milk, sat, and took a cookie.

"He didn't happen to mention Bernie Kusher, did he?" asked Marlene.

"Bernie Kusher?"

"Yeah, Fein's and Panofsky's old law partner."

"Excuse me, but why . . . ?"

"Later," said Marlene.

And later, in the bedroom, Karp under covers, Marlene placed the Sony machine on his lap and said, "I swiped your Sony. You should listen to this tape. It's Vivian Fein Bollano."

Karp pushed the play-back button and listened in silence.

"Oy vey," he said when it was done.

"Yes. *Infamia*. Big-time. That's why the don didn't want me talking to Vivian, and why Little Sal practically committed murder to get the woman back into his hands. They didn't much care about the Fein murder, but *this*"—she tapped the Sony—"this is the end for them."

"What are you going to do with it?" Karp asked.

"I'm not sure. Any chance of nailing the Bollanos in court?"

"I doubt it," said Karp after a moment's thought. "It's supposition and stories. Nobile provided a key. So what? Jake might know something, but I doubt he'd say anything in court and we got no way to make him. Bernie's dead, having first manipulated and unleashed Leung. Of course, as you say, Bernie always was something of a joker. Panofsky? Lots of luck! I agree with you that if it went down the way we think, only the Bollanos and Charlie Tuna know the whole story, and I doubt that they're going to come forward out of remorse. Also, we still got no idea *why* they killed him."

"They wanted the girl," said Marlene without hesitation.

"You think?"

"Yeah. As long as he was alive, neither of them was going to get close to the princess. And there could have been something else. Maybe Fein found out that Panofsky framed him, found out about Panofsky running bribes for the Mob. Maybe it pushed Jerry over a line he didn't want to cross. There was that missing ledger she talked about . . ."

"Which it was we'll never know," said Karp. "I'd like to nail the bastards, but absent a confession . . ." He made a helpless gesture.

Marlene picked up the little tape recorder and bounced it in her hand. She looked at Karp and down at the machine and back at Karp.

"No," he said in a voice that allowed no argument.

"He'd confess to JFK and Hoffa both to—"

"No. We don't blackmail people into signing confessions, Marlene."

"No, we don't. Or *you* don't." She pulled the microcassette out of the machine and slipped it into her night table drawer. Then she got under the covers and placed her head on his shoulder. "And you have thereby proved once again that you are a finer, better person than I am."

"Marlene, if I even suspect that you are using

that tape in violation of the laws of New York state, I will throw your ass in jail."

"What, *this* ass?" she said, wriggling same against his groin.

"Yes, this round, solid, warm, perfectly proportioned, *juicy* . . ."

"Then you better enjoy it while you got it, buster," she said.

In the morning, slipping into his tropical-weight suit jacket, Karp reflected that he would not be getting any more suits at cost from Chinese tailors, and then rejected the thought as unworthy. His daughter had lost far more from the Chen disaster. On the other hand, she seemed to be getting along with Marlene again. Clearly another chapter in the ever fascinating childhood of Lucy Karp was about to open. He could hardly wait.

Marlene was still in bed, groggy and warm. He bent over and mushed his face into her neck.

"No, no, not *again*," she murmured.

"I'm going."

"Like the man from Kent, for a change. Mm, you look spiffy. Big day, huh?"

"Fairly. Have you got any plans?"

"I don't know. I thought I'd run up to Brearley and apply for a job teaching French."

"Sounds good. You could coach the pistol team, too."

She made a face and a nauseated sound. He said, "Let's have lunch today."

"What, you and me? In a restaurant?"

"Unless you prefer the cancer wagon."

"No, but this better not be you want a divorce."

"Nope, but it *is* a surprise. Meet you out front at twelve."

Hot day, the air like taffy, white sky, New York at the start of July: not a day for a vigorous walk if you wanted to preserve any crispness. Karp hopped a cab downtown and offered the turbaned driver an absurdly large tip to make up for the mingey fare. At his desk, he called and briefed Roland Hrcany on the Leung affair, called the ADAs in charge of the cases against Little Sal Bollano, Brenda Nero, and Reginald P. Burford, and informed them that the never sleeping eye was upon them and would be upon them until these particular defendants were prosecuted to the full extent of the law, and forget any hint of a plea bargain. He called Ray Guma at home and told him that the fix was in, that he should stop worrying and return to work whenever he felt like it. He made two calls to Washington, D.C., one to the office of the U.S. attorney for the Southern District of New York and one to a private home in East Hampton, Long Island. Then he engaged himself in routine until nine-thirty, when he had an hour reserved with the district attorney.

The D.A. heard the story of Mr. Leung and the Asia Mall murders and the Catalano murder told in the disciplined, precise, logical way that it would be presented to a jury, which is how he liked to hear about a case, which is how he himself had taught

Karp to do it fifteen years before. He asked no questions until Karp had finished.

"So all you have on the Catalano is this dying declaration?"

"Thus far. Of course, now that we're looking in the right place, we should find forensic evidence linking Leung and the Vo brothers to the crime scene."

"Will the Vo boys roll on each other?"

"I think so. We have the two of them on the kidnap charge, so they're not going anywhere. The dead one, Kenny, was the brains of the outfit. I don't think either of them is going to want to do the full jolt for the kidnap and get deported back to sunny Vietnam afterward. They'll go for it."

"Good. The homicide double, you got the dying declaration and the two girls. What about the third one, the Chen girl? She going to be a defense witness?"

"Well, I don't think there's any question that they'd perjure her if they thought it would do any good. But it won't. The Chens will do what Mr. Yee tells them to do, and Mr. Yee is not in good shape right now. Detective Wu is singing his head off about Mr. Yee's various dealings in Chinatown. So I think after I've got Mr. Yee to understand the position, he'll do the right thing."

"I presume there's no need to bring in the Kusher angle, the Macao connection, into the Leung prosecution."

"No, that's a bit rich for a New York jury, and we don't need it. We'll establish a basis for the Chinatown murders, because juries like motives. Triad rivalries—end of story. The witnesses and the kid's declaration are enough to sink him."

"Going to take the case yourself?" asked the D.A. sourly.

"No. Not unless you *really* want me to," said Karp, straight-faced.

Keegan burst into laughter. Karp continued, "I thought Vasquez should do it, but it's really up to Roland. What I'd really like to do is nail the don. But we don't have the stuff."

"No, we don't. The bastard skates again. Still, he can't be very happy. His kid's gone, and his big *capo* Pigetti has got to be counting the days until he can take away the whole thing."

"My heart bleeds," said Karp. He had not told the D.A. about the horrors recorded on Marlene's tape.

"Yeah, but now we come to the cherry on the top. Mr. Tommy Colombo and how we grind his face in it. Any ideas?"

"Yeah. I'd like to hold a joint press conference at which I'll announce these arrests and Colombo will announce the formation of a federal-state Asian crime task force, with federal funding, of course, and—"

"You're kidding, right?" said Keegan uncertainly.

"Not at all. And, at which Mr. Colombo will offer a formal public apology for irregularities in his office that besmirched the spotless rep of our own Raymond Guma. Fade to black. Applause."

Keegan chortled again. "Jesus, Butch, you're a

piece of work. Remind me never to piss you off. What makes you think Tommy will go for that?"

"Oh, I think he will. Tommy was vacationing at East Hampton until just a few hours ago. He was going to attend some big-time political clambake out there. I was able to get hold of him and inform him about the parts of this weekend's events that he might have missed on television, and I told him that if he didn't want to play nice, then at the press conference at three this afternoon you would announce that while he was chasing nickel-dime garbage-collection rip-offs, there had been a massive infiltration of Asian killers into our glorious city, which he had refused to acknowledge, and had even given immunity to the chief murderer, also that his organization was so incompetent that one of our fine ADAs, Ray Guma, was about to start a civil suit against him personally, for defamation, and that his superiors in D.C. were thinking seriously about an internal investigation of prosecutorial malfeasance. I still have some people in D.C. who owe me favors."

"A certain amount of bluff there, am I right?"

"A certain amount, which he is in no position to assess, but there's enough pastrami in that sandwich to make a big, embarrassing splash on the slowest news day of the summer. Tommy wants to *bury* this, and get back to sucking ass out on the Island. I expect to hear the blades of his helicopter momentarily, circling the Javits Building."

"You made a friend for life there, son."

"Oh, Tommy will come around. He's so paranoid and ambitious that the best approach is enthusiastic and open-handed cooperation. It drives him nuts. If he plays nice, I'll give him something sweet to chew on."

"Like?"

"Like Judge Herschel Paine."

"Hah. You don't have anything solid on Paine."

"No, but something could turn up," said Karp.

Marlene was wearing white sandals, a crisp, palest-yellow shirtwaist in which it was impossible to conceal a large handgun, and a round French schoolgirl's straw hat with a dark band. To Karp's eyes she looked barely older than Lucy.

"How about a cooling chopped liver sandwich and a frosty celery tonic?" Karp asked after a discreet kiss.

"Lead the way, Jewboy," said his wife.

They ate in a brightly lit, noisy deli around the corner from the courthouse. During the meal Karp filled her in on the morning's various coups, with which she was well pleased, but after which she said, "This was the surprise?"

"Oh, no, the surprise is for last, like the cherry on top of the charlotte russe."

"I always ate the cherry first," said Marlene.

"Queens *goyim*, feh!" said Karp. "What do *you* know?"

As Karp had expected, and as he had determined from a window high above, the woman and her shopping cart were at their accustomed bench. Karp walked up to her and said, "Shirley Waldorf, I presume," and was rewarded by the astonishment on his wife's face.

The old woman was startled, however, and stood up, looking wildly in all directions. Karp put a gently restraining hand on her shoulder.

"Miss Waldorf, I'm Roger Karp. I'm the chief assistant district attorney. We're interested in reopening the investigation of the murder of your employer Gerald Fein, and we understand you may have some information relevant to that case."

The woman blinked several times, and then she cocked her head and her eyes narrowed. "Are you real?" she asked.

"I think so," said Karp. "This is my wife, Marlene Ciampi. Marlene, say hello to Shirley Waldorf."

Marlene extended her hand. "Pleased to meet you, Miss Waldorf." The woman hesitated and then took her hand and watched the two hands as they shook, as if observing a new phenomenon. Marlene wondered how long it had been since someone had shaken her hand, and then the old woman looked up and into her eye. Shirley's face was weatherbeaten and grimy and had the bemused, slack look of the typical street dweller, but Marlene could see another face, her real face, beneath this, as if it were trying to swim up out of a depth of filthy water.

Shirley Waldorf said, "I sometimes see things that aren't there. I was in the hospital for my nerves."

"Yes," said Karp, "you've had a hard time. But, we'd really like to take a look at what you have. I understand you have some records that belonged to Mr. Panofsky."

"Yes, him," said Shirley, as if referencing Beelzebub. "He kept it locked up tight in his desk. I knew there was something fishy going on, because I had keys to all the filing cabinets in the office and we had a big Mosler safe, but he wouldn't put his things in the safe, oh, no. I started looking for evidence against him after Mr. Fein pleaded guilty. And there it was, right in that desk."

"But how did you get the records out without Panofsky knowing?" Marlene asked.

"Oh, it was easy. I'd purchased all the office furniture, and I had the original invoices. I sent a copy of the invoice for Panofsky's desk to the furniture company and said we'd lost our keys and could they send me another one. He's a very bad man, you know."

"Yes, we know," said Karp. "Okay, Shirley, why don't we go up to my office and look at what you have and make copies and all that? And then we'll talk about finding you a place to stay."

So they did, the two of them and the bag lady, into the courthouse through the D.A.'s entrance, and into Karp's office, prompting a certain amazed interest on the part of the office staff, and Karp ordered a bagel and coffee delivered for his guest, and they sat around his big table and unwrapped Shirley's treasures from layer upon layer of plastic bags.

"My God, this is the tag book!" Marlene exclaimed, holding a thick ledger bound in brown leatherette. She thumbed through it, shaking her head, and uttering little whistles of astonishment. It was all there, the record of over a decade's worth of political corruption, implicating many men who had since become powers in the land, all in Panofsky's neat handwriting. There was a rusted paper clip on one page, and Marlene turned to it.

"Why is this marked, Miss Waldorf?" she asked.

"Oh, that's the payoff for the two jurors in the Gravellotti murder case. It came, as you see there, from Mr. Bollano. I told Mr. Fein about it, and he became very excited because, you see, it cleared him of the bribery charge. He called up Mr. Bollano, and he said Mr. Bollano had set up a meeting to talk about it. And the next morning, that's when the meeting was, and when they pushed him off."

She started leaking slow tears then, and Marlene gave her a pack of tissues. That was the last piece of the puzzle. Poor Shirley had set up the death of her beloved. Fein must have threatened to blow the whistle on the bribed jurors, and that would have involved Panofsky, which would have led to the uncovering of the network of corrupt payoffs. Marlene could imagine Panofsky's mind racing to find a space to crawl out from under, recalling Nobile had once worked for the building, getting him to obtain a key, selling the idea to Bollano. Take him out, make it look like a suicide. Okay by them, and the delicious little Vivian as an extra on the deal. Jake Gurvitz gets Nobile to procure the key. Selling the meeting to Fein: Jerry, let's meet, but not in the office. There's a couple other people involved, major big shots, don't want to be seen going into a meeting with Sally Bollano. We'll step up to the observation deck, talk there, keep it private. Yeah, it could've worked that way. No way to prove it now, but there was enough in this book to knock Heshy the Armpit clean off the bench.

"That's what I was trying to show Detective Mulhausen," said Shirley, "but he insisted in treating me as if I were crazy. He wanted the book, of course, but I hid it. Nobody else was looking for it, because that . . . *man* had told his mobsters that it was destroyed."

"Of course he'd do that. Where did you hide it?"

"In Bernie Kusher's safety deposit box. No one knew he had one except me. Then when Mr. Kusher ran away . . . I can't quite recall what happened then. You know, if you're all alone in the world and everyone's telling you that you're out of your mind, pretty soon you come to believe it, too. In any case, I took all the things out of the box and carried them from place to place. They kept them for me in the hospital, and when I left I just carried them around. You don't think I'm crazy, do you?"

"No," said Marlene, "but I do think you need to get off the street. I have a place attached to my office, just a room with a bath and little kitchen. You could stay there."

"I really couldn't accept charity, Mrs. Karp."

"It wouldn't be charity. I run an investigations agency, and I happen to need a legal secretary—part-time, but you could stay in the room for the time being."

"Oh, in that case," said Shirley Waldorf.

• • •

The next day was the Fourth of July, and in the late afternoon the entire Karp *mishpocheh* went over to V.T. Newbury's East Side penthouse apartment, where every year he threw an immense party for his large family and his many friends to feast and drink and watch the fireworks over the river. The tradition at V.T.'s was Moët and pâté rather than beer and burgers, but the Karps did not mind this at all.

"Hail to the hero," said V.T., greeting them at the door. He was cradling a magnum of champagne in his arms like a beloved infant and was wearing a tall Uncle Sam hat made of paper. "I saw you and Tommy on the tube the other day. His chin was covered with little black feathers. It was heartwarming. Here's Marlene. Mmm. God, what lips. You're wasted on him; for a true sensual treat you can't beat a tiny little WASP. No? And who's this? Not little Lucy! You let her walk the streets unprotected? All in black, too. Have you turned intellectual? God, I hope not. Sweetheart, later we'll find a dark corner and say nasty things to each other in French. And the tiny twins! How *do* you tell them apart, et cetera. There are about a thousand kids here, Marlene—Martha has kid food in the kitchen. You can get drunk if you like, I am. Or have already."

The party absorbed them. V.T. had the rare knack of assembling old-money people with lovely manners and no-money people with interesting lives and ideas into a mixture that bubbled nicely, neither exploding nor falling flat. Marlene observed her daughter among a group of girls her age, all dressed in the best, and inclined to be snooty, but none of them had been kidnapped by Asian gangsters. Lucy was in full Claudine fettle, using her natural wit and talent for mimicry to great effect. She looked from a distance like a regular teenager.

Marlene drifted away, searching. There was just one person she had to see before relaxing into the limitless champagne, and she saw him in a corner of the terrace, looking out across the darkening East River.

"Goom."

"Marlene, what's happening, baby? Come here, let me give you a squeeze. Uh, that's enough, I'll embarrass myself here."

"I hear you're a solid citizen again."

"Yeah, that *stronzo*. You know, there are Italians and there are *Italians*. I got no use for a guy won't come and talk to you, treat you like a human being. Anyway, Butch pulled it off, and what can I say, you married a classy guy. Too bad he's Jewish."

Marlene laughed. "Speaking of *stronzi*, have we heard much from the Bollanos lately?"

"I hear they're laying low. The don's got some reshuffling to do. You know, it's like the chimps, they all got to sniff each other's crotches to see what the new dominance hierarchy is."

"You think the don is losing his grip?"

"Well, it could go either way. Pigetti gets impatient, he could try something, but the don's built up a lot of respect over the years. The older *capos* . . . you know how they are."

"I do. Which is why I'm going to slip this little tape into your pocket."

"What is it?"

"It's Vivian Bollano describing the Bollano version of 'Happy Days.' Truly heartwarming. Listen to it, and I think you'll want to share it with some of your pals in the Bollano organization."

"Uh, Marlene . . ." said Guma nervously.

"Or, I could just mail it to half a dozen *capi regimes*. But I figure you'd want the credit. These guys like to think they're like Al Pacino with *la famiglia*. They wouldn't want this to get into general circulation. I think they'll buy you a box of cannoli."

Guma stared at her for a moment, took the tape from his pocket, tossed it once, and put it away. "You really are something. Butch know about this?"

"No, and you know he doesn't want to know. Will you?"

Guma nodded slowly. A grin broke out across his face, horrible to see. She grinned back. It was a Sicilian moment. "Yeah," said Guma. "Yeah, I think I will. As a public service to the Mob. Besides, I never cared for the old *cafone*. What if they want to know who gave me the tape?"

"What tape is that?" said Marlene sweetly, and skipped away back to the champagne.